Soul Integrity

a Soul Identity novel

Dennis Batchelder

NetLeaves

Soul Integrity

Copyright © 2016 by Dennis Batchelder

Published 2016 by NetLeaves.

ISBN   978-0-9798056-4-6

For my loyal and impatient readers.

Thanks for the encouragement and the reminders that I need to get this book out of my head and into your hands. I'll try to never make you wait this long again.

Soul Identity books
  Soul Identity
  Soul Intent
  Soul Integrity

prologue

Claudia–Benares, India–December 11, 1980

They both linger outside the door to her hotel room. She hands him an envelope and says, "Please ensure this letter gets placed in the depositary."

"I shall attend to this tonight." Then he bows and says, "Take good rest, Madam-ji."

"There is no alarm clock. Can you schedule them to wake me at seven thirty?" she asks.

"Assistance for your awakening will be unnecessary, Madame-ji."

When she wrinkles her brow, he clasps his hands behind his back and recites, "Priests will be singing mantras at five thirty, and their voices will be penetrating the dreams. If Madam-ji finds their melody is causing sleepiness, fires will be lit and parathas will be cooking at six, and the smell of cow dung burning will be tickling the nose. If yet Madam-ji finds herself slumbering, the sun will be starting its duty at six thirty, and this Benares sun is a stubborn one."

"And if my sleep is also stubborn?"

"If none should bring awakefullness, at seven thirty I will be knocking this door." He demonstrates with a light rap.

"And then?" she asks.

"At eight o'clock we will take some chai in the hotel canteen."

"After that, Anup," she says softly. "Tell me what we'll do next."

"At eight thirty we will hire a rickshaw to take us back to the Ganga."

"Did you arrange the boat?"

He waggles his head back and forth. "The boat will be hired while Madam-ji sleeps. The man we used tonight seems a lazy chap, but rest assured; I will find one well suited to the task."

"And he'll row us back to the temple."

Another waggle. "Yes, Madam-ji. Back to Kashi Temple, and then on to Dashashwamedha Ghat, where we visited tonight and floated three deepas during the aarti. One for your late husband, one for baby Valentina, and the last for..." Here his voice trails off.

"The last was for me." She shakes her finger at him. "Be strong, Anup. You mustn't fail me."

"I will not, Madam-ji. I am here to serve you very well."

She stares into his eyes. "I believe you will. Now tell me what comes next."

"At ten o'clock we leave the boatman behind, and I row us exactly one quarter mile upstream. We will make our own contemplations. And at precisely 11:04, I will..." he swallows and licks his lips.

She drills her stare into him. "Tell me what you will do."

His gaze falls away. A moment later he peeks at her, then casts a glance down the empty hallway. He clears his throat then whispers, "I will do the needful, Madam-ji."

She smiles. "It's very needful. Good night, Anup." And with that, Claudia Famosa steps into her room. She turns back to the man into whose hands she has placed her future. She reaches out, but quickly lets her arm fall. Before he can offer anything else, she closes the door.

Midnight. She rubs her palms over the tiny table's cool marble top. Rocks into the short leg of the rickety chair. Flails her arms when the mosquitos whine. Stares at the blank sheet of paper.

Two o'clock. She closes her eyes and sees deep blue skies. It is January 1956, and she's almost sixteen. The fishermen have begun their return to the harbor around the point. Their masts barely scratch the pink skies above the calm sea. They have this cove to themselves. Young Claudia hikes up her white skirt and runs barefoot into the waves. After a moment Fico follows. He catches her around the waist, and they are falling, falling onto the beach, falling into their love. Their very first time, and afterward, he strokes her face and wipes the tears from her eyes. The tide chases them up into the grass, and she weaves a crown for her prince's head. He strings pink and purple flowers through her black hair.

Four o'clock. Her pen has yet to make a mark. The mosquito whine fades. She hears Fico Valdes in his firm revolutionary soldier voice swearing to love and cherish her forever. A strong and confident seventeen-year-old Claudia answering back. The ringing bells and firing rifles joined in their own raucous union. The drums and guitars and singing and stomping and laughing and whistling. The hearty congratulations from Fidel and Che. The whispers and gasps and moans and cries of man and wife overwhelming the nighttime clangor.

Six fifteen. The sharp smell of burning cow dung succumbs to memories of salty Caribbean air. Diesel fumes. Body odor three weeks in the making. A gag-inducing wave from putrefying flesh. And after the rescue, the pure scents of bleach and soap and starch and rice and beans and bread.

Seven thirty-five. Claudia scrawls her signature, puts down the pen, folds the paper in half. She runs her fingers through her long hair. She answers Anup's knock and hands him the paper.

"May I read it, Madam-ji?"

She nods.

He unfolds it and clears his throat. "To the Indian Authorities," he reads aloud. "This letter is to inform you that the bearer, Anup Chatterjee, son of Vijay Chatterjee, has my express permission to arrange my affairs in India. He is in no way responsible for the actions I, Claudia Famosa y Valdes, take today. If you require any clarifications, please contact Mr. Chatterjee's employer, Michael Rafferty of The Alert Foundation."

He folds the paper and slips it into his pocket. "This is protecting me from any over-zealous functionary who may be stumbling across our path," he says.

She swallows a lump in her throat. She hefts her suitcase onto her bed and double-checks its buckles. She lingers at the mirror, then again at the door.

"Shall we, Madam-ji?"

"We shall." They step into the blazing sun.

Almost four minutes past eleven o'clock a.m. India Standard Time. Anup glances at his watch and says, "The time has come, Madam-ji." He grasps the gunwales of the rowboat and crawls to the bow, crouching behind her.

She gazes at the water but sees nothing. "I am ready," she whispers. "Do the needful."

Seconds crawl by. She hears the water running from the oars. Each drop jars her senses, but she can't afford to lose focus.

Anup unsheathes the razor. "Lean forward over the bow, Madam-ji," he says, his voice trembling.

She stares at her palms, her wrists, her forearms, then grasps each elbow and hugs her knees tight. She rocks forward and stretches her neck over the water. "Like this?"

"Just so." Anup's voice is a whisper in her ear. "We are waiting a few more seconds."

Her knees are baby Valentina in her arms, nuzzling into her breast. His hands are Fico's caresses, kisses scorching a line of fire across her neck. She exhales slowly, confident that her next breath in will be in less than a year. Will she remember?

Will Valentina?

A shudder against her back, and a groan in her ear. She opens her eyes and spins around. Anup is shaking, his eyes wide but seeing nothing, his lips moving but speaking nonsense.

"I cannot I cannot I cannot," he mumbles.

"You must!"

His wild eyes lock onto hers, then break away to stare at the razor in his hand. He raises his arm and extends it over the side. "I will not," he says.

He opens his hand. The razor drops. And Claudia watches eternity fall from his fingers, the blade catching the sun as it slices through the filthy water.

She launches herself over the gunwale. She kicks down, arms waving, fingers grasping. Searching, seeking, hoping, praying.

And then she has it. The blade bites into her fingers as she squeezes it tightly.

No time to surface, no time to think, only time enough to act. A slash across her right wrist, then another to be sure. The blade drops from her numb fingers.

I'm coming, Fico. Wait for me, Valentina...

one

I'm standing in the shadows, just offstage, next to my ex-husband. I haven't had a chance to share with him the good news that the ex- is now official, and I'm hoping it won't piss him off too much. I certainly was thrilled when the email popped onto my phone a few minutes ago, complete with a scanned attachment of our finalized divorce decree from King County, Washington.

Rain and I are about to walk on stage for the last performance we owe Soul Identity under the contract we rushed to sign two years ago. Back when we were giddy with the promise of reuniting our soul lines. Back when I was trying to prove that somehow our shared past mattered more than anything else going on in my life.

When it's done, I'll head home, eat the last of my ice cream, and say goodbye, hopefully forever, to the Pacific Northwest.

Our emcee is at the podium. He's been building up our entrance. He's pausing a little too long between sentences, like he's telling a half-remembered joke, but finally he says, "And now we're at the moment you've all been waiting for." Big pause. Then, "It's my privilege to welcome back to our stage Soul Identity's most famous living couple, Rain and Val Ekko."

We walk out arm in arm to the standing ovation of Soul Identity's three hundred high-producing soul seekers. They've won this weekend trip to Seattle, and gosh darn it, they wanted—needed—a performance from the world's best living example of cross-generation soul mates. We are their inspiration, and the huge commission that my ex-husband's soul line paid out is their aspiration. We are the closing story these guys tell to prospective new members. We are viewable on the top Internet video sites, the reincarnation darlings featured on countless blogs.

I wonder how these seekers would take it if I told them that today Rain and I put the final nail in the coffin of this whole soul mate idea. But we won't be doing that; my ex-husband and I agreed to keep our pending divorce under wraps until the contract ends. As far as the audience knows, we're still happily married to each other, still as in love as our previous incarnations were.

The spotlights follow us, and I glance at Rain. He looks great in his tuxedo. His handsome face with its broad jaw, Slavic cheekbones, dark eyes, and high forehead is frozen in what he calls his studious look. You'd never guess he's also a thug. His emerald green bowtie, chosen to match my gown, is cocked slightly to the right, and when I reach up and fix it, he leans forward and whispers, "Let's make this the best show of all."

"Just stick to the script," I whisper back.

But he's ignoring me, already in character of the Rain he wishes he could be. The Rain he thinks they want. And they do want that Rain—when I glance down to the front row, I see a half dozen twenty-something-year-old girls squeezed in the front row seats at the base of the stage, cute in their stretchy tops, their shapely little butts squeezed into half as many chairs as the rest of the audience would need, their eyes only on my ex-husband.

They can have him.

I press my clicker, and a photograph lights up the giant display panel behind us. The image is dominated by the faces of a young and beautiful couple. The boy's right arm wraps around the girl's shoulders, his fingers entwined in her long black hair. The girl's lips are parted, as if the photographer caught her in mid-sentence. The tip of her tongue peeks over the ridge of her bottom teeth. Both have flushed cheeks. Both are dressed in white. Both have little bits of rice stuck in their hair.

Just like the first time I saw the image, I'm overwhelmed by the intensity of the joy the photographer has captured. Even almost sixty years later, print this on the cover of any bridal magazine and you'd triple its sales.

"Does anybody know this happy couple?" I ask.

Everybody knows, of course. But one of the bimbos in the front row actually stands up, puts her hands behind her back like she's reciting a poem, and steals my line. "That's Frederico Valdes and Claudia Famosa in 1958, on their wedding day." She holds up a finger, wrinkles her brow as if she's constructing some great insight, and adds, "It's also the only known photograph of Fico."

Rain beams encouragement, and I wonder how long he spent practicing my line with her. "Then it's lucky for us the image is so clear," he says. "Otherwise we'd never have been able to determine his soul identity."

I'm not sure if Claudia and Fico's story will still generate interest once everybody knows Rain and I are done with each other. My guess is that Claudia's demonstration of her faith by slicing her wrists in India will lose its relevance, or even be considered an act of fanaticism. It will be a pity to lose her story, but it's not worth saving if it means I'm stuck with this guy.

Rain nods at me, and I press the clicker. The image zooms in until we see just the couple's brows, eyes, and the tops of their hooked noses. Claudia's honey eyes are flecked with green, and Fico's look like pumpkin pie, each slice outlined in chocolate. The irises are mesmerizing on the display, over a foot tall and perfectly clear. All four pupils reflect images of the photographer and his camera, and if you look closely, you can make out some of the wedding party standing behind him.

I click again, and we zoom in on one of Fico's pupils. At this magnification it's like watching cars on a satellite map, but slouching behind the photographer are two lightly-bearded men wearing black berets and olive-green jackets. Rain says in a deep voice, "Fico and Claudia asked only two comrades to stand with them at their wedding, and both Che Guevara and Fidel Castro graciously accepted."

I remember how excited Rain and I were when we first identified the revolutionaries. They gave credence to Claudia's story, and they gave us a fleeting brush with real-life bad boys. After the obligatory applause from the audience, I click the image back to the four eyes. Time to get technical and pump some tablet video into the presentation.

I drag the four eyes to the top half of the display. "First I'll calculate both soul identities," I say. I tap on my tablet to highlight Fico's irises, then select "calculation" from my own reader program. I do the same for Claudia. The screen shows a whirling donut, and then it paints the identities dead center between each pair of eyes.

"And now we have Fico and Claudia's soul identities, calculated from their 1958 wedding photograph," Rain says.

I'm still using the algorithm from two years ago, the fast one Scott and I developed before our relationship unraveled. I wonder if he's come up with better ones since.

We're at the proof point of our presentation. "Next we'll overlay Rain's and my identities," I say.

Rain nods and smiles like he's supposed to, but then he says, "And as a special demonstration as part of our final show, we'll be doing this one live."

I whisper, "I've got our eyes already baked in. We don't need to do this live."

"It's our last show, Val. Let's make it our best." He indicates with his chin at the now-buzzing audience. "Our fans seem to like the idea."

He must have promised some razzle-dazzle to the bimbo. I decide to make him fight for it. "They're here for the love story, not for your showmanship."

He stares at me. I want to outlast him, but I can't hold his gaze. Not with the "I haven't told you yet, but our marriage is finally over," guilt running through me. So I light up a smile and nod.

"I knew you'd play along," he whispers. He turns and asks the audience, "Which one of our top soul seekers happens to have a reader app on their phone?"

That produces quite a few chuckles. The same bimbo comes up the stage stairs and prances over to us. Her sequined top dazzles the audience as the spotlights catch her, and she tosses her head, showering her blonde hair over her shoulders as she hands her phone to Rain. He's fast, but I catch the extra caress he plants on her wrist.

The bimbo dances away to the side of the stage. Maybe she'll twist her heel and land on that tight little ass. I'm really not jealous, just pissed that he's flaunting her in public.

"Ladies first," Rain says as he hands me the pink plastic-sheathed phone.

I see that it's loaded and ready to go. This app is Scott's, which I've heard through the grapevine is the best reader available these days. I motion Rain to face the spotlight, and I snap an image of his face.

As the app is processing, I plug a cable into the phone and attach it to my tablet. Then I drag Rain's face to rest right under Claudia's eyes on the overhead display. I widen the image so just Rain's eyes are showing, and after a moment the app displays the same soul identity as Claudia's.

"Ladies and gentlemen, we have a match between me and Claudia," Rain intones, and the audience breaks out in applause.

I grab a screen shot and keep it up on the display, then disconnect the phone and hand it to Rain. He takes my picture, and I plug the cable back in and enlarge and drag my own eyes to rest under Fico's.

And there's my soul identity—the one I share with Fico. I learned his his story a little over two years ago, just before I decided to take this side trip on my life journey.

Again Rain declares a match, and again the audience applauds. But before I disconnect the phone from the big display, my eyes disappear, and Scott Waverly's face appears.

Scott Waverly, my ex-boyfriend, ex-lover, ex-soul mate. He was all of these until Rain came along and everything was ruined.

For a minute I think I must have selected a wrong button, but then Scott begins to speak.

He taps the screen, and I hear the thunks resonating through the hall's sound system. "Hello soul reader, whoever you are," he says. "I see you have just read Val Nikolskaya's—I should say Val Ekko's—identity, and I have a very important message for her. Can you hand her the phone, please?"

This is a recording, a gimmick he inserted into his smart phone application. I rush to unplug the cable and get him off the overhead display.

Rain grabs my arm and shakes his head. "Let him make a fool of himself," he says.

"You planned this?" I hiss at him.

"No, I guess I'm just lucky," he whispers back. "But now that he's stuck his nose in, I want everybody to see how pathetic he is."

Rain always gets excited when my ex-lover shows his anguish at losing me. Scott has escalated his attempts to send me messages over the past two years, and I've rebuffed them all. The rebuffing gets Rain strutting around our house, his face aglow with what I assume are his primeval joys of besting another man.

I'm ashamed to admit that Rain's strutting used to get me going, but not lately. Especially not tonight.

But I let Rain have his silly victory. My inner geek is impressed with Scott's latest attempt to contact me. Credit where credit's due: embedding recognition code and a message inside a widespread smart phone application is a pretty creative way of reaching me. I walk over to the tablet and adjust it so the phone's app fills the screen.

And right on cue, Scott says, "Okay, Val, you're either there, or I've got a serious bug in my software."

The audience laughs at this. Scott is popular with them. They like the software he writes, and they love their extra commissions they've been earning ever since he published his adventure novels, creating a flood of new members. His two books have lifted Soul Identity out of the backwaters of obscurity and into the deluge of public opinion.

Scott holds up his hand. "But I want to make sure it's really you, and not somebody holding your photograph up to the reader," he says. "Can you please tell me the name of the Moscow train station where we met Archie on our trip to visit your parents?"

That was two and a half years ago, right after we got engaged, and right before we broke up. I'm about to respond, but then I wonder if it would be better to stay quiet. Why should I let Scott make a fool out of himself?

And then I think about the novels Scott wrote, where I've heard he portrayed me as a nice but one-dimensional Russian chick with little else besides sex on my mind. And I think about the explaining I've had to do at these performances from those who want to know how I could leave Scott after I'd killed that Nazi skinhead for him. And I think that maybe it's time for Scott to get a taste of what he's been serving me these last two years.

So I lean down and speak the train station's name into the phone's microphone. "Yaroslavsky Vokzal."

Nothing happens for a second, but then Scott's image breaks out into a smile and he says, "It really is you! Thank you, Val." He takes a deep breath. "I want you to know that I finally understand why you left me. When you found out about Fico, I was excited for you learning about your soul identity's past. But then Rain butted into our life, and I handled it poorly."

That was quite the understatement. Scott first panicked, then shut down and gave me the silent treatment. Not to mention what he tried to do once Rain came to visit. He was responsible for converting my curiosity into an anger at him for daring to tell me what I couldn't do.

"I know you think I'm a jerk," he says.

He's got that right.

"And I want you to know that I'm taking responsibility for my actions."

I glance at Rain, and I get the impression that he's not so thrilled that he let Scott's broadcast continue. He signals at me to unplug the cable, and I'm about to, but then Scott starts speaking again.

"Val," he says, "I still think you were wrong to choose this whole in-herited soul mate business over us. I know I screwed it up and I deserved to lose you, but of all the people in the world, did you have to end up married to Rain?"

This is interesting. My newly-minted ex-husband walks toward me. He's signaling again, more frantically this time, but I decide to let Scott's message keep playing.

Scott points his finger right at the camera. "I know you believe in soul mates," he says.

I used to.

"But would your true soul mate do this?" And all of a sudden Scott's face is replaced by a bunch of images shown rapid-fire. They're all of Rain, and in each picture, he's either kissing or fondling one or more half-naked girls.

The noise in the room fades and time downshifts to a crawl. Rain runs toward me in slow motion, his mouth, lips, and tongue moving but making no sound. I am leaning too far to the right, and I grasp the table's edge before I fall over. I feel a flush spreading up my neck and onto my face. My stomach has turned into a brick.

But Rain asked for this. And with that thought, time speeds up to normal. I hear the audience gasp. In the bimbo row, the girls are shrieking, which makes sense, as they're heavily featured in the photographs Scott has thrown onto the display.

Rain skids to a stop, his face now bunched into a snarl. Without thinking, I slap him as hard as I can. His head jerks to the right. My hand stings, and I want to hit him again and again.

But I don't. Scott's show is still playing, after all. After at least twenty damning images, his face is back. "Rain is using you," he says. "He's not your soul mate, no matter how much you want him to be."

Rain's hand darts for the phone, and I slap it away. "Back off," I say.

Scott says, "There's something much more important for you to worry about."

Like how to recover from this mess.

"You're in danger, Val." His eyes grow wide. "Watch out for–"

And this time Rain is successful at reaching the phone. He rips out the cable and with a great bellow he slams the cute little pink thing down onto the table. The screen shatters in his hand and he jerks back. Blood runs out of gashes on his palm, and both he and I stare at it dripping down onto the phone fragments.

Then my ex-husband wipes his bloody hand on his tuxedo pants and walks into the shadows and off the stage without even once glancing back at me.

two

Val–Seattle–Present Day

I go straight from the evening's debacle to hot yoga practice. I figure I need the ninety minutes of mind-clearing hellish torture before I dare reflect on and maybe even obsess over what happened tonight.

And the Bikram yoga class works. I get myself so caught up in stretching one more inch and balancing one more second in the 105-degree room that I have no time to focus on the horror.

Until the camel pose. Tracy, our yogini, says that camel always brings a gift, and she's right. After stretching, pulling, and prodding my body for most of the session, she makes us kneel down with our legs and ankles spread six inches apart, our hands on our butts. We arch our head, neck, and bodies backward. She makes us grab our ankles and force our hips forward while looking upside-down at the back wall.

I'm grinding my hips so far forward that I'm afraid if my fingers lose their grip on my ankles I'll spring forward and crash into the mirror. And right then my heat-addled and toxin-flushed brain sends me a replay of the evening's events, but it's all mixed up. I smell Scott. I hear the pictures of my now-ex-but-then-current-husband's escapades, and I feel my body crushed in Rain's big hand, as if I've become the bimbo's little pink phone. Sharp pieces of me break loose and dig into his hand and rip it open, and I revel in the blood I draw, feeling its warmth flow over me.

Yikes. I pull myself upright. I look in the mirror and see tears mingled in with my sweat. Quite the gift from Mr. Camel. I'm not sure I can do the second pose.

And then I notice that everybody is staring at me, their foreheads laced with concern.

"You screamed bloody murder, Val," Tracy says. She's wearing this little loop-over-the-ear microphone. "Are you okay?"

I shrug and give a shaky laugh. "Camel dumped a load on me."

She nods, and instructs us all to lie down and enter savasana, the dead man's pose. Then she comes over, switches off her microphone, and kneels next to me. "Bad day?" she whispers.

"The worst."

She squeezes my shoulder. "You're in the right place. Get it all out on second camel." Then she's up and telling us, "It's normal to feel a bit weird after this pose."

I grit my teeth and do my sit-up and continue on. Camel, rabbit, and the rest of the poses all help.

Afterward while driving home, I call my friend Anastasia. I plan to pack up my final suitcase and head over to her condo for my last night in town. I've transferred the title of my car to her, and she'll drop me off at the airport in the morning for my flight east.

I love that Seattle is chock-full of Russians. I can buy the food I grew up eating, and even better, I can hang out with other ex-Soviets. Friendships are easily established between those with common growing-up experiences. And even though sometimes our predilection to find the bad news and conspiracies in any situation can suck the excitement out of the air, tonight I need a good dose of support from someone who, like me, is a trained expert at dealing with situations so rotten and hopeless that the only valid response is to laugh.

"Why are you calling me early?" she asks me. We Russians are also pretty direct with each other, which tends to sound rude to overly-polite Pacific Northwest native ears.

"I caught the earlier yoga class," I say. I'll fill her in later.

"Let me clear the house," she says. I hear her talking to somebody in Russian. "Change of plans. Get dressed and get out of here. Take your vodka with you."

"Nastya, wait!" I use her Russian nickname. "Have him leave the vodka."

"*Ladno, ostav vodku*," she says to him. I hear him grumble, and then her giving him a kiss. "Get out," she says.

"I'm still at least a half hour away," I say.

"Mishka! Don't leave quite yet." More grumbles, then another kiss as I hang up.

In ten minutes I park half a block down the street from my place.

Back when I first moved out west, Rain and I bought both halves of a duplex in West Seattle. His grandfather Mikk moved into the ground floor and we lived on top. Six months ago when we separated, Mikk bought the house from us, and he and I swapped places. Until this morning, that is, because that's when the couple who bought most of my furniture hauled away everything except my small traveling suitcase filled with the little I will keep from this life.

I had planned to spend a few minutes alone with my ice cream. But now the thought of staying even a minute longer than necessary in this house disgusts me. I dash inside and grab my suitcase, not bothering to turn on the lights. But on the way out, I think that I might as well bring the ice cream to Nastya's place. So I enter the kitchen and fumble around the freezer in the dark.

"If you're looking for that pistachio ice cream, I finished both containers a half hour ago." The voice comes from a man on a bar stool at my counter. He's speaking in Russian.

It's Mikk. He's almost eighty, only a bit over five feet tall. He's wrinkled like an elephant with a head like an emu, complete with the big beak, hairy eyebrows, and huge red eyes on top of a skinny neck. But now I can just barely see his outline. "Why are you sitting in the dark?" I ask him.

"It was light when I got here." He lets out a sigh. "You were going to sneak out without saying goodbye to me?"

I walk over and put my hands on his bony shoulders, which are encased in a fuzzy baby-blue bathrobe. "I was going to come up after I put my bag in the car."

He sighs again. "Maybe it's better you don't. My grandson's not in a good mood."

I stay silent for a moment, then ask him, "Did he tell you what happened?"

"No, and I didn't ask. I've never once gotten in the middle of your problems."

I give his shoulders a squeeze, then lean forward and kiss his cheek. "I'm grateful."

Mikk's hands are clenched in his lap, and he's keeping his head down. He takes a deep breath and blurts out, "My grandson, such a precocious child, grew into such a stupid asshole adult."

He sure has. But I can't say that. I'm very fond of Mikk, and I hate that my ending it with Rain means I'm going to lose him. But really, nothing good can come out of commiserating on what a lousy person his last living descendent has turned out to be.

I pull my hands back. "He's your grandson, Mikk. He loves you, he knows he's lucky to have you, and with me heading back east, he's going to need you even more."

"He has a funny way of showing me his love." Mikk lifts his head, and I see that his right eye is almost swollen shut and his bottom lip is puffed up and split right in the center.

I draw in a deep quick breath. "Rain did that?"

He tightens his face, but after just a second it crumples. "I must have tripped coming down the stairs," he mutters.

"Mikk." My nails are digging into my palms. "Did. He. Hit. You?"

He closes his eyes. Finally he nods.

"That bastard—I'll kill him."

"Val, stay away from him. Please."

Like hell I will. I reach into my purse to get my keys.

He grabs my arm, and I help him stand. He reaches into his pocket and pulls out his glasses. The right temple is broken off, but he's able to loop the left one over his ear, and the glasses hang lopsided.

I wonder how he's going to get them fixed with me no longer around.

"Look," he says, "I'm a tough old bird. I can handle that sack of shit treating me like a punching bag. But if he were to hurt you..." His voice trails away.

He's already hurt me enough. "Is there somewhere I can bring you?" I ask. "Maybe for a few days while Rain cools down?"

"Not anymore." And I know this is true; Mikk's last buddy passed away three months before. He's been spending his spare time feeding the sea gulls along Alki Beach during his days and trolling the Internet's social networks most of his nights.

"How about a hotel?"

He gives a half smile. "And pay for Internet access?" He grabs and squeezes my hand. "Don't worry about me, Val. I'll be fine. But you should go."

I wrap my arms around him and pull his head tight against my chest. "I'm going to miss you, Mikk. You'll email me?"

"Email's so old school. I'll message you, though. Count on it." He pulls back and rearranges his bathrobe, which has come open in the front. "Your itty bitty sweaty yoga outfit is going to kill me. Get out of here before I embarrass myself."

I rest my palm on his cheek. "Stay tough," I say.

He gives a growl, and I laugh. But as I turn to go, the kitchen lights flash on, and Rain's standing in the door. He's still in his tuxedo pants, but somewhere he's lost the jacket. And found the beer, by the smell of it. He's holding a thin sheaf of papers wrapped in a rubber band in his left hand.

"So my ex-wife is running away." This in a monotone, in English. Rain doesn't speak Russian very well.

"You've read the email," I say. "I wonder if fucking those girls will be as fun when it's not considered cheating."

He shrugs. "Probably not. I'll have to find a new diversion."

"Like beating up your grandfather? Come on, Rain."

His face twists into a snarl. "You stay out of my family business. And get your ass out of this house."

"I'm going." I step toward him, close enough that my pointed finger is almost touching his nose. "If you touch him again, I swear I'll call the cops."

He grabs my finger and bends it backward. "Fuck you, bitch. Leave before it's too late."

"Don't hurt her!" Mikk cries. He's somehow lifted the bar stool up over his head.

"Stay out of this, old man."

"Let go of her."

"Or what?" Rain asks. He gives my finger a twist, and I cry out from the blaze of pain.

Mikk throws the bar stool at Rain, who drops his papers and easily deflects it. The stool crashes to the floor, and Rain reaches out and shoves his grandfather backward.

I scream as I watch Mikk fall onto the counter and bang his head. His glasses fly off and skid under the refrigerator. Then Mikk slowly slides to the floor.

I wrench my finger free. "You sonuvabitch, you killed him!"

"He's fine," Rain says. "Stand up and toss me another chair, grandpa. I wanna hit you again."

My father used to say that once the sleeping Russian bear has been woken up, beware. And the evening's events are definitely waking mine up: Rain flaunting the bimbo, me enduring the photo show, Mikk's eye and lip beaten, and now this. My leg flies up with all its yoga-earned strength, and I slam it as hard as I can into my ex-husband's crotch. I feel his balls, through his tuxedo, flattened against my bare thigh.

Rain's knees give way, and he collapses to the floor and onto his side. He curls forward into himself, I guess to protect what's left of his manhood.

I'm afraid he'll get up and kill us. So while he's gasping and moaning, I plant a kick on each of his knees. In between these kicks I check on Mikk and see that he's opened his eyes. Thank goodness.

"Are you going to kill him?" Mikk asks me as he struggles to his feet.

"No, but if I let him up, we're dead." Rain rolls over and raises himself up to a kneeling position, so I kick him in his lower back and he falls forward. Hopefully I got his kidneys, and he'll piss blood for the next two weeks.

"I don't think he can get up." Mikk's face is all scrunched up.

He's probably right. But to be sure, I take Mikk's bathrobe tie and use it to bind Rain's feet together. I tie a huge Gordian knot, and I hope it'll hold. "That should buy us enough time to get out of here," I say.

"We're leaving?" Mikk looks troubled.

I stare at him. "You know you can't stay here."

He looks at me, then at Rain. "Eeney meeney miney mo, grandson," he says. "I'm leaving with your ex-wife. God help you."

Rain's eyes open. "I'll hunt you both down," he gasps.

"Let's go," I say to Mikk. And on the way out, I see the sheaf of papers that Rain dropped when he dodged the bar stool. I pick it up and examine it. The papers are yellowed with age, and the top sheet has writing in the script font of the old Selectric typewriters. It reads, "Just in case, by Claudia Valdes y Famosa. December 1980."

I wave the papers at Rain. "Where'd you get this?" I ask. "Your soul line collection?"

"Give it here," he says. "It's private. None of your goddamn business."

He's right. I realize I don't want to know anything else about Claudia or any life lessons she's left this loser. I toss the stack of papers onto his chest.

And then we leave, Mikk holding his bathrobe together and shuffling in his slippers, me in my yoga outfit. Because it's lying too close to Rain, I decide to abandon my suitcase. A clean start on my new life.

I look at Mikk as we're getting in my car. A small gash on his forehead leaks a trickle of blood down to his cheek. His eye is purple, and his lip is swollen twice its size.

Half-way to Nastya's apartment, I veer to the side of the road and slam on the brakes. I open the door just in time to get my head out before I'm sick. When I'm finally done heaving, I reach behind my seat, grab a bottled water, and rinse out my mouth.

"I still can't get over how you kneed him in the nuts," Mikk says. "Now I'm never gonna get a great-grandchild." He darts a look my way, then back out the windshield.

When he looks back at me, I smile, he chuckles, and then we both lose it. We laugh for a good five minutes, so hard that we've both got tears running down our cheeks.

"That felt good, but now what?" Mikk says when we calm down. Rain knows you're sleeping at Nastya's tonight."

Good point. We shouldn't endanger her, so I get her on the phone and tell her that I won't be able to come.

"Don't ask why," I say.

"Why?"

I'm silent for a moment. "Nastya, you should sleep somewhere else, too. Rain's mad, and he may come looking."

She understands, and I tell her I'll leave her car at the airport. "I'll call you with the spot in the garage," I say. "You have the spare set of keys, right?"

"Da. Be careful, okay?"

"You too." I hang up. "Where are the cheap hotels?" I ask Mikk. I want to pay cash and leave no trace, as Rain has too many connections to Seattle's underbelly of crime.

"Down past the stadiums." He chuckles. "And if you frizz up that gorgeous red hair a bit and stick out your chest, we'll fit in with the rest of the local talent."

"In your dreams, mister." But maybe he's onto something; acting like a prostitute and a john may be the best way to remain anonymous.

We hit an ATM and cruise the streets and eventually find a motel that is well-lit and next door to an adult club. We sit in the car for a minute and watch the dancers with their clients scurrying between the two buildings. We park on the brightest side street I can find, a half block away. I grab what little belongings I have in the car. It' s not much: my purse, my tablet, and the gown from this evening's event.

The hotel clerk sits locked behind a glass cage. He glances at me, then his eyes widen when he sees Mikk parading in his bathrobe, black eye and fat lip, squinting at the safety signs. At least I wiped the blood off his face.

"Got any rooms?" I ask into a dented and rusty speaking grill.

He's already shoving a keycard into the machine. "For just the hour, or do we roll till the morning?"

"I can go all night," Mikk says. "It's been building up for quite some time."

The attendant shakes his head and looks at me.

"Keep it rolling," I say.

He nods. "You're new here, so I need two hundred on deposit." He taps his hand at the base of the window. "Slide it on through."

I slip ten twenties into the slot.

"Another buck seventy-five for the room," he says. "You've got a half-dozen sets of towels and sheets—make sure I get 'em back or I dip into your deposit."

I slide another nine twenties his way.

He pulls a thick roll out of his pocket and slaps on my money. Then he peels off a grubby five-dollar bill and slides it and the keycard back to me. "Room 138. Down at the far end."

The room is clean and has a funeral home odor of flowery perfume hanging in the air. It's got a king bed and two arm chairs. No television, but several sets of mouthwash, toothbrushes, and towels. The bathroom has no door, but it has a stand-up shower with a curtain, so I strip off my yoga outfit, rinse down, and put on the emerald evening gown. I use one of the shampoos to wash my shorts and top in the sink. Then I wring them out and pat them as dry as I can with another towel.

Mikk gets up and goes into the bathroom. I hear his pee dribble in the toilet, then him washing his hands. He comes back and flops himself down on the bed. His bathrobe falls open, and he quickly pulls it shut.

I toss him my almost-dry shorts. "I think you'll fit in these," I say.

"Thanks." He pulls them on, takes off his bathrobe, and crawls under the covers on the left side of the bed. He's silent for a moment, staring at the ceiling, and then he says, "I really don't want to be a burden to you, Val."

Too late for that. But I reply, "You're fine, Mikk. I'm glad you came."

"So what happens next? To me?"

I know Mikk's got no other family. His friends are all dead. And until Rain calms down, I won't let him go back home. Even with the divorce, I consider him family.

But I have neither answers nor comforting words for Mikk tonight. "We'll figure it out tomorrow," I say. I keep the evening gown on and crawl into the right side of the bed. "Meanwhile, old man, stay on your side."

"I was just gonna confess that I lied to the hotel clerk," he says. "I wouldn't last more than a minute, let alone all night." He turns onto his side and faces me. "You've supplied me with more than enough fantasy material for a man my age."

I reach out and squeeze his shoulder. "Sweet dreams, Mikk," I whisper. But his eyes have closed and he's already snoring.

three

I sleep better than I thought I would, but all of a sudden I'm wide awake. The clock slowly swims into focus; it's five-fourteen on the first morning of my new unmarried life.

Mikk's already up and brushing his teeth. I lay in bed and think about changing my flight: I can't leave Seattle until I get Mikk settled somewhere safe. And until I find myself some traveling clothes.

I call to him. "You going to be long in there?"

Mikk sticks his head into the room and smiles, hotel toothbrush hanging from his mouth. "Ten minutes and the bathroom's all yours."

I get up and straighten my gown. The only mirror is above the bed on the ceiling, so I stand on the mattress, look up, and yank my mop of curls into some semblance of order.

I glance at my phone. It's time to listen to the rest of Scott's message. Does he really think I'm in danger, or is this just another ploy to get me back?

I've made quite an art out of ignoring his pleas to talk to me. But sometimes when I'm being stretched and twisted in hot yoga class, I find my mind wandering into the forbidden territory of my life with Scott. I try to stop myself, but I can't, and I end up with this longing feeling for a life as good and as simple as what we had together.

I'm able to counter this with some righteous indignation at how he treated me and what a jerk he became once we discovered how my soul ancestral line was entwined with Rain's. Getting pissed at him has been an effective way for me to cope. I try to keep this in mind as I go online and download Scott's latest Soul Identity reader app.

Scott's become quite the Soul Identity entrepreneur since we split. He's got his books, presumably he and his parents are still doing security consulting, and he's selling lots of apps.

My phone asks if the app has permission to use my camera, my GPS, my Internet connection. Do I really have a choice? I turn on the bedside lamp, hold it away from my face, and snap my picture. The app calculates and displays my identity, just like it did at the dinner last night.

And then I wait for Scott to appear, but this time he stays away. I'm left staring at my eyes and my identity. Dammit. I recall him saying last night that it was my last message from him. I guess he meant it.

I'll have to call Scott if I want to know the rest of the message. I sit and stare at my phone for a minute.

Three rings, and then it's voice mail. I don't know what to say, so I hang up.

Mikk comes out of the bathroom. He's back in his bathrobe, and I see he's using my sports bra as a belt. "What do you think?" he asks.

"Looking sharp."

He chuckles. "We need to find clothes before you get bored with my fashion statement."

"Is anything open at this time?"

"A Freddy's is our best bet. They open at seven," he says. "And we even have time for a Grand Slam at Denny's. My stomach's thinking my throat is cut."

I hadn't even thought of eating. "How can you be hungry?" I ask.

"It must be all the adventure," he says. "This is the most fun I've had in years, Val. I could eat a cow."

"I'm glad one of us is enjoying this." But I smile as I head into the bathroom.

We gather up what little we brought to the room. The hotel guy smirks when Mikk gives him a double thumbs-up. "We have a weekly rate which works out to seven nights for the price of five," he says to me. "You interested?"

I shake my head, and he returns my deposit. "Next time, then," he says.

I hope not.

Outside the sun's already popping up over the Cascades. The skies are white on the horizon and deep blue above. No clouds, no mosquitos, and the thermometer never above the high seventies: our two months of summer are worth Seattle's ten months of gloom.

Denny's is right down the road. The waitress seats us at a big round corner booth, and the patrons don't give my gown and Mikk's bathrobe a second look. Mikk can't see the menu without his glasses, but he orders his Grand Slam, and I get chocolate chip pancakes off the kid's menu.

"Looks like you're enjoying the adventure," Mikk says after I succumb to an offer of whipped cream.

Maybe. But it's time to get down to business. "So what are your options?" I ask.

He shrugs. "I thought about this all night. I either go home and make peace with Rain, or..." he pauses and stirs some sugar into his coffee.

"Or?"

He's looking at the table. "Or I come with you."

"Hmm."

"I won't be a bother, Val." He still won't look up at me.

I'm silent for a bit. Then I ask, "Do you think last night was a one-time thing?"

"What, Rain's punching me?"

I nod.

He's quiet for a long moment. "Once it starts..." Now he looks up. "I never told you how Rain and I survived before you came along."

"You don't talk about those days."

"That's how Rain wanted it," he says. "But now that we've hopped in bed with each other, I feel I owe you the whole story."

Neither of the Ekkos, nor I for that matter, speak much about our past. They know some stuff about me from Scott's books, and I've figured out that Rain's mildly criminal background never really went away. Mikk acts like he's been in academia. But other than these hints, the only past we've spent time recounting has been that of Claudia and Fico.

"Tell me," I say.

"I'll give you the whole story." He smiles and says, "I'm a Russian literature professor in Tallinn. In eighty-nine my wife gets massive headaches, and we discover her body's full of cancer. This brings our son back home, along with his wife and their little boy, Rain. When my wife dies a month later, a former student who's now a bureaucrat tries to cheer me up with a tourist visa for me and my seven-year-old grandson."

He smiles. "I'll always remember the day Rain and I arrived in New York City: the twenty-third of August. We get to our hotel and watch the Baltic Way on the news." He looks at me, his eyebrows lifted.

I shook my head. "Baltic Way?"

"Two million Estonians, Latvians, and Lithuanians form a human chain, hundreds of miles long, to protest the fiftieth anniversary of Russia and Germany's sneaky deal over the Baltics. I have tears streaming down my cheeks, so proud I am of my countrymen standing up to the Soviets.

"When I call my son that night, he tells me he's being followed by the police. And a week later I find out that he and his wife have been killed in a car crash."

I wince. "Accident?"

"Who really knows? Just another mysterious death from the waning days of the Soviet Empire. I stay in America, apply for political asylum, get Rain listed as my dependent, and end up driving a cab in Seattle.

"But that's what passes as the happy beginning of our story," he says. "Now comes the middle drama. Rain and I somehow are scraping by, and maybe I'm too busy to spend enough time with him. We stop communicating around his fifteenth birthday."

"What do you mean stop?" I ask.

"Stop as in we become two ships passing in the night. No 'what's for dinner,' no 'can I have some money,' no 'what time will you be home?' We each do our own thing."

"You two communicated just fine when I met you."

"Well, some of this you know already. Rain starts hanging out with hooligans. Now fast forward fourteen years. Rain's still living at home, and we're still not talking. Who knows how he makes his money, because I'm not giving him any. He ends up owing some serious cash to his gang, and the leader has this bright idea that he can work it off by stealing equipment from the dockyards. There's an explosion and Rain's eyes are injured. He can't see for three weeks, and all of a sudden he needs me again."

Now I'm on familiar territory. Rain incorporated his thug-to-good-guy conversion into our presentation—the one we should have given last night.

"We're moving toward the climax, so pay attention," Mikk says. "I take Rain while he's still blinded to a private, no-questions-asked eye doctor. She checks him and goes off somewhere, and we're sitting there just waiting to hear whether he's gonna spend the rest of his life being led around by a guide dog. She re-examines his eyes, and we wait again. All this time Rain's getting jumpier. After an hour of suspense, the phone rings, and I think Rain's gonna fly out of his examining chair.

"Rain listens to what the doc is muttering into her phone, and all of a sudden he shushes me. 'The bitch ratted me out,' he hisses, and when she comes back and leans over him, he grabs her around the neck and holds a knife to her throat."

Mikk chuckles. "The doc and I are both so scared we pee our pants. Rain's half-ready to slice her open, but then she spits out that it wasn't the cops but Soul Identity who called, and that they'd been trying to find Rain for the last ten years.

"That's really when Rain and I become buddies again. His eyes get better, we go together to the local Soul Identity office, and he's officially read and matched. He finds Claudia in his past, and the pile of money she left behind. So he pulls a couple hundred grand out of his soul line collection and pays off his debts. I help him open a bank account, get a credit card, and teach him how to act like a respectable human being. Then he goes looking for you."

Not quite the story Rain told when he did find me. "And you can see how that worked out," I say.

He shrugs. "He fucked up a good thing. Obviously he didn't inherit my brains."

We finish our food in silence and I signal for the bill. "So you're saying that there's nothing to go back to."

"That's what I'm saying."

I reach out and pat his baby-blue terrycloth lapel. "You prefer us walking around in evening gowns and bathrobes?"

"Only until we get to Freddy's."

I look at my phone. It's now seven, and the store should be open. But as I'm about to stand up, I spot a familiar middle-aged couple enter the restaurant. What are they doing here?

Mikk follows my gaze, then notices my consternation. "Do you know them?"

I nod.

The man looks at his phone, then points in our direction. He catches my eye for a minute, but then quickly looks away. He and his wife hold hands and advance slowly toward us.

"Who are they?" Mikk asks.

The couple reaches the table. Both of them have funny half-smiles plastered on their faces. The woman eyes my wrinkled gown, flick over Mikk's bathrobe, then land on her husband. "Maybe we should come back later," she says to him.

I stand up and give them both a hug, and I can feel relief radiate through them. "Mikk," I say, "I'd like to introduce you to two of the nicest people in the world. Mr. and Mrs. Waverly."

Mikk stands up, pulls his bathrobe together, and shakes their hands. "Sit with us," he says. And when they do, we all stare at each other.

"Mikk is my ex-husband's grandfather," I say to Scott's mom. Might as well get it all out in the open.

"Ex-husband?" she asks.

I nod. "The divorce was finalized yesterday."

She shoots a glance at her husband, then says to Mikk, "Val used to live with our son, before he stupidly chased her away."

Mikk raises his bushy eyebrows. "A week ago I'd have said tough tooties. But now I know my grandson's never gonna be nothing but an asshole. I'm on Team Val."

Scott's dad clears his throat. "We are too."

I turn to him. "How is your son?" When he's not busy wrecking my performances.

"That's why we're here," he says. "He's been missing for a month now. We need your help."

four

GREETINGS TO THE ME THAT IS TO COME!

This is my very first time writing, so perhaps I should introduce myself.

You and I are privileged to share a soul identity. I lived my life as a previous incarnation of you, and now I live inside your heart. You are me, and I am you. I carried our soul identity since I was born in 1940, in Cuba. Today is my 36th birthday, and I live in the United States. My name is Claudia Famosa. I'm very glad to meet you, and I am bursting to tell you more about me!

Here's a sobering thought: I almost missed meeting you! If I hadn't rear-ended that Gypsy fortune teller Madame Flora and almost killed her, I wouldn't have visited her in the hospital. And if I hadn't visited her, she wouldn't have introduced me to Soul Identity. And if she hadn't introduced me, I'd never be able to write you this, or to help you in your current incarnation.

I'm getting ahead of myself. I want to tell you all about me, and about what I've learned in this first-to-be-recorded incarnation. Maybe I can spare you some grief. Maybe I can help you find meaning. I get the chills just thinking that by writing this, I'm helping myself.

Most importantly of all, I need to tell you about Fico. He's the reason I survived. He's the reason I loved. And he's the reason I'm writing to you, because I can't bear the notion that we might be living without my (and your) soul mate alongside of us. You'll just have to trust me on this.

Maybe you've found Fico, or he's found you. It's easy to check; I've enclosed a copy of my one photograph of us, and I've also included a copy of his Soul Identity, calculated by Madame Flora, who's one of their readers. Your lover's eyes should produce the same identity. If they don't, get rid of him (or her), as there's somebody much better coming your way. I know this to be true, and I believe it with all my heart.

I was just re-reading what I wrote, and I'm afraid that I may scare you away with all of these instructions. I think that I should step back and tell you more about Fico. Then maybe it will all make sense.

I grew up in southeastern Cuba, below the foothills of the Sierra Maestra mountains, in Oriente Province. I lived on a coffee plantation, or cafetale. Fico was born in Havana. Our souls merged when I was almost sixteen and he seventeen, on a beautiful beach on a magical day.

It was January 19, 1957. We had that Saturday morning off from work. I had planned to go to the sea with my two girlfriends Sissi and Prissy, so we got up early and rode down on the burros, way up on top of the bags of coffee beans. The bags swayed back and forth down the steep mountain trails, and more than once I worried that the unanticipated top-heaviness would cause my burro to stumble over the edge of the cliff. But she was sure-footed, and we slowly descended into the valleys below.

Yesterday I asked Madame Flora if she thought you lived in Cuba, but she just stroked her chin and said your location hadn't been revealed to her yet. So since you may not live in Cuba, I must tell you about the views from the Sierra Maestra trails, for they are the absolute most beautiful trails in all creation. The air is clear and crisp, the sky is blue and dotted with bright, billowing clouds. Below you can see the green rows of yams and bananas in the lower plantations, their leaves stretching toward the sky. Behind them is the city of Santiago de Cuba, and the towers of El Cobre gleam in the distance to the left. The turquoise Caribbean glitters on your right, and when you draw close to the edge of the cliffs on your trusty burro, you'll see a thin strip of beach clinging to the base of the mountains, white-tipped waves crashing to shore. Above you the birds are singing, your skin is both heated by the sun and chilled by the mountain breezes, and your nose is filled with the lush scents of coffee beans and jungle decay.

I hope you have been blessed with growing up in a place like this. I am sure that you have made the best of where you were placed, but if you haven't already done so, please travel to the province of Oriente de Cuba and spend a week, a month, even a lifetime in the foothills of the Sierra Maestra. And of course bring Fico.

Back to the magical day. At the base of the mountains the trails joined the road to Santiago. The coffee packers helped us climb down, and as they continued to Santiago de Cuba, we three girls headed down to the beach. Our plans were to swim, collect some shells to decorate our shared room in the cafetale, then find some local boys for evening dancing.

Are you a dancer, future me? Have you danced the Cuban Rumbas? The *Guaguancó* is my favorite. The seduction and conquest and eventual capitulation lets us dance to the oldest story in the world. The twirling and spinning and brushing and thrusting up against your partner leaves your heart racing, your breath shallow, and your head light. Fico's and my life together was one long dance of the *Guaguancó*.

But I am getting ahead of myself! At this point in my story Fico and I have neither met nor danced. I am still on the beach with Sissi and Prissy. We have a nice collection of shells, and we've been wading in the water, lifting our long skirts to avoid the foamy waves.

We had always been best friends. I was the oldest, but Sissi was only a week younger than me, and Prissy nine days. Everybody in the cafetale called us las trillisas. Well, almost everybody; our mothers insisted on referring to their daughters not as the triplets, not as Sissi, Prissy, and Didi, but as Isabel, Preciosa, and Claudia.

We didn't look like triplets. Sissi and Prissy resembled the cafetale: dark coffee skin, coffee husk-colored curly hair, and coffee bean eyes; whereas my skin was café con leche, my hair was long and straight, and my eyes the color of honey.

I looked more like my father, and less like the local coffee workers. But that's a story for another time, my dear future me. This story, eventually, is about Fico.

I know who you are, my dear me, but since I don't know when you are, I'd better share bit of Cuba's history with you. History gets rewritten over the years, and I don't know what you may have learned about my times.

My 800-mile island home was first "discovered" by the Europeans when Columbus stopped by in 1492, not far from where I grew up. Cuba was owned by the Spanish until the late 19th century, when it became an American protectorate. The Americans treated the island as a source of nickel, sugar, coffee, and leisure. They bought most of the flatlands for their sugar cane farms, turned many of the local farmers into migrant workers, set up casinos in the cities, and used puppet governments to protect their economic interests. The last of the American-sponsored dictators was President Batista, and his iron fists caused the death of more than 20,000 citizens before Fidel Castro led a rebellion and forced him to flee Cuba at the end of 1958.

Fidel's rebellion was headquartered deep in the Sierra Maestra mountains, just a few miles behind my father's cafetal. He and 81 revolutionaries sailed a boat from Mexico to Cuba at the end of 1956 to kick-start an uprising. Batista's forces spotted the boat, and on December 5, three days after the revolutionaries beached, Batista attacked. Only 18 escaped into the mountains, but over the next two years, this tiny kernel of revolution grew.

The day Sissi, Prissy, and I waded on the beach was only six weeks after Fidel's forces were almost annihilated. Nobody knew if Fidel was alive or dead, and Batista was claiming that he had killed him. On the 15th of January, Batista declared a state of emergency and suspended the government and its Constitutional guarantees. He installed a cruel Chief of Police in Santiago de Cuba, whose counter-terrorism operations only fueled more anger at the government.

Nowadays, any news of Fidel's death would be met with much weeping and wailing in Cuba, and a lot of rejoicing in the States. But almost twenty years ago, nobody outside of the local revolutionaries in Santiago de Cuba and maybe the university students in Havana thought much of him. He and his brother had failed to take the Moncada Barracks and got a lot of locals tortured and killed four years before, but then Fidel left first for the US and then for Mexico when Batista granted amnesty in the lead-up to his new government.

My cafetale sympathized with the rebels. Batista's forces stomped over the coffee bean trees and confiscated our vegetables and livestock, while the rebels always paid for their food. The army set up checkpoints and harassed the packers as they delivered their loads of beans, and the rebels hired the packers as scouts. The only problem caused by the rebels was a labor shortage; the men and even some of the women were leaving the farms during harvest to join up with the revolution, and there were still beans to pick and dry and haul to the city.

Just two days before, Fidel and his rebels came out of hiding and attacked a State Police guard barracks on the mouth of the La Plata River, just west of the beach where I've left the story of Sissi, Prissy, and me. Fidel treated the surviving soldiers, then tied two of his own scouts to the trees and killed them because he thought they might be spying for Batista.

Now back to my story. It was Saturday, the 19th of January, and we three girls came out of the water, sat under some bushes, and unwrapped our empanadas and bananas. I remember we were talking about the evening, and which boys we wanted to dance with. Sissi was worried that the entertainment would be cancelled by the new curfew, and Prissi was afraid that the two boys she was currently enamored with had left to join the rebels.

I don't remember why, but we started arguing with each other. Those two girls started gossiping about my father. I got mad, our insults grew, and instead of making up like we usually did, this time it ended with Sissi and Prissy stomping off to town ahead of me. "Walk by yourself," Sissi said, as she and Prissy left.

It was barely mid-day. I didn't chase after them right away, but instead I stayed under the bushes on the beach and watched the fishing boats on the horizon. I thought about life in the cafetal, and I wondered how different it would be to live in the mountains with the rebels.

After a while of sitting alone, I must have dozed off, for the next thing I remember was waking up and seeing a young man not much older than I crouching over me.

I opened my mouth to scream, but he clamped a hand over my mouth. "Shh!" he hissed.

The boy had the most beautiful orange-brown eyes, and when they caught my own in their steady gaze, my fear disappeared and I felt calm and safe. I nodded, and after a few seconds, he slowly removed his hand from my lips.

He tilted his head toward the far end of the beach. "I can't get caught by the soldiers," he breathed. "They'll kill me, and probably you too, if they figure out who I am."

My heart trilled. "Revolutionary?" I whispered.

He nodded. "The day before yesterday we kicked their puta asses at La Plata. Batista's mad as hell, and he's sent out new troops."

"Why aren't you in the mountains?"

"I delivered a message in the city and I'm on my way back, but now these guys are in my way."

I couldn't wait to get to the dance and gloat to the girls about helping a revolutionary. Especially one so dashing. "What do you want me to do?"

"Stay still. If they do see us, we'll have to pretend we're a couple."

I nodded, hoping with all my heart that the soldiers would see us. "How would they know you're a rebel?" I asked.

He grimaced. "A small bullet wound on my left arm. My remembrance from La Plata."

"You're hurt?"

"It's not much more than a scratch. I was lucky; many men died."

I can tell you, future me, my heart was hammering away and I could barely catch my breath. Of course I didn't recognize it then, but I had that sexy feverish rash working its way up my tummy and across my breasts, giving me an itch that I didn't even understand needed scratching. A handsome, wounded, revolutionary who needed my help. And who just threatened that he may act like my boyfriend. Why, why, why weren't the soldiers seeing us yet?

I risked a glance at the soldiers; they had set themselves down and were unpacking what looked like their lunch. They were looking out to sea, pointing at the boats.

The young man looked like he was about to crawl away, so I said to him, "Should we practice acting like a couple, in case they turn around?" Crossing my fingers and toes, and feeling that rash creep up my neck.

Now he was looking at me differently. His eyes grazed down my body, across my not-so-flat but not-quite-as-big-as-I-wanted chest, pausing at my hips. Then back up again. "I guess we could practice, just in case." He smiled. "I'm Frederico, but you can call me Fico."

"Claudia, but I go by Didi."

"Have you ever kissed a boy before, Didi?"

I shook my head. "But I'm old enough."

He raised his eyebrows.

"Fifteen," I said. "And a half."

He smiled. "I'm almost seventeen. Now tilt your head just a bit to the side."

Future me, he lowered his head and licked his lips and brushed them against mine and I thought I had reached heaven sixty years ahead of schedule. And if you've inherited anything from me at all, I'm sure you know exactly how that feeling shoots out from your lips and down your sides and across your nipples and then dips into the center of your womanhood.

Or maybe your manhood. Madame Flora told me that you may not be a girl at all. If that's the case, I'm positive that you know the feeling, just as I'm positive that I felt Fico's manhood poking at me that very first time as our lips stayed together and as our tongues first met.

I pulled away, breathing hard. "Am I doing it right? Do you think it will fool them?"

"I think you need just a bit more practice, Didi." He reached out with his left arm, but then groaned, "Mierde, you made me forget my wound."

I tilted my head back and saw that the soldiers had heard Fico groan. "They're coming," I hissed. "Kiss me again."

Fico's glanced up at them, then swiftly dropped his gaze and kissed me, this time with a lot more passion. His tongue went deep, and his legs wrapped themselves around one of mine. His crotch was thrusting against my thigh. He hid his wounded arm under my back, groaning deeply into my mouth as he did so.

He was such a brave revolutionary. And it worked, too, the soldiers walked to twenty feet away and stood for a minute. Fico and I both stared into each other's eyes, kissing our way to safety. I thought that if it didn't work and the soldiers did catch us both, this moment in time was worth dying for.

And we kept kissing and thrusting and clinging to each other, and the next time I looked up, the soldiers were gone and we were alone.

Would you have told him the coast was clear and he could go? I think not, if you're anything like me. We're not stupid, are we? I suspect Fico also knew the soldiers were gone. Or maybe he forgot about the soldiers. In any case, we practiced acting like a couple until we didn't need to act any more.

January 19, 1959 was a perfect day. When I told him that I was missing the dance, Fico taught me the *Guaguancó*. We moved and swayed for hours. And right before sunset, when the fishing boats were back in view and heading to shore, Fico continued his *Guaguancó* lesson, only this time we were lying down, with him using the dance's distinctive vacunao thrust on top, then inside, me as he made me his woman.

And there you are, my dear future self, you have now met Fico. Now you know why we must find him (or her) again. What we had was too perfect, a one-in-a-million combination. Until you dance the *Guaguancó* together with him, you won't have lived.

In the morning Fico brought me to Fidel's camp in the Sierra Maestras and I became a revolutionary. I never went back to the cafetale of my youth.

five

GREETINGS, CLAUDIA-OF-THE-FUTURE:

Or maybe I am Your-name-of-the-past. Either way is fine with me.

It took me a long time to write again. I just re-read the letter I wrote you two years ago, and I must say that I sound so young.

It is August, and Miami is hot and humid. I am 38 years young today. My dentist husband of almost two years, bless his old and rich soul, is too cheap to buy air conditioning, so I'm sitting in the shade, outside by the pool. The pool boy, who looks like he could have been Fico's little brother, has just left, so it's time for me to stop staring and dreaming and remembering. Time to tell you more about my current (and your previous) life.

I'll start with my father. He was the eldest descendant of one of the original French coffee plantation owners who ran away from Haiti when the slaves revolted and took over the country. Their family lived on a cafetale in the foothills of the Sierra Maestra, the south-eastern mountain range made famous by Che Guevara and the Castro brothers. Their cafetale, like the other 170 around them, was falling into disrepair, as more modern techniques for growing coffee had undercut their once-lofty prices. My father was an aristocrat at wrong end of a family tree dipping into obscurity, and doing his best to recover.

My mother was a famous Cuban Salsa dancer who worked the casinos in Havana. She and my father met while he was on a three-month trip to the capital, trying to attract investment for establishing a cultural heritage center on his plantation. Although unfruitful from a money raising point of view, the seed of our own life was, you may say, planted into my mother on the bed, in the bathroom, and once even up against the wall in the elevator in one of the swanky capital hotels.

You may be asking how I know these details. After Batista fled, the revolution succeeded, but before we left Cuba, my mother came to visit Fico and me in Havana. She only stayed the night, but the stories she told after downing almost a full bottle of rum would've made a stripper blush.

You can imagine the ruckus my father stirred up when he brought his pregnant dancer home to meet his wife and the rest of the family. From what I heard from the other servants, his wife clamped down so hard on his cojones that he never left the safety of the cafetale again.

Their whirlwind romance sounds kind of like the books my husband's large-bottomed sisters live their lives through. They lounge around this same pool, ooh-ing and ahh-ing over the adventures and affairs of dashing heroes and blushing maidens. I watch them fan themselves when they reach the steamy parts, peeking up to see if anybody notices. If they think I'm not paying attention, they spread their legs and burrow through their rolls of fat and maybe even find a way to rub some joy into their miserable lives.

Never mind them. When I get that old I'll be slender and sexy and living my life on my terms, not sucking on the tit of my younger brother's generosity. But by then both of them and my husband will all be dead, anyway.

So why did I recently marry an old fart, we may be asking ourselves? The answer is simple: money. Not just for me, but money for us. I need it, we need it, to ensure your future is filled with at least as much happiness as I had with Fico.

With the prices of gold shooting up these days, I want to get as much funds deposited into our account as possible. Madame Flora told me that Soul Identity uses the current price in gold to measure my deposit. The sooner I make a large deposit at a lower price, the more we'll have in the future. You need to have enough to find Fico, woo him, and live out the good life that ended too soon for us.

Back to the story. You'll remember that I left the cafetale to join the revolutionary camp with Fico. We put our lives on the line so our people could be free. At least that's what we were told; I spent my days cleaning up after all the men, and my nights, when he wasn't on sentry duty, with Fico. We'd creep away into the jungle, along with other couples and the camp whores, and when we were done, whisper back and forth about our life and our future.

I learned that Fico's last name was Valdes, which meant that he was an orphan raised by the Casa de Beneficencia in Havana. All orphans raised in this church were surnamed Valdes, which, minus the apparently offending accent on top of the "e", was the name of its founder, Bishop Valdés. Fico's being an orphan didn't bother me, the daughter of a casino dancer and a cafetale scion. We used to pretend that our mothers had once been best friends in Havana, and that our union was a way of bringing them back together when they couldn't do it themselves.

Now it occurs to me that I'm counting on you, future me, and future Fico too, to reunite us in a similar way. Please don't let me down.

The early days we spent in the revolutionary camp knitted Fico's and my relationship together so tightly that I was convinced that nothing would ever pull us apart. One starlit night Fico asked me to marry him, and of course I said yes. I was the happiest girl in the world, drifting from one happiness to another just like the mariposa de cristal, our mountain butterfly with the transparent wings, went from flower to intoxicating flower.

By July, after I had been there seven months, our contingent had grown to over 200 revolutionaries. Fidel split us up into three columns to take the fight directly to Batista's army. Fico and I went with Raul. By the next spring, we kicked Batista's forces out of the Sierra Maestras, and even though they came back and surrounded us with ten thousand troops and dropped enough bombs to chase us out of our camp, we beat them, and when they retreated, many of his soldiers stayed and joined our side.

Fico was growing noticeable in the camp. As he was excellent with numbers and logistics, he became a supply master for Camilo Cienfuegos, one of Fidel's *Comandantes*. Cienfuegos was one of 19 survivors from the 82 revolutionaries who sailed with Castro from Mexico. In the fall of 1958, Fidel put Cienfuegos in charge of the western column of his army.

Fico was asked to quartermaster for Cienfuegos. He didn't want to leave me behind, but we both knew how important he was to the success of the rebellion.

The day before the column was to leave, Fico came to the small casita that I shared with some of the other girls. He was carrying a large package and a serious expression on his face.

"What is it, my love?" I asked. "Did Cienfuegos decide to leave early?"

He shuffled his feet and shook his head. Then he flashed me a big toothy grin. "A wonderful opportunity," he cried. "We're getting married tonight!"

Future me, believe me when I tell you that the camp was the last place on earth that I expected to hold my wedding. Since I was a child I had dreamed of a church, with Sissi and Prissy at my side. But holding the ceremony that night couldn't have been more perfect.

The large package Fico was carrying contained white wedding clothes for me and him, family clothes lent by Camilo Cienfuegos. A priest was visiting Fidel that day, and he was drafted to officiate. And my Fico even worked a miracle; somehow he had gotten Sissi and Prissy to take the perilous journey into the camp to be there with me!

The cooks had prepared a goodbye feast for Fidel's army, and they added a wedding cake to their menu. Fidel and Che stood in for my father, and they both gave me away. After the ceremony we danced all night long. All of us, that is, except me and Fico, who snuck off at midnight to a private cabin graciously supplied by Fidel himself. We watched the full moon rise, and then Fico, my husband, took me to bed.

In the morning, as I said goodbye to my husband, and also to Sissi and Prissy, I didn't know if I would ever see any of them again.

The rest of the story of the Cuban Revolution should be in your history books: how our army split the island in two; how Cienfuegos, with Fico's help, won the Battle of Yaguajay; and how they met up with Che Guevara the next afternoon, on the final day of 1958, in Santa Clara to wrap up the war. How Batista fled Cuba that very night.

But that belongs in the history books. The story for you, dear future me, is what happened to me and Fico. How our perfect life was ripped from us, and why you must help us get it back.

With the war over, Cienfuegos asked Fico to join the treasury, because, he said, he had the knack for ensuring that just enough, but not too much, supply was available at just the right time. The country needed capable people like Fico.

I was thrilled that my husband had distinguished himself. After all, the Hero of Yaguajay was an important man in Fidel's circle, and having Cienfuegos as Fico's sponsor was a privilege. Also, it kept Fico out of the tribunals, where they were herding Batista's men through quick and dirty trials and executions.

So Fico took the job and sent for me to join him in Havana. We rented a small apartment on top of a convenience store, and while Fico was at work, I cleaned, cooked, and did my best to be a good wife. The noisy and vibrant city was different from the cafetale, and nothing at all like the revolutionary camp, and we both preferred life in the capital.

This afternoon I asked my ancient sisters-in-law what happens in their romance novels once the hero and his blushing maiden realize that their destiny is bound together and they have their big love scene. "What comes next?" I asked.

They looked at each other and cackled. "Why, that's when the book ends," the younger one said. "Nobody cares after that."

"I guess they realize pretty soon that their life is mundane, and that's when they start reading their own romance novels," the older one mused.

It sounds sad and trite, but I suppose that's exactly what was happening to Fico and me. After the first few months filled with the joys of midnight (and early morning) sex with nobody else listening in, and of the purpose-driven work of transforming a government, we settled into a routine that wasn't so exciting. It was normal. And maybe we both were missing the excitement, for just as I started noticing that the young man who delivered my groceries was actually quite handsome and flirty, I also noticed the faint scent of cheap perfume and the blush of almost-wiped-away lipstick on Fico's white shirt collars.

Did I say anything, future me? I didn't. I had seen this drama play out many times in the camp over the previous year, and it always ended with the girl kicking the man out of her life, to her later regret. I wasn't going to be a wife who couldn't hang on to her husband. Besides, Fico was my soul mate, and he just needed to figure out how good he had it with me.

So instead of picking a fight, I devoted myself to being the best wife to be found in Havana. I never looked at that grocery boy again. I made sure Fico's food was always hot, his clothes always clean, and his fantasies in bed always satisfied. I am proud to say that it worked; within two months there was no more perfume, no more lipstick, and no more excuses why he had to work late. Fico couldn't wait to get back home.

Future me, I hope you don't think me weak. I prefer to think I was the strong one, managing our relationship as well as Fico was managing the finances of the country. Sometimes you have rough spots, but your job is to keep the train on track and headed forward and not let it get derailed.

One day soon after the lipstick disappeared, Fico came home with a worried expression on his face. "What's wrong, my darling?" I asked as I led him to the table.

"I made a very big mistake," he said.

I quickly looked away and squeezed my fists together, counting to ten. If Fico was ready to confess his indiscretions, I wanted to be composed. "I'm sure every mistake is forgivable," I said.

"Not this one," he said, and he gulped his wine even before he sat down. "This mistake could destroy our happy life together."

Was he over the other puta? Or maybe there was a new one? I did a quick mental review of his behavior. He had come home straight from work. Our time in bed was more fabulous than ever. In fact, it was probably so good that he felt the need to get his past indiscretions off his chest.

So I told him, "Fico, darling, if you made a simple mistake, no matter how bad you think it is, the best thing to do is just to put it aside, never mention it, and work doubly hard to be sure it never, ever, happens again."

My husband gazed at me for a few minutes, and I watched his expression go from fear to worry to understanding. Then he offered a tentative smile, stood up, and gave me a big kiss on my lips.

"Didi," he said. "You are the best and wisest wife in the world, and I am so lucky you married a miserable shit like me!"

I hugged and kissed him back and hoped that he had learned his lesson.

Oh, future me, you see me all smug and content with how smart I was, but how wrong it all turned out to be! Fico wasn't confessing his indiscretions, and the advice I gave him was the worst possible I could have offered. For what Fico did was something that, in hindsight, was considered traitorous to our newly formed country: he cashed the monthly lease check that the US paid Cuba for the use of Guantanamo Bay Naval Base, and then, based on my ill-formed advice, covered it up.

Now, I'm not sure what's happening in your future world, but here in mine the US has been renting the naval base from Cuba ever since 1898, when in gratitude of helping free them from Spain, the Cuban government offered them the land. The US preferred to lease it instead, and paid them the monthly amount of $2,000 in gold coins. By 1959, the lease amount was no longer in gold, but was paid as a check of $4,085, made out to the "Treasurer General of the Republic." That title ceased to exist when Batista fled Cuba and Fidel's government took over.

Even though the country changed hands, the US kept paying. And Fico, poor Fico, in the early days of his helping in the treasury, cashed the check he received in January and used the funds to pay some of the bills that Fidel's tribunals were incurring.

Why was this so bad? Because some time in February, Fidel used his treasury department to inform the US that the base, just like the various plantations owned by the American corporations, was Cuban land, and it belonged to the Cuban people. It was time for them to move out of Guantanamo.

Of course the US had other ideas. They replied with a copy of the treaty granting them the land in perpetuity. This letter reached Fidel, and he instructed the treasury department to politely inform the US that their treaty was with the previous country and not the current one, therefore the treaty was null and void.

On the day Fico came home worried, he had just received a letter from the US that in essence said, sorry Fidel, but your new government confirmed the treaty when they cashed the monthly rent check eight months before, in January.

You see the problem? Fico was the man who deposited that check. Fico was the man who must deliver to Fidel the letter that condemned his actions. Fico was the man who would be blamed.

And my advice, future me, my silly advice is what killed Fico. For in my self-centered and smug assumption, I assumed he was talking about me, and I told him to cover up his misdeeds. Poor Fico did just that; he destroyed the letter, and tried to remove all traces that tied him to the deposit of the original check. This worked for a couple of months, until that terrible day in October when Camilo Cienfuegos himself came to our house with a warrant for the arrest of Frederico Valdes.

Fortunately for us, the *Comandante* came alone. After announcing his intentions, he put his finger to his lips and motioned me to pull the shades.

"What really happened?" he asked Fico.

Fico told a story of following his best intentions, but then getting trapped as he tried to cover up the mess he made.

"It was stupid of you to try to hide," Cienfuegos said. "You should have told Fidel immediately what you did when you got that letter."

Fico hung his head. "I am ashamed, *Comandante*."

Cienfuegos reached out and gripped Fico's shoulder. "We must leave immediately," he said. "Or you, Fico, will die."

"You will help us?" I asked.

The Hero of Yaguajay glared at me. "Four days ago, against my better judgment, I followed Fidel's orders and arrested my best friend. He will be executed shortly. I don't ever want to do something like that again."

He continued after a long moment of silence, "I have grown tired of watching people who fought with me die. Especially when their deaths come from the hands of other comrades. I am beginning to think that all rulers, no matter how noble their original cause, grow into despots."

The *Comandante* told us his plan. He would "chase" Fico and me to Camagüey, where his Cesna six-seater airplane was hangered. There he would arrest us and fly us back to Havana. But we wouldn't reach Havana, for Cienfuegos had a plan: we'd ditch the plane in the ocean and board a speedboat to Florida. Everybody would assume we died in the crash, and the three of us would all start new lives in America.

"But this is the country we fought for," Fico said. "These are our people."

"If we stay, you'll die," Cienfuegos said. "I'll probably be assigned to kill you, as you are also a hero of the revolution. And if I have to kill any more heroes, I'll kill myself."

Fico squeezed his eyes shut for a moment. Then he turned to Cienfuegos and whispered something in his ear. Cienfuegos nodded and said, "I've taken care of that already," as he stood up to leave.

The *Comandante* pointed at me. "Leave now, Didi. Don't pack anything. Just get out as fast as you can."

And so we went. I disobeyed and grabbed one wedding photo as Cienfuegos opened the shades, leaned his head out the window, and beckoned his driver to come upstairs. We jumped out the back window and stole his Jeep. Then we drove directly to Camagüey, where we were "caught" by Cienfuegos the next evening. He boarded us on his plane that evening and registered to fly us back to Havana to stand trial.

Only we all know now that this plane never got there. I am sure that you can read this in the history books, future me. Cienfuegos' plane disappeared. He died a war hero, and the schoolchildren of Cuba still throw roses in the ocean on 28th of October to remember the country's loss. Even now you can find Camilo Cienfuegos' face on Cuba's 20-peso bill.

Cienfuegos did crash his plane in the ocean. It was a rough landing, and Cienfuegos did not survive. And it was a rough voyage for me and Fico. Our boat was adrift for three weeks before we were rescued by American fishermen, but by then, Fico, my dear dear Fico, had perished. Only I was rescued, along with the one photograph of our wedding.

I killed him, future me, with my selfish advice. You need to get him back for us.

Chapter 6

"What do you mean missing?" I ask. I glance at my phone, as if Scott's face is going to pop up and he's going to start talking like he did last night. But he doesn't, and I reach out and grab his mom's hand.

She squeezes back. Her palms are cold, like she and her husband have been outside for a while. "He told us he was chasing something down," she said. "Something big enough to make him go underground."

Scott's dad says, "He said if he was still gone after six weeks, you'd be the only one who could help."

They're two weeks early; but it is their son who's missing. "So you found me in Denny's?" I ask.

Scott's dad digs into his pocket and pulls out his phone. "He gave me this new app. It's supposed to track you both."

He hands me his device. The screen shows a map of Seattle zoomed into SoDo. A little tiny picture of me is hovering over Denny's. I tap on my face, and it enlarges to fill the screen. I'm in my wrinkled emerald dress, my hair a mess. You can see the back of Mikk's bald head in the bathroom behind me.

Scott may not have answered when I read my eyes, but he kept the photo I took. Clever. I ask, "So I popped up on your phone this morning?"

"No, last night it showed us your face on top of a downtown theatre," he says.

"Same dress, better hair and makeup," Scott's mom adds. "But you were gone by the time we got there."

That must have been the image from the bimbo's phone. The one Rain smashed.

"Then later that night we saw you at an ATM about a mile from here, but again we missed you," she says.

"The app only really started to track you this morning," Scott's dad says.

I look at the screen and I notice there's a time overlay mode. I slide and pinch to bracket yesterday and today. I see the image Rain took at the event, then a fuzzy fisheye image of me and Mikk at what must be the ATM. It shows a breadcrumb trail tied to the picture from this morning, leading from the hotel to the car to Denny's. Scott's app is impressive; he's pulling data from readers, phones, and even the bank's video.

"Is this one of the apps he's selling?" I ask.

He shakes his head. "He says we'd get shut down if they found out what it can do."

"I think he's right," I say. I give the phone back. "So why are you in Seattle?"

"We're staying at Scott's place," he says, and when my jaw almost falls into my lap he adds, "Wait. Didn't you know he moved out here?"

I shake my head. Guess that explains how he got his photos of Rain's indiscretions.

"It's gorgeous," Scott's mom says. "I could live in the Pacific Northwest."

"You say that now," Mikk says. "But try it in March when it's been raining every damn day since October and you haven't had a sun break in six weeks."

"But why here?" I ask. As if I don't know.

Scott's dad shrugs. "He can do his contract work from anywhere. Currently he's conducting a search for new overseers."

Whatever. "Where's his place?" I ask Scott's mom.

"West Seattle, along the sound. A bit south of Alki Beach," she says. "He bought the place back in June."

"Actually, it's a company house," Scott's dad says. "So technically it's one-quarter yours."

"Sounds like you've got a stalker," Mikk says to me.

I sure do. I glare at my ex-boyfriend's parents. "Look, you two," I say, "Scott's been intruding on my life for two years now, and I've been consistently ignoring him. Now you tell me he's moved into my city. My neighborhood, even. Maybe you should find someone else to help."

"I knew this was a bad idea," Scott's dad says to his wife.

But her eyes narrow and she points at me. "Listen, missy. Do you think we'd have interrupted your perfect pre-destined soul mate life if we had a choice?" She's breathing pretty hard now. "My son is missing, and apparently you're our only option. You're going to help us find him. You owe it to us."

I try to get myself offended by her comments, but I can't seem to summon up the rage. I look across at Mikk's baby-blue bathrobe held together with my yoga top, then down at my gown, then out the window. "If this is the perfect life," I say, "then I seriously need to reset my expectations."

"It's pretty perfect for me," Mikk says. "I'm having a ball."

"Not last night you weren't," I point out. "Not at home."

He shrugs. "Details. It's one day at a time for a man my age. And it got better at the hotel."

I face Scott's parents. "I was planning to fly back east this morning," I say. "I've got no house, no job, and after last night's screw-up, not as much money as I hoped to have."

"Our company's got plenty of funds," Scott's mom says. "Just come back."

"You've got two years' worth of profit sharing we've been holding for you," his dad adds. "That's over six hundred grand."

Mikk raises his hand. "With money like that, I vote we help find this kid–what's his name again?"

"Scott," his mom says.

Mikk nods. "I'll try to remember that." He looks at me. "Val?"

Mikk needs a place to stay, and he probably needs a distraction. I think about the implications of stashing my ex-husband's grandfather in my ex-boyfriend's house. Maybe it could work. "Can you squeeze me and Mikk into Scott's place?" I ask.

"There's more than enough room," Scott's dad says.

Really, if Scott's in trouble, I have to help him. Regardless of our past. He'd do it for me.

I look at each of them in turn, then give a short nod.

"Hooray, our adventure continues," Mikk says. "Now can we go and get some clothes? The ladies here may overheat from all my indecency."

Scott's parents give me the address to the company house, and on the way Mikk and I stop at Freddy's for clothes and toiletries. We get ourselves a week's worth of outfits and two roller bags, then we change in Freddy's restrooms. We head to Scott's, which is less than a mile from my old place. In my book, that makes Scott a stalker.

The Waverly family security business apparently had a couple banner years. The house is an old Cape that got its last facelift just recently: granite countertops, old-growth fir floors, a wall of windows overlooking the Puget Sound, covered balconies, stone-tiled bathrooms, and an in-out gas fireplace. Mikk and I are given our own floor in the former attic, complete with two bedrooms, a bathroom, and a small kitchen.

We move our new clothes upstairs, then gather with Scott's parents on the patio. Mikk stands at the railing and squints at the waves slapping against the sea wall. "Why would you trade a life like this for one with my loser grandson?" he asks.

A question I've caught myself pondering too many times over the past two years. But I'm not about to tell him that.

"She didn't trade Scott in," Scott's mom says to Mikk. She gives my arm a squeeze. "We know what happened, Val. You made the right decision at the time."

At the time is an interesting choice of words. "What did he tell you?" I ask.

They look at each other for a minute. "He didn't tell us exactly," Scott's dad says.

Another glance between the two of them. His mom says, "Did you read Scott's books?"

I shake my head. "But I know about them."

"Well, he started writing a third one. But..." She grimaces. "He only wrote as far as your breakup before he deleted the whole draft."

"If he deleted it, how did you read it?" I ask.

"I saw it on his laptop one day."

"Just say it like it is," Scott's dad says. "He got moody and stopped talking to us. Then you got nosy, and you broke into his computer."

"Don't be the pot calling the kettle black," she says. "You read it too."

Scott Waverly, self-proclaimed security zealot, snooped on by his mother. "Does he know you read it?" I ask.

"Of course not," she says.

"You hope not," Scott's dad says.

"So what did it say?" Mikk asks.

They both stare at him, and Scott's mom sputters, "I beg your pardon."

He holds out his palms. "Just keeping us on plot," he says. "Tell Val what Steve wrote. I want to know too."

"It's Scott," she says.

Mikk nods. "Yup. Your son. I've been paying attention."

"You said Steve."

"Did I?" He crinkles his brow. "I think I'm doing pretty good for an eighty-year-old. Maybe if you told us the rest of the story, your boy's name will start sinking in."

She points her finger at him, and it looks like she's about to give Mikk an earful, but after a moment of standing there and pursing her lips, she turns to me and asks, "Is the grandson anything like the old man?"

I grab both their hands. "He doesn't mean any harm," I tell Scott's mom. And to Mikk I say, "Try to be a bit more patient."

Mikk drops into a deep bow. "I apologize, madame," he says, his head almost on his knees. Then he groans and says, "Val, can you help me get back up?"

I lift his shoulders and get him standing again. Scott's dad leads us over to a cluster of patio chairs, and we settle into them.

Scott's mom turns to me. "Scott started the third book with you two meeting Archie in Moscow. You were on your way to visit your family."

That releases a flood of memories. Scott and I had gotten engaged on Valentine's Day, and we flew to Russia the next week to tell my parents. Archibald Morgan had embarked a few months before on a new career as philanthropist after retiring as executive overseer of Soul Identity. He was working with various Roma groups, and we had agreed to meet up at the Moscow station for a quick reunion before Scott and I took the overnight train to my parent's village.

"I remember how Mr. Morgan had really changed," I say. "Instead of his limo, he climbed out of the back of this old beat-up car. And no green outfit, either; his coat and scarf were a rainbow of colors." Like he was rebelling against his lifetime of self-control.

"You know he returned to Soul Identity a few months ago," Scott's dad says.

That seems odd. He was so happy with his retirement that I can't imagine anything dragging him back. Unless Soul Identity was in trouble. "Did something happen to Berry?" I ask. Berry is the current overseer in charge of the organization.

He narrows his eyes. "Aren't you and Rain their poster children?"

"I don't keep up with the gossip," I say. And that's an understatement. Except for what I need to know to do our quarterly presentations, I avoid all other Soul Identity interactions and information. It's still too painful for me, especially since I no longer believe.

"Berry had a heart attack," Scott's mom says. "We flew up for the funeral back in May."

Berry used to be Scott's neighbor in Maryland. Almost four years ago I helped Scott get him in and get a bad overseer out. That's also when Scott and I hooked up in one of those love-at-first-sight cases. We had been the perfect couple, until we screwed it up. He screwed it up.

"If Mr. Morgan came back, that must mean that there's been no new overseer recoveries," I say. When I left their employ, Archie and Berry were the only two living overseers.

"Archie's the last one," Scott's dad says.

"And he's getting nervous," Scott's mom adds. "His first night back, he cut a deal with Scott to use his new apps to quickly find an overseer." She shakes her head. "The key word was quickly. Archie's what, eighty-five now? Maybe eighty-six?"

"That's barely past prime," Mikk says. "But what's an overseer?"

Time to get Mikk up to speed. "You already know Soul Identity's like an eternal safety deposit box that lets its members pass things to future members of their soul lines." I say.

He nods. "That's where Rain got his money. From Claudia."

"Correct. They have millions of members and a couple trillion in assets, so they need some kind of oversight," I tell him. "That's the overseers. They're like a board of directors."

"How come I've never heard of these overseers?"

"Most members haven't," Scott's dad says.

"How do you become one?"

"You have to be born one," I say. "A long time ago, this Greek philosopher Thales started the organization with some Egyptian priests and their paintings of people's irises and soul identities. Then King Darius moved everything to Babylon, and he had his entire empire's soul identities read. He found matches against thirty-five of those paintings. These people became the original overseers."

Mikk massages the top of his bald head. "I think I get it. This old guy Archie has the same soul identity as one of those original Egyptian paintings?"

"He does," Scott's dad says.

"Where's the other thirty-four?"

"Berry was one, but nobody knows about the rest of them," I say. "Historically Soul Identity has been led by three to five overseers at any given time."

"Nobody knows what will happen to Soul Identity if Mr. Morgan dies before another overseer comes along," Scott's dad says.

"Ah," Mikk says. "That makes your ex-boyfriend's current search pretty important." He points at Scott's mom. "See? I have been paying attention."

"It makes his search crucial," Scott's mom says. "But let's get back to Scott's deleted story. You and Scott have dinner with Archie, and then you head off to see your parents. There's some hanky-panky on the train–"

"–In Scott's books, there's always some hanky-panky going on between him and Val–" Scott's dad tells Mikk.

"–And your parents pick the two of you up in the morning in some Russian city."

"Nizhny Novgorod," I say. "They really liked Scott, you know."

She raises her eyebrows. "That's not what he wrote. He said they glared at him the whole week, and your mother kept whispering things in your ear while making some funny hand gestures at him."

"She was protecting us from the evil eye," I say. Then I remember what my mother told me on our last day in town. "What did Scott write about the necklace?" I ask her.

"I was just getting to that," she says. "Your parents tell you this story of a Cuban lady visiting you when you were a baby, the necklace she left for you, and the promise that one day a man would come to marry you."

And that, in a nutshell, is the story that Rain and I were supposed to tell last night at the Soul Identity dinner. Before Scott interrupted the speech with those pictures of Rain and the half-naked bimbos. The story of Claudia finding me in the Soviet Union and telling my parents that I was the reincarnation of her dead husband Fico. Her promise to return in her next life as a man in time to marry me, and her gift of several thousand rubles to help raise me.

The story my parents never hinted at when I was growing up, and didn't bother telling me until I was engaged to Scott. The story that Scott couldn't handle. The very one that led to our break-up and my impulsive marriage to Rain.

But that's my version. Now I guess I'll have to hear Scott's mom's version.

"He claimed that was the beginning of the end," she says. "You barely spoke to him on the train ride back to Moscow. You seemed distracted on the flight home. And once you were back in Maryland, you wore that necklace." She points to my neck. "I see you're not wearing it anymore."

"It's in my soul line collection," I say. The necklace was half a pendant: when Rain later found me, he brought the matching half Claudia left for him. I buried mine in the depositary four months ago, on the day I filed for divorce.

"I remember when we picked you up at the airport," Scott's dad says. "There was something not quite right between you."

But that's just parental revisionist history. I say, "We were fine then." I remember those days, the last month before our breakup. I spent my evenings searching the archives for Claudia, excited by the possibility that I was part of a story bigger than this life. Scott helped me dig for clues on Fico, but we came up short. It was as if he and Claudia were ghosts, figments of my parents' imagination.

But then in April, just as we started flirting with the idea that maybe Claudia had been Scott's undocumented soul line ancestor, Rain knocked on our door. He showed me his half of my necklace and told me about Claudia and Fico's past. "Our relationship only fell apart after Rain arrived," I say, "And only then, after Scott almost killed him."

"He wasn't trying to kill him," Scott's dad says, "He was just trying to scare him away."

By the time Rain and I had finished talking the night he came, it was the wee hours of the morning, and Scott was sound asleep when I crawled into our bed. In the morning Scott offered to take Rain on a kayak ride, and somewhere along a deserted beach of the Chesapeake Bay, he almost drowned him.

Scott's dad says, "Rain blew it all out of proportion."

A coast guard patrol happened to motor by, and they apprehended Scott after they caught him holding Rain face-down in the water. They brought the kayak and the two men, one in handcuffs and one on a stretcher, right to our dock.

"I saw the coast guard video," I say. "They had to resuscitate Rain."

Scott's dad shakes his head. "You only saw what they saw. And you've never given Scott the chance to explain."

I rode in the ambulance with Rain. And while I brooded all night in a hospital chair, I let Scott stew in jail, neither informing his parents nor arranging bail until late the next morning. He tried to talk to me on the drive home, but by then it was too late; by then I had already decided to give Rain and me, the soul line heirs of Claudia and Fico, a chance.

"Scott knows he made a mistake," Scott's mom says.

"He actually wrote that in his draft?" I ask.

She nods. "Even though he knew Rain was wrong for you, he should have let you discover that yourself."

And just like last night when Rain earned my knee in his crotch, an almost uncontrollable flash of rage courses down my spine and shoots out my arms and legs. That smug, self-righteous bastard!

"That's not it at all." I try to keep the anger out of my voice, but it's not easy after two years of replaying these events in my head. "When push came to shove, your son didn't trust me. He didn't have faith in us, and he tried to solve the problem without me." I wipe away the tears that spring into my eyes and I whisper, "That's what chased me away."

Scott's dad brings me a box of tissues, and thankfully nobody says anything until I get my sniffling under control.

"In any case, Scott's still missing," I say. "Did he actually claim I was the only one who could help?"

Scott's parents both nod.

"Anything else you can add?"

They both shake their heads.

I ball the wet tissue in my hand and stand up. "Can I get connected and start digging?"

"Of course you can," Scott's dad says as he rises. "I'll take you up to the office."

seven

Scott's office is above the main floor and under the attic where Mikk and I are lodged, and it's giving me the deja vus. The layout is almost a copy of the office we shared on Kent Island. The same fabulous west-facing water view through huge picture windows tempts my eyes away from the four laptops and two wall-hanging flat screens. Though the Puget Sound is crystal clear, not Chesapeake Bay brown, and the view below is a patio instead of a sloping Maryland lawn.

He's still got four desks, though. One for himself, two for his parents, and one extra, butting up to his own. In Maryland that was my desk. A nameplate sits on top, but it's face-down. I flip it over: Val Nikolskaya. Seriously, Scott?

Scott's dad clears his throat. "Before you think he's totally crazy, let me tell you that I dug that nameplate out of the closet and placed it here only this morning. After you appeared on my phone."

I point at the sleek aluminum laptop resting in the middle, secrets locked inside its closed cover. "And this?"

"Now that was parked there when we got here last week," he says. He lifts it up and shows me a note stuck to its underside. "For Val, when she comes," it reads in Scott's scrawl.

Not if, but when. I brush my fingertips over its paper-thin shell, but I take a moment before cracking the laptop open. I'm not sure I'm ready to hurtle down this path. Especially when there's a good chance that Scott's just pulling my strings, executing some elaborate game to try to win me back.

If I catch him gaming me, I'll squash any lingering hopes he has for us.

I open the lid. A tiny blue light blinks on, and straightaway the camera embedded above the screen splashes my live image across the screen's background.

My tears on the patio have left my eyes bloodshot. My red curls are less lazy and more unruly than I like. But I'm feeling good about this hint of determination that both tightens and plumps my lips. It thrusts my head up and jaw forward, even when I'm looking down at the laptop. Goodbye, Ekko, and welcome back, Nikolskaya.

Scott's dad interrupts my mental surname re-alignment. "I'll be outside," he says. He heads to the door, and then turns back and adds, "No need to admit it, because it's written all over your face. This office. This work. Being here. It suits you."

That brings on a grin and even a little blush high in my cheeks, because he's called it. He leaves, and I reach out and tap the "Identify" ribbon that's splashed across the top half-inch of the display.

On the screen my face fades to a bleached-out gray-and-white, except for three remaining swaths of color across my eyes and mouth. The words "Don't Blink" appear under my chin. I comply. A border around the screen darkens, then flashes twice.

A second later my name appears in the top ribbon along with "Identified", and "Don't Blink" is replaced with "Stick Out Your Tongue," followed by an underlined "Why the hell would I do this?" link.

That's the question going through my mind, so I tap it, and Scott's face appears in a video window on the bottom right. "You are helping me test out a new two-factor authentication and laptop personalization product," he says. "First I identify you. Then I make sure you're not a photograph by flashing your irises and giving you a random command to execute. If you can do it and you're one of the good guys, the laptop's yours." His eyes go wide. "But if you can't, or if you're not, then I wipe the laptop clean."

Sounds fair. I stick out my tongue, and the top ribbon changes from "Identified" to "Authenticated", and a second later to "Authorized". My face is gone, replaced by the desktop. Application tiles start populating the left side, and a row of people's faces appear across the bottom: Scott, each of his parents, me, Rain, and Mr. Morgan.

I zoom into my face. Underneath it reads, "Location: West Seattle Office. Confidence: High." His parents show the same. Rain's image shows he's home, but with only a medium confidence. I tap my ex-husband's face, and a map of Seattle pops up. It contains little breadcrumb paths; I'm assuming these are Rain's last movements as tracked by his mobile phone. I see the path Rain took from West Seattle to the Soul Identity talk yesterday evening, and a jaunt to Bellevue he seems to have made on his way home. So the bimbo lives on the Eastside. There's a small spreadsheet at the bottom, and it shows that Rain's last update, from his mobile at his place, came in just after midnight.

Scott's turn. I slide the screen over to his image. "Location: Unknown. Confidence: N/A." I tap his forehead, and his map contains no breadcrumbs, his spreadsheet no data. Scott's off his own grid.

And Mr. Morgan? According to this, he's spent the past seven hours in his office at the Soul Identity headquarters in Sterling, Massachusetts. I can picture the room, spartan furnishings with the organization's logo hanging on the wall behind his desk.

Maybe the overseer can tell me something about Scott's whereabouts. I tap on the screen until I get Mr. Morgan's contact information. There's a button labeled "Video Call," and I tap it.

The computer emits a Euro-phone-like beep, and then I'm face to face with Archibald Morgan for the first time in two years. He's wearing a white shirt and a green bow tie like before, but his full white hair is longish now, and his glasses are more oval, with thick green frames.

"Right on schedule, Ms. Nikolskaya," he says. "It is good to see you again."

"You too, Mr. Morgan," I reply. "But whose schedule am I on?"

"Scott said you would be calling me today. I have been sitting at my desk for the last two hours, waiting for this new computer to ring." He leans forward, and I see a twinkle in his eyes. "I dared not leave, even to use the facilities."

"When did Scott tell you that I'd be calling?"

He scrunches up his forehead. "It must be around three weeks ago. He put an appointment on my calendar, so I wouldn't forget." He spins his laptop around, and now his camera's pointing at his desktop computer screen. His daily schedule runs down the right hand side. Then I see his hand in the image, and his finger waggles right over a small box of text.

"Valentina Nikolskaya will call you," I read. "Please have that new laptop turned on." Scott has blocked from four to eight p.m. Sterling time.

I eye the clock as Mr. Morgan spins the laptop back around. It's three here, six in Sterling. "Did he tell you what we'd be talking about?"

Mr. Morgan nods. "How did he phrase it? I am to 'bring you up to speed' on the task I assigned him. He told me that you two are back working together."

"We're not, really," I say. "I told his parents that I'd help look for him. Nothing else."

"Is he missing?"

"Out of touch from them for the past month," I say. "Do you know where he is?"

He shakes his head.

"I just heard about Berry," I tell him. "I'm sorry, Mr. Morgan. I remember how much you were enjoying your foundation work."

"It seems my place is here," he says. "And to be honest, I have enjoyed being back in the thick of things."

"That's good."

"It is." He crosses his arms and stares at me for a moment. "We miss you here."

Before Scott came along, I spent almost three years running Soul Identity's software development division. My teams wrote and maintained the identification systems, the depositary applications, and all the code behind the web pages. I continued doing this remotely from Scott's place in Maryland, but I gave it up once Rain and I got married.

Writing software for the world's largest private bank was tough. Working for an organization that connected people's lives together gave me a sense of purpose that I haven't had since. This is partly why I'm moving back east; I need to find how to do something that matters again.

But I don't want to have this conversation. Not now, and not with Mr. Morgan. So I smile and nod and prompt him, "So you hired Scott to find your replacement."

"Yes," he says.

"How long has he been looking?"

"Just over three months."

"Has he had any luck?"

Mr. Morgan stares at me. He purses his lips, and then says, "In a way, yes."

I lean forward. "So he found you a replacement overseer? Where is this person?"

"Not one person. Persons," he says. "Those new programs Scott developed are quite amazing. He found three overseers in less than a month."

"So there you go," I say. "When will they make their debut?"

He sighs. "They will not, for two reasons. One, they are too young to be Soul Identity members. They are only eight, twelve, and fourteen years old. Which means we must wait almost five years before the oldest can serve."

"And the second reason?"

"They and their families were killed in horrific accidents within a week of Scott finding them. Two home fires and a vehicular crash."

I'm about to interrupt him, but he raises his hand to fend me off. "We have been able to keep this quiet, and I am expecting you to do the same," he says. "If some of our members heard that three overseers had died, they would assume all kinds of conspiracies."

"Would they be right?"

He shrugs. "Scott certainly believed something shady was going on."

"And he's off trying to figure it out?"

Mr. Morgan nods.

"Where did he go?"

"He would not tell me. He claimed it was for my own safety."

That sounds like Scott. But Scott would also have left some information with Mr. Morgan, otherwise he wouldn't have had him wait for my call. "What message did he leave for me?"

He shakes his head. "I received no special message."

"Nothing?"

He raises his hands and lets them fall onto the desk. Then he stands up, and I can only see his chest and waist. "You will forgive me, Ms. Nikolskaya," he says, "but I must use the facilities after all. Can we continue in a moment?"

"Of course."

I watch Mr. Morgan turn and disappear from view. A moment later, the laptop spins around, and he is leaning into the camera from the other side of his desk.

"That was quick," I say.

He smiles. "I have yet to go. But I remembered something else. Scott said you should talk to nobody at Soul Identity except me. He said, 'I don't know who can be trusted.'"

I raise my eyebrows. "That sounds scary."

He nods, no more twinkling eyes. "Most scary." Then he straightens up, turns around, and walks out the door and into the hallway, leaving me to watch his empty room.

Talk to nobody? This would explain Scott going underground. I look at Mr. Morgan's open door, and even though it seems a bit over the top, I decide to mute my microphone and camera. No sense showing myself to people walking by the overseer's office.

I can still see his office, and out his office door, and even a bit into the hallway. Two people walk by, but they flash past, and I don't recognize them. I decide to record the video stream so I can look later at who these people are. I find the record conversation control and slide it on.

Somebody walks up to the office door, but it's not Mr. Morgan. I don't recognize him; he's probably no older than twenty-five. He's dressed in black jeans and a tight black turtleneck that shows off a well-muscled chest.

Employees all wear green, so the black outfit marks him as a contractor. A cute contractor, though. The kid's got model looks, with high cheekbones, a nice cleft in his strong chin, and thick, dark-brown, medium-length hair that sprouts curly locks in the front. He must be Mr. Morgan's assistant, and he must be giving the old biddies at Soul Identity heart flutters.

I'm about to un-mute and introduce myself, but the kid glances quickly to the left and right, then scoots into the office. He disappears from my display as he steps around the desk, but I can hear him open and close the drawers.

"Bollocks," I hear him mutter in a British accent. Then I hear him click on the keyboard, pause, and do it again. "Bloody hell."

He's trying to log into the overseer's computer. I wonder if Mr. Morgan knows his assistant is snooping. And then I wonder if Scott knows, and he's pulling the strings in some elaborate puppet show to rope me into his life again.

I'm acting way too suspicious, I realize. If Mr. Morgan's assistant needs access to the old man's office, it's not really any of my business. I decide to give him his privacy, so I get up from the desk and walk over to one of the huge picture windows.

I can see Scott's parents below. They're chatting with Mikk, lounging on benches around an unlit fire pit. Beyond them the Puget Sound sparkles in the sunlight. And the Olympics, with just a bit of snow at their peaks, shimmer through a light haze. A windsurfer, dressed head to toe in a black wetsuit, zips to the south a couple hundred yards offshore. Two seagulls trail him. A seal breaches the surface fifty feet out. He snorts some water from his nose and slides back under the surface.

Scott's pad makes the little duplex Rain, Mikk, and I lived in seem a shack. What was he thinking when he moved out here? Was it to show off? Woo me with his possessions?

It doesn't add up. Scott and I spent almost two years on the Chesapeake Bay enjoying the simple life. We donated our profits to Mr. Morgan's foundation for the Romas in Central Europe. He never was attracted to expensive things. My leaving couldn't change him this much.

I'll grill his parents about it later. I glance back at my screen to see if Mr. Morgan has returned.

His office appears empty, but then I see the assistant step into view, apparently from behind Mr. Morgan's desk. He pokes his head into the hallway and looks both ways. He pushes the office door closed and positions himself flat against the wall, opposite of where the door swings open.

The assistant reaches into his back pocket and pulls out a short black metal rod, like the bully sticks the British police carry. He grasps the handle at its base and smacks its head into his other palm.

This isn't good. He's going after Mr. Morgan, and I've got to stop him, somehow, from almost three thousand miles away. I rush back to my desk. I'm about to un-mute the connection, but then I realize that yelling at the assistant, if that's what this person is, won't work, and will only make me lose the connection.

Maybe I can scare the guy away. I grab my phone and find Mr. Morgan's office phone number in my address book. I swipe right on by it, though, in my haste, and I force myself to take a deep breath as I backtrack and dial.

I can hear the ring both in my ear and over the laptop, but the assistant, cool as a cucumber, doesn't even glance at Mr. Morgan's office phone. He doesn't move a muscle. And the phone stops ringing and switches to voice mail.

I hope Mr. Morgan's prostate is as constrictive as Mikk's, and that his bathroom visit will drag out until I can find somebody to dislodge the intruder. I'm searching my phone for other Soul Identity numbers.

I see the number for George's cell phone and stab at it. He and Sue will know what to do. They better know what to do. I keep my eyes glued to the laptop screen, the phone jammed to my ear.

The assistant pulls his arm back and freezes, a coiled spring. Is Mr. Morgan at the door? Come on, George, answer your goddamn phone.

Again voice mail. And now the door's opening, so with no other options, I un-mute my laptop connection. I wait for the door to open half-way, and then I poke my finger at my camera and shout, "Mr. Morgan, stay in the hallway!"

Then everything happens almost too fast for me to watch over the video connection. The assistant leaps toward Morgan's desk, and the door flies open and crashes into the wall. A man rushes in, and it's not Mr. Morgan but somebody else dressed in black. He's got what looks like a sawed-of shotgun in his hands. A net flies out of its top, but it hits the wall where the assistant was but no longer is. The assistant uses some Karate-type move and flips the man to the floor and jumps on him and swings his club into the side of his head, just above the ear.

And just as I realize that the man crumpled on the floor is Scott and the assistant is about to take another swing, Mr. Morgan walks in the door. The assistant leaps up and bounds toward the hallway. He lashes out with his foot and catches the old overseer in the temple and then he's gone.

Mr. Morgan stumbles and falls on top of Scott.

"Mr. Morgan!" I scream into my microphone. "Can you hear me?"

He groans, and I swallow a lump in my throat, but then he shakes his head and raises himself up to his hands and knees. His glasses sit askew and his eyes look dazed, but he's nodding his head and then he's straightening his back.

If I hadn't spooked the assistant, Scott would have caught him with that net. But I put that horrible thought on hold and call the Soul Identity front desk and plow through the automated attendant until I get to a human.

"Mr. Morgan has been attacked in his office," I say. "He needs urgent medical attention."

"Who is this?"

"Val Nikolskaya. I used to work there. Get some medical care upstairs, fast." I watch Mr. Morgan shake Scott's shoulder, but Scott doesn't move. "Two people are hurt, please hurry!"

While I'm overcoming the operator's questions of how I know about things going on inside the executive overseer's office, Scott's parents and Mikk rush into my room.

"We heard you scream," Mikk says.

I motion them forward and point at my laptop, and they cluster behind my desk.

"That looks like Archie," Scott's mom says.

"Somebody attacked him." I point at the screen. "And Scott's there, too, on the floor. A bad guy hit him in the face with some sort of club. Pretty hard."

Scott's dad catches his wife as she stumbles forward.

"Help should arrive any second," I tell them.

Scott's mom is staring at the screen. She's leaning forward and gripping the desk with both hands. And a horrible thought tries to wriggle its way up to the surface. I push it back down. It's not my fault. Not yet.

I un-mute and lean into the microphone. "Mr. Morgan, help is coming."

"Thank you, Ms. Nikolskaya." The overseer is still kneeling on the floor. "Scott appears to be unconscious," he says in a faint and groggy voice. "But I can feel his pulse."

Scott's mom clasps her husband's hand.

Three Soul Identity security agents burst into the room. They're followed by two paramedics. We watch them check both Mr. Morgan's and Scott's pulse, pupils, and breathing. Then we can't see anything but the paramedics' backsides.

Scott's dad walks over to his desk. "I'll find the next flight to Boston," he says.

The paramedics help Scott into a wheelchair. The one eye we can see is only a slit. He's got gauze covering the left side and the bottom half of his face.

"Scott, can you hear me?" his mom asks.

Scott gives a thumbs-up, and one of the paramedics says, "We've got his mouth bandaged shut, just in case his jaw is broken."

"Where are you taking him?" Scott's mom asks.

"The nearest hospital, ma'am." And they roll him out the door.

Mr. Morgan is in a discussion with the security guards. After a moment, he turns to the camera. "Ms. Nikolskaya, I will have a private jet waiting for you and Scott's parents at Boeing Field within the hour. Come right away."

"We'll be there," I say. There's no choice after I almost got Scott killed. "Get yourself checked out—that was a big kick."

"It certainly was. See you soon." And with that, he leans forward and disconnects the call.

Mikk clears his throat. "We're leaving, and we only just got here."

Scott's mom spins her chair around. "Archie didn't invite you."

"There's no way Val's going without me," he replies.

"You sure you don't want to hide out here for a few days?" I ask him.

Mikk shakes his head. "Your ex-boyfriend seems hurt. You need somebody to keep things straight. Somebody who's thinking beyond Sam's needs."

"His name is Scott," his dad says.

"Right, I know that."

"Learn his name or you're not coming," Scott's mom says.

"Scott. Scott. Scott-Scott-Scott. See? I can do this. Do you think the old man's jet has a bar inside, like they do in the movies?"

I shoo the three of them out of the office and suggest they start packing. Once I'm alone I click back to the recording of my video call with Mr. Morgan. I advance frame by frame from the door opening until Scott is on the ground. My fears are confirmed: Scott was fully expecting the assistant to be standing next to the door. In fact, I can see a look of surprise in his eyes when his net hits the wall. I did make him miss... I screwed up his take-down.

But it's his own damn fault, I tell myself. Scott was overly clever, setting up my call to the overseer and waiting for the assistant's ambush before trying to stop it. He shouldn't have counted on me following his script; how could I possibly be in synch with him after two years apart?

I doubt his parents would see it my way. I won't show them the recording until after we get to Sterling and I talk to Scott.

eight

DEAR FUTURE ME

It's been another two years since I wrote you, future me. I thought I was done with my instructions to you. I was sure I had wrapped them up, along with my memories worth keeping, in a nice, neat package and put on a big bow. But, oh, how wrong I was!

First, you can wish me a happy birthday. I turned forty today. This one is special, as it shall be the last birthday I celebrate.

Second, you may be wondering why I won't reach forty-one. It's simple; you need to hurry up and be born. For you see, future me, my darling Fico has appeared in the form of a precious baby girl, and soon I will find a way to visit her. Then I need you, a fine strapping young man, to get here and play your part in the great drama of our souls' lives.

My husband, God rest his rich old soul, is now filling angels' cavities in the great dental office in the sky. A heart attack, said the coroner, but I suspect it had more to do with the two bottles of tequila that he drank starting promptly at noon every day. The week after he was planted, I bundled up his sisters and sent them on a one-year round-the-world excursion. That gets them out of my way until I'm also gone.

Third, if you don't know already, you're probably wondering how we found Fico. This is the real miracle: Madame Flora got a flyer in the mail from Michael Rafferty, the head of The Alert Foundation. Mr. Rafferty's wife Xinya, a physicist originally from China, has spent a large chunk of her young life perfecting her formulas that predict where and when the next incarnation of a soul line will appear. Mr. Rafferty was looking for an initial set of Soul Identity members who were interested in finding lost soul line connections from their past.

On my weekly visit to Madame Flora, she showed me the flyer. She said they had a good reputation in the business, and we could probably trust them when they said that they may be able to predict where and when Fico's soul line would reappear. Where and when! At first that sounded like cheating, but after thinking about it for less than ten seconds,

I realized that this was an opportunity to reunite my and Fico's soul lines, and that I should seize it.

So together Madame Flora and I dialed Mr. Rafferty, who promptly told us in his strong New York accent to please call him Raff. We did, and I described my quest for finding Fico's soul line heir and reuniting with him. I said that I had a wedding photo that showed Fico's eyes, but it was my only one. He asked a few questions about where Fico had lived, and before you could say 'reunited', I had paid for an airplane trip to New York City for me and Madame Flora to visit The Alert Foundation's headquarters.

Raff looks like one of those Italian mafia family dons you see in the gangster movies: straight black hair slicked back; a heavy gold bracelet, cuff links, and a pinky ring; a shirt opened halfway down his chest; expensive hand-tooled Italian shoes. He brought us into his office and offered us cigars and whisky. He showed us pictures of soul lines which he and Xinya had recovered. Then he put his feet up on his desk and told us about how he and Xinya had started The Alert Foundation.

The two had met at a mid-town social event for Soul Identity seekers. Raff was a brand-new hire, and Xinya was making quite a reputation for herself in finding heirs to long-lost soul lines. Raff was determined to discover her trick. "So I wooed her," he said. "Besides, it was easy, as she's drop-dead gorgeous."

At that point, Xinya walked into the office. She is tall and slender, with dimples in both cheeks when she smiles, which is almost all the time. She doesn't talk often, but her black eyes are alight with curiosity, and her straight black hair is cut in a shoulder-length bob. She was wearing a fancy embroidered Chinese silk top over sleek black pants tucked into black leather boots with four inch heels.

Raff eventually learned how Xinya had spent years at university perfecting her predictive formulas. She came to work as a Soul Identity seeker, and her success rate with locating these soul line heirs was proof enough to Raff that she was on to something big.

But what Xinya really wanted to do was to reunite living souls from previous lives, not just find the heirs to lost soul lines. "We need to help these couples," she said. "Once souls have been entwined, they need to be together again and again. It's the natural order."

Music to my ears, my dear future me. Xinya and I were on the same wavelength.

"When Xinya told me this dream of hers, I proposed," Raff said matter-of-factly. "Xinya needed a partner who could take her work and make it available to everybody." He smiled. "For a price, of course."

Xinya leaned forward and put her hand on my knee. "Raff talks tough, but he has a good heart," she said in her musical voice. "We will reunite you and Fico, and then we will be ready to take it to…" At this she turned to Raff.

"The masses, honey," he said. "We're going to take it to the masses."

She flashed him a smile. "And make the world happier."

Raff made a copy of my and Fico's wedding photo. I endured two and a half hours of Xinya's deep and probing questions about where Fico lived, where he was born, and where he traveled. She seemed most interested in the events I could remember the most clearly. The next morning, I did it all again, and once more the next evening. Xinya said it was absolutely crucial to remove any uncertainties in the data she used. She claimed that people don't realize that their memories change over time.

Xinya tried to explain the basics of her formula to me. Apparently she calculates a soul's journey through the universe by identifying a few "flashbulb moments" where she can pinpoint the soul in a specific place and time, and how that soul interacts with others. The more points she can identify, and the more incarnations she can verify it across, the better chance she'd have of locating the current soul line heir.

I was worried when I heard this, as I had no idea about any of Fico's previous soul lines. Also, Fico never knew his actual birthday (he was an orphan), so we couldn't start with his entrance into his life. But I did have a few points where I was very clear as to specific dates and times: our first time on the beach, our wedding, where he was during some key battles of the Cuban revolution. Xinya said that even though I wasn't sure of Fico's exact birthdate, I was lucky that Fico had never traveled beyond Cuba, as this limited range constrained his future incarnation's options.

Xinya was right about the flashbulb moments that I had treasured for so long; I found my memories had changed over time. We spent an afternoon in the New York City public library map room, and I found that Fico and I met on a different beach than the one I remembered. Somewhere along the way my memory shifted to the beach Sissi, Prissy, and I used to hang out at. We consulted the solar and lunar and even weather calendars for that day, as well as our wedding night, and the vivid image of the full moon I remembered rising over our wedding cabin was apparently a figment of my imagination. She decided to not rely on the moment and location of Fico's death, because every time I told her about it, my story shifted just enough that she said it would throw off the results. This raised a lot more questions in my own mind about the quality of my memory, and it got me worried that we'd never find Fico, but Xinya seemed positive about my chances.

Five days later, on our last day in New York, Xinya showed me a drawing she had created. At first, it looked like a picture of a plate of blue spaghetti. But then she slipped a map of Cuba behind the thin paper, and she explained how it was a space-time rendering of Fico's movements from one p.m. on January 19, 1957 (when we met on the beach) up until five p.m. on October 28, 1959 (when Cienfuegos flew me and Fico from Camagüey toward Havana).

"You provided almost three years of information," she said. "It should be enough to pinpoint where Fico's soul line heir will appear."

"How can you be sure?" I asked.

She was silent for a troubling minute. "We cannot be sure," she said eventually. "But you must have the proper amount of faith."

Raff had prepared a contract for me to sign. He gave me a discount on the finding fee, as we were Alert's first living customers, and we were helping to establish the foundation's reputation. Not that I cared; my husband left me loaded, and I'd pay anything to find and reunite us with Fico. He charged me half the fee up front, with the balance due when Fico's soul line was pinpointed. I agreed to pay a bonus for Fico's name and location if he was alive. When we left, Xinya gave me a hug and told me she'd do her best to pinpoint Fico's pathway. She told me that in Chinese, her name meant "proper faith", and that's exactly what I needed to have.

Then Madame Flora and I flew back to Miami, and I waited. The anticipation was killing me, but at the same time my happiness knew no bounds. I was sure that they'd find Fico, just as I know that you and Fico will be together soon. Faith is a powerful force, future me.

The next three months seemed to crawl by slower than the twenty years since Fico left my life. Each day I would stare at my telephone, willing it to ring. Each day I would call Madame Flora to see if she had heard anything, only to fret that Alert might have called when the phone was busy.

But then, future me, then came the day when I received the call that changed everything. You might say that it was the call that put you on your own journey of life. For Michael Rafferty informed me that not only had Xinya been able to pinpoint Fico's soul line, but with a bunch of research and local help, the foundation had also identified his soul line heir: a baby girl named Valentina Nikolskaya who was born just this past March in the closed city of Gorky, deep in the heart of the Soviet Union.

That was two weeks ago. Since then, Raff has called me back twice more and told me that his associates in Russia have made contact with Valentina's parents. He has hinted to me that Xinya's formulas can also be used to pinpoint where you will be born. He has suggested the possibility that if I travel to the appropriate places at specific times, I can even influence where and when my future incarnation will occur.

That sounds almost too good to be true. And to be honest, the almost three years of my life that Xinya had graphed out in those blue squiggly lines were my happiest, most magical, most meaningful years. I'd do anything to get them back for me, and for you. Anything at all.

I gave Raff the information about my own birth location, and he promised to pass it on to Xinya to begin the calculations for me.

Xinya is right: it takes faith. Proper faith. And even as I write this, I wonder if my faith in our future is strong enough.

Last night I visited a priest for the first time since Fico's memorial service. I told him that I had to make a very difficult decision, and I wasn't sure of the outcome. I asked him how to achieve the proper level of faith.

The priests in America are a bit different than the ones I remember from my childhood in Cuba. He was well-dressed and well-fed. Not too overweight, but enough to give him a middle-aged pot belly. He smiled a lot, which was a nice change from the frowns I got whenever the priest saw me at the cafetale.

"May I tell you a story about living a life of faith?" He asked me.

I thought he was going to recite one of the parables, or maybe tell me something about Moses, so I hesitated. The last thing I wanted to hear was how some ancient perfect person followed God well enough to get themselves written about in the Bible.

"Don't worry; it's not religious."

So I agreed.

Once upon a time, he told me, there was a priest who served in a parish in Miami. My suspicion is that his story was autobiographical, but he refused to confirm that.

The priest, along with two nuns, had been with the local congregation for a few years. The three of them used to eat breakfast together every Monday morning to plan out their acts of God for the week.

One Monday, the older of the two nuns was sick, and the priest and the other nun met alone. The conversation strayed a bit from the proper businesslike tone that he usually maintained, and they found themselves talking about their own backgrounds, their favorite colors, and even some gossip about the other nun.

That was it for a couple of years, for the older nun recovered. But then one of their parishioners was nearing the end of their life, and the priest and the younger nun walked together to the hospital for a visit. Again they enjoyed their time alone with each other, commenting on the flowers they saw along their path, the pet dogs they had in their child-hood, and other silly things that people say when they're interested in how the other feels about them.

The priest gave a few more examples of how he and the nun got closer and closer. I didn't pay too much attention, future me, for really, I was struggling with my own faith and wondering how the story was rel-evant. Suffice it to say that this priest and his nun were slowly falling for each other.

One fine day the priest was called to run a seminar on a topic he was sort of an expert in. I think he said it was about dealing with rich and an-gry church members. Apparently this is an interesting topic for priests and nuns all over the country, for he was called to present a two-day seminar in Denver. The priest brought the younger nun with him to assist.

And that, future me, was the beginning of an affair of the heart be-tween the priest and the nun. I know it sounds like the set-up for a joke, but it's not. I could hear in his voice how deep his love was, and I started paying attention.

The priest told me that on their trip to Denver, and all during the seminar, they were well behaved. But coming back to Miami, they missed a connection and got stuck overnight in Dallas, and the airline put them up at a hotel.

It was St. Patrick's Day. They drank a beer together at the hotel bar, they shared a few laughs. She complimented him on an excellent presen-tation, and they said good night sometime around midnight and went to their own rooms.

And the priest couldn't sleep. He kept thinking about his nun, and even more about the woman underneath the habit. Every conversation they ever had, every smile she had ever given him, and every glance she had made in his direction, replayed itself inside his head.

And then he thought about the hotel, and the gift of anonymity it brought them that night. He got up, put his robe on, grabbed his key, strode down the hall, and knocked on her door.

She opened her door, said that she too had been lying awake, and admitted that she too had been thinking of him. They discovered a whole lot more about each other, and about the fun that God had given every other person in the world except the poor bastards who swore vows of chastity. (That's my editorial, not the priest's exact words, future me.) They spent the night together, beginning an affair that continued for the next thirty years.

"So where's the faith?" I asked him. "This sounds more like a story of illicit love."

"Ah," he said. "I haven't gotten to that yet. But I'm glad you're now paying more attention."

The priest said that at sunrise, after a sleepless (and I suppose energetic) night, they flew back to Miami and re-entered normalcy in the parish. They stole away together to discuss what happened between them, and after a bit of stammering and beating around the bush, they both realized that their church family was more important than indulging themselves in each other.

"I don't believe you," I told the priest. "If they're both still at the church, they're finding ways to be with each other."

He looked sheepish, then admitted to me that yes, indeed, the priest and nun do get together once a year, around St. Patrick's Day. And for the first few years of this arrangement, in early July they'd start counting down the days of their next get-together. After a magical night of bliss, the second half of March would pass in a warm glow, and then they would mope around, upset and even angry at God, from April all the way through June. During those three months they'd wish they had met each other before they both married the church, and they would wonder why God made life so difficult for them.

But after fifteen years or so it started making sense, he told me. Their love included a lifetime of spending every day in each other's presence, punctuated just once a year with the deep expression of that love. If anything, their love for each other increased their faith in God, and made them better servants to the church.

"And faith?" I prompted.

"Here's the point," he said. "If you believe in something so much that you do what defies all logic, you have the proper level of faith. This priest and his nun believe that if they serve their parish and keep their vows, then God would reward them with the gift of spending eternity together."

"Except for once every year," I pointed out.

He nodded, with a twinkle in his eye. "That annual reunion is when they renew their faith and remind themselves about how good their reward will be."

I think the priest is right. And I think he's deeply in love with his nun. Faith is believing so much that you can't act logically. I have faith that Fico's and my soul lines will be together. I am willing to defy all logic to help make it happen.

I'm going to visit baby Valentina, future me. It won't be easy getting to the Soviet Union, especially since they live in a closed city, but I'm sure that I'll figure it out. And then I'll figure out how to get out of your way, so you can, we can, meet her and reunite our soul lines.

nine

"Hey, Ms. Xia," Brandon whispered. "I'm back!" He stood in front of her, his skateboard in one hand and knapsack in the other.

Xinya looked up from her formulas on the blue-lined graph paper, smiled at the boy, and stifled her urge to rake his sticking-up hair into some order. "Hey, Brandon," she whispered back. "So you are. Did you have fun this summer?"

"Counselor at summer camp, are you kidding?" He scowled. "All they did was BMX this, BMX that. Nobody skates anymore. Even the ramps were busted up. I had to rebuild them."

"It sounds awful."

"Well, it wasn't that bad," He said. "Except maybe the food. But I missed the city." He looked at his watch. "I've got a couple hours free. Have you got any work for me?"

"I always have work for you," she said. "Do you have time to do some elimination tasks?"

"Which country? I've been practicing my Japanese ever since we found that last heir."

"Here in the States. Boston."

"Piece of cake." He sat down next to her and shoved his skateboard and knapsack under the library table. "Hey, I turned eighteen. A raise would be an awesome adult birthday present."

She smiled. "You got one in January when they increased minimum wage. And you still share profits when we recover. If you want a raise, find faster, and we'll all make more."

He rolled his eyes. "Whatever." Then he grinned. "I've made almost as much as Mom this year, and that's with the whole summer off. Let's find this heir fast, so I can take her to California for Christmas."

"Deal," she said. She handed Brandon a folder and slid a stack of books over his way. "This case is different."

He opened the folder. "It looks like we're still researching vectors for possible matches."

"Yes, but this is only a few vectors. You know how most times we look through hundreds of them?"

He nodded.

"This time we only have three."

"Did your formulas get better?"

She shook her head. "We have better facts. A man died in Cuba in 1959. His wife hired us, and she gave me accurate information."

"Hold on, this isn't for a lost soul line?"

"No, we will reunite her with her husband's soul line heir."

"But you said the lost soul lines pay the best."

"Don't worry about the money," she said. "Raff negotiated a huge finder's fee. Our job is to find the heir."

"Okay. So what do you want me to do today?"

"We're looking for a Boston girl born in December 1962 who died in April 1974."

"The wife will pay us even if the heir is dead?"

"Of course." Xinya folded her hands under her chin. "But I hope we don't find her in Boston. The other two vectors predict the heir is alive."

"Yup, that's your dream. Reunions and all," he said. "How far did you get?"

"I'm seventy percent done." Xinya pointed at the top page. "That list has the known births. I crossed out the recorded deaths that don't match, and then I used high school yearbooks to eliminate the girls still alive." She rapped on the stack of books. "You can go through these."

Brandon nodded and opened the first yearbook, and for the next two hours, every time he found a match, he half whispered, half sang, "and another one gone, another one gone, another one bites the dust."

"Brandon, it's a library," Xinya whispered for the tenth time. "You have to be quiet, or they'll kick us both out."

"Sorry, but the song fits so well." He put down the last yearbook and stretched. "We're done. The chicks are all alive. This vector has been eliminated."

Xinya sighed. "That is a relief. I did not want Fico's heir to be dead. Claudia doesn't either."

"Shall we start on the other vectors?"

She shook her head. "Not yet. Raff has local teams looking into them. They're in Brazil and Russia. Tomorrow I will bring some lost soul line work that you can do."

"Okay, I'll go home then. Put me down for two hours." Brandon picked up his skateboard and knapsack and headed out of the reading room.

"Please pass your mother my regards." She watched him leave, returning his wave as he exited the room.

"A good boy," somebody said behind her. She turned and saw it was Lily, one of the newer and younger librarians. She wore a white sweater, black slacks, and big round glasses. Her long hair was gathered into a pony tail, and her lips contained a few remaining smudges of a bright red lipstick.

"I am glad Brandon is back," Xinya said. "I missed him this summer."

Lily pointed at the stacks of yearbooks. "I've meant to ask what you're working on, Xinya. You're here almost every day. Are you researching a book?"

Xinya smiled. "You could say that I'm a detective, looking for missing people."

"A detective." The librarian seemed to mull this over. "Do the people you find want to be found?"

"So far they have," Xinya said. "Because I reunite them with their lost inheritance."

"I see." But then Lily frowned. "How do they get lost in the first place?"

Xinya pulled a folder out of her briefcase and pulled out a Soul Identity match sheet. She showed Lily how the differences between a person's two irises made an identity, one that was unique as long as that person was alive. "After I die, somebody else eventually comes back with my soul identity," she said.

"So it's like reincarnation," Lily said.

"With a bank account," Xinya said. "Soul Identity lets you leave money and memories to your future soul line carrier. But when nobody claims the soul line account for at least a hundred years, we seekers get bonus commissions."

"How can seekers find the heirs?" Lily asked.

Xinya explained how some seekers scanned through photographs, looking for matches. The older ones trained themselves to recognize identities, and then watched people closely in public places. And recently a new group of optometrists had signed up as seekers. "They have a big advantage, since they're already looking at your eyes," she said.

"If you have bad vision, I guess," said Lily. "How about you and Brandon?"

Xinya smiled. "Ancient Chinese secret." And when Lily raised her eyebrows so they peeked over her glasses, she said, "Many Chinese people believe that life follows a rhythm, and if you can figure it out, you can predict what will happen."

"So you use those horoscopes that are printed on the Chinese restaurant place mats?"

"It's the same principle, but what I do is more similar to tracking comets. I plot a soul's speed and orbit around the world, and then I predict vectors of where and when that soul will return. That gives me a list of a few hundred dates and places to work with." She gestured at the papers and books on the table, "Then we research to see if we can find the heir."

"Far out," Lily said. "Can I help? They don't pay us librarians very much."

Xinya had worked with various New York City Public librarians, and she found them to be very meticulous. "Of course," she said. "I pay minimum wage for the research, and you'll get a share of the commissions. Sometimes we have big payouts."

"I'd love to be paid to do research," Lily said. She sat down across from Xinya. "How'd you get into this line of work, anyway?"

Xinya explained that she'd been dreaming of reuniting people her whole life. She was born in China on October 1, 1949, the day Chairman Mao pronounced the start of the People's Republic of China. It was also the day her father sold her unnamed twin brother.

"How could a father do that?"

He had been a solider and had lost both legs in the war, Xinya told her, and the family couldn't afford to raise the twins. A communist government official and his childless wife were moving to the new capital, and they were only too happy to pay for the privilege of claiming the boy as their own.

"So you grew up knowing you had a lost brother?"

Xinya shook her head. When she was ten, one of her playmates, in a burst of tantrum, shouted that her family should have sold her off like they did her brother. "Suddenly it was clear, and I understood why every night I lay in bed feeling I was missing somebody in my life." She had a twin soul somewhere in China, waiting to be found and reunited with her.

Xinya told Lily how she had excelled at school, and had been accepted at Tsinghua University in Beijing as a physics major in 1965. Her intent was to develop predictive formulas for finding lost people. "But when the Cultural Revolution shut down the school the next year, my professor helped me transfer to Columbia University on a scholarship. My parents had both died, so I was free to move and continue my research."

After a year in the States, Xinya attended a Soul Identity seeker meeting, and discovered that she could apply her research to something that would pay her mounting living expenses.

The ancient files contained lots of variability. Xinya's formulas weren't that forgiving, and even in the best of cases, when she felt she had precise time and location information from several of a soul's incarnations, she was left with several hundred predicted vectors to research by hand.

Each vector had to be chased down until the heir was found. Her apartment was just a block from the main branch of the New York City public library, which she haunted most days, alternating between the gigantic, high-ceilinged history, astronomy, map, and microfilm rooms. "This is where Brandon and some of your coworkers help me with research," she said. "We have to process and eliminate lots of people before we find the match."

She met Brandon four years earlier when he and his mother had lived in the same apartment building and he was an awkward teenager. Brandon's mother worked nights and slept days, and she was grateful when Xinya offered to hire him to help her in her library research.

Even with all the misses, she had earned enough commissions from her finds over the years: enough to pay for her apartment, fund her research, and enshroud her reputation in a layer of mysticism. Enough that Raff had sought her out and helped her transform her dream of helping reunite living people, not just matching people to dead files, into a reality.

She explained how she had met Michael Rafferty, and how he had swept her off her feet just two years before. "I'm so shy, and he's so outgoing," she said. Raff taught Xinya how to eat trendy foods, and dance in the SoHo clubs, and dress in ways that accentuated her long legs and slim body. He showered her with compliments and attention. And when he proposed to unite their lives and their business plans, she said yes with no hesitation at all.

"The Alert Foundation is a real company," she said. "We have our first live client, and if we can find Fico's heir, my formulas will finally have been used to reunite two souls."

"This job sounds perfect. When can I start?" Lily asked. And after Xinya gave her the address of the office, she agreed to stop by after work the next day.

ten

Xinya wanted her first live case to be a huge success. If her formulas could pinpoint Fico's heir, The Alert Foundation would be able to help many other souls reunite. That would satisfy her immensely, and it would make her business-oriented husband excited about the new opportunities.

What she and Raff hadn't told Claudia was that Xinya's vectors had proven to be wrong many, many more times than they were right. Raff warned her that if she told Claudia how shaky the science really was, they'd lose this client, and they might as well shut down the foundation. Instead, he suggested, they should focus the conversation on the "razzle-dazzle" of Xinya's previous successes, not on their many failures.

She trusted Raff's business sense. And besides, Xinya hoped that Claudia's memories would yield more precise times and locations, which in turn would produce less vectors and make it easier to locate her heir.

And so the day her Alert Foundation found Frederico Valdes' soul line heir was the most satisfying day Xinya could remember since she immigrated to America. Especially after the many days of arduous work, and the sleepless nights worrying if she had calculated everything correctly.

While she and Brandon researched and eliminated the Boston vector, Raff worked the Rio and Gorky vectors by negotiating and contracting with local Soul Identity seeker teams.

Two days ago Raff brought bad news: The Rio team had no luck. The birth records for the city were abysmal, and although a search through the schools found many ten-year-old boys born in July 1970, not one of them matched Mr. Valdes' soul identity. That made two dead ends.

The bad luck in both Brazil and the States had Xinya examining her formulas yet again. Even though there was still some hope for the Russian vector, she had gotten a sick feeling in her stomach. The more she looked at her derivations for calculating the soul's orbit, the less they added up.

She must have gotten it wrong. For as long as she'd been calculating vectors, not a day had passed without some level of doubt creeping into her mind. She had always viewed this as healthy, and she had made some good finds. But the clarity of Claudia's information also brought clarity to the results; there was a problem in calculating the orbit. And it wasn't fixable.

She stared at the calculations. Even though she had done it hundreds of times over the past week, she painstakingly re-ran the proof. And yet again she was confronted with the realization that her past decade's work was wrong. Soul lines could not be predicted. Period, end of story. Which meant that no matter how much she wanted them to, her formulas would never lead to reuniting living people.

As Xinya sat contemplating the depressing thought of spending the rest of her life doing nothing but treasure hunting for Soul Identity's lost soul lines with Brandon, Lily, and the other librarians, Raff walked into the map room and straight up to where she was sitting at the corner table. The echoes of his quick footsteps bounced off the cavernous walls.

He turned to Xinya, a frown on his face, and whispered, "You won't believe what we found."

Xinya sat back and put her hands in the lap of her black slacks. Willed them to relax. Raff must have discovered the problem with the formula? Would he demand that they shut down Alert? Would he find himself a better business partner than she could be?

She opened her mouth to speak, but nothing came out. She took a deep breath, closed her eyes and whispered, "You found the problem." Then stared at the table.

"I found something," he said, "but it's not a problem." Her husband and partner opened a manila folder and, with a flourish, extracted a color photograph of a baby girl. "May I present to you Miss Valentina Nikols-kaya? You did it, Xinya—we found her right where you said she'd be!"

And all the doubt dissolved as Xinya jumped to her feet and let out a squeal. She quickly covered her mouth with both hands and gave a short bow to Lily, but the librarian just smiled and threw a mock tut-tut her way. Xinya touched both of her husband's shoulders and kissed him on the cheek. "Are you quite sure?" she whispered.

Raff nodded. "I had the seekers run the soul identities of both Fico and Valentina." They sat down, and Raff placed the two identity sheets on the table, alongside Valentina's photograph. "See how they match?"

She traced her fingers over the colored swirls and whorls of the shared identity. "It is a match indeed. But can we trust the identity of a baby?" Hoping you could.

"I asked that same question," he said, "and they told me that if you can read the iris, you can trust it. Valentina's eyes are almost neon green, which makes them easy to read."

She allowed herself a moment of silence, to think how she was ready to throw it all away. "Have you told Claudia?" she asked.

He shook his head. "You deserved to hear first."

That earned him another kiss on the cheek. "It works after all," she said as she sat back down, thinking it shouldn't, but somehow it did. She whispered, "We can help others now."

He held up his hands. "Whoa, honey, not so fast. Let's get Claudia happy and willing to give us her reference first. You wanna come over for the call?"

She nodded, then gathered her research into her black leather portfolio. They walked the three blocks to The Alert Foundation's offices, and Xinya sat on the couch while Raff dialed Miami.

"Claudia? It's Michael Rafferty. Hey, we have great news for you. Are you sitting down? Yes? Xinya was able to plot out your husband's soul line." Raff gave Xinya a thumbs-up.

"Yes, it was quite difficult… And it took us more expenses than we anticipated, too. But that's okay, there's even better news." Now he was pumping his fist.

"The news? Are you ready? Yes? We spent considerable resources in our research, and we had to get the identities verified, but we now know that your husband's soul line heir is alive and well."

Xinya could hear nothing for a few seconds, then a loud cry came over the phone. Raff grimaced and pulled the receiver away from his ear. He covered the mouthpiece with his hand and whispered, "She's lapsed into Spanish. No idea what she's saying."

Xinya smiled at him, thinking how happy Claudia must be. As happy as she'd be herself, some future day once she located her brother.

"Claudia, are you there? You're still speaking Spanish…. That's better…. Yes, I said alive, right this very minute… Where, you ask? Deep in the heart of Russia, ma'am. In a closed city, which means that no foreigners are allowed… yes? Um, I'm not sure if you'll be able to visit. But I'm sure Alert can check for you, and arrange a trip if it's possible." He covered the mouthpiece again. "She wants to go there," he whispered.

Xinya couldn't blame her. The whole point of finding the heir was to allow the souls to reunite. But it did pose a problem that baby Valentina was in a closed city. She and Raff both understood the difficulties of traveling to a Communist country; Raff had yet to submit for his own visa to China, complaining that the application form asked too many personal questions.

Raff was still talking. "Her name? It's Valentina Nikolskaya." He spelled it out slowly. "She's just a baby, only three months old... What was that? Yes, of course I will send you her picture, along with the soul identity cards and our invoice." He smiled again at Xinya.

"Okay, Claudia," he said into the phone. "I'll get those to you by Federal Express.... Yes, you'll have the documents by tomorrow afternoon... Of course I will pass on your regards... okay then, bye bye." He hung up the phone.

Raff leaned back in his chair, fingers interlaced behind his head. "Our first satisfied customer," he spoke to the ceiling. "Boy, that feels good." He reached into his desk drawer and pulled out a bottle of whisky and two small glasses. He poured a large one for him, and just a drop for her.

He carried the glasses and sat next to her on the couch. "A toast to my brilliant wife, and to our foundation's future."

They clinked glasses and drank. With the burn in her mouth from the golden liquid, Xinya looked at her husband and thought what good partners they made. One happy about the business potential, and the other happy about the spiritual potential. Two necessary sides of any important endeavor.

"We should celebrate again once their souls have been reunited," she said.

"Yes, we will," he said.

She imagined Claudia holding baby Valentina in her arms. "I want to go with Claudia to meet Valentina," she told Raff.

"Do you think that's safe?"

She was silent for a minute. "No," she admitted. "But I will go anyway."

Her husband-cum-business partner stood up, poured himself another whisky, and said, "Of course, honey. I'll get the local team to figure it out."

eleven

Getting a visa for Claudia wasn't easy. The Soviets had marched into Afghanistan the previous Christmas Eve, and the US responded by leading more than sixty countries in a boycott of the summer Olympic games in Moscow. Tensions between the East and West were taut.

Xinya could travel under her Chinese passport, and she didn't anticipate any problems for herself. But when Claudia's visa application was rejected for the second time, she called Xinya to commiserate.

"This is crazy," she wailed. "Why are these bureaucrats keeping me and Fico apart?"

"I'm so sorry, Claudia."

"I thought you Alert people had local resources who were going to get me there."

Raff had told Xinya he had tried everything. They had bribed the embassy staff, and even passed on a strong suggestion to the Nikolskiy family to emigrate out of Russia. But nothing had panned out. Only communists could visit Gorky, as apparently this city on the Volga River was where the Soviets built and launched their nuclear submarines.

"There's no way an American is going to get there," he had said. "Good thing you kept your Chinese passport. We tried to arrange a meeting at the Moscow airport on an international transfer, but we can't figure out how to get the Nikolskiys into the transit terminal. And now Claudia's tried so many times that she's been blacklisted."

"There must be a way," she had insisted, but Raff had just shrugged.

On the phone, she told Claudia, "We have run out of options. I'm sorry, Claudia." And she had to wipe away her own tears when the sobs came over the line.

"It's been twenty years, Xinya. Twenty years of Cuban exile, waiting for Fico. Two decades, and the whole time I stayed strong. You found baby Valentina, Xinya. Don't tell me that I won't meet her. She's so close."

"Yet she is so far." And then a bell dinged in Xinya's head. "Wait," she said. "Cubans can visit the Soviet Union. Do you still have your Cuban passport?"

"Defectors don't have passports," Claudia said.

"So defect back to Cuba." And as the words came out of her mouth and flowed into the handset, they sounded so ridiculously simple that she wondered why this idea had eluded them.

"Me go back to Cuba—are you crazy?" Claudia asked. "Mother of God, Fidel would hang me in the middle of Havana, then throw my body to his dogs."

Silence for a long moment. And then Claudia said something in Spanish and laughed and laughed. She switched back to English and said, "Xinya, my darling best friend, you are brilliant! Defecting to Cuba is the most amazing idea ever."

"You just said they wouldn't take you back."

"That's because I forgot about Cienfuegos."

"The general."

"*Comandante*. Yes. He's still a national hero in Cuba."

"He is dead."

Claudia sounded impatient. "But the Cuban people don't know that Cienfuegos tried to defect. Fidel will want to keep that embarrassing detail under wraps. He'll let me in just to keep my mouth shut. I'm sure he'll even get me my Russian visa."

It sounded a bit tricky to Xinya; something Raff would understand better than she. After a minute of goodbyes, Xinya hung up and stared at the phone. If she had just three percent of Claudia's conviction, she and Raff would have reunited hundreds of living souls by now.

She went to Raff's office to discuss her idea with him. He stroked his chin while listening to her. "I suppose it could work," he said. "But boy, defecting back to Cuba… that's quite a sacrifice just to visit a baby girl. What if Fidel locks her up when she returns from Russia?"

She struggled for a moment to put her thoughts into words. "Claludia is the strongest lady I have met," she said, "and you are the best dealmaker I know. So make the deal with Mr. Castro. I'm sure she can handle any consequences."

He nodded. "I'll make some calls."

Two weeks later, Raff stopped by the library and sat across from her in the weather room. He placed a stack of papers, bound at the top, on the table. He flipped to the last page and showed her the notarized signatures of both Claudia Valdes y Famosa and Fidel Castro. "Your crazy idea worked," he said. "Castro agreed to everything Claudia demanded.

It cost her over five million, and she coughed it up before I could even negotiate it down."

"Will she come here before she goes to Cuba?"

He looked at his watch. "She should have landed in Havana a few minutes ago. She'll never be able to come back to the States."

She hoped the single trip to Russia would be worth Claudia's lifelong sacrifice. "Have you organized the dates for the reunion?" she asked.

He slid a paper across the table. "I talked to the travel agents and had them prepare your tickets. Here's your Inturist itinerary, leaving three weeks from today. You'll be there for a week. You meet Claudia in Paris and travel together from there. You'll need to get that visa application submitted, okay?"

She took his hand. "Thank you, Raff."

He bent forward and kissed her fingers. "Come back safely. We have much to do."

twelve

Three weeks and one day later, Xinya met Claudia at Charles de Gaulle Airport in Paris. They flew together to Moscow, where they were greeted by Olga, a dour looking Soul Identity matron dressed in a dirty green skirt and jacket. She held a sign with Alert written in big red letters.

"I bring you to train station and get you to your cabin," Olga said. "You meet my colleague in Gorky. She has same sign."

They arrived at the train station with a few minutes to spare. As they boarded, Olga pointed at them and said, "You arrive six a.m. in the morning. Do not miss stop, or must you wait eight hours for turnaround at next station."

"Did you find that Cuba has changed?" Xinya asked Claudia as they sat in the dining car drinking extra-sweet black tea with stale rye bread and hard cheese.

Claudia shook her head. "It's like I travelled back in time. The same cars on the road, the same food in the stores. The same politics argued in the bars."

"This time you have money," Xinya pointed out. "That must make a difference."

"Not as much as you might think. I invested most of it into my future." And when Xinya raised her eyebrows, Claudia added, "It's in my soul line collection, so in my next life, I'll have enough for both me and Fico... I mean Valentina."

Back in their sleeper cabin, they ordered more tea off the provodnitsa's cart, then climbed into their bunk beds.

Xinya spent most of the night staring out the window at the moonlit, snow-covered countryside flowing by. She wondered how Claudia was so sure that her future incarnation's vector would overlap with baby Valentina's lifespan. This is where faith would really count.

She thought about Claudia's quest to find Fico's soul, and wondered if baby Valentina would exhibit any signs of recognition.

Then she thought about her own quest to find her twin brother. Xinya had no photograph, no papers, not even a name. Her father had executed a cash transaction on the day she and her brother were born, then claimed he had forgotten the names of her brother's purchasers. He outlived his wife, and died in 1965, before Xinya left China. Other than a shared birthdate, she had no facts to go on.

If Valentina recognized Claudia, she knew that someday, somewhere, she'd recognize her own brother. When she did doze off, Xinya dreamed a time-worn reunion scene, and woke in the morning with tears on her thin pillow.

When the train arrived in Gorky, they alighted and stood with their luggage in a rain and sleet storm. Ten minutes later another Soul Identity lady, also carrying an Alert sign, and also named Olga, showed up. She ushered them off the platform, through the station, and into a waiting Gaz taxi. "Twenty minutes," she said as she climbed into the front passenger seat. "We stop at cozy cafe in Kremlin and discuss rules of behavior."

"Will Valentina be there?" Claudia asked.

Olga shook her head. "Parents are very nervous. They learn in schooling all foreigners are dangerous. And more afraid that neighbors say they are dissidents and get them arrested. We first make sure you act in ways that do not scare them, or neighbors."

"This place sounds just like Cuba," Claudia said. "We need to bribe the authorities so they leave the family alone."

"That is bad idea for you to bribe," Olga said. "Police not to be trusted. But don't worry. Mr. Rafferty has already solved. Family will be safe."

"Are you sure? Baby Valentina must have the best of everything."

Olga shook her head vigorously. "Best of everything will only get parents arrested and baby Valentina disappeared. We protect her with Soviet way."

"What do you think, Xinya?" Claudia asked.

Xinya frowned. "I would trust Raff on matters of protection," she said.

The taxi pulled up in front of the Kremlin. Olga hopped out and held the door for Claudia and Xinya. "Leave luggage inside. Cab will wait," she said.

The three stepped over the dirty slush as best they could and walked up the sidewalk on the left side of the building. "Good café here," Olga said as they reached a large red door. She held it open and waved the ladies through. "Some days they have good hot chocolate."

"I just want to see Valentina," Claudia said.

"Five minutes. We talk, then we drive there." Olga pointed out an empty table off to the left, half-way down a narrow corridor. "Sit, I order drink."

In a moment, Olga sat down and handed each of them a plain brown scarf. "Rule number one: cover heads to look Russian, and no talking to babushkiy outside of apartment. They chatter too much."

"Chatter?" Xinya asked.

"Spread gossip. Cause big problem." She put her elbows on the table. "Rule number two: drink tea when they serve. It is rude to say no. And if too hot, we drink out of saucer, yes?" She pointed at the tables around them. "Like these people."

Xinya and Claudia both nodded. At dinner on the train they had watched the Russians pour small portions of their cups of hot tea into their saucers, then pick up the saucers to drink. Some of the ladies had even held sugar cubes between their teeth.

"Rule number third: do not ask family opinion of government or religion."

The ladies nodded again. "Can I tell them about Fico?" Claudia asked.

"You may."

"Can I give them any gifts?"

Olga frowned. "What gifts?"

"A necklace for Valentina," Claudia said. "And some money for the parents."

"Rubles?"

Claudia nodded. "I exchanged in Havana."

Olga scowled. "You exchanged for Comecon foreign rubles. Nikolskiys get themselves arrested if caught with hard currency. You must convert to Soviet rubles."

"Can you help me with that?"

"How much to convert?"

"Ten thousand."

"Too much. Not only they will be arrested: you will make entire Nikolskiy family vanish."

"Ten thousand," Claudia repeated.

Olga stared at her for a minute. Then she sighed. "For this much, I must make telephone call. Rule class dismissed." She got up, adjusted her coat and scarf, and walked outside the café.

The waitress brought three hot chocolates in porcelain teacups, and Claudia and Xinya sipped the steaming hot drinks.

Xinya asked, "Do you plan on giving the family the whole ten thousand rubles in cash?"

"It's a bit over six thousand dollars, so it's only a start," Claudia said. "I left more with Alert. I want to be sure Valentina has the best."

Xinya was silent as she gathered her thoughts. Then she said, "I read that people here only make a hundred rubles or so a month. She may be endangered if the neighbors think the family's rich. What then?"

Claudia sighed. "I don't know, Xinya. She must grow up well, and get a good education, so she's ready to meet my own future incarnation. How else can I convince her parents to invest in her?"

As they drank the rest of their hot chocolate and waited for Olga to return, Xinya thought through Claudia's assertion, and eventually decided that Claudia was right. No matter how Xinya looked at it, she reasoned that the chances that the parents would remain true to their word and raise Valentina to look for a future Claudia were slim anyway. If life in the Soviet Union was as hard as she had heard it was, then the additional money may just help them feel indebted enough to keep their promise.

Maybe, but maybe not. Again Xinya was impressed by Claudia's determination.

"Maybe you and I should trade names," she told Claudia. "You seem to have more proper faith than I have."

"Oh, you don't want my name," Claudia said. "It means 'lame'. And besides," here she looked meaningfully at Xinya, "without your predictions I'd have never found Fico again. If you didn't have the proper faith in your formulas, we wouldn't be here today."

Xinya felt a pang of guilt as she remembered how desolate she felt when she thought the formulas were broken. "My faith is not as strong as it seems," she said.

"Strong enough," Claudia said. "I trust you and your formulas. I trust them enough to place my future in your hands. I'm ready to let my soul line heir carry on from here."

Xinya put her hand on Claudia's arm. "Why not stay here in Russia and become part of Valentina's life?"

Claudia gripped Xinya's hand in hers and looked at her in the eyes. "Xinya," she said. "Is there something you're not telling me?"

"No."

"Are you absolutely sure of the accuracy of your formulas?"

Xinya hesitated for a moment. She remembered Raff's reminder: show no lack of confidence, or The Alert Foundation is doomed. "I am sure."

Claudia squeezed her hand and leaned close in. "Then all will be fine," she said softly. "In less than twenty years, Fico's soul and mine will be together again, as part of Valentina and a strong young man. My staying alive is getting in their way."

Xinya took her hand back. "But how are you so sure?" Xinya asked. "What if—"

"—it's not if," Claudia interrupted. "But when. I trust your formulas." Her eyes were wide.

Xinya wanted to explain how her formulas for Valentina didn't apply to Claudia's own soul line, but Olga came back and gulped down her now-cold hot chocolate, and the three of them hopped back in the taxi and headed out for a quick detour to the Soul Identity branch so Claudia could exchange her foreign rubles before meeting the Nikolskiys.

They would have to sort this out on the train ride back to Moscow.

thirteen

We march into Archibald Morgan's office, Scott's parents behind me, Mikk holding my arm.

My ex-husband's grandfather has been peppering me with questions about the Soul Identity headquarters. "So whose office is this?" he asks.

"Mr. Morgan's," I say. "He's the executive overseer."

Mikk take a look around. "It's rather empty." He points at the wall behind the desk. "Just some photos. Are you sure he works from here?"

"No, I'm not." I step behind the desk to see better. On the wall hangs a large framed black and white picture of a young Madame Flora. She looks to be in her early twenties, and she's holding the hand of a cute toddler boy. They're both smiling into the camera. This picture is flanked by a dozen or so recent snapshots of Rose and Marie.

"Who's the chick in the middle?" Mikk asks.

Scott's mom answers. "That's Flora, Archie's life partner. The boy is their son." She steps up to the wall and gestures at the small pictures. "These girls are their twin great-granddaughters." She points at Mikk. "Flora passed away a couple of years ago, and Archie loved her deeply. He's our host, so respect him and don't call her a chick."

Mikk steps up close and studies the picture for a minute. "She looks mean," he eventually says. "And not a bit happy, even though she's smiling."

Scott's mom opens her mouth, but before she speaks we hear somebody behind us say, "She certainly had plenty of anger boiling inside of her. It was not until the very end when she seemed to mellow out."

"Hey Archie," Scott's dad says, shaking hands with the executive overseer. "How's the bump?"

Mr. Morgan taps the bandage on his forehead and grimaces. "Apparently I have a head hard enough to absorb a karate kick. Other than a mild headache, I am fine."

"Mr. Morgan, I'd like to introduce you to Mikk Ekko. He's my…" I look at Mikk for help.

"Grandfather," Mikk says. "In-law. Or at least I was until Val here signed the divorce papers." He smiles at me. "Now I guess we're just friends."

"I still can't believe you're divorced," Scott's mom says to me as Mikk shakes Mr. Morgan's hand.

"Like I said, don't get your hopes up." This is a replay of a conversation we had once on the flight from Seattle to Boston, once in the back of the Soul Identity limo that picked us up and brought us to the hospital, and once again on the ride from the hospital to Sterling.

She sighs and looks at her husband, who shrugs. Then she steps up to Mr. Morgan and gives him a kiss on his cheek. "It's good to see you again, Archie."

"It is a pleasure to see you too, Mrs. Waverly." He motions us to sit down on the couches in the corner to the left of his desk. Once the five of us are seated, he looks at Scott's mom and asks, "Were you able to see Scott?"

She shook her head. "He's still in surgery. His temple is fractured, and the internal bleeding put pressure on his brain. They have to pick out the bone bits and relieve the pressure before they'll know more."

"I am sorry," Mr. Morgan says. "Apparently Scott was trying to save my life. Once again he is a hero."

I bite my lip and think how my interruption caused Scott to be surprised and injured.

"I want to know who did this," Scott's mom says. "I want to kill him myself."

The executive overseer closes his eyes and sighs. Then he looks at Scott's mom and shakes his head. "We do not know yet. My security team tells me that I have to prepare myself for the possibility that it was somebody I know and trust. They are digging through our security tapes, and of course we will learn more when Scott wakes up."

I look around the ceilings to see if there is a camera. "You recorded the incident?" I ask.

Mr. Morgan frowns. "Apparently not," he says. "There are no cameras on this floor. But we do have tapes from the rest of the building."

"I saw him," I say. "I can give a description." But not the tape. Not yet.

"While you guys do that," Scott's dad says, "Val suggested that instead of waiting at the hospital, we come to Sterling and freshen up. Can we crash at the guest house?"

"Of course," Mr. Morgan says. He walks to his desk and makes a call.

After a few minutes more of small talk, Bob arrives at the door to chauffeur them to the guest house, and Scott's parents and Mikk leave. Then I turn to Mr. Morgan and say, "The guy I saw hit you was dressed in black, and he seemed to know your office. Do you have any contractors working for you?"

He nods. "We have been short-staffed, and I brought in a team of six to help run the office and provide security while I dedicate myself to finding my replacement."

"This guy had a British accent."

"They all have British accents," he says. His eyes widen behind his glasses, and he stares back at me. "George and Sue had this team vetted pretty well. I assume they are beyond reproach."

"Can I meet the team?"

"I will assemble them now," he says as he picks up the phone.

Two minutes later, six black-suited contractors crowd onto Mr. Morgan's two couches. Four women and two men. Three of the women are middle-aged and overweight, and I dismiss them, then focus on the two men and remaining woman.

Neither man looks like the guy who bludgeoned Scott and kicked Mr. Morgan.

"Are you the only guys on the team?" I ask them.

The older of the two men answers me. "That is correct, ma'am." He sticks out his hand and says, "I'm Nigel, and my cohort is Hans."

After I shake their hands, I turn to Mr. Morgan and ask, "How long have you had them here?"

"A tad over two months," he says.

I turn back to Nigel. "And you're the same six who started two months ago?"

"We are."

"No substitutions?"

He shakes his head. "Our contract does not allow it."

I look closely into both Nigel's and Hans's faces. The assistant who clubbed Scott was more fair in his skin than either of the men here, and these two have more girth. No way it was either of these guys.

So I turn to the one possibility, the one girl who seemed in shape. I'm thinking that she could have dressed as a guy, but it's not likely; her boobs are too big, her figure too curvy, and she's at least a foot too short. On top of that, her skin is dark like she's at least half Indian.

So I ask them, "Are there any other British contractor men working in headquarters?"

Nigel shakes his head. "It's just us, and of that I'm positive, ma'am. Mr. Beringer made all contractors redundant back when he was the chief; Mr. Morgan brought only us back."

Mr. Morgan stands up and says, "Thank you for your time, but that will be all. I apologize for the questioning."

After they left, I ask him, "Why did you dismiss them so quickly?"

"It was not them. Why keep them here?"

It's a good point. Besides, I want to get back to the hospital and talk to Scott without his parents around.

fourteen

From the front of the taxi, Olga pointed at a concrete block apartment building. "We go to sixth entrance, over there," she said, pointing. "Apartment 192."

The three of them got out of the taxi and looked at the nine story building. Xinya saw five old ladies, protected from the cold air by fur hats, mittens, and patched woolen coats, sitting on two benches that flanked the entrance. "I assume those are the babushkiy?" she asked.

Olga nodded. "Put scarves up," she whispered. "Look Russian." And she led them past the ladies and into the building.

"We go to third floor," she told them.

Xinya wondered why apartment 192 was on the third floor, but then she noticed that the first floor's apartments were numbered 181-184. "How would I know to use this entrance?" she asked Olga.

"Simple math," Olga replied. "Building has nine floors. Always four apartments on each floor, and numbers start at 1. So we go to sixth entrance. Nikolskiy family are on third floor in last apartment."

The three trooped up the two flights of stairs, and Olga knocked at the door.

"*Kto tam?*" A girl's voice asked from inside.

"*Eto Olga Borisovna,*" Olga replied. "*S dvumya gostyami.*" She looked at Claudia. "I said I am here with her guests."

The door opened right away, and a tall, pink-cheeked girl of no more than nineteen with curly red hair and startling green eyes stood in the doorway. "*Zdravstvuite,*" she said. She wore a dark blue hand-knit sweater and a brown skirt, with white tights and red slippers.

"*Zdravstvuite,*" Olga said. "*Eto Claudia Famosa i Xinya Xia.*" She turned to Claudia. "This is Valentina's mother, Natasha."

"So young," Claudia whispered to Xinya.

"So beautiful," Xinya whispered back. "Lucky Valentina."

Claudia extended her hand toward Natasha. "Pleased to meet you."

Natasha took it in both of hers as Olga translated. "*Ochen priatno,*" she replied. "*Prohoditye, pozhaluysta.*" She motioned them forward.

The three ladies stepped into the apartment. "Boots off," Olga said. She pointed to a pile of red slippers in the corner. "Keep feet warm with those."

Once they put on the slippers, Natasha led them into the living room. There were two divans at one end. A hanging red carpet partially covered the pink wallpaper above them. At the other end, next to a yellow-curtained window, a small table with four chairs held a large electric samovar. The samovar was topped with a small gold and white teapot. Six teacups in saucers were placed around the table.

As Claudia, Xinya, and Olga sat on one of the divans, two men, one considerably younger than the other, came into the room. Natasha spoke to Olga, who said, "This is Valentina's father, Vladimir Andreiovich, and his father, Andrei Vasilivich."

The two men came over and kissed Claudia and Xinya's hands. Then they sat with Natasha on the other divan.

After a half minute of silent staring at each other, Natasha spoke to Olga, who told Claudia and Xinya, "Family will serve you tea. We sit at table."

They all stood up and went to the tiny table. The ladies sat in the four chairs, and the two men dragged their divan across the room and up close. Natasha took the teapot from on top of the samovar and poured a half-inch of hot black tea into each cup. Then she filled each cup, one by one, to the brim with hot water.

When everyone was served, Olga showed them how to pour just a bit of tea into their saucers, then pick up the saucer in both hands and sip. "We use saucers only when tea is hot," she explained. "After two times, you can drink from cup."

Valentina's father said something to Olga, who turned to Claudia and said, "Vladimir Andreivich asks how was journey."

"Good," said Claudia. "The flight was long, but the bed on the train was comfortable."

After a few minutes of small talk, Claudia leaned over to Olga. "Where is Valentina?" she asked.

Olga said, "She is with grandmother. We meet after tea is finished."

Claudia turned to Xinya. "I'm so nervous," she said. "Do you think Fico will recognize me?"

"You should call her Valentina," Xinya said. "Don't scare them."

Claudia nodded. "I keep reminding myself to only say Valentina, but I find it very hard to do." She picked up her cup and gulped down the remaining tea. "I'm ready," she told Olga.

Olga frowned. "We wait a few more minutes to be polite."

After another five minutes, the husband and father-in-law finished their tea, and Natasha removed the teacups and saucers. At Olga's suggestion, they moved back to their divan, and the men dragged the other one back to the wall.

Claudia put both hands on her knees and looked at Natasha. "Can we meet Valentina?"

After Olga translated, both Natasha and Vladimir started to speak in loud and sharp voices. Xinya thought they were arguing with Olga, and eventually Natasha held up her hands and gave a two-minute-long speech to the translator.

"What's going on?" Claudia whispered to Xinya. "Are they tricking us?"

"I hope not," Xinya said.

Olga replied to Natasha, and then the father-in-law stood up, shouting. He stalked out of the room, still speaking over his shoulder.

Olga threw up her hands and spoke to Natasha. Then she turned to Claudia and Xinya. "We have problem. Russians believe no strangers should look on child for first year of life. Natasha does not want you to meet Valentina—"

"—Now wait just a minute," Claudia said. "We came a long way for this meeting." She was sitting forward and breathing heavily.

It seemed to Xinya that Claudia was about to stand up and shout, which would not help resolve the problem. She put her hand on Claudia's shoulder. "Let Olga finish what she's saying," she suggested.

Claudia nodded, and Olga continued. "Natasha does not want you to meet Valentina until you no longer stranger. You need proper conversation first, so evil eye does not interfere."

"Ah," Claudia said, and she sat back. "That's a good idea."

"Good," Olga said. Natasha has question first. What was husband's favorite color?"

"Azul turquesa," Claudia said. "Turquoise blue, the color of the ocean."

After the translation, Natasha nodded. She spoke to Olga, who said, "Do you have any keepsakes of your husband?"

"Just one photograph, and many wonderful memories."

Natasha then pointed at Xinya and spoke to Olga, who translated, "Natasha wants to know how magic formula works."

Xinya bit her lip. She wasn't even sure if it really worked. But she thought about Raff's advice, so she said, "Every soul is on its own journey. The formulas help me find the path, so we can find the next heir."

Natasha listened closely to Olga's translation, then she replied, and Olga said, "Natasha thinks you are better than Gypsy fortune tellers. Can formula predict when in future Claudia's soul will return?"

Xinya took a deep breath and glanced at Claudia. She wished she could have had this conversation alone with Claudia, and not here in front of Valentina's parents. She started to shake her head.

But Claudia held up her hand and told Olga, "Xinya has already predicted my path, and I am ready. Tell Natasha that I will pass on very soon and return as a boy in Estonia ten months later. Tell her that very soon The Alert Foundation will help that boy and Valentina meet."

Xinya stared open-mouthed at Claudia. Was she delirious? She realized that although Claudia may be a bit over-excited, if this was true then something was terribly wrong with Alert. With Raff. Her husband had lied to Claudia about Xinya's formulas. He was running a con.

And Claudia's heir born in ten months? Claudia was planning to die, and die very soon. Raff was sure to be helping her.

Xinya had not run her formulas on Claudia's soul line. In fact, ever since the day they discovered Valentina, she hadn't run any formulas at all.

Raff must have produced some fake charts and convinced Claudia that she could choose her own heir, her own destiny. And all of a sudden the strange comments Claudia had made during their conversations on the train, and in the café, made sense.

But what could she say? She looked at Claudia, her face bright and animated. Natasha and Vladimir seemed a bit shaken as Olga translated, but they nodded their heads, and both were speaking.

And then she realized if she stopped the conversation, she'd only make it worse. It wouldn't do to cast doubt on Alert's accuracy. She still had time to dissuade Claudia, and Valentina's parents would have years to think about this conversation. Who was she to jump in the middle and mess up the good feelings? Especially as she didn't have all the facts about what Raff had done.

So, as uncomfortable as she felt, Xinya remained silent and listened as Claudia painted a bright future for the Nikolskiy family. She smiled and nodded when Natasha looked at her with questioning eyes.

Claudia handed over the ten thousand rubles. She took two necklaces out of her purse, demonstrated how they joined to form a completed engraved circle, and gave one of them to Natasha.

Natasha went to a back room and came back a minute later with Valentina in her arms. The baby girl was a miniature of her mother, with curly red hair and even brighter green eyes.

Natasha handed Valentina to Claudia. The baby looked up, gave Claudia a three-toothed grin, and nuzzled into her breast.

Maybe all would work out, Xinya thought. She wiped the tears from her eyes. Instead of worrying about Raff and her formulas and whether Claudia was going to kill herself, she focused her mind on the day when she would be reunited with her own brother.

fifteen

On the way to the train station, Xinya listened with only a half an ear to Olga's reassurances of how The Alert Foundation would support Valentina and her family.

When they said their goodbyes and finally sat down on the beds in their cabin, Claudia pulled out a brown leather-bound diary. "I want to record everything," she said. "My future self needs to know how incredible Valentina is."

Xinya watched her write and thought about how she would approach the subject of Claudia's future self, and, more importantly, what Raff had told her.

"Will you put the diary in your soul line collection?" she asked.

Claudia nodded. "I started keeping it a few years ago, when I first joined Soul Identity. Now that I know exactly where I'm going, it's important that I record all my instructions. I want my future self to find Fico as soon as possible."

"What you told the Nikolskiys surprised me," Xinya said.

"I was surprised too. Valentina is as beautiful as I had hoped. Did you see how she smiled at me?"

"I mean what you said about coming back soon."

Claudia's eyebrows raised. "We've talked about my next incarnation many times on this trip."

"Yes. But you seem so sure about when your future self will be back. You mentioned something about an Estonian boy appearing ten months after you die."

"Yes, I did. Was I not supposed to share your data with them?"

Xinya shook her head. "Sharing is fine. It's part of the reunion. But Claudia…"

She saw Claudia lean forward, eyes open wide.

How could she say this gently? "Claudia, you cannot trust the formulas on your own soul line."

"Of course you can."

"I did not run the formulas yet."

"Of course you did. Raff sent them to me."

Xinya shook her head. "They are not mine. But even if they were, my formulas only tell me where to look. I have to research lots of predicted vectors. And most are wrong."

Claudia crossed her arms and looked into the darkness out the train window. She was silent for a few minutes. Then she said, "Okay, I get what's happening."

Xinya let loose with a big sigh of relief.

"You've got cold feet, haven't you?" Claudia asked.

"Excuse me?"

"You're chicken. Afraid. Frightened." Claudia punctuated with her pointer finger. "You got scared when you heard I was going to kill myself, didn't you?"

Xinya looked at her, open-mouthed.

"Just when I need you the most, you're backing out, aren't you?" Claudia shouting this.

"No, I—"

"—you asked me to trust your formulas. Well, what do you know, I do trust them. And do you know why?"

Xinya shook her head.

Claudia made a fist. "They work. You found Fico. You saw for yourself how Valentina recognized me. You know they work."

"But—"

"—Don't you dare back out on me now, Xinya. Don't try changing my mind, just because you think I should stay alive." She balled her hands into fists and pressed her knuckles together. "It's time for me to pass on. And I really need your support if I'm going to do this."

Xinya pulled her legs up and grabbed her knees in her arms. "Oh, Claudia, I want to support you. But you need to know—"

"—I know everything I need to know. It's you, Xinya, who has to be strong. You knew right from the beginning that I wanted to be with Fico again."

"I did."

"So support me."

She realized that only Raff could put a stop to Claudia's nonsense. Claudia trusted him, and once he explained that he had lied, Claudia would want to spend her life watching baby Valentina grow. Not trying to force her own soul to return faster.

But could she convince Raff to do admit his wrongdoing? She would make him, she vowed. In the meantime, it was important that she stay on good terms with Claudia.

"I support you, Claudia." She took a deep breath before continuing. "And if you die," here she failed to hold back a shudder, "then I'll do everything I can to reunite your and Fico's soul lines."

Claudia stood up and motioned for Xinya to join her. They both embraced.

"You brought joy to my life by finding Fico," Claudia said. "Thank you for helping me finish this difficult journey."

Xinya patted Claudia on the back. She must convince Raff before it was too late.

sixteen

Xinya looked for Raff as she came through customs, but he wasn't there as he had promised. So she took a cab directly to the Alert offices, dragging her luggage behind her. She had to talk to him immediately about the damage he was about to cause Claudia.

She entered the empty lobby and headed to his office. The door was closed, so she opened it quietly and stuck her head in, not wanting to interrupt a customer meeting.

Raff stood facing his desk and the window, his back to Xinya, and his pants around his ankles. The new receptionist was bent forward, skirt hiked around her hips, elbows on the desk, mouth open, and also looking out the window. Neither of them seemed to have heard her.

It took a few seconds for Xinya to process the scene. When she did, she quietly pulled the door shut and slowly released the knob. Then she leaned against the wall, her hands covering her mouth.

A minute later, when she was able to walk again, she left and walked to her apartment. After taking a shower and putting away her luggage and taking several deep breaths, she called the office.

"The Alert Foundation, how can I assist you?" The receptionist's cheery voice betrayed nothing.

"It's Xinya," she said, gritting her teeth. "May I speak to Raff?"

"Of course, Ms. Xia. Let me connect you."

After a few moments of imagining the receptionist going to Raff's office and hugging and kissing him before delivering her message, her husband came on the phone. "Xinya, has your flight landed already?"

"It arrived early," she said.

"I was going to call the airlines, but I got pulled into a customer meeting."

Xinya remained silent.

"Should I come get you at the airport?"

"I took a cab," she said. "I'm at my apartment. We need to talk."

"Sure, honey. I want to hear how it went with Claudia and Valentina. You want to come to the office?"

She closed her eyes and imagined herself sitting in his office, trying to concentrate on what he was doing to Claudia instead of what he had done to the receptionist.

"Meet me at the library," she said. "I have some research to wrap up. Can you come to the map room?" It had the best chance of being empty.

"Aren't you tired?"

"No, I was able to sleep on the flight."

"Let me look at my appointments." Then a minute later he said, "I need to wrap up something important. How about I meet you there in two hours? Say, at four o'clock?"

"Fine." She made sure a smile could be heard in her voice as she brushed away a tear. "I can't wait to see you, Raff."

"Me too, honey. Be there soon."

In the map room, Xinya opened her portfolio and removed a pad of graph paper and two pencils. She tried to focus on the work, but she ended up spending the next hour replaying the sex scene starring Raff and the new receptionist. She imagined what it would have been like to march up to Raff and slap him across the face. And she contemplated her future now her dreams for Alert were crushed.

Claudia was right. She was a big chicken.

She spent the next hour and a half working through her formulas, comparing the soul lines she had found to the predictions the formulas had made about their future lives. And the results were not at all what she had expected to see.

She heard fast footsteps, and turned to see Brandon carrying his skateboard and knapsack.

He had a big smile on his face. "Hey Ms. Xia, how was Russia?" he asked.

She forced herself to smile back. "Good, Brandon. The reunion was magical."

"Awesome." He pulled out a chair, turned it around, and sat down, arms wrapped around its back. "I've decided to change the way I research."

"Oh?"

He pointed across the room at a world map covering half of the wall. "I tried going country by country instead of file by file. This week I eliminated every Japanese vector from the unfinished lost souls. It went so much faster than hopping all over the place."

He paused, and Xinya nodded.

"Today I'm starting Spanish-speaking countries," he said. "They will take a bit longer because of their lousy records and my lousy Spanish. But still, it will be faster this way."

"Good. You're recording your hours?"

"Of course." He looked at her. "Did you hear anything I said?"

She tried to replay the conversation. "I'm sorry, Brandon," she said. "I have two major problems I need to solve."

"What can I do to help?"

She shook her head. "They're not research problems."

He shrugged. "Try me anyway. You know I love to learn new things."

Xinya stared at his pointy hair, his skateboard, his knapsack, his smile. "I will give you a hypothetical problem," she said. "Imagine we had a customer who we helped reunite with her lost soul mate."

"Like the reunion in Russia?"

"Hypothetically speaking."

"Of course."

"Now," she said. "Imagine that our customer wanted to use our formulas to plan her own next incarnation to intersect with that soul mate."

Brandon scratched his head. "You mean she wants to die and come back to be with the little girl. Can she do that?"

Xinya shrugged her shoulders. "On the surface it seems possible. We use where the soul has been to plot its trajectory. I suppose you can alter your trajectory if you choose where and when to die."

Brandon ripped a piece of graph paper out of the back of her pad. He grabbed a pencil and drew two parallel arrows going up and to the right. "So this would be her and her soul mate's trajectories, right?"

Xinya nodded, and then circled a segment of the top arrow, halfway up. "Imagine if she adjusted the time and place of her death." She drew a radius from the circle that detoured down, crossing the bottom arrow. "That could modify her trajectory to make it intercept."

"Far out," Brandon said. "Your formulas can predict this?"

"It's never been tested. But given the existing trajectory, I suppose the formulas would calculate possible new vectors." She tapped her pencil on the paper. "But there are two issues."

"Only two?" He scratched his head.

"The first you know." She drew an array of lines radiating out of the same circle. Some intersected with the line below, and some didn't. "My formulas predict many possible vectors, and we don't know which vector will be the one that works."

"That's why we research and eliminate them. But obviously you can't research the future," he said. "I get that issue. What's the other one?"

She sighed. "The formulas don't work."

The pencil fell out of Brandon's hands. "What do you mean?"

She dropped her voice so it was barely audible. "I found a paradox in my calculations. And it cannot be resolved. At best it guides our search, but I am now convinced that there is no way to calculate a soul's trajectory."

He pointed at her portfolio. "But you find souls all the time! You pay me to find them, too."

"Like I said, it guides our search. But think about how often my predictions are wrong. And even the soul lines we've recovered don't exactly follow the vectors that were predicted."

"They don't?"

She sighed. "I can't believe I didn't do this earlier. I looked at the three soul lines we recovered this year, and then I tried to go backward and predict the past."

"You started with the living person?" Brandon asked.

She nodded. "But it didn't work."

He raised his eyebrows. "Not at all?"

"Not a single prediction was close," she said. "We've been tricked by confirmation bias." She opened her folder and showed Brandon the graphed lines. "The formulas don't work. The predictions are not real."

"That nineteen grand you've paid me so far this year was real enough. Something in your formulas must be working."

She raised her hands and let them drop to the table. "Maybe they work just enough to give us a good hint," she said. "And maybe we have just gotten lucky."

They were both silent for a moment. Then Brandon said, "Hint or luck, your formulas pay well."

"True. But we can't use them to help people choose their next life."

He nodded. "That is quite an issue. Have you told your Cuban lady that you can't predict her future?"

Xinya shook her head. "It may be too late. Raff has already told her that it works. She is planning to die so her future self can meet with Valentina."

"That's crazy." He planted both hands on the table. "We can't let her kill herself! Especially since we know it doesn't work."

Xinya gave him a sad smile. "Claudia seems set on destroying herself. I was hoping that Raff will convince her to stop, but even he…" her voice trailed off as she saw her husband approaching.

seventeen

Raff oozed smiles as he stepped up to the map room table. He pecked Xinya on the cheek, slapped Brandon on the back, and said, "Hey, kid, what say you give me some privacy with my wife?"

"Sure, Mr. Rafferty." Brandon grabbed his knapsack and skateboard. "I'll be in the stacks," he told Xinya. Then he left the room.

Raff sat down in the chair Brandon had vacated. "Not sure I trust that kid," he said. "He needs to dress like a professional."

Xinya stared at him. "He's just eighteen, Raff."

"Even so. He's an adult. When I was his age, I was already wearing suits to work."

And probably already seducing the receptionists. But she kept that inside, and said, "Claudia wants to die as soon as possible."

"Of course she does."

She noted that he didn't even try to act surprised. She looked closely at his eyes. "Is our foundation part of this scheme?"

He glanced away, rubbing his nose.

"Are we?" she asked again.

"She mentioned it to me," he said.

"Did you send her vectors from my formulas?"

Again he glanced away. And then he said, "I thought we agreed that I'd run the business side of things, and you'd focus on the recoveries."

"Raff, I never calculated her formulas. Yet she was sure I had predicted her next incarnation. Why would she think that?"

He shrugged. "I might have sent her some mock-ups of what we could provide her."

"Mock-ups? Raff, she's ready to kill herself."

"That's her problem, honey. Our job was to find Valentina. What she does next is her own decision."

Xinya put her hands to her temples and willed herself to stay calm. "Raff," she said evenly. "If you provide fake information, and she uses that information to kill herself, that makes you a murderer."

He slammed his palm down on the table, then glanced quickly around. He put his finger to his lips and grimaced at the librarian, mouthing sorry.

"Xinya. Honey. You need to let me handle the business details."

"I do not wish for The Alert Foundation to be known as fakes." She pointed at Raff. "You must stop this."

He stared at her for a full minute without saying anything. Then he leaned forward in his chair, put his elbows on the table, and spoke softly. "Xinya, there is something you need to remember."

She waited.

"Before me, you were just a girl with dreams and formulas. And without me doing what I do, keeping my eye on the company's future, you won't be able to..." He paused for a second. "Strike that. You will never reunite any living people."

What had happened to her business partner? To her husband?

"Tell me," he said. "Did you enjoy the reunion between Claudia and Valentina?"

She closed her eyes briefly, seeing it again in her mind. "It was very special."

"Do you want to have more of those?"

"Of course I do."

"Then let me do what I do, and stay out of the dirty parts of the business."

"But you are lying to Claudia. How can I be happy if I know you are lying to our customers?"

"It's the way the world really works. And anyway, it's what customers expect."

She scrunched up her face. "They expect to be lied to?"

"Claudia wants the illusion that she's in control of her destiny. That she can mold fate to suit her needs."

Xinya thought about that. "She may be able to change her fate, but that does not make her soul vectors predictable."

He shrugged. "Nobody knows that, Xinya. Only you know where the soul lines will go."

Here she leaned forward, palms down on the table. "Raff," she whispered. "Even I don't know. My formulas don't work."

"Stop," he hissed, holding up his hands. "Don't you ever disparage the formulas in public. Of course they work. Everything we do is based on the illusion that those formulas are perfect."

How could she make him understand? She assembled her thoughts. "I know I'm not the businessperson you are," she said, "But what happens to our reputation when Claudia's soul doesn't return in ten months?"

He leaned back and put his hands behind his head. "Of course her soul will return," he said with a big grin. "The Alert Foundation will discover him in just a couple of years, and we'll have the greatest reunion that a Soul Identity member could ever imagine."

"How can you be so sure?"

His grin only grew wider. "For somebody so smart, you're awfully slow on the uptake. Just think about it."

So she thought about how Raff could be so sure that Claudia's soul would return. And she said, "The boy is already alive, isn't he?"

Her husband nodded and tapped his nose. "Bingo."

"But his soul identity doesn't match Claudia's."

He smiled. "Oh yes it does." He leaned forward. "Do you want to know how?"

She tried to think how it was possible that two people could share the same identity, but she was stumped. The organization would have collapsed centuries before if soul identities weren't uniquely possessed by a single person at a time.

"Tell me," she said.

He grinned. "Before Claudia moved to Cuba, we opened a brand new soul line account for her, using the identity of the boy."

"She let you do that?"

"I told her that a new account was the only way she could get her account linked with Fico's."

Xinya sighed. "And I suppose she's already put her money and memories in the boy's soul line account?"

Raff nodded.

"How did you get that account through the depositary screening?"

Raff stood up and paced around the table, hands on his hips. "Their security efforts are aimed at those trying to steal existing accounts. It was easy as pie to open a new account with a faked identity." He stopped directly across from her. "When she moved to Cuba, she gave us power of attorney to her accounts. I've transferred everything else over."

"What happens when she accesses her soul line account and sees that everything is gone?"

He sat down again. "She won't do that. We've told her that her account has been sealed, with us keeping an eye on it as we wait for her next incarnation. And we've got her on a ticking clock. She thinks she only has a couple of weeks."

"Claudia's real incarnation won't have any knowledge of her past, because you put everything in the wrong account."

He shrugged. "She'll never know that. And if the boy has any doubts, he'll have plenty of money to help him remember."

"This is crazy."

He smiled. "We'll have lines of customers stretching around the block once we pull this off. Reunions galore, Xinya."

She closed her eyes. "But they won't be real reunions, will they?" she whispered.

He steepled his hands. "They'll all be real to them, Xinya."

"But we'll know that they're fake."

She spent a few minutes in contemplation, staring at Raff while he smiled back and played with his cufflinks. She wondered how she would be able to continue working for Alert when she knew her own company's reputation was established on a lie.

He had no respect for her beliefs, or for her reputation. And she decided that it was time to get everything out on the table and see if she did have a backbone after all. She took a deep breath and asked, "Are you having relations with your receptionist?"

He stared at her. "Why are you changing the subject?"

She tried sharpen the edge in her voice. "Just answer the question, Raff."

"I can't believe you'd ask me that. You of all people, who spend nights in your own separate apartment." He stood up. "Look, Xinya, I have to get back to the office. We can talk later tonight, or tomorrow. But I'm not having this silly conversation now."

She must let him go. Though every ounce of instinct screamed at her to stop him, find an excuse for him, and let him off the hook yet again.

When Raff reached the door, he pivoted to face her and said, "Stick with the plan, okay?"

She stared back at him, using all her strength to keep from nodding. "Do what's right, Raff," she said loudly.

She watched him turn away.

eighteen

I open the door to Scott's hospital room. It's dark inside, and I see the silhouette of what I think must be Scott on the bed, and a larger person sitting in a chair at his feet.

"Scott?" I whisper.

The larger person stands up and walks over to me. It's a middle-aged man in his early sixties, with a largish belly, a clean shaven face, and long grey hair pulled into a ponytail.

"Valentina?" he says, sticking out his hand. "Michael Rafferty. Remember me?"

I take his hand. "Of course, Raff. How could I forget?" Raff is the head of The Alert Foundation, the organization that got me and Rain together two years ago. "How have you been?"

He nods at the door. "Let's go in the hallway and let Scott sleep," he says.

As we step out, I size up Raff. A sharp charcoal suit and a button shirt open halfway down his chest covers his paunch. A fat gold chain and grey chest hair curls are lapping against the edges of the shirt. He's wearing brightly polished black leather shoes.

"You haven't changed a bit," I say.

He smiles and pats his forehead. "Maybe a bit more face to wash, and maybe a couple extra pounds, but time has treated me well."

I wait for him to continue.

"I heard you and Rain called it quits," he says.

I nod. "In a very public way."

He winces. "I hope you haven't hurt my business."

I stare at him. "Really, Raff? That's all you can say?"

After a minute he says, "You're right, Val. I'm sorry it didn't work out between you two. But you can't blame me for thinking about the welfare of my employees."

"Of course not," I say. "I blame you for talking business when I want to know how Scott is doing."

"I'm not sure, he hasn't woken up since I've been here," he says.

I already know from Archie and Scott's doctor that Scott is sleeping off the anesthesia from his surgery to repair his cheekbone and jaw.

We share a minute of silence, then Raff says, "You're probably wondering why I'm here."

I nod again.

"Scott and I are partners."

"I find that hard to believe," I say. "Last I knew, he hated Alert."

"That's water under the bridge," he says. "Scott and I are helping Soul Identity find a new batch of overseers. Scott supplies the tech, and I supply the formulas." He brings his fingers together into a steeple. "Our unique technologies are a match made in heaven."

I think about this. "You've really become business partners?"

"Actually, Soul Identity contracts both of us separately, even though I asked them to make me prime and save themselves the hassle. But regardless, I run the search, and he's on the team."

I remember all the bitter words Scott had to say about The Alert Foundation when they united me with Rain. He was deeply suspicious of their formulas, claiming it was just luck that they predicted Claudia's soul line reappearance in Rain. I can't see him and Raff as partners; Scott could never tolerate a businessman oozing charm instead of brains.

Unless something changed Scott. But I have no idea what that would be.

"Have you had any luck?" I ask.

Raff shook his head. "Just some false alarms. We're still digging."

I think back to the call with Mr. Morgan. He said three discovered overseers disappeared, along with their families, in terrible accidents. Raff doesn't appear to know I know this. And I remember what Mr. Morgan relayed from Scott: he didn't know who could be trusted.

So I ask, "How are you searching for them?"

Raff rubs his hands together and says, "My historians fleshed out the overseer soul line data, which in some cases was pretty frigging sparse. Then my mathematicians ran the predictive formulas. With all the guesswork, we had to cast a wide net, hoping to find something, anything at all."

"And Scott's part in the search?"

"He's got his cameras around the globe, but not everywhere. When Alert predicts the cities to check, we tell Scott, and he acquires more eyes and does his magic."

"What does acquiring eyes mean?"

He smiles. "Hacks. Borrows. Taps into. I don't know the right word here. Scott says that the whole world is wired to the Internet, and that includes millions of cameras. But we have to give him a prioritized list, as he can't boil the ocean by himself. We tell him which cities, and maybe even the neighborhoods, and he takes it from there."

"And the false alarms?"

He holds up his hand and see-saws it. "Scott's tech found a lot, too many actually, potential overseers. But when my ground team checked them out, the matches were off." He leans close to me and whispers, "When he wakes up, don't tell him I said his tech needs more work; he'd be pretty embarrassed."

"He's rather confident about his technology," I say.

"Some would say defensive." He jerks a thumb at Scott's door. "If you tell him I tattled, he won't work with me, and then where would Soul Identity be? Up shit creek, and with Archie on his last legs, we really can't afford to take too long."

"That's true." I incline my head toward the door. "I want to see Scott."

"I'll keep you company," he says.

I shake my head. "I need to do this alone."

He scratches his head, shifts his stance, and seems about to say something.

"What is it, Raff?"

"Nothing," he says. "I hope the kid recovers. But I'm afraid that his memory is addled. Maybe not even accurate anymore."

"Did the doctor tell you that?"

He shrugs his shoulders. "Not in so many words. But apparently he got brain pretty hard." He reaches into his suit jacket and pulls out a business card. "You'll call me when he wakes up? I need his help in the search."

I take the card. "Of course."

He seems about to add something, but then changes his mind and walks over to the elevator. When the doors close, I turn the handle to Scott's room and mentally steel myself.

nineteen

From the parts of him I can see, Scott hasn't changed much in the past two years. Maybe his curly hair is a bit thinner, and he's acquired more laugh lines around his eyes.

But I can't see all of him. The left side of his face from the cheek downward is covered in a bandage. A hospital gown covers his chest, and a bedsheet snugs up to his waist. He's got an IV pole next to him, and a tube from it running into his arm.

I step up to his right side and lean my face in close to his neck. Call me weird, but I have a sudden urge to lay my head on his shoulder before he knows I'm there. I lean forward and down to him.

"Is that Irish bastard finally gone?" he whispers.

I jerk my head up. "You're awake."

"Come back," he says, eyes still closed. "It's been a long time."

So I lean in again and nuzzle my nose into his neck, halfway between his ear and shoulder. He lifts his arm and strokes my cheek.

"You ok?" I ask.

"I should be. I think a kiss will make me heal quicker."

I kiss his finger. "That's all you're going to get."

"That's all I need." He points across the room to a cabinet. "Do me a favor and get my clothes and shoes."

"You're not going anywhere," I say. "Doctor's orders. I spoke to him and he says you need to rest for at least a few days."

"What does he know, anyway? Just get my stuff."

I stand up straight and put my hands on my hips. He looks at me for a minute and then eyes the cabinet.

"My clothes?" he says. "I want to show you something."

I sigh and walk over to the cabinet and open the door. Inside there's a black t-shirt and jeans, a pair of loafers, and a wallet. I scoop it all up and turn around in time to see Scott rip the IV tubing out of his arm.

His head must still be addled. "Scott, you need that tube in your arm... what are you doing?"

"Getting out of here," he says. "While I still can."

Is paranoia associated with head injuries?

"I'll explain later," he says. "Right now we have to go." He points to his clothes. "Where's my underwear and socks?"

I look in the cabinet, but it's empty. "Not here."

"I'll just have to go commando."

"Are you sure you should be getting up?"

He looks at me solemnly. His eyes hold mine. "I want to live," he says. "And that won't happen if we don't get out of here."

I might as well humor him, so I hand him his clothes. He pulls his gown over his head and puts on the t-shirt. He looks at me and purses his lips, then swings his feet over the side of the bed, letting the bedsheet fall.

And I see my first difference down there. "You've started shaving," I say.

"It's what modern singles do." He pulls up his jeans, arranges himself before zipping up, and steps barefoot into his loafers. "Ready?"

I point to his bandage. "Does it hurt?"

Scott snaps his fingers. "I almost forgot," he says. He grabs the bandage and pulls at it. He winces, then unwinds a band of gauze that is wrapped around his head. The dressing is stained an angry reddish brown, and it catches his skin as he pulls it off. Underneath is an ugly patchwork of cuts and stitches.

"Ouch," I say.

"Ouch is right," he says. "This adhesive is really catching the hairs on my face."

"I meant your wound."

"Oh." He catches my eye. "Watch this." He digs his fingers into the cut, and I suppress a scream as he pulls at the torn skin. Then with a sucking sound, the entire wound pulls away from his face.

"Latex," Scott says. He holds it out, and it jiggles in his hand. "Just like the movies."

I close my wide-open mouth and stare at the piece of plastic. "You faked this?"

"I had no choice. I had to hurt myself before they really killed me."

"But—"

He holds up both his hands, the fake wound tucked into his palm. "Not now, Val. We have to get out of here before Raff, or somebody else, returns and realizes I'm not incapacitated."

I nod, and he heads for the door.

"Hold up," I say. I point to his cheek. "You still have some stuff there."

"Where?" He looks toward the mirror.

"Let me get it," I say. I lean in toward him, and then I rear back and slap his cheek as hard as I can.

Scott's head snaps to the side and his hand flies up to the white spot on his cheek.

I stare at him, breathing hard, and feeling great. "That," I say, "was for your stunt during my speech."

"I guess I deserve that," he says, rubbing his cheek.

"And so much more," I say. "We'll get there. But let's go."

twenty

Both the jetlag and her troubled thoughts made the first night back in the States seem to last forever. Finally, the workday started, the sun rose, and Xinya got up and stood in front of the mirror in her bathroom.

"I am strong," she lied to her image. "I am courageous."

She called in a favor with one of her librarian friends to get dinner reservations for that night at Tavern on the Green.

Then she called Alert. When the receptionist answered, she tamped down her feelings of disgust and said, "I have a dilemma that you can help me with."

"Do you want to speak to Mr. Rafferty?"

"No, it's a favor I need," she said. "I had surprise dinner reservations for Raff and me for eight o'clock tonight, but I now realize I cannot make it. Would you be able to accompany him? It's his favorite restaurant, Tavern on the Green."

Silence on the line. Then an uncertain, "Are you sure you want me to go with him?"

"Of course I am," she said. "He shouldn't miss the restaurant because of my mistake."

"Okay, Ms. Xia, I'll do it. And don't worry, I'll take good care of him."

Of course she would. That afternoon, when Brandon met her at the library, she asked him, "Can you come with me to the office at eight o'clock tonight?"

He looked at his watch. "I could, if I go home now and get my homework done first. What are we doing?"

"Investigation work," she said. "We need to discover exactly how, when, and where my husband intends to help Claudia die."

"You couldn't convince Mr. Rafferty to stop."

She shook her head. "I feel so stupid."

"Will he be there tonight?"

"He has an out-of-office appointment."

He nodded. "See you at eight."

After Brandon left, she went back to her apartment, found an unused toolkit under the kitchen sink, and slipped its screwdriver and hammer into her purse.

Then she packed her suitcase with a few days' worth of clothing. After sitting and thinking for a few moments, she replaced half the clothes with items that she couldn't imagine living without. This included the few photographs, documents, and trinkets from her life in China; her diploma and a bound copy of her doctoral thesis from Columbia; and her address book.

When the packing seemed complete, Xinya swept her tiny kitchen, washed the tea cups in her sink, threw out the remaining food in her refrigerator, and unplugged the appliances. She tossed her garbage down the incinerator chute. She put on her coat and took a last look at the apartment where she had spent most of the past fifteen years. She carried her suitcase to the hall, locked the door and deadbolt, and put the keys under the mat. The super would find them before too long.

Down on the street, she hailed a cab, and asked the driver, "Can you take me to a hotel?"

"Which one, lady?" the cabbie asked.

"The closest one to the library," she said. "With at least two stars."

"There's a Howard Johnson's three blocks from here."

"Perfect."

The hotel lobby was empty. Xinya rang the bell on the desk, and after a few minutes, a bald man in a brown suit came from the back, wiping his nose on his sleeve.

"Do you have any rooms available?" she asked him.

"I might," he said. "For how many nights?"

"Seven." She bit her lip. "But I may leave early."

He checked the register on his desk. "We have a non-smoking queen room available on the fifth floor." He slid a registration card to her. "If that works, fill this out, and I'll get it organized."

She used Claudia's name and address instead of her own.

He scanned the card when she handed it back. "I would have pegged you as Chinese," he said.

"Half." She hoped the lie didn't show. "My father was Cuban."

He nodded. "Thank you, Miss Famosa," he said. "How will you be settling your bill?"

"Cash."

"Then I'll need payment up front," he said. "As a security deposit."

Xinya paid, the manager handed her the key, and she lugged her suitcase to the room. She stood for a minute at the window and stared at the yellow taxis below. Then she took the elevator to the lobby, stepped outside, and walked to her bank.

"I need to make a sizeable withdrawal," she told the pretty teller. She slid the withdrawal slip under the glass.

"Of course, Ms. Xia," the girl said. "But you left the amounts empty. How much would you like?"

"All of my private account, and half of the joint account," she said.

The teller nodded, then busied herself on the computer terminal. After a few minutes, she slid an envelope under the window. "Here's the money from your private account," she said. "A little over eight thousand dollars."

Xinya put the envelope in her purse.

Another minute, and the teller frowned. "I'm afraid the joint account is empty," she said.

"Empty?"

The girl nodded. "A Mr. Rafferty was here this morning." She held the bank record up to her side of the glass. "We wrote him a cashier's check for sixty-eight thousand and four dollars."

Was she that predictable? "Thank you," she said, and she left the bank and returned to her hotel room.

At seven forty-five, she headed over to The Alert Foundation's offices. She arrived five minutes early. The lobby was dark, but she checked to be sure that Raff's office was empty. Then she called Tavern on the Green, and confirmed that Mr. Rafferty and a guest had indeed arrived, and no, she didn't want to pass along a message.

She looked through the papers on and in her husband's desk. She leafed through his appointment book, and didn't see anything referring to Claudia.

Brandon arrived precisely at eight o'clock.

"Is your homework all done?" she asked him. "This may take a few hours."

He nodded. "I didn't know how long we'd be, and Mom's at work, so I'm good to go. Have you started already?"

"I just went through his desk, and found nothing. I think we can look through the client files next."

"What exactly are we looking for?"

"We need to find where and when Raff told Claudia to die. It is probably a place, and maybe a time. Or maybe we'll find a schedule, or a graph, or a copy of a letter he sent her."

"Wasn't Mr. Rafferty hiding this information from you?"

"He was. We'll have to go through each file to see where he hid it."

"How will I recognize it?"

"You probably won't," she said. "I'll have to check to see if it's what I'm looking for. Your job is to put the files back in order so he doesn't know we were looking."

For the next hour and a half, Xinya reviewed every paper in each client file, and Brandon put everything away. But they didn't find anything that seemed to relate to either Claudia or Fico.

As he closed the last client drawer, Brandon asked, "Where's his secret hiding place?"

Xinya frowned. "What do you mean?"

"Before Dad left and we moved to your apartment building, I discovered where he kept all the things he didn't want Mom to find."

"What kinds of things?"

"You know, old letters from girls before Mom, some dirty magazines, an address book. He even had a pack of cigarettes and a half-empty bottle of scotch in there."

Xinya pursed her lips. "I don't think Raff has a secret hiding place."

"Mom probably never knew that Dad had one, either. But every guy has one, I'm sure of it."

Xinya pursed her lips. "Where was your father's hiding place?"

Brandon smiled. "Dad had this wooden chest in the back of the closet. It had some old books and games in it. And it had a false bottom."

"How did you find it?"

"When I was thirteen, I was looking for him, and I found him kneeling down in front of the chest. When he heard me, he slammed it shut and shoved it to the back of the closet. Then when he and Mom went out that night, I tore that chest apart." He smiled. "I was thirteen, and those dirty magazines were like finding gold."

"I'll bet. Do you have a secret hiding place, Brandon?"

"I said every guy has one, didn't I?"

"What's in yours? And where is it?"

He sucked in his breath through his teeth. "Ooh, I'm not telling."

She sighed. "Interesting as your story may be, it's not helping us find the papers."

"I told you, they'll be in his secret hiding place. We just have to find it."

"Okay, Brandon." She put her hands on her hips. "If this was your office, where would your hiding place be?"

He stood in the middle of the room and slowly turned in a circle. He scratched his chin, then his head. Then he said, "Got it."

"Where?"

"Behind or under the desk drawers. It's the only logical place."

"There's logic when it comes to hiding places?"

"Of course. Look, a hiding place has to be easy to get to, and it has to be somewhere you can cover up quickly." He waved his hand around the room. "This office doesn't have many options—the filing cabinet faces the door. So do the couches. The only place it could be is the desk."

"I already checked the desk before you came. It has no hiding places."

"Let me look." Brandon walked over to the desk and pulled out the center drawer. He stuck his hands in the back, and after a moment, frowned.

"Did you find it?"

He shook his head. He opened the top right-hand drawer and dug through the papers. Then the middle drawer. Then the bottom drawer.

"Any luck?"

He gave a big grin. "It's here. This drawer only slides halfway." He tugged at the back panel, and it lifted out with a loud click.

Xinya stepped around the desk as Brandon withdrew three manila folders and placed them next to Raff's telephone.

"Told you," he said.

"You were right." Xinya slid the top folder to her and opened it up. Inside was a cashier's check made out to Michael Rafferty and Xinya Xia, in the amount of $68,004 exactly.

"It's got today's date on it," Brandon said. He lifted it up.

Xinya took the check from him, folded it, and put it in her purse. "I'll hold onto that," she said. "What's in the next folder?"

Brandon opened it up. A carbon-copy of a telegram addressed to Claudia Famosa was inside. Xinya picked up the flimsy paper and read it out loud.

FORMULAS PREDICT BENARAS INDIA ON DECEMBER 11
AT EXACTLY 1104AM INDIA STANDARD TIME STOP YOU
WILL RETURN AS BOY IN ESTONIA ON OCTOBER 3 STOP
AIRLINE TICKETS AND INSTRUCTIONS ON THEIR WAY
STOP XINYA AND I AWAIT THE SOON RETURN OF YOUR
SOUL STOP

Silence in the room. Then Brandon said, "She's going to die in India."

"He's going to kill her, in just five days," Xinya said. "I have to stop this."

"But how?"

"Let's look in the last folder," she said. Inside was a single sheet of notebook paper with four sentences written in Raff's bold and large handwriting.

"Kashi Temple. Dashashwamedha Ghat. Anup Chatterjee. 10AM." Brandon read these out loud, then looked at Xinya. "What does this mean?"

Xinya shrugged, took the page, and put it in her purse. "You can research this at the library tomorrow, while I figure out how to get myself to India in time."

twenty-one

Xinya–New York City–December 1980

While Xinya procured her tourist visa at the Indian consulate, Brandon researched Benares. Now they were back at the library, and he provided a quick summary: Hindus believed that Lord Shiva established the city. Buddha gave his first sermon on the outskirts, under a tree in the village of Sarnath. The Ganges River was sacred, and pilgrims came from all over India to bathe, pray, give offerings, and even die along the banks.

Brandon passed her his hand-drawn rendering of a city map, where he had marked both the Kashi Temple and the Dashashwamedha Ghat. "They're next to each other, along the banks of the river," Brandon said. "It seems you will have to walk the final half mile to reach them, though. The road stops short."

"Thank you, Brandon," she told him. "I need you to do two things."

"Anything, Ms. Xia."

"First, take your final payment. I am sorry that I cannot spare any more than this." She slid him an open envelope containing a stack of crisp one hundred dollar bills. "Twenty thousand dollars."

He peeked inside. "You didn't have a finder's fee," he said. "I can't accept so much for so little work."

"Of course you can. Because I have another favor to ask of you." She handed him a small sealed envelope. On the outside she had printed, "Please read this if I wronged you."

Brandon took the envelope and asked, "You want me to read this?"

"Have I wronged you?"

"No way!"

"Good. I want you to place this envelope inside my dissertation in the library stacks at Columbia University. Someday it may become important."

He looked at her solemnly. "I will do it this afternoon."

"Thank you, Brandon."

"Am I going to see you again, Ms. Xia?"

She reached out and grabbed his hands. "I don't believe so, Brandon. After I stop Claudia, I plan to return to China and reunite with my brother."

He squeezed her hands so hard they went numb. "Ms. Xia…"

"Yes, Brandon?" she whispered. Her tears flowed down each cheek.

He stood up and walked around the table, and beckoned her to stand up. When she did, he grabbed her hands again and stared into her eyes. "I'm not a child any more," he said. "Let me come with you."

He had indeed become an adult. For a minute she yielded to the idea of continuing to work together with Brandon. But she mustn't be selfish.

She pulled her hands free and set them on his shoulders. Her fingers reached out to the nape of his neck and stroked his curls of hair.

He closed his eyes, and moved his hands up to her waist, fingers reaching toward the small of her back.

"Brandon," she had said. "Your life is just starting."

"Everything in my life revolves around you."

She shook her head. "Your mother needs you. Take her to California like you planned. Finish school. Get a great job. Find a wonderful person to marry. And live a happy life."

He stared at her, his lower lip trembling. Then he suddenly pulled her into an embrace, and kissed her on her lips.

She lingered for just a second before she drew back. She looked at him, and he at her, and they came back together, their lips searching, seeking, opening. Her tongue touched his, and the tingle in her lips grew into a bright flush across her chest.

And only then she pulled away, but slowly.

They stared at each other, breathing hard.

"You will do amazing things in your life, Brandon."

"I will be miserable without you."

"I will find happiness in my memories of you." She disentangled herself from his hands and wiped her eyes and turned away and walked out of the library.

twenty-two

Claudia–India–December 10, 1980

Dear future me:

Or maybe I should say, almost me. Almost because you're coming soon. I know it in my heart. Plus, I have proof. You are an Estonian boy, and your birthday is October 3, 1981. Isn't it incredible that I know this? Especially when you realize that I'm writing this in December 1980. Someday in the next month or two you will be conceived, and part of me will become part of you.

It's been only four months since I wrote last. That was when I learned that Fico had returned as baby Valentina in the Soviet Union. I've been around the world since then, planning our future. And here I am, sitting in a hotel in Benares, India, waiting for tomorrow to come and the next stage of our life to start.

I am trying to picture where you will be when you first read this. Hopefully it is warm, and you are close to the sea, and you're not so old that you will have to ditch some girlfriend in order to reunite us with Fico and Valentina. I wonder if you're right-handed like me, or if you have my eyes. How about my laugh? And my temper? God, I hope so.

I flew to India a week ago from Havana, Cuba. The plane refueled in Angola, and then somehow wheezed its way into New Delhi. The Alert team helped me get from there to Benares. But you don't know yet that I was in Cuba. So I should back up and tell you the whole story properly. I'm sorry, future me, my mind is racing.

When Raff and Xinya told me that Fico had returned as Valentina Nikolskaya in Gorky, I knew I had to see her, no matter what. But as it turned out it took a lot more than I first expected.

The Soviet Union denied my visa request, twice. Apparently they did not want a Cuban turned American to give their tovarishi any uppity thoughts. I was stuck, and Raff couldn't find a way to have Valentina's parents to visit me in Florida, either.

Then Xinya and I spoke and she had this crazy idea that if I returned to Cuba, I could wrangle a visa to the Soviet Union out of them. Sounds insane, right? Especially, as you will recall, that Fico and I escaped from Cuba. There was no way that Fidel and Raoul would take me back.

Unless I had something to blackmail the Brothers Castro. Do you remember what it could be, future me? I am sure you do, as I'm sure our minds work alike. Think about it for a minute.

Did you figure it out? Of course you did. It was the story of what really happened to Camilo Cienfuegos, the war hero who is still remembered in Cuba on the 20-peso bill, the general for whom the schoolchildren toss roses into the ocean.

Camilo Cienfuegos, the same general who defected alongside Fico and me. If that story ever gets out, Fidel and Raoul would have a cow, and you'd see the fastest history book changes in the short life of the republic. This scandal would make Che Guevara's perfidy seem like a schoolboy prank.

So I had leverage, future me, and I chose to use it to get what I needed for our future. Raff helped me with the negotiations, and when it was all done, we had a deal: if I promised to keep my mouth shut about dear Camilo, Fidel would procure me the necessary visas to get to the Soviet Union, and then I could live out my life in my home province de Oriental, in the city of Santiago de Cuba. Just a few miles from the cafetal where I grew up, and just a mile from the beach where I met Fico.

A deal made in hell, but it was worth it just to see Fidel's angry face and wild eyes when I was whisked off the plane, into a 1950's Cadillac, and driven to his palace. He grabbed me by the shoulders, stuck his face right into mine, and told me that I was a dead woman if I even thought too hard about Cienfuegos, but that he would graciously allow me to live out my pensioner years as long as I behaved.

You know how we are, future me. I couldn't let that comment pass by without a proper response. I warned him that if anything happened to me, if my littlest fingernail broke when I wasn't expecting it, the truth about his dear friend and patriot Cienfuegos would come out. And I reminded him that the five million bucks that I was required to send to his government's Swiss bank account before he let me return was more than enough compensation for any troubles than I could possibly cause.

And with that, he roared with laughter and gave me a kiss on each cheek. "America must have turned you into a conniving bitch, Didi. We've sent over a hundred thousand of our unhappy comrades to the States on shrimp boats this summer, and here you are coming back home. Let me be the first to welcome you."

"Just get me my Soviet visa, Fidel," I said.

And he did. In less than a month, I flew to Moscow, rendezvoused with Xinya, and took the train to Gorky. We met Fico's current self, baby Valentina Nikolskaya. Who, by the way, is the most beautiful, perfect baby in the world, future me, with red hair and sparkly green eyes. I can't wait for you to meet her.

I saw Fico, future me. He was there, inside baby Valentina's body, his soul shining through her eyes, just like I will through you. He pleaded me to come back soon and join him, and I must honor his wishes.

I'm scared for Valentina. Scared she won't ever find you. Scared the Soviet regime will find a way to fuck up our future together. She needs somebody to help her and Fico thrive, especially in that crazy country. She needs for you to find her and join her and continue the perfect life we had.

And that's why I'm in India. It's time for me to do my part to bring you into this world, so you and Valentina can be together. Raff and Xinya worked their magic and found a predictive soul line that has you being born just ten months from now, in Estonia. That's part of the Soviet Union, and it means you'll be able to visit Valentina, once Alert finds you.

But to make it all work, I have to give everything I have. Otherwise you won't be born. It will take a lot of courage on everybody's part, more courage than most people have. Already I've seen Xinya falter and back away, but Raff understands me, and he has remained strong, even though he knows his advice means my life will end.

Raff sent me a telegram, telling me the time and place I needed to die in order to come back as you. Tomorrow morning, at precisely 11:04, I will take my last breath until you burst out of your mother's womb in October. You and I will spend a few years learning to survive in the world, and then when the time is right, we'll find Valentina and Fico, and we willl be reunited with them. Just like it's supposed to be.

Let me tell you what India is like. Imagine you haven't cleaned your home in two months. The clothes are piling up in corners, and the dirty dishes are stacked in towers both in and around the sink. Multiply this disorder by ten, and you can begin to picture the slummy parts of India. I've watched children bathing in the same pond that old ladies were washing clothes and buffalos were pissing in. I stepped over, around, and only sometimes in piles of human shit outside the train station. In India, nobody seems to care about hygiene.

But maybe it's just their attitude to shit and piss that's different than the rest of the world. They're pretty clean otherwise; I see the Indians showering outside, brushing their teeth, the women wearing the most brilliantly colored clothes. The food is so full of flavor that it bursts on your tongue.

The people here don't smile much when you catch their eye. Usually they just stare back. I guess that's because I'm an outsider. They have tight communication between themselves, and the family members appear to work well with each other as they prepare their food, sweep their dirt floors, carry wood on their heads, and do whatever else they do in this city.

Benares is on the banks of the Ganga, a holy river in India. My guide told me a story of how the river flows as milk out of some goddess's tits, but I don't remember the details. This is the place the Hindus come to burn their dead and toss the ashes into the river.

Yesterday evening, we hired a boatman to paddle us up the river. There were thousands of floating lamps in the water around us. I saw fires in pyres along the banks, burning the wood that everybody was carrying on their heads, and burning the bodies of those who died. I even saw an old lady throw herself onto a burning pyre and into the flames, her family members just watching. My guide said she was following her husband into their next life together.

I admired her faith, and her ability to recognize that it was time to move on. And I was jealous of how easy it was for people in this culture to reset themselves. Unlike the path that I've had to take these past twenty years.

But all of that is behind us now, dear future me. Like the old lady, I will have the courage to leap into our future, forsaking everything to reunite our soul with Fico's and Val's.

I will spend tonight reflecting on my and Fico's life. The Indians have a delightful English phrase: when they want you to do something for them, they request that you "do the needful." Tomorrow, for our future, I will do the needful.

See you soon, dear me. I can't wait!

twenty-three

The train ride took all night, with over a hundred pilgrims crammed into her carriage. Xinya found a spot at the corner of a wooden bench, and she was able to rest for only the second time in four days. She smiled at the thought that just a week ago she would never have been able to sleep with babies crying, people passing gas from both ends of their bodies, at least six radios playing different songs, and strange singing and humming coming from the older men.

At sunrise, the train pulled into Benares, and she stepped down onto the platform. She carried just her purse; her luggage was probably still in Lucknow. The coolies didn't keep up when she jumped onto the running boards before the engine picked up too much speed.

It was already seven in the morning. Less than four hours to find Claudia and stop the madness. She pulled the paper with Raff's writing out of her purse, along with a small map Brandon had drawn for her. "Kashi Temple. Dashashwamedha Ghat. Anup Chatterjee. 10AM."

Would it have been better had she let Brandon come with her?

She put that thought of her assistant out of her mind, strode through the beggars milling around her, and caught the attention of a man standing next to a two-wheeled rickshaw.

"Can you take me to Kashi Temple?" she asked.

He waggled his head.

"How long to get there?"

"You will be getting there in thirty minutes, Madame-ji." He stood up and grasped the shafts, tilting the rickshaw back. She climbed into the seat, and with a grunt, he started pulling.

The rickshaw runner swerved his way around two cars, a truck, and some camels. He squeezed between a donkey cart and another truck, and Xinya closed her eyes when it appeared they may get crushed.

She leaned forward and asked, "Is it always this busy?"

"This season is slow, Madame-ji. The roads are empty. If we were in April, you would be sitting at the train station, still waiting to push off." He stopped and turned around. "Are you here on a pilgrimage?"

She shook her head. "No, I am looking for my friend."

"May I be of assistance?"

Why not? "My friend's name is Claudia Famosa," she said. "She is with a guide named Anup Chatterjee. They are supposed to be at either the Kasi Temple or the Dashashwamedha Ghat at ten this morning.

"Anup Chatterjee?" the runner asked.

She nodded. "Do you know him?"

He waggled his head. "I am finding out, Madame-ji." Right in the middle of the street, he set down the rickshaw's shafts, and said, "I shall be returning in two minutes."

Xinya looked around. The stream of cars and trucks and bicycles and motorcycles, as well as other rickshaws and tractors and even a small herd of cows, moved around her rickshaw without any discernable problems. After twenty minutes of waiting, her rickshaw runner returned, picked up the shafts, and started walking again.

"Did you find Anup Chatterjee?"

"Nobody knows him, Madame-ji."

"Then are you taking me to the Kashi temple?"

"No, Madame-ji. My cousin thought he knows somebody who may know of Anup Chatterjee. Do you happen to know his father's good name?"

She sighed. "I do not. But please note that I must be at the temple by ten o'clock. I cannot be late."

He waggled his head again. "As you wish, Madame-ji." And with that, he spun the rickshaw in a u-turn and headed against the traffic, causing Xinya to shut her eyes tight.

At nine forty-five, the rickshaw runner found somebody who knew of Anup Chatterjee, and they headed to the hotel where he was rumored to have stayed. The runner talked to the hotel manager, and then came back.

"We just missed him, Madame-ji. He is heading to Dashashwamedha Ghat, along with a foreign lady."

She felt her heart pound. "Can you take me there?"

"Of course, Madame-ji." And at nine fifty-five in the morning, he stopped along the banks of a dirty grey river that looked to be at least a half mile wide.

"The Ganga, Madame-ji. This is our holy river." He set the shafts down and gestured with his arms. You will see thousands of pilgrims bathing and making poojas to their gods. Some of them will be drinking the water."

"Where is the Ghat?"

He pointed. "Down the banks, a fifteen-minute walk for you to make."

She looked at her watch. "You didn't get me there on time."

"So sorry, Madame-ji."

"Can't you take me the rest of the way?"

"I would love to, Madame-ji, but alas, there is no road for me. You must either walk or take a boat."

Xinya looked at the water, and indeed there were several long wooden boats waiting at the shore. "Is the boat faster than walking?" she asked.

"Most assuredly, Madame-ji."

She paid the rickshaw runner and ran to the water. "Who can take me to Dashashwamedha Ghat?" she asked the five boatmen standing there.

The boatmen looked at each other, and one stepped forward. "My boat is available for your rental, Madame-ji. I will give you a tour of our splendid city."

"I don't want a tour; I need to get to the ghat by ten o'clock."

The boatman stepped back, a confused look on his face.

Another boatman said, "I can take you to visit all eighty Ghats."

"I need to get to Dashashwamedh Ghata straightaway. I must meet somebody there at ten o'clock."

"Madame-ji, the Dashashwamedh Ghat is closed until this evening, when the fires are lit and singing starts. Let me show you the rest of the city until then."

Xinya looked at her watch again. She wasn't going to be able to save Claudia. But even as she thought this, she remembered she needed to be strong.

So she pointed at the man and said sharply, "You will take me to Dashashwamedha Ghat immediately."

The man's eyes went wide, and he waggled his head. "Please, Madame-ji, take rest in my boat, and I will have you there in three minutes."

"Thank you." She sat in the stern of the boat, on a dirty wooden seat, facing the bow. The boatman sat in the bow and picked up his two oars.

"Dashashwamedha Ghat?"

She nodded.

"Consider it done." He put the oars to the water and gave a mighty pull. The boat surged forward, and they were underway. Then he said, "Ten horse sacrifice."

"Excuse me?"

"Dash means ten. Ashwa means horse. Medh is sacrifice. Long ago Lord Brahma sacrificed ten horses to welcome Lord Shiva to this place."

"The poor horses," Xinya said.

He smiled. "Being sacrificed by a god would have granted the horses moksha."

"Moksha?"

"Instant trip to heaven. No more reincarnation, no more coming back to earth again and again."

"Moksha seems like a short cut."

"The shortest short cut of them all, Madame-ji. Everybody wants to find the shortest path."

She was silent as she thought about the short cuts Raff had taken with Alert's business and her formulas, and the terrible short cut that Claudia was about to take. Maybe the shortest path wasn't always the best way to get somewhere.

"I don't like short cuts," she told the boatman.

"Yes, Madame-ji," he said. And he stayed quiet while he rowed up the river.

The gentle rocking the boat was soothing her. But the next thing Xinya felt was the boatman tapping her arm. "Wake up, Madame-ji," he said. "We have reached the ghat."

She opened her eyes and glanced at her watch. She looked up at the boatman, horrified. "It's already ten-thirty! How could you let me sleep?"

His eyes opened wide. "Madame-ji needed to take rest. And you will see no people milling around."

"Never mind." She grabbed his arm. "I am looking for an American lady, accompanied by a guide named Anup Chatterjee. Did you see any-body at all?"

The boatman screwed up his forehead. "At our first arrival, a boat-man I've never seen before brought two people to the ghat in a yellow and red boat. A Hindustani man and a Gori woman."

"Gori?"

"Skin whiter than yours."

She squeezed his arm. "Where did they go?"

He shrugged. "They paid the boatman, and the fellow took the money and left them alone in the boat."

"Where is this boat?"

The boatman pointed upriver. "The Hindustani man rowed it himself." He chuckled. "A lousy boatman he was."

"I believe those were the people I needed to meet. Can we go look for them? I must get to them very soon."

The boatman gently disengaged her hand from his arm. "Madame-ji, I believe you are suffering needlessly from a lack of sleep, and from possibly too much sun. Why don't you take more rest, and we can find them tonight?"

"You don't understand. I must reach them." She looked at her watch and said, "In the next thirty-one minutes." She looked up at him. "It is a matter of grave importance."

He regarded her for a moment, and then he nodded. "Please arrange yourself to be comfortable. I will follow the path they have taken."

"Thank you." She tilted her head as he grabbed the oars. "What is your name, sir?"

"My good name, Madame-ji?"

She nodded.

"Nitin," he said. "And what is your good name, Madame-ji?"

"Xinya."

He smiled and wagged his head. "A very good welcome to India, Madame-ji Xinya."

She smiled back. "Thank you, Nitin. Now please, let's find that boat."

"Consider it done." And he heaved the oars and headed upriver.

twenty-four

I follow the abundantly healthy Scott out of the hospital and into the parking garage. He bounds up the stairs two at a time, but there's no way I'm going to show him I'm struggling to keep pace.

He looks back at me. "You okay?"

"Fine," I manage to say, trying not to pant.

He smiles. "It's only been five flights. Two more to go."

"I haven't slept since you got hit in the head," I say. "Give me a break."

"Yeah, about that." He looks at me, then down at the ground. "Val," he says, "I'm sorry that I put you through this anxiety. But I really needed you here, and I needed my parents safe. This was the only plan I came up with that got you all out to Sterling while buying me some valuable time."

We start climbing again the stairs again, and I think about ways I could push him over the railing. "We're definitely all in Sterling," I say. "But playing dead really buys you time?"

"Of course it does," he says.

I stop mid-flight and put my hands on my hips. "Cut the bullshit. You just sat in bed and wasted two days."

He chuckles and I'm getting even more pissed.

"I've been working like crazy," he says. "That eight-hour surgery I just went through?"

I nod.

"I was up here."

"In the parking garage."

He nods. "You'll see in a second."

So I follow him up the next flight and a half of stairs, and he leads me to a green Jeep Cherokee with dark windows parked facing the wall in the back corner of the garage. He opens the driver side back door and says, "Step into my remote office."

I peek inside. The interior has been modified: a leather bench seat runs long-ways down the driver side of the car. A narrow desk with two laptops sits opposite, and the back passenger windows have been fitted with widescreen monitors.

Scott climbs in, slides along the seat, and beckons me to enter.

"No way," I say.

"I need to show you something."

"Tell me."

"It's about our search for a new overseer."

"I don't care about the goddam overseers anymore. Haven't you heard?"

His eyebrows shoot up. "Is that really true?"

I sigh. "I need to go," I say. "Your parents will be happy that you're well. I'll let them know."

"Val, please don't go."

I lean my head against the Jeep's door frame. "Scott, I'm tired. You fucked up my final speech, and your very public photos caused Rain to almost strangle me. Then I spent the last day and a half worried that I killed you. I don't want anything to do with you, or with Soul Identity."

He holds up his hand. "Can I just get fifteen minutes to make my case of why you should help? I promise that if you walk away after that, I will never bother you again."

I stare at him for a minute.

"Ten minutes," I say. "And when you say never, that means never, ever, ever bother me again."

He closes his eyes, then looks up at me. He holds out his hand and says, "Deal."

I shake his hand, then climb into the back of the Jeep, closing the door behind me.

Scott sits staring at me. He purses his lips, then says, "I'm wondering where to start."

"The beginning is a fine place."

He nods, leans forward, and taps the screen of the closest laptop. The desktop comes up, and Scott logs in using his fingerprint.

"No facial contortions?" I ask.

He smiles. "I thought you'd like that." He brings up a folder and opens a document. "I want to start with some history about The Alert Foundation."

"Raff's company."

"Yup. But I'm talking about 1978, when it was only half his. Back when Michael Rafferty's wife Xinya was still alive and working with him."

I knew that Raff started the business around his wife Xinya's formulas, and after she died of breast cancer in 1981, he persisted through many lean years. Until finding me and Rain as the carriers of Fico and Claudia's soul lines gave The Alert Foundation its big break.

But all I knew about Xinya was what Raff told me when he met with me and Rain: she was the genius behind the prediction formulas, and his was a labor of love, a dedication of the company to her memory, ever since she passed away after just a few precious years.

Scott navigates through the document and double clicks a photo of Raff and a pretty Chinese lady standing with their arms around each other, on the campus of Columbia University. The lady is wearing a black graduation gown. "This is Xinya and Raff in June of '78", he says.

"I've seen this picture before, hanging in Alert's lobby," I say.

He nods. "Me too," he says, holding up his smart phone. "I was there a couple months ago, and just for giggles, I scanned Xinya's eyes."

"For giggles?"

"Archie hired both me and The Alert Foundation to find overseers as quickly as possible. I wanted to compare my own image search tools with Alert's predictive algorithms."

"And you used Xinya's soul line for this."

"That's the giggles part. I really don't trust that guy."

"Don't you think Raff would have already predicted where and when Xinya would return?"

Scott shrugs. "Maybe. Maybe not. My thinking was that if I could find her soul line carrier before he did, it would be obvious to everybody whose technology was better."

"And?"

He smiles. "My cameras found her."

"Not her," I point out. "Her soul line carrier."

He clicks on the laptop and turns it toward me. "No," he says. "I found Xinya. She's alive and well in Beijing."

On the screen is a Chinese lady in her mid-sixties, standing in a park. Her arms are folded across her chest, one leg extended behind her. She's surrounded by other ladies her age, each in the same pose.

"Tai chi," Scott says. "Chinese exercise. I tapped into a Beijing Parks camera and there she was. She practices tai chi every other day."

"Xinya's alive?" I look closer at the photo on his laptop. "You're sure it's her?"

"See for yourself." He brings up both pictures side by side, then kicks off another program, which calculates both soul identities and displays them below. "A perfect match."

"What about image recognition?" I ask. "Not that I don't trust you."

He launches another application. He selects both faces and gets a partial match. "Seventy-five percent match isn't bad for photos taken almost forty years apart," he says.

I sit back and cross my arms. "Did you tell Raff?"

He shakes his head. "I just said I don't trust that guy."

I glance at my watch. "Seven minutes left. Xinya's alive and well. So what?"

"Her predictive algorithms don't work."

I roll my eyes. "Not this again."

"I mean it, Val. I've been working with Raff for a few months now, and the algorithms are bullshit."

"So you say. But they did predict me and Rain."

"No, they didn't."

I stare at him. "Alert found me when I was a baby. Can you explain that?"

"Last month I took a field trip to Cuba. It's a bit easier to get there these days." He clicks on the laptop, a photograph pops up. This time he drags the image to the monitor hanging from the window in front of me. "Recognize this guy?" he asks.

I squint at it, seeing something familiar in the face. What is it?

Then it hits me. "He looks like Fico," I say. My soul line ancestor.

"Very good," he says. "I found this picture of him at the Casa de Beneficencia orphanage in Havana. Apparently he was almost adopted when he was thirteen, and this picture was in his records."

"I thought the wedding photo was the only one we had," I say.

"Everybody thought that because Cuba's been closed for so long." He sends another image to the screen, a copy of the photograph of Fico and Claudia at their wedding. The same image I used with Rain in our Soul Identity speeches.

"Watch this," he says. He runs the image recognition, and this time it's a ninety-nine percent match.

"And the soul identities match?"

"That's the interesting part," he says. He runs his app on both sets of Fico's eyes and displays the results.

"They're different."

"Of course they are," he says. "You can't trust Raff."

I look at him. "But let's be sure. Put my identity up there."

Scott smiles. "I knew you'd ask me to do that." He holds up his smartphone and snaps a picture of me, then sends it to his laptop. He puts it up on the screen, and I see myself sitting in the back of his Jeep, arms crossed and a scowl across my face.

"Next time, you should smile," he says. He runs his matching app, and I see that my soul identity still matches the one from Fico's wedding picture.

"The other picture could be Fico's twin brother," I say.

Scott shakes his head.

"You seem sure about that."

"I am."

"So, how did they do it?"

"What, fake Fico's identity?"

I nod.

"It's not that hard. They had yours already, and they just had to make his match." He selects young Fico's picture and zooms in on the eyes. They fill the top half of the screen. Then he lays Fico's wedding eyes just below.

I lean in. The left eyes are the same, but the right eyes are different. Not much, but there are two whorls at the top of the iris that exist only in the wedding picture.

"My guess is that they went through a lot of babies' eye photos, looking for somebody that didn't require a lot of changes, and your eyes fit the bill."

"So they changed the wedding picture?"

He nods. "It's a great job, too. Maybe Raff knew a forger from his criminal years."

"Criminal?"

"I told you; you can't trust him." He opens up another doc and drags it in front of Fico's real and modified eyes. "Here's Michael Rafferty's New York State rap sheet. I couldn't get his juveniles, but I guess I don't really need it to prove the point."

I read through the first page: a young Raff has a photo on the top right. It shows his AKAs as Mickey and Raff, and eight Burglary and Petit Larceny convictions between 1972 and 1977.

"How did you get this?" I ask.

"Do you want to know?"

I look at my watch. It's been nine minutes. "I guess not. Do you have more to show me?"

"You need more before you commit?"

I think about what he's shown me so far. Xinya alive, a doctored photo that means Fico is not my soul line ancestor, and Raff a criminal. Destiny did not guide Rain to me. As I turn this over in my mind, I feel the guilt of not being able to make my marraige work melt away, and I am overcome with relief.

"This could ruin Raff's entire business," I say. "He's going to kill you if this comes out."

"That's one of the reasons why I pre-empted with my own faked attack."

That seems backward to me. "What was the other reason?" I ask.

"I believe the three overseers are alive. Raff made it look like they died with their families, but he's taken them hostage."

"How do you know this?" I ask.

"My tech spotten one of them just before the accident that supposedly killed him." He pulls up a video of a car waiting at a traffic light. "This is England; see how the car is on the wrong side?"

I nod.

"Watch what happens in slow motion," he says. He presses play, and I see two gunman approach the car, crash the rear window and yank out a small, wriggling boy. Once the men drag the boy away, a huge truck runs the red light and smashes head-on into the car. Its windshield flies over the truck. The truck stops, goes into reverse, slams into the car again, and then drives away.

I stare at the crushed car. "Nobody could survive that," I say.

"Nobody did," Scott says. "Except the kid, who is one of the child overseers. He and his parents were declared dead at the scene, and the municipal copy of the traffic video is missing. My guess is that Raff has this kid, as well as the other two overseers."

Raff is playing a much bigger game against Soul Identity. But it will take me time to process everything; more than the single minute more I offered to hear Scott out.

"There is one other thing," I say. "You said in your message that I was in danger. Was it true?"

"You were in danger," he says. "But you don't seem to be any longer."

This feels like Scott attempting to raise the stakes and get me back involved. But when he tries to tell me more, I hold up my hand and say, "I promised your parents I would help find you, and I did. I will let them know that you're safe and sound."

"Thanks," he says.

Then I take a deep breath and add, "And thank you, Scott, for the information. But I'm not going to join you."

He looks at me, his mouth hanging open. "Val, I need your help."

I open the door and climb out of the Jeep, but just before I slam the door, I ask him, "And where were you when I needed your help two years ago?"

twenty-five

Despite Nitin's assurances, Claudia and her guide Anup Chatterjee proved to be elusive. As Nitin rowed them up the Ganga, Xinya scanned each boat ahead. This wasn't easy, as the river was a quarter-mile wide, and the left bank teemed with pilgrim-filled wooden boats.

She took a peek at her watch. 10:59–five minutes before Claudia would die. She would throw away her life, and baby Val would end up with an Estonian boy who had no more in common with her than they were both being exploited by Alert.

If she couldn't find Claudia in the next five minutes, that's exactly what was going to happen. Baby Val and the boy would believe that they were destined to be together. Soul Identity would have a great recruiting story. The Alert Foundation, and Raff, would flourish. Everybody would win except Claudia, who would be dead.

Claudia would have traded her present life for a future that she desperately needed to be true. A future that Xinya desperately knew was false.

Where, where, where was Claudia? She closed her eyes for a minute and thought about where the feisty Cuban lady would go. She was the most determined person Xinya had ever met, which meant that she wouldn't be in the middle of all these boats; there was too much risk that somebody would mistakenly save her from dying.

Xinya glanced again toward the empty right bank. Empty or not, Claudia had to be there. She looked back and forth close to the shore, and then she saw it: a wooden boat with two people, neither of them rowing.

"There!" she cried. "That boat on the other side!"

Nitin glanced across the river. "It is possible that boat is the one I saw earlier. But it is hard to tell from this distance."

"Row there, Nitin, as fast as you can!" Xinya glanced at her watch. It was 11:01. "You have three minutes to reach them."

He stopped rowing. "No, Madame-ji. I cannot cross the Ganga in three minutes."

"Why not?"

"There will be a swiftly flowing current, and it is a wretchedly long distance."

"Please do your best. My friend will die if we cannot get there in time."

"I will most assuredly try my best." And Nitin resumed rowing with mighty pulls against his oars.

Please back out, Claudia. Please, please, please back out. Don't make me watch you die.

They reached the middle of the Ganga, and they were only a hundred yards from the boat. Xinya watched as Claudia knelt in the bow, her arms wrapped around her legs.

"We're almost there, Nitin, faster, faster!" she cried.

"Yes, Madame-ji," the boatman gasped.

The man in the boat with Claudia walked forward and knelt behind Claudia. Xinya could see his lips move as he said something, and Claudia stretched her neck out over the gunwale of their boat.

They were only fifty yards away. Xinya screamed, "Claudia!" as loud as she could, but neither of the boat's occupants looked her way.

Xinya saw the man reach into his pocket and withdraw something metal. He flipped it open, and she saw it was a wicked-looking straight razor. She gasped, and cried, "Nitin, faster!"

"Yes, Madame-ji," he said, but she heard a loud crack, and when she looked back, she saw that the left oar had snapped at the oarlock. She watched as the front half of the oar broke free and slipped into the water.

She gave out a moan. Only twenty yards to go, but no way to get there. "Tell me you have another oar, Nitin. Please tell me you have one."

The boatman pulled the right oar out of the oarlock and started paddling, but the progress was not enough.

Xinya whirled around to face Claudia and saw the man behind her raise the razor over his head. She screamed, and the man turned and looked at her.

Her heart pounding through her chest, Xinya waved her arms. The man groaned, said something that she couldn't make out, and crab-walked to the stern, leaving Claudia alone at the bow.

They were only ten yards away. A flush of relief washed over Xinya. She saw Claudia open her eyes and look at the man. She said something indecipherable and he shook his head. Claudia yelled, and the man held the razor up in the air and let it fall into the water.

And just as Xinya was about to shout for joy, she watched Claudia launch herself over the side of the boat. She screamed at Nitin, "Paddle as fast as you can!"

"Yes, Madame-ji," he gasped, but after a minute with little progress, Xinya couldn't wait any longer. She kicked off her shoes and jumped into the water and swam to the red bloom of blood that marred the surface of the filthy river.

twenty-six

Mikk and I stand outside of The Alert Foundation's midtown offices, and I'm wondering why I'm here.

I should be starting my new life, as far away from Seattle (and Rain, and Soul Identity) as I can get. This is my plan. But instead, here I am, digging into Alert and Raff and God knows what else Scott has planted in my head.

After I left Scott in his Jeep, I ride-shared to Sterling, where I found Mikk annoying Scott's parents at the Soul Identity guesthouse. I passed along the news that their son was alive and well, and they were pretty pleased.

"Why would any son put their parents through so much grief?" Mikk had wondered aloud.

Scott's mom then begged me to take Rain's grandfather off of their hands and out of their lives. I sympathized with them, so I called up Mr. Morgan, told him I'd be leaving, and Mikk and I headed to Boston to catch the train to New York City.

While we chugged south, I searched online and found a gorgeous two-bedroom Upper East Side apartment that was available for the next three weeks while the owners were in Aruba. Mikk and I split the cost and ride-shared up from Penn Station.

That was two days ago. Yesterday we bought groceries and some more clothes and caught up on our sleep. But today I can't get Alert out of my mind.

If Scott is right and Xinya is alive, does Raff know? And if Raff modified Fico's eyes to match my identity, can I get him to admit it? And, the biggest question of all, is it true that Xinya's predictive algorithms are useless?

I know I should do what I told Scott I'd do, and just leave this all behind me. Dammit, Scott's right again. I can't just walk away.

So Mikk and I ride the elevator up and traipse into the Alert offices, and the first thing we see is a huge wall-dominating picture of Rain and me on our wedding day. Emblazoned across the bottom it reads "Trust Alert to keep your soul lines together."

"That's my grandson, Rain," Mikk tells the receptionist.

She shakes her head. "Then you should slap some sense into that boy. We're gonna have to take that down, you know, now that he called it quits."

"It was me who ended it," I say. "Is Raff here?"

"Right now he's with somebody, Mrs. Ekko."

"Call me Val."

She nods. "He should be available in thirty minutes. Did you want to wait?"

I think that I might as well throw some of my fame around before it's all gone. "I need to talk to him right now, and I don't want to wait."

She stares at me, probably trying to gauge how serious I am, and if she would be blamed if I did leave.

I just stare back and try to scowl.

Mikk, however, has different ideas. "Just get the dude, missy," he says. "My bladder and my back can't handle waiting."

The receptionist lets out a sigh. "Have it your way." She stands up and walks to the office on the right, and with a quick knock, opens the door a crack.

We hear Raff say, "I asked not to be disturbed."

"Mr. Rafferty, Val is here to see you, and she says it can't wait."

"Tell her I will be there in five minutes."

By then it's too late. I reach around the receptionist and push the door the rest of the way open. I walk into the office, with Mikk right behind me.

Raff is sitting behind his desk, leaning forward on his elbows. A fifty-something man in round black-rimmed glasses, jeans, and a camouflage t-shirt is sitting on the other side of the desk facing him. The man is holding a sheaf of papers in his left hand and gesturing with his right, but stops when he sees us.

I walk up to him and hold out my hand. "Val Nikolskaya," I say. "I'm the reason that Raff's still in business."

His mouth goes into a big "O" and he stands up.

"Brandon Drumm," he says. "You're that Valentina, Fico's heir?"

"The one and only," I say. Try as I can, I can't help but steal a glance at Raff to see how he reacts to this, but he betrays nothing.

Brandon smiles. "I was The Alert Foundation's very first employee. I was here when they found you the first time, and when Xinya traveled to Russia to meet you."

"That must have been exciting times," I say. "Do you still work for Alert?"

"Gosh, no," he says. "I left when Xinya did." He looks at Raff. "That was what, thirty-five years ago?"

Raff's frown tells me he's not pleased that Brandon and I are talking. "What brings you here, Brandon?" I ask.

Another quick look at Raff, and he says, "I stop by every now and then to check on Xinya's legacy." He turns to Raff and says, "I'll be on my way."

Raff nods, and Brandon leaves the office, closing the door behind him.

"A nice-enough guy," I say to Raff.

"He's just a librarian," he says. "Same boring books for the past thirty-five years. In fact, thank you for saving me from a useless conversation with him."

"You talk that way about your first employee?"

"He became a city worker. If he'd have stuck with me, he'd be rich." He shakes his head. "But Brandon is trapped in the eighties. He never did get over Xinya's passing. I tried to hire him back a few months ago when we started the Soul Identity contract, but he claims he's too happy at his job to budge."

"He seems pretty easy going."

"He seems naïve," Raff says. "And now that you've relieved me of him, introduce me to your friend and tell me why you're here."

"This is Rain's grandfather, Mikk."

Raff smiles at me. "You came here to tell me in person that you're back together with Rain."

"Over my dead body," says Mikk.

Raff turns to face Mikk. "I'm sure we could arrange that."

"No you won't; I like Mikk," I say. "Leave him alone."

"Anything for you, Valentina. Now, why are you here?"

"Actually, I want to know more about Xinya," I say.

He squints at me. "You came all the way here to ask about my wife who's been dead for thirty-five years?"

I nod. "What happened to her, anyway? You said she had breast cancer."

Raff let out a sigh. "I remember it was just a week or after she returned from meeting you and your parents. She came into my office, right where you're standing, and told me that she was dying." He paused and wiped his eyes. "Xinya made me promise that I would keep her formulas going, and that I would spend the rest of my life reuniting people."

"And you've kept that promise," I say.

"I have. There isn't a day that goes by that I don't think about her and thank my lucky stars that we had two good years together."

"Speaking of reuniting," I say. "Did you ever run your prediction algorithms on her soul line? To see if you could find her new carrier?"

Raff looks up sharply, and I stare back with what I hope comes across as concern.

"I haven't," he says. "The formulas rely on knowing lots of information about a person's exact timing and whereabouts, but I know so little about Xinya's past."

"You must know when and where she was born, and where and when she died," I say. "Plus where you got married, and where you vacationed. Isn't that enough?"

He shrugs. "Probably, but honestly, Valentina, I don't really want to reunite with Xinya's carrier in this lifetime. Save that kind of thing for my customers."

"Wouldn't finding her soul line descendant help juice your business?" I ask. "It would make a great story: scientist's algorithms are used to find her own carrier."

Raff strokes his chin. "You may have something there. If I ever need a public relations manager, I'll offer you the job first."

"Actually, that's the other reason I stopped by," I say. I'm making this up on the fly.

"You want to do public relations for me?"

"No, I want to help you find the overseers. With Scott out of commission and the clock ticking on Mr. Morgan, I'm guessing you need help."

Mikk's giving me a strange look. And I don't really want to help Raff; I just want a chance to go through his files and learn what really happened to Xinya, to Rain, and to me.

Raff frowns at me. "What would you do if you worked here?"

"What do you need?"

"I need Scott's technology to work. My algorithms find cities and towns, and even approximate times of birth, but the searching went much faster when we used his cameras to sweep through the general population."

"I can't work for Scott. He's incapacitated. His business is effectively shut down."

"Can you tap into his network?"

"I can try."

"Let me know when you figure it out, and we can talk about a salary."

"Can you share with me what he's done so far?"

He shakes his head. "The day Scott got hurt, all his data disappeared from our machines, and we lost the ability to query his systems."

"You're kidding me," I say, feigning outrage. But inside I'm pretty happy for Scott.

"I kid you not," he says. "That's why I went to Sterling; I needed to talk to Scott the minute he woke up."

"Did the doctors give you any indication when that would be?" What I'm really wondering is if he knows that Scott's been faking.

"They're still not sure he's even going to recover," Raff says. "In the meantime, we'll keep researching and re-running the algorithms. Even without Scott's tech we'll find an overseer soon."

"You hope," I say.

"No, we'll find one," Raff says, his eyes shining. "Remember, we found you."

"Of course you did," I say. And now I know he's lying.

twenty-seven

"Where to next?" Mikk asks as we leave Alert's offices and head east.

"Let's see if we can find Brandon Drumm," I say.

"The kid who was in the office?"

"Kid? He's got to be twenty years older than me."

"And at least 30 years younger than me. That makes him a kid in my book." Mikk points at the grey building on the right. "New York Public Library," he reads. "That jerk Raff said he's a librarian. Maybe he works here."

So we go up the stairs to the entrance, ask at information for Brandon Drumm, and what do you know, he works there. After five minutes he comes out and shakes our hands.

"Didn't I just see you?" he says.

"You did. But I was hoping we could talk a bit more," I say.

Brandon leads us down the back of the library and into the employee area. He has a tiny office, with just enough room to cram two chairs in front of his desk. I have to stand while Brandon closes the door, and then we all sit down.

"Cozy," I say.

"To me it's a palace. It took me twenty years for enough seniority to get out of a cubicle," he says. "Now I can hang my pictures."

I look at the wall to my right, and I see that he's hung a half dozen photos of himself with an Asian woman. They range from a teenaged Brandon to one that looks like it was taken in the past few months.

"Is that Xinya?" I ask, pointing to the first one.

He smiles. "It is. This was taken after our biggest soul line recovery, which was Fico's. I remember I earned a twenty-thousand-dollar commission, which in those days was almost more money than a nineteen-year-old could spend."

Mikk stands up, reaches into his pocket and pulls out a pair of reading glasses, then puts them on and peers at each picture. "Why is it that men age, but women always look the same?" he asks. "It's a shame that you've gained at least fifty pounds and she looks no different."

Brandon lets out a chuckle. "It's not the same lady in the pictures." He waves at the wall. "After Xinya, the rest have been a whole string of girlfriends." He points to the last one. "That was Wei. She and I broke up a month ago."

"Sorry to hear that," I say.

"Don't be," he says. "I find that my relationships only last a few years before I go on the prowl again."

Mikk points at Xinya in the first picture. "You're chasing after this first one, aren't you?"

Brandon sighs. "Guilty as charged. Xinya was my goddess, and I'm doomed to spend the rest of my life attempting to recreate her from mere mortals."

"Do you tell them that when you meet then?" Mikk asks.

"They figure it out pretty quickly."

"And yet they stay with you," Mikk says. "An amazing power you have."

"I'm a nice guy," Brandon says. "But eventually I realize that they're not Xinya, and that they never will be Xinya, and that it's time to start over."

I wonder what Brandon would say to Scott's conviction that Xinya is still alive.

"Speaking of Xinya," I say. "Did you ever try to track down her soul line?"

"Of course," he says. "That's why I drop by Alert and visit Raff soon after every breakup. I want to know what he's found. He says he's not looking, but he must be."

"Why would he even answer your questions?" I ask. "Wasn't Xinya his wife?"

"That doesn't mean much to a guy like Raff. He screwed around and only loved her for her formulas. They didn't even live together."

"Were you two together?" Mikk asks.

"I wish." Brandon lets out a sigh and makes a fist. "It was my hope, but then she ran away and died."

"Ran away? I thought she got breast cancer."

"That's Raff's story, but it's not true. Xinya left him once she realized he was cheating."

"She knew he was cheating on her?"

"She knew. And when she learned he was also cheating their customers, she left. But you know Raff cheated customers." He gives me a stern
look. "Don't you?"

I pause for a minute and wonder if I should tell him what Scott said
about me and Rain not being soul line descendants of Fico and Claudia.
I'm not ready, I realize. I don't even know how close he and Raff are.

"Why would you say that?" I ask.

"Come on, Val. The only reason that you'd possibly look me up in the
library is if you thought your past was a lie."

"The force is strong in this one," Mikk says to me.

Brandon smiles and says, "I am the droid you're looking for."

twenty-eight

Xinya gulped another breath of air and dove beneath the surface for her fourth attempt. This time she had waited for a minute to let the river water settle to better show the source of the red bloom.

She could only see a few inches, but it was enough to chase the trail of blood. Twice she stopped and swam in circles to find it again, but eventually it led her the right way.

And then her body told her, rather forced her to stop. Her diaphragm was contracting, straining to breathe deeply, and she experiencing weird bursts of blue and red light across the edge of her vision.

So she gave up, but as her hands desperately cupped the water to pull her to the surface, her fingers brushed past wispy hair. And without thinking, they grabbed hold, worked their way down to a scalp, and then she was clasping Claudia's head.

With a renewed burst of energy and even a sense of triumph, Xinya kicked to the surface, dragging Claudia by her hair.

"Help me," she screamed to her boatman, whatever his name was, who had managed to free the one remaining oar and was using it as a paddle to bring the boat close. He reached out and grabbed Claudia under her left arm and levered her into the boat. Then he helped Xinya aboard.

Was she alive? She had to be, after all this effort. But when she checked, Claudia was not breathing.

"The blood is flowing," the boatman said.

Xinya looked at Claudia's left wrist and the two nasty gashes across it. Dark red blood was flowing freely out of both cuts, dripping to the floor, and pooling in the boat well.

But it was not pumping out, so if she hadn't drowned, Claudia might yet be saved, as it seemed she didn't slash her arteries. Xinya pulled off her blouse and ripped the bottom off of it. She wrapped this bandadge tightly around Claudia's wrist.

Only then she turned back. "We have to get her breathing," she said.

"There is nothing to do," the boatman said. "Take comfort that she passed on in the most holy of waters."

"But she's not dead!" She couldn't be dead. Not Claudia. Xinya rolled her onto her side and used her fists to thump her between the shoulders. She continued the roll until Claudia was face-down. Again she pounded her fists into her back. But Claudia didn't respond.

"Help me turn her over," she commanded the boatman.

And he pulled on Claudia's arm while Xinya lifted her at the shoulder, and Claudia lay lifeless on her back.

Xinya straightened Claudia's neck. She pinched Claudia's nose, pulled her jaw forward to open her mouth. She put her lips on Claudia's and blew into her mouth. But when she made sure her lips created a seal, no air left her own lungs.

She arched Claudia's neck a bit, hoping it would help the flow. She tried again, eyeing Claudia's chest. This time the air passed easily, and Claudia's chest rose.

Xinya pulled back, and Claudia exhaled. She waited a few seconds, and again breathed into her, and watched Claudia's chest rise and fall.

After ten or so these breaths, she starting thinking about Claudia's life. She remembered how impressed she had been with the Cuban lady's determination the first time she came to New York. And how the reunion with baby Valentina was full of joy. Xinya realized that even though she had failed to save Claudia, she should celebrate her friend's strength. Her courage. Her faith.

Claudia Famosa y Valdez was the strongest, bravest, most convicted woman she had known. Even though Xinya discovered the future soul lines were a lie, Claudia believed in them, and she acted on that belief. Xinya vowed to spend the rest of her life being as strong and brave as Claudia had been.

And then Claudia coughed once, twice, and rolled onto her side and started gagging. She vomited out at least a quart of greyish water and lay gasping and choking.

Xinya held her friend's head in her hands and used the rest of her tattered blouse to wipe the vomit and mucus from her face. She stroked her scalp while Claudia coughed and then whimpered.

Claudia reached out her hand to the side of the boat and grasped the gunwale. Xinya helped her sit up. "Easy, Claudia," she said. "You just came back from the dead."

"No!" Claudia shouted hoarsely. She grabbed the gunwale with both hands and tried to heave herself over the edge.

Nitin and Xinya both held onto Claudia's legs as she writhed to break free.

Xinya bent down to her ear and screamed, "Claudia! You must stop!"

"I must die!" she growled. "You have fucked up my future!"

"You mustn't! It was a lie!"

"It's the truth, and you know it." Claudia struggled all the harder.

Xinya thought about strength. And courage. And wondered what Claudia would do if the roles were reversed.

She would stop Xinya. Of course she would.

So she held onto Claudia's legs, even when Claudia turned around and hit her, tried to strangle her, and bit her arm until blood flowed.

"I won't let you die," Xinya gasped. "Not for Raff's lies."

"Let me go!"

"I won't let you die," she repeated. "Not for Raff's lies."

"I hate, hate, hate you, Xinya. With all my heart I curse you for keeping me alive."

"I won't let you die. Not for Raff's lies."

And eventually, when Claudia was coughing and gagging and vomiting up more water, Xinya took the opportunity to wrap her arms around her friend and squeeze her as much as she dared.

She held on until Claudia stopped coughing and the two of them sat weeping in each other's arms.

"I must tell you about Raff's lies," she said as Nitin paddled them back to the far shore.

twenty-nine

I stare at Brandon's camouflage t-shirt, not yet ready to meet his eyes. I notice that the shirt's shoulders are creased, like it's been ironed. "Why do you think I'm here?" I ask him.

"You figured out that you and Rain are not the soul line descendants of Fico and Claudia, and now you want to know if there are any more lies."

I nod once, still not meeting his eyes, as I remind myself that it was Scott who figured it out. Not me.

"Hold up," Mikk says. "I was hitting every pitch, but then you threw out this curve ball. What did I miss?"

I look at Brandon while he answers Mikk. "Raff is a lying scumbag," he says. "He borrowed Xinya's reputation to start The Alert Foundation, and when it didn't work out the way he hoped, he faked everything."

"How is that even possible?" Mikk asks. "I thought this soul identity thing we have is real."

"It is real," Brandon says. "When Claudia gave us Fico's photo, somehow Raff must have had the eyes doctored so that Val's eyes matched." He turns to me. "And that was rather straightforward, compared to what he did with Claudia and Rain."

"What did he do?" Mikk asks.

"Let me ask a question first. When was Rain born?"

"October 3, 1981," I say. I know this date well, as it was part of our joint speech.

Brandon turns to Mikk. "Do you agree?"

"Of course. He's my grandson."

Brandon leans forward. "Where you there at his birth?"

"No." Mikk looks at the ceiling and purses his lips. "I wasn't even in Estonia when Rain was born; I was lecturing at Lomonosov University in Moscow those years."

"When were you gone?"

"That was the fall of '79 until the summer of '82. My wife and I only met our grandson when we returned to Tallinn." He chuckles. "Rain was an amazing baby, very advanced for his age. Did you know he was walking and talking at eight months?"

Brandon reaches under his blotter and slides out a manila inter-office envelope. He slowly unwraps the strings. "Maybe he was so advanced," he says, "because he was born exactly one year earlier, in 1980."

Mikk shakes his head. "I find that hard to believe."

Brandon reaches into the envelope and slips out two sheets of yellowed paper. "Look at these," he says. "Two birth certificates. One for each year. I had to go to the hospital myself, learn to read cursive Cyrillic, and dig through thousands of moldy boxes to get to the truth."

He slides them over to Mikk and I, and we read that indeed, there is a discrepancy between the two birthdates: the handwritten hospital record says 1980, and the typed official version says 1981.

The old man shakes his head. "It can't be true," he says.

"It is true," Brandon says. "I found it myself."

"Nope," Mikk says.

Brandon starts to sputter, but I hold up my hand and say, "Tell us why not, Mikk."

"Because my son and his wife hadn't even met in October 1980," he says. "They met at a New Year's party in 1981, she got pregnant within a week, and they got married in March. They sent my wife and me pictures of their wedding ceremony, their pregnancy, and bringing the baby home from the hospital."

"But look, Mikk," I say, pointing at the hospital certificate. "On this 1980 one, it only shows Rain's mother." I show him the blank space where the father's name was to be listed.

"So my son's not his father?"

I think about this. "Maybe your son adopted his girlfriend's baby boy?"

His shoulders slump and he lets out a sigh. "And then spend a year fooling me and my wife into thinking that the kid was his?" He looks at Brandon over his glasses. "Why would he do this?"

"Maybe he wanted you and your wife to accept her. Maybe he was preserving her reputation. Or maybe he did it for money," Brandon says. "Times were tough in Estonia in 1981, I would imagine."

"They were definitely tough," Mikk says. "But we weren't that broke. Reputation I can believe; my son was an honorable man. So I suppose it is possible." He goes quiet for a minute. "I've always wondered how Rain went from such a smart little boy to a nothing-too-special adult, anyway."

"Alert must have made your son an offer he couldn't refuse," Brandon says. "That's been Raff's approach, as long as I've known him."

Mikk shuts his eyes and goes quiet for a minute. Then he clears his throat and whispers, "I brought Rain to the states in 1989, and while I was there, my son and his wife died in a car accident."

Brandon scratches his chin. "You and Rain got a free trip to the states, didn't you? From somebody in the police department?"

"That's right," Mikk says.

"I am positive that the trip was Raff's doing. I've seen copies of your and Rain's airline tickets in Alert's files," Brandon says.

"He paid to get me to America?"

"He paid for Rain and you," Brandon says. "because you didn't know the real story. I think Raff was afraid that he'd lose Rain with all the upheaval in the Soviet Union, and he needed to spirit him out of Estonia and over to the States."

Mikk stares at Brandon. "So what are you saying?"

Brandon stares back. "What do you think I'm saying?"

"Did Michael Rafferty kill my son and his wife while I vacationed in America?"

Brandon's got a somber expression on his face. He says, "I believe Raff contracted somebody to kill them, Mr. Ekko. Though I can't prove it." A beat later, he adds, "But I'm still working on some leads."

Mikk's fists are balled up as tight as his face. He growls, "You let me know when you can. I'll kill that bastard myself."

"Mikk," I say, reaching out my hand to pat his knee.

He grabs my hand and squeezes it hard. Then he turns to me and asks, "How much of this did you know?"

"I heard a rumor two days ago that Claudia and Fico aren't on the same soul lines as me and Rain," I say. "But Rain being adopted and Raff having your son killed?" I shake my head. "It sounds so far-fetched."

"But it's all true," Brandon says.

"So you say," Mikk says.

Brandon holds up his hand. "Mr. Ekko, I have no reason to lie to you."

"Don't you?" I ask. "You hate Raff, you think he betrayed Xinya. Aren't you a just little bit too biased?"

He crosses his arms. "We both know Raff faked Claudia's and Fico's soul identities to match yours and Rain's. These birth certificates show how he got Rain into a respectable family."

Then I start wondering about my own birth certificates. "And what about me?"

"Your parents?" Brandon asks. And when I nod, he says, "Unlike Rain, both your parents are really your parents. I checked. Remember that Raff only had to find somebody who was a close match. Because Fico was already dead years before, he didn't have to predict your return.

That made sense to me. But something was still not right. "Why are you telling us this?" I ask. "You don't know us at all. If we're friends with Raff, you're dead."

"I know you're not friends with Raff," Brandon says.

"You met us in his office," I say. "How do you know we weren't there to catch up on old times?"

"No way. You were there because you were questioning the past. You were there because you think he may be a fraud."

"Is this what you wish, or is this what you know?" I ask.

Brandon stares at me for a couple seconds. "It's what I know," he says.

I consider how he could possibly know why he can trust us.

And then I let out a big sigh. "Okay, Brandon. Where is he?"

Brandon's face breaks out into a big grin. "Gosh, you're good." He points at the door. "If you wouldn't mind getting up, you can let Scott in. It'll be tight, but we can squeeze."

thirty

Brandon, Scott, Mikk, and I are crammed into Brandon's tiny office. I introduce Mikk and Scott to each other.

"I finally get to meet the famous Slava," Mikk says.

"It's Scott," Scott says.

"Whatever. You're the dude who broadcasted the photos of my grandson sleeping around?" Mikk growls.

"I am," Scott says. "Sorry about that."

"I was led to believe that you were at death's door," Mikk says. "We busted our asses getting from Seattle to Boston. Did you tell your parents about your miraculous recovery?"

"I told them, Mikk," I say. "You were there. Remember when I picked you up?"

"I told them too," Scott says. "I visited them late last night, before flying down here." He turns to me and says, "Val, I met Brandon for the first time this morning. He's agreed to work with me."

"What does Brandon know?" I ask.

"Xinya is alive!" Brandon says. "And we're going to talk to her soon."

"But we have to be careful," Scott says. "If Raff finds out where she is, it'll be bye-bye Xinya."

"So you have a plan?" I ask.

Scott points at us. "Our plan was to arrange for you to meet Brandon and follow him back here. Then we'd work together on what came next."

I think for a minute about how Scott still is able to maneuver me. "I wanted confirmation that Raff faked Fico and Claudia's soul lines." I point to the envelope on his desk. "But you already have it."

"We do," Scott says. "But Raff won't give a shit about our evidence. He'd kill us before negotiating."

"So just walk away," I say. Not that I've been able to do it.

"Because it's not about us. It's about finding an overseer," Scott says. "Soul Identity needs at least one before Archie dies. Otherwise they fall apart."

No matter how upset I have been at the organization, I don't want to see it collapse. I turn to Brandon. "Are Xinya's algorithms any good?"

He shakes his head. "One of the last things Xinya told me was that she discovered they didn't work."

"They don't," Scott says. "My technology found the overseers. All Raff did was waste everybody's time by directing deep searches in the wrong cities."

"Raff said your systems shut down after you were attacked," I say. "He offered me a job if I could get them working."

"Why would you help him?" Brandon asks.

"I guess it would make sense if we wanted to keep an eye on what he's doing," Scott says. He looks up at me. "But then we'd either have to re-enable my tech for him, or waste time faking it. And we don't have much time. Archie could die at any moment."

"What's he got?" Mikk asks. "Cancer? Bad ticker?"

"Tumor in his brain," Scott says. "It's in a bad spot, and it's inoperable. The doctor said a month ago that he's probably got only a few weeks left."

"I had a friend drop dead from an aneurysm in his brain," Mikk says. "A taxi driver. It burst while he was driving. The accident made the news. Not a bad way to go for him, but his poor passenger had quite a ride."

Scott looks at Mikk, his mouth open. "Thanks for that little tidbit."

"You'll get used to him," I say. "About your tech: I saw this crazy app on your dad's phone. He tracked me to Denny's."

He smiles. "My tech for finding soul identities is un-fucking-believable."

"It can't be that great, or you'd already know if there were other overseers."

He frowns. "Either they live where there are no cameras, or we have already found them all."

I think about a world with no Soul Identity. Even though I've lost my faith in the significance of soul lines, I know it means a lot to the many who still believe.

I also think about the past few days, and how much I've enjoyed working with Scott again. I've missed his sense of purpose, his curiosity, and his exuberance. Working with him was always exciting, always an adventure.

"I realize that I told you no," I tell Scott, "But you're right: we need Soul Identity to survive. How can I help?"

"I have one condition."

I raise my eyebrows. "We're not getting back together."

He smiles. "Even I'm not that stupid." He pauses for a moment. "Come back to work with me."

"But you don't need me," I say. And when he's about to interrupt, I hold up my finger. "Don't talk."

He nods.

I turn and ask Brandon, "Can you help Mikk find the restroom?"

"I'm fine," Mikk says. "And I want to hear this."

"Let's give them some alone-time, Mikk," Brandon says. And we maneuver around the tiny space to let them escape.

"You have exactly two minutes to explain what happened that morning," I say as we both sit back down.

"Which morning?" But when I stare and say nothing, he mutters, "Fine." He takes a deep breath and closes his eyes. Then he says, "You had come to bed so late, but I pretended to be asleep."

"I thought you might have been faking it," I say.

Scott grimaces. "I got up at five, made the coffee, and then sat and stewed on the porch. At six-thirty, I woke up Rain and offered to take him on a kayak ride."

"Why would you do that?"

He opens his eyes and looks at me. "I wanted to tell him about you. And about us. About how great a life we had together, and how perfect we were." His bottom lip is trembling. "I wanted Rain to realize that his timing was all wrong. And if that failed, I wanted to ask him, man to man, to leave us in peace."

"And how did that work out for you?"

"You saw the video," he says. "I tried to drown him. And I would have if the coast guard hadn't come by."

I cross my arms.

He sighs. "We stopped at the creek and walked along the beach. Rain did most of the talking. He told me that he had been looking for you for a while, and was relieved to finally find you. Apparently he did his homework, because he thanked me for keeping you safe in India and Slovakia."

Rain and I never talked about my time with Scott. The subject was off-limits between us.

"I tried to tell Rain about you, but he cut me off. 'I don't really care,' he told me. 'This is a financial transaction, nothing more.'"

"Rain said I was just a financial transaction?"

He nods. "He said that bulk of the money Claudia left for him was locked up until you two married. He offered me a million bucks if I would just disappear."

"And you said?"

"No fucking way."

"But that doesn't explain why you tried to drown him."

"Because I haven't told you what else happened. Rain claimed that you two were already together and just waiting for a good time to tell me. That the reason you were up so late the night before was that you were fucking in the guest bedroom."

"That's a lie," I say.

"Obviously. And when I didn't fall for that, Rain admitted he had paid big bucks to assemble your psychological profile. He said he could appeal to your sense of needing to belong to something big. He mocked you, Val. He said the lure of a soul line and a great love-through-the ages story would eventually drive enough instability into our relationship that it would tear us apart."

Ouch.

"I dared him to try," he says. "I knew he couldn't pull it off. We were too strong." He's speaking faster now. "Next he told me he was well-connected to organized crime, and he'd use his contacts to harass, maybe even kill, my parents."

"I've never seen you give in to a threat."

"I sure as hell didn't start then. My parents can hold their own, any-way. But then…" he looks at me and bites his lip.

I wait.

"…then he said that if you wouldn't marry him, he'd just move on down your soul line. He showed me a list of possible death dates that Alert said would work to bring your next carrier back soon. He told me he'd kill you, Val, if I didn't let you go."

I stare at him, not saying anything.

Scott says, "And that's when I snapped. Next thing I know, I had him face-down in the creek and the coast guard had me in handcuffs."

I hear tapping, and I realize it's my own fingers on the desktop. I say, "He was such a prick. I just couldn't see it at the time. I was so caught up in living somebody else's destiny."

"Prick or not," he says, "Instead of telling you what I knew and trusting you to work it out, I tried to solve it myself. That was stupid. I am so sorry, Val."

I stare at him, his crestfallen face, his sad eyes, and somehow we're both standing up and in each other's arms, crushing our bodies together. His lips find mine, and a host of repressed physical memories wash over me as I kiss him back. We're perfect together, we really are. He's right; we need to be partners.

"I've missed you," he whispers.

"Me too. But stop kissing me."

"Are you crazy? I can't stop."

I pull my head back and look up at him. "You dumped a lot on me. I need some processing time before I forgive you and become your work partner again."

"Another kiss first? I want the odds stacked in my favor."

My desire easily trumps my self-control; I do want the odds in his favor. So we kiss, and we hold each other, and we curse when Brandon and Mikk open the door.

thirty-one

Xinya looked into the kind eyes of the doctor standing before her. "How is she this morning?" she whispered.

Claudia had picked up a bad infection in the dirty water of the Ganges, and she had not found a way to shake it off. It had been almost a year since Xinya saved her from killing herself, but she'd been in this hospital bed ever since.

The small man frowned. "Hope is something you must never let wriggle from your grasp, Madame-ji." Then he sighed. "But the eventuality looms. Your friend, she is most unwell. Her body is supremely tired of fighting the infection."

"Is she able to talk today?"

"She possesses her wits, but the darkness is returning, so waste no more time conversing with me."

Xinya patted his arm. "Thank you, doctor. I will be free to assist you with your rounds afterward."

He wobbled his head back and forth. "Thank you, Madame-ji. It is much appreciated."

She took a deep breath and entered the room, leaving the door open behind her. The room was dark, as Claudia's eyes were sensitive to the light. She peeked inside the ancient refrigerator on the right side of the bed, checking that nobody had taken the precious antibiotics.

"Claudia?" she whispered. "It's Xinya."

"I heard you in the hallway."

She approached the bed and took Claudia's hand in both of hers. "The doctor said we shouldn't give up hope."

"He also said I had an... what did he call it? An eventuality. Never mind that my Cuban blood still boils at his indirectness, but the meaning seems clear. I'm nearing the end."

Xinya's eyes brimmed with tears. "I don't want you to go, Claudia."

"Me either, which is pretty funny after I tried so hard to rush it." Claudia let out a long sigh. "Xinya, I'm already feeling the dizziness coming, so let me say something quickly."

"Please go ahead."

"You have treated me better than I deserve, and I thank you from the bottom of my heart for the love you have shown me."

"You are most welcome, Claudia. You are very dear to me."

"I need a favor from you. A big one."

"Anything, my friend."

Claudia let go of Xinya's hands and reached up under her pillow. She withdrew a small yellow pad of paper. "You probably don't know this, but I have been keeping a journal."

At Claudia's request last month, Xinya had purchased the pad and three felt-tip markers. Now she took the pad from Claudia and flipped through it. Claudia's print filled at least half of the pages. "Is it for me?" she asked.

"It's meant for my fake soul line carrier. That Estonian boy will need to know what really happened before he makes a mess with his and Valentina's lives."

"I won't be able to deposit this, Claudia," she said. "Raff misfiled your information, and he isn't going to let me mess up his plans."

Claudia nodded. "I've been thinking about this. It seems to me that once the match is found, Alert is going to make a big deal out of the news. At that point, you can give my journal to the boy or his parents."

Xinya tapped the pad. "And you expect that this will clear everything up?"

"Of course…" Claudia's voice faltered, and after a moment she started again. "Honestly, I don't really know. I have learned first-hand that the pull of destiny is pretty damn strong." She grimaced as she twisted her body toward Xinya. "This is my last shot at fixing the mess I made."

"You will recover, Claudia."

"Bullshit. I'm dying. I'm at peace with it."

The two were quiet for a moment.

"I was dreaming about our trip to the Soviet Union to meet Valentina," Claudia said. "She was so pretty and perfect and innocent. Shame on me for thrusting her into a false future."

"But what if the future is good for her?"

"What do you mean?"

"Maybe Valentina will fall in love with the Estonian boy, and they will live happily ever after."

Claudia's eyes narrowed. "What are you suggesting? That they meet and see what happens? Even though we know that their shared past and destiny is a lie?"

Xinya patted Claudia's hand. "I'm saying that if Valentina and the boy get together, we should wait and see if they need this extra information. It's possible that the story of you and Fico, and their belief that they are carrying your love story through the ages, will help them."

Claudia started shaking her head back and forth. "No, no, no, no. It's a lie, and we know it. It won't work."

"It may, Claudia."

"It won't," Claudia whispered. She swallowed and said, "Fico and me..."

A long pause. Then Xinya asked, "What about you and Fico?"

Claudia twisted away and faced the wall, breathing hard. She remained silent for a long while. When Xinya thought she must have fallen back into her delirium, she finally whispered, "It wasn't true," and refused to say another word.

thirty-two

After she helped the doctor with his rounds, Xinya peeked from the door at Claudia, who was twitching and moaning in her unsettled sleep.

"The painfulness will be gone by the morning, and she will be sleeping most of tomorrow," the doctor whispered. "We do not expect another wakeful moment. Were you finding an opportunity to offer your final farewell?"

"I did," Xinya said. "Thank you for all you have done, doctor."

He smiled and bade Xinya goodbye at the hospital door.

She reached out and grabbed his arm as he was turning away. "Can I ask you for a favor?"

"You have no need to ask, with what I am owing for your assistance," he said.

She held out the yellow pad that Claudia had given her, now sealed in a large envelope she got from the supply closet. "I stay at a hostel, and I don't have a secure place to store this. Can you keep this for me until I leave India?"

He wobbled his head. "I will take it to my home. When you are preparing your departure, kindly ask for it, and I will be bringing it to the hospital."

As she walked back to the hostel where she'd stayed since she rescued Claudia, Xinya thought about whether it was possible to be both prudent and brave.

Xinya understood prudence well. It taught her to bide her time and wait for the right moment. It advised her to not stick out, but to fit in and make well-thought-through decisions. Prudence led her to marry Raff, apply respectful interpretations to his business dealings, and to forgive his marital indiscretions.

But her marriage was over, Raff's business dealings remained unethical, and Claudia's life was ruined. Prudence, with its wait-and-see advice, had failed not only Xinya, but also Claudia. Maybe even Brandon, who seemed wretched when they discussed her departure. And likely baby Valentina and the Estonian boy whom Raff had chosen to be Claudia's fake soul line carrier. A life with prudence leading the way could be devastating. A life of too much prudence produced too many victims.

If lack of prudence led to Claudia's bravery and allowed her to have control over future events, Xinya was determined to lose it.

As she crossed the street to stop at the vegetable stand, and avoided the rickshaws and bicycles that seemed intent on mowing her down, it dawned on her that people called on prudence only when they didn't think they could change the future. Claudia's bravery was based on her belief that her actions mattered. Conviction led to courage, and allowed Claudia to risk everything.

If Xinya wanted to fight her fears and stand up to the injustices she felt, she needed to believe that her actions would matter. She needed to believe that she mattered.

She needed conviction.

Almost a year ago, Xinya was so horrified by the thought that Claudia was going to kill herself based on Raff's lies, that she left New York, flew to India, and somehow stopped Claudia just in time.

This wasn't prudence; her conviction that Raff's evil plan must be thwarted spurred Xinya's single act of bravery. Which seemed miniscule when compared to Claudia's life of joining a rebel army, escaping Cuba, returning to face Castro, and fighting to redefine the history of her soul line.

But Xinya's action was a start, and one thread of conviction could be built upon. As she carried the okra and onions back to her hostel, Xinya swore that she would spend the rest of her life becoming more convicted and acting with bravery to improve the world.

She reached her tiny room and opened the door and nearly dropped the vegetables on the floor when Raff grabbed her by the back of the neck.

"Hello, wifey," he growled. "Fancy finding you in Benares."

She tried to take a deep breath. "You know exactly why I am here."

He let go of her neck and shoved her across the room.

Xinya slammed into the far wall and slid to the floor. Nothing seemed broken, though her cheek and shoulder throbbed with pain. She summoned an image of Claudia to her mind: Now was the time to be brave.

"Why yes, Dr. Xia, I do know exactly why you came here," he hissed. He pulled the door closed and turned to face her, his hands on his hips. "You came to fuck up my plans. Alert's plans."

"I did fuck up your plans," she said. "Claudia lives. You can't have her come back as your Estonian boy."

He laughed. "One would think that spending almost a year in this hellhole would cure you of your naivety. But you're wrong. Claudia died in the Ganges River in this city on the eleventh of December, 1980. I have a certified death certificate to prove it."

"But she can refute it."

He shrugged. "Her doctor says she's going to die tonight or tomorrow. Which is fortunate, as it means I won't have to kill her."

She slowly got to her feet, wincing as she straightened her shoulders. "What do you want, Raff?"

His face darkened, and he shouted, "I want you gone, Xinya!"

"I've been gone for almost a year now."

"Then let me be more clear. I want you dead and gone. Just a memory for Alert, so we can inspire people through you. So customers will see my efforts at The Alert Foundation as my devotion to you.

"You think people are that easily fooled?"

"It's a well-worn path. Stalin did it to Lenin. Augustus did it to Julius. Nehru did it to Gandhi. People love when somebody dedicates their lives to a cause. It looks self-sacrificing. It looks brave."

She took a step toward Raff and pointed at him. "If you kill me, you will lose everything."

"Let's find out." He pulled a knife out of his pocket and unfolded it.

She could change this outcome. She was convinced that she must. She eyed the knife and tried to close her mind to prudence's insistence that she make peace with Raff. "If you kill me," she said in a clear and steady voice, "you will be exposed as a fraud."

He shook his head. "Xinya, my dear wife. Don't you think I've learned by now when you're lying?"

She lowered her head. "I never lied to you, Raff. Never."

"That's not true!" he shouted.

"It is true." She forced her chin up. "If you kill me, my account of what you did to Claudia will be published in the New York Times." Her very first lie.

"Bullshit."

She pointed to a small table next to her bed. "See for yourself."

He strode over to the table.

"The large envelope on the right," she said. "My deal with the lawyer is that if he doesn't hear from me for a week, he assumes you had me killed, and he sends my information to a reporter who owes him a big favor."

If Raff opened the envelope he would know she was lying.

He stood holding the envelope. "You call him every week?" he asked.

"Every other day. I was planning to stop once Claudia died." She glared at him and said, "You need to be exposed, Raff. You tricked her, and you lied to her, and now her life is over. Shame on you." She swiped at the tears that ran down her cheeks. "Shame on what you've done."

He slapped the envelope back down on the desk. "You're trying to shame me? After all the shit I put up with to make Alert work?"

"All will be for nothing when the story gets published."

"It will never be published!" Raff pocketed the knife and grabbed the envelope. He ripped it into tiny pieces, which he threw in her direction. They floated to the floor between them. "I'll do that to every copy of the New York Times if I have to."

She could do this. "You make no sense," she said. "If that story gets out, you and I both know that you and Alert will be finished." Then, as his hand reached into his pocket, she added, "But maybe you're right."

"Of course I am right."

"I mean about my dying. Maybe I need to die for Alert to succeed."

"Damn right you do." He cocked his head to one side. "Finally you see it my way."

"Not quite. Your way of dying is too violent." She took a deep breath. "Let me die of cancer. That would be even more compelling to your customers."

"You don't have cancer."

"You can say that I have been in treatment this past year, and that the end was peaceful, and you are committed to run The Alert Foundation in my memory."

"And where will you be during all of this?"

"China," she said. "I promise to return to China and stay away from you."

"And the New York Times article?"

"I will instruct my lawyer to destroy it the day I reach Beijing." She thought for a minute. "And today I will write you a goodbye letter from my cancer deathbed, urging you to keep Alert going, expressing my faith in my algorithms, and giving you my full support for Claudia and Fico's heirs."

Raff pursed his lips. He regarded her for a few moments.

Xinya lowered her head and kept it there.

Then Raff said in a gentle voice, "In your heart, you really don't want Alert to fail, do you?"

She shook her head, not daring to speak in case she broke the spell.

He continued, "Is that why you're doing this?"

Living and finding her brother and learning how to face Raff in the future was much more important than dying here in India. She took a chance and looked up at him. "I believe that it is not my job to punish you. You will get what you have coming to you, but not from me."

He smiled. "That's what you think. But I know the world better than you do, Xinya. The weak get punished, not the strong. Not the smart. Not the brave."

She considered his words. "Quite possibly you are right."

"Of course I'm right." He pulled the knife out of his pocket and flipped it open. "But Xinya, I want you to listen very carefully."

She tried to not stare at the knife. "I am listening, Raff."

"If you publish anything that even remotely harms me or Alert." He slashed the knife down. "You're dead. I have associates in China. I can reach you anywhere in the world."

She nodded. "I get it."

"And furthermore." He stopped, waited.

"Yes?"

"I will kill Brandon. And your brother, if you ever do find him. Nobody you love will be left alive if you decide to go rogue on me."

It was impossible to stop from shuddering. "I understand, Raff. You have my word that I will not publish. Just let me remain dead to the rest of the world."

He stared at her for another long moment. "I believe you. Write me that letter. Now."

She nodded, sat down at the desk, and composed her farewell letter.

thirty-three

Scott drops me and Mikk off at our rented brownstone and gives me a lingering kiss. It's late evening now; we talked and plotted with Brandon, then we stopped for sushi before calling it a night.

"How long do you need to decide about our partnership?" Scott asks.

I shrug. "At least one night. Maybe more. I'll let you know."

He nods and says, "I'm flying back to Seattle in the morning." Then he turns to Mikk, and says, "Take care of her for me, old man."

"Old man my foot," Mikk says. "I can still bust a move. You should be worried that I'll steal her from you."

Scott laughs and says, "I hope I'm as cool as you when I'm a hundred years old." And he leaves, with me watching him until he turns at the street corner.

I really don't want him to leave. But he can't just waltz right back into my life either; he's got to work for me a bit.

"The sparks are flying between you two," Mikk says. "Don't worry about me, Val. I won't really steal you away."

I wrap my arm around his shoulders as we climb the stairs to the house. "Thank you for being such a gentleman."

We get inside. Mikk goes right to bed, and I sit at the kitchen table with a cup of tea and my laptop. I'm going to look into Xinya's algorithms and see if I can understand them.

First up is a web search. I look for The Alert Foundation and Xinya Xia, and that takes me to Alert's web site. I find an image of the final letter Xinya wrote Raff, before she supposedly died of cancer. It's a tear-jerker: Xinya asks Raff to continue to reunite people, and tells him that he has a sacred duty to do so. She encourages him to stay strong even though she knows he's missing her horribly, and that maybe in the future they'll be able to reunite their own soul lines.

Too bad I know that it must have been faked. Xinya's still alive, and Brandon told me earlier today that the two didn't even live in the same apartment when they were married.

But maybe Xinya's letter was her price of escaping Raff, much like my and Rain's final speech marked the end of our marriage.

There's a big difference between Xinya and me: thirty-five years later, Xinya's letter to Raff still carries weight, a moral imperative, for Alert customers, while Rain's and my charade fell apart during the speech.

I search Alert's site for references to the algorithms, but I only find blurry images of diagrams and time-based graphs. The site says that the formulas are secret and proprietary.

That's not good for me. But I get to thinking about this: didn't Xinya earn her Ph.D. around her formulas? Maybe I can find her paper online.

And with only three more searches, there it is; Xinya Xia's dissertation from Columbia University has been recently scanned and uploaded. There's a link to a press release touting the generosity of the corporate donors who helped get all the dissertations online, and I'm certainly grateful to them.

I download her thesis to my laptop, and an hour later, my brain feels like it's been put through a strenuous workout. I've read through half of it, and I barely understand more than the verbs. And now my tea is cold.

Xinya's dissertation is about predicting orbital change from imperfect data. Say you discover a new asteroid, and you want to know when it may hit the earth. Xinya came up with a way to solve this that doesn't require knowledge of the orbit.

I know Xinya was observing soul identities and not asteroids. I doubt her Physics professors knew this at the time, otherwise she probably would not have been awarded her Ph.D.

If you pull data out of the asteroid's interaction with other objects, Xinya says, then you can measure micro-fluctuations and build a prediction model of the orbit. The more events you gather, the more refined your estimates will be, and this leads to accurate orbital change predictions. The interactions, Xinya claims, are the key to predictions.

Xinya's interactions are also the key to my headache. I enter skimming mode for the rest of the paper and hope my eyes will latch onto anything significant.

And as I jam the down arrow and let the pages roll by, I see a flash of handwriting where there should be typeface, but it's gone by the time my brain registers it. I go back up, and there it is: an envelope taped to the center of page 124. Somebody has neatly hand-written, "Please read this if I have wronged you" on the outside of it.

I stare at the envelope. Is there still a letter inside? And if so, was the letter written for me to find? After this past week, I know I've been wronged. But it's hard to blame Xinya; Brandon's story makes Raff seem the bad guy, and Xinya an innocent party.

But maybe Xinya saw it differently. Maybe this is an apology. Maybe it's more. Not that it matters; I'm reading the document online, so there's no way that I can look in the envelope.

But I do want that envelope, really badly. I need to see what Xinya might have written. So I pull out my phone and message Brandon.

"Still up?" I type. It's almost midnight, but this is important, so I press send.

"Yup," he writes back after only a moment.

"Do you have library privileges at Columbia U?"

"I do." Then a second later, he sends, "Why you asking?"

"Can we go there?"

"Now?"

"Need to see Xinya's dissertation."

"You know you can read online?"

"Yup. But I need the hard copy."

"Uh oh." And a minute later, he types, "Columbia destroyed all dissertations after they went online."

Shit. I call Brandon, and he answers on the first ring. "Are you sure they destroyed the hard copies?" I ask.

"I saw the machines, Val. First they cut off the binding. Then they automatically scan. When they're done, they shred the originals."

"But there was a letter."

"A letter?"

"There was a scan of an envelope, taped to page 124." I look at my screen. "It says, 'Please read this if I have wronged you.'"

"Sorry, Val. They don't have it anymore."

I hold on tight to the phone and squeeze my eyes shut, but now I'm thinking about how I've been wronged, and my tears are running down my cheeks.

If the letter is from Xinya, when did she write it? When she realized her algorithms were crap? When she realized Raff was using them to get Claudia to kill herself?

Maybe. But maybe Xinya wrote it when she figured out that my life was going to be up-ended, and I would realize that the Fico and Claudia thing was a lie, and I would come looking for her.

"She did wrong me," I tell Brandon, trying hard not to sound choked up. "I just wasted two years with a guy based on the idea that I was living out my destiny."

"How's that different than everybody else?" he asks. "I'll bet most couples on their wedding day believe that the stars have aligned just for them."

He makes a good point, and he makes me think a bit harder. "There is a difference," I say, "Xinya knew I would believe in her algorithms, and she knew Raff would trick me, and she never told me otherwise. That's wrong. The letter was meant for me."

Silence on the phone. Then Brandon asks, "Can you come over to my place?"

"Now?"

"I have the letter, Val. I saved it from the shredder the day they scanned her dissertation."

"What does it say?"

"Come and read it for yourself."

thirty-four

I catch a ride-share to Brandon's building. He lives in the basement, and I wonder if this is standard for all librarians. I smile at the doorman and head for the stairs.

When I knock on Brandon's apartment door, a dog starts barking. I hear Brandon shout, "Settle down, Bob!"

A minute later he opens the door and says, "Come on in." A big black Labrador pulls on the leash in his hands. "Meet Bob the Dog," Brandon sas. "He doesn't bite, but he does slobbers a lot."

I reach out my hand, and Bob laps it. Brandon lets go of the leash and says "Settle, Bob."

Bob darts to me, rears back, and plants both of his front paws on my shoulders. I'm able to avoid his tongue's swipe at my lips, but his cheek catches mine and coats it in drool.

"He likes you," Brandon says as I wipe my face.

"He's cute." I shrug, Bob goes down, and I step in to Brandon's apartment.

Brandon points me to the yellow leather couch, and as I sit down, Bob the Dog jumps next to me and puts his head into my lap.

I look around the room. Japanese anime posters cover every wall. A desk, sagging under the weight of the many books stacked on it, sits where I'd expect a television. It is flanked by a dog bed on one side and a reclining armchair on the other.

Brandon sits in the recliner and leans back. His bare feet go up, and I notice huge blisters around his toes.

"Have you been walking more than normal?" I ask.

He sighs. "When your ex-boyfriend told me this morning that he found Xinya, I left work for a long walk. I ended up walking down to Battery Park, across the Brooklyn Bridge, and back. Twelve miles."

"Thinking about the past?"

He smiles. "Re-living the past is a better way to describe it. Xinya was my first crush. She was classy, smart, gentle, beautiful. She was dedicated to her cause of reuniting the world. And I was head over heels in love with her."

"Did she know?"

He grimaces. "I was just the neighborhood teenaged boy whom she hired to help The Alert Foundation get off the ground. I was too chicken to tell her how I felt; too scared that if I did confess, it would ruin everything." He sighs. "That's not totally true. The day she left New York City to try and save Claudia, I almost got up the nerve. We shared a single perfect kiss, and then she was gone."

"Thirty-five years is a long time," I say as I scratch Bob between the ears. "But I'll bet you remember that day perfectly."

"That memory has gotten me through some bad times." He leans over to the desk and picks up a small yellowed envelope. "Right before she kissed me," he says, "Xinya asked me to place this inside her dissertation. She said that one day it would become important. When I heard that Columbia was putting everything online, I rescued it, hoping that whoever saw the scan would somehow find me."

"Have you read it?"

He shakes his head. "She said it wasn't for me, that she would never wrong me." He's got tears in his eyes.

He uses both hands to offer me the envelope, and I lean forward and take it from him. It's got old tape marks on the top and bottom edges. It looks exactly like the one I saw in the online file.

I hesitate for a minute, and Bob the Dog lifts his head and stares at me. "Maybe you should get off my lap," I tell him. "We don't want your drool on this very important piece of paper."

"Bob, go lie down," Brandon says.

Bob gives a gentle growl, turns his head to look at Brandon, and when Brandon points his finger at the dog bed, he gets up and goes to it. He turns around a few times, then lies down, nose on his paws, looking at me with mournful eyes.

"He's got quite the personality," I say.

"He's the best," Brandon says.

I hold up the envelope. "Are you sure I should open this?"

"It's been waiting for thirty-five years, Val. I'm sure."

I examine the envelope. It's sealed, but I'm able to lift up the flap. I go slowly enough to keep it from ripping.

Brandon is watching me with wide eyes.

I pull out a two sheets of paper and unfold them.

"What do they say?" Brandon asks.

"I'll read it aloud," I say.

DEAR ESTEEMED AND HONORABLE PERSON:

If you are reading this letter, it means that you are unhappy with me, and you are now blaming me for causing you pain. (If this is not the case, please leave this letter intact for a future visitor who will need it even more than you.)

"That was pretty trusting of her," Brandon says.

"Group reliance is all she had," I say. "Shall I continue?"

"It's up to you. Are you blaming her?"

I think about it for a minute. "I am," I say. "She should have stopped Raff long before I was introduced to Rain."

He nods, and I keep reading.

I have wronged you, and I submit my utmost apologies for your consideration. This letter is my attempt to explain what happened to me, and what I promise I will do. I cannot undo the pain I have caused, but I want you to know of my commitment to improve.

I was born a twin, but my father sold my brother to a Communist official on the day we were born. I have lived thirty-one years with a hole in my heart, wondering if we would ever be reunited.

When I discovered Soul Identity and saw how they could reunite people with their past lives, I was seduced by the idea that soul lines could be predicted into the future. I spent years developing and testing my formulas. I hoped that one day I would use them to find my brother.

And then I met Mick Rafferty, my husband. He was funny and charming. He loved my work, and together we dreamed how The Alert Foundation would serve people searching for purpose in life.

"This is the same old crap that Alert spouts," Brandon says. He stands up and paces around the living room, hands on his hips.

But over the past year I started seeing another side of Raff. Where he once was funny, I saw him as sarcastic. No longer charming to our clients, but obsequious. Raff cared more about Alert's money than its mission.

And even though I was concerned, I did nothing. I didn't want to ruin what we had, or say something that would make it even worse. So I compromised. I convinced myself that all would be fine, and I just had to try harder to grow the business with him until he could settle down and pay attention to what was really important.

We foolishly seek reasons for our bad behavior so we can tolerate living with ourselves.

I lacked the courage to face Raff and stand up for what was right. It wasn't until now, when I know he is leading Claudia to her death, that I am able to do something. But I am afraid it is too late. Claudia Famosa is probably going to kill herself, and my false predictions will have caused you immense pain.

I paused and looked at Brandon. He was in front of his desk, staring at a picture of Xinya. Tears streamed down his cheeks.

"Are you okay?" I ask.

He nods. "I wish I could go back in time and kick my eighteen-year-old self in the ass."

"And tell him what?"

"To get off his skateboard, pay more attention to Xinya, and help her be brave." He looks at me. "And then maybe she would still be here."

I tap the paper. "Want me to finish?"

He nods.

I spent last night thinking through what I should do to save Claudia. I have decided to fly to India and attempt to reach her before it is too late. I will do my best to keep her alive.

But I may fail, which is why I have two promises for you.

First, I solemnly promise I will spend the rest of my life learning how to stand up for what is right, to act with courage no matter how strong the adversary.

Second, I solemnly promise that if I am still alive when you are reading this letter, I will dedicate my life to help you right whatever wrong I have caused. I want you to find me as soon as possible after reading this, and allow me the opportunity to make things right.

If you need assistance in locating me, Brandon Drumm is somebody you can trust. He is very special to me. He is a good person, strong in character, and full of surprising capabilities.

Sincerely,
Xinya Xia

Brandon has left the desk and is now towering over me. "Let me see that," he says.

I hand him the paper, and he reads the last paragraph.

"Very special," I say.

He swallows and repeats, "Very special." Then he pulls his phone out of his pocket and starts tapping the screen.

"Who are you calling?"

"I'm calling Scott." He flashes me a smile. "She said it herself: it's time to go and get Xinya."

thirty-five

Xinya double-checked the address on the slip of paper she held in her hand. She rapped hard on the apartment door. Two minutes later, she heard coughing and shuffling, then the door opened and a bald man, his face lined with wrinkles, stood on the threshold.

"Even the neighborhood rooster is still asleep," he said as he rubbed his eyes.

"I apologize for my disturbance," she said.

"Is it important?"

"The utmost."

He beckoned her forward, and she followed him into the house and sat when he pointed at a couch.

"I have no tea," he said. "But I can offer you water."

"May I prepare some for both of us?" When he nodded, she went to his kitchen, lit the stove, and soon brought back two teacups of hot water.

They sat on the couch and sipped in silence. Xinya looked around the clean apartment. Government propaganda on the walls, a poster of Chairman Mao. A couch in the front, and a bed and dresser along the back wall. The furniture was new, the floors spotless.

At last the old man put his cup down. "How can I be of assistance?" he asked.

"There is a rumor that you can find missing people."

"It is dangerous to blindly believe rumors."

"I need help to find my brother. I heard that you have reunited many who have been separated."

He stared at her for a moment. "Where did you hear this?"

"A mutual acquaintance in the Department of Vital Statistics."

He nodded. "I have visited there before. To whom did you speak?"

"Li Xiaohong. She said to tell you that you don't have a rooster in your neighborhood."

He smiled. "You should have told me that right away, instead of leaving me to wonder if you were here to arrest me."

She smiled back. "I also had to ensure I was safe."

He raised his eyebrows. "Is there something in my apartment that gives me away?"

She pointed to the dresser. "Bald men don't need combs and hair tonic."

"Oh!" He reached up and removed a bald wig, revealing his mane of pure white hair. "You can see my hair is quite memorable. Sometimes I go where I would rather be forgotten."

"I see."

He stood up and bowed to her. "My name is Zuo YunTian."

She also stood and bowed. "Xia Xinya."

After they sat back down, he said, "Tell me about your brother, Xinya. What is his name?"

"I don't know. I haven't seen him for thirty-six years."

He raised his eyebrows. "Surely you're not that old."

"We are twins, separated the day we were born. My brother was adopted by a party official and his wife, here in Beijing."

"Do you have the family's name?"

She shook her head. "My father thought they came from Xi'an, but he was not sure."

YunTian Zuo rubbed his head and sat silent for a moment. Then he asked, "Do you have your own birth certificate?"

Xinya reached into her purse and handed him a stamped sheet of paper.

The old man read it, and said, "I see you were born on National Day, 1949."

"I was."

"But this paper says you were a single birth. Not a twin."

"My father said my brother got his own certificate, with his new parents listed."

YunTian Zuo looked over the paper at Xinya. "Of this you are certain? You are convinced he is real?"

Xinya sat quietly for a moment. She noted the old man's curious gaze, warm face, and even some concern etched into his expression. "I have felt, missed, and longed for my brother's presence my entire life," she said. "I have faith that he is out there, waiting to meet me."

He considered her for a moment with eyes half closed. "Tell me where you have searched," he said.

"I came back to China six years ago, and I've spent every day seeking him. I've been to Xi'an many times. I've criss-crossed Beijing and the surrounding towns. I've visited more libraries and government buildings than I can count." She wiped at the tears that had escaped as she spoke. "But I can't find him myself," she said. "I need your help."

YunTian Zuo rubbed his head again. He sat frowning at his own belly for a full five minutes. Then he looked up and said, "I will help you find your brother, Xia Xinya. But on one condition."

"What is it?"

"First you must assist with another reunion."

"Another lost brother?"

He shook his head. "Ever since our wise Chairman Mao went from urging many children on our citizens to enacting his new One Child Policy, there haven't been many brothers. Or daughters, because when one has limits, every family wants only a son." He sighed. "This is a case of an only child, a son, who went missing last winter."

"He is young?"

"He just turned eight. When Peng was almost seven, his parents and he rode the train home after a visit to Beijing, and he was snatched somewhere before they reached Tianjin." YunTian Zuo stood up and walked over to the small table with the hair tonic. He opened the center drawer, reached inside, and pulled out two large black and white photographs. He brought them over to Xinya.

She saw a picture of a small smiling boy in the arms of what was presumably his mother, a plain-looking lady in traditional peasant clothes. Next to her stood a man. He was shorter than the mother, and his smile had a gap between the top front teeth.

"This is the boy?" she asked.

"Yes, this is Peng, along with his parents, who remain devastated since his disappearance."

Xinya looked at the next picture. It was a photograph of a beggar boy standing on a street corner, clutching a money cup and staring at the camera. His left arm ended in a stump where his hand should have been. His right eye was missing.

"This is the same boy, almost one year later. He was taken by the beggar king, who wants to expand his street empire. The beggar king knows that maimed boys raise more money than normal ones, so little Peng lost his hand and eye."

"This is horrible!" Xinya said. "That beggar king ought to be stopped."

YunTian Zuo nodded. "And that is what you will help me to do."

"Me?"

"You and me together. We will rescue Peng and bring him back to his parents. We will remind the beggar king there is no value in stealing little boys."

"Will it be safe?"

"Probably not. But it must be done. Peng's parents need him, and he needs them." He looked at her. "Are you brave, Xinya?"

She stuck up her chin. "I found you, Mr. Zuo. And I came here alone. My desire to reunite with my brother makes me brave."

At that he smiled and stood up. "Of course it does. Meet me here at six this evening. Peng's street corner shift starts at seven, and we want to be there first."

thirty-six

"Is that Peng?" Xinya asked YunTian Zuo. She watched a young boy dressed in filthy clothes move to the edge of the street corner. He held a metal cup in his good right hand.

The old man nodded. "He's right on time. This organization runs like clockwork."

"Are you going to talk to him?"

"Not yet. Look." He indicated with his chin at the man standing a half-block away. "We must wait for that man to leave."

"Who is he?"

"The beggar king's lieutenant. He watches the beggars on duty in this quadrant. Twelve of them at a time, and they rotate every two hours to different corners. He's got four children, four women, and four old men."

"Sounds like he's busy."

"It's a good business." He looked at her and narrowed his eyes. "I'm going to destroy it, Xinya."

"Today?"

"Today we're taking another bite out of their profits." He shook his head. "There are many more children to rescue. Today is Peng's turn."

"Do Peng's parents know that he's been maimed?"

"They do. And they are eager to get him back." YunTian Zuo sighed. "Not all parents are at first, you know. Sometimes it takes a few weeks for me to persuade them."

"You are a good man, Mr. Zuo," she said. "How long have you been finding lost children?"

"Five years, when my neighbors lost their son to a kidnapping. I used to play with him in the afternoons. One day I saw him on a corner, very much like this one, begging like Peng is doing now." He scowled. "He'd been maimed by the beggars. I had to look twice to be sure it was him."

"What did you do?"

"What anybody would do. I scooped him up and brought him home to his parents."

Xinya smiled. "I know how it makes me feel when I help people find each other. It makes me want to do it again and again."

He turned toward her. "You also reunite people?"

"I did," she said. "When I lived in America, I started a company that helped connect people back to their ancestors. But I left it all behind me when a bad man abused it just to make money."

He scowled. "When will you return to fight this bad man?"

She stared at him. "Why should I return?"

"Because we must always fight against evil," he said. "Always."

Xinya closed her eyes and thought how her world had fallen apart seven years before. She thought about her mad dash to India to save Claudia. After a few moments she said, "I have spent my life following others' advice, even when I knew their morals and methods were wrong. Except for once, I never thought I could stop them."

"Allow me to share a secret with you," YunTian Zuo said. "When you are convicted your cause is righteous, nobody and nothing can stand in your way."

Xinya's thoughts turned to Claudia's ability to accomplish great things even in the face of great adversity. "You are a wise man, Zuo YunTian," she said. "I will find my brother, strengthen my conviction, and return to fight the bad man who stole my company."

The old man smiled. "Work with me, Xinya," he said, "and I will help you prepare for that battle." He then pointed at the lieutenant, who had started walking to the next street corner. "But now the watcher has left, and we must rescue Peng."

They crossed the street, dodging the onslaught of bicycles and pedestrians. When they reached Peng, he held up his cup and looked down at the ground.

YunTian Zuo stood in front of the boy. "How would you like to go home?" he asked him.

The boy kept looking at the ground. "I have no home," he said.

"But you do," the old man said. "Your parents miss you very much, Peng."

The boy's good eye flitted up to peek at YunTian Zuo. "My parents don't want a ruined boy."

"Of course they do," YunTian said. "I have showed them your picture, and they told me to bring you home as fast as I can, because they miss you so much." YunTian touched the boy's left arm, right above the flap of skin where the hand should have been. "They love you, Peng."

The boy looked up the street. "The lieutenant will hurt them if I leave my post. He tells me that every evening."

"We won't let them hurt your parents," Xinya said. She knelt down in front of Peng. "Come with us and we will keep you safe."

The boy shook his head. "I must not leave my post."

Xinya looked at YunTian Zuo. "What now?"

The old man pulled a frayed blanket out of his bag. "Wrap him in this and carry him. Just make sure he doesn't scream."

As Xinya took the blanket, Peng dropped his cup and darted away between them.

"Catch him," YunTian Zuo called as Xinya chased him.

Xinya followed Peng down the street and finally caught up when he skidded to a stop just before the next street corner.

"The lieutenant," he whispered. "If he sees I have left my post, I will be whipped."

"Come with us, Peng. You won't be whipped, and your parents are waiting for you."

He looked at her. "My parents really want me back?"

"They do. I promise."

Still he hesitated.

She asked, "Are you scared, Peng?"

He hesitated, then said, "Maybe a little bit."

"I will keep you safe." She held out her hand and smiled as he grabbed it. "Let's get you home to your mom and dad."

thirty-seven

It took Brandon a day and a half to organize his time off and pack. I call Scott after Mikk, Brandon, Bob the Dog, and I land at SeaTac airport.

He's waiting for us in a green SUV at arrivals. "You brought a dog with you?" he asks when we reach him.

"He's a certified therapy dog," Brandon says. "And I have a prescription."

I shake Scott's hand, but he turns it into a hug and kiss, which is nice. The boys pile into the back and I climb into the passenger seat. "Where are we staying?" I ask.

"At my place," Scott says. "There's plenty of room now that my parents have returned to Maryland."

"We saw your house just last week," Mikk says.

"Only for a couple hours," I add. "Then we flew to Sterling after watching you get beat up online."

"But you see, he didn't get beat up," Mikk says to Brandon. "He faked the whole thing."

"I know," Brandon says. "You told me three times on our flight here."

After another half hour of similar banter in the backseat, Scott pulls up to his house. "Welcome home," he says.

"I live right down the road," Mikk tells Brandon. "With my dumbass grandson."

"Why not stay there?" Brandon asks.

"I don't want to miss anything."

We follow Scott into the house. He shows Brandon and his dog the basement where his parents. "This will be best for Bob getting out," he says.

"It's perfect," Brandon says. He unzips his single piece of luggage, takes out a red and black checkered blanket, and lays it at the foot of the couch. Bob the Dog jumps on it, spins in a circle, and lies down.

We head upstairs, and Scott shows Mikk the same attic room where Scott's parents had put us. "You'll be okay here, old-timer?" he asks.

"Of course," Mikk says. He asks me, "Are you staying here too?"

I look at Scott, who says, "I was hoping..." he points downward. "I'm on the same floor as the office."

I don't like his presumption, so I say, "I'll stay up here with Mikk. Somebody has to keep him out of trouble."

Scott sighs, but he's able to put on a smile. "Come down to the office after you get settled," he tells me.

After he unpacks, Mikk declares he needs a nap to recover from the flight. I head downstairs to the office, sit at the desk holding my name-plate, and open the laptop. After I authenticate by touching my nose, I open a browser and start a search.

"What are you looking for, partner?" Scott has come up behind me and is resting his head on my shoulder.

"Visa requirements for China," I say, spinning my chair around to face him. "Xinya's said she's willing to help make things right. I intend to take her up on that offer."

"You're holding her to a promise she made thirty-five years ago?"

"I am."

He pulls his chair right up close to me and sits down. "I guess it makes sense," he says. "She probably would appreciate closure on the harm she caused you and Rain."

I look into his eyes. "Brandon is super-motivated in re-establishing contact."

"It's been a long time since they've talked," he says. "I hope he doesn't get disappointed."

I reach over and fix the collar on his shirt. "It's been over two years since you talked to me. Were you disappointed?"

He grabs my hand and lightly strokes my fingers. "Point taken."

I like this guy. And his fingers feel great.

"Maybe Xinya can help us, anyway," he says. "One of the overseers I located was from China, and Xinya could help translate once we find her again. If she's alive." He pulls out his phone, taps for a second, and holds it for me to look at.

I hold his hand to steady the phone. On the screen I see an Asian girl with what must be her parents standing next to a double-decker bus. "The child?" I ask.

"That's her," he says. He pinches open the image. Still in pigtails, but wearing grown-up tights and boots.

"She looks to be around fourteen," I say.

"Which makes her five years too young," Scott says. "Archie's not going to last that long." He puts the phone away.

"What about the other two you found?"

"The boy was eight, and the girl was twelve."

"Any luck spotting them?"

"No," he says. "I talked with their neighbors and the local police departments. Nobody saw them get kidnapped. It seems Raff's guys were good. I'm betting that he's taking good care of them, but keeping them out of sight from any of my tech."

"So you think they're alive."

"They have to be," he says. "They're not worth anything dead."

I have been chewing on this ever since Scott hinted that they may have been kidnapped. Raff must know that Alert is useless without Soul Identity. His only business is to predict soul lines, and Alert will go bust if Archie dies with no new overseer and Soul Identity disappears.

"Raff is a great businessman," I say. "He turned the Claudia and Fico story into lots and lots of customers. He'll want to position The Alert Foundation as the company who saved Soul Identity by finding the overseers."

"Yes, but remember that this is the guy who helped Claudia Famosa kill herself so he could grow his business. He's got three young overseers; what do you think he's going to do?"

Scott and I have some experience dealing with sociopaths. I ponder this. "He's going to ransom them to Soul Identity," I say. "And he might even demonstrate his ruthlessness by killing one of them."

"That's where my thoughts ended up," Scott says.

"So we have to find them and rescue them before he gets any bright ideas."

"Then somehow keep Archie alive until they grow up."

"So let's find them and get them."

"Not so fast," he says. "We have to be sure Raff isn't tracking us."

"How would that happen?"

"He somehow outsmarted us and grabbed these three. I still don't know how he did it."

"But you were working with him then."

"If Alert hacked my system, then he already knows we're onto him."

I get a lurch in my stomach and I stand up. "Something's not adding up here," I say as I cross my arms.

He sits quietly as I get my thoughts in order.

I say, "You told me at the hospital that you faked getting hurt so you could buy time. Explain your logic to me again."

"Once I suspected that the children overseers were alive, I needed to shut down Alert's access to my systems, without letting on that I knew Raff was a bad guy. Plus, now he thinks there's another player out there that he has to worry about."

"It seems very strange to fake your own attack, if all you wanted to do was remove Alert's access."

His eyebrows go up. "And how would you have done it?"

I play different scenarios through my head, but each one ends with Raff knowing that Scott has figured him out.

"Maybe you're right," I say.

"There's another reason, too," he says. "I needed your help, Val. And so did Soul Identity. Having you watch the attack got you on that plane so you could at least hear me out."

I take a deep breath and try to relax my fingers gripping my arms. "So you used me."

"No." He looks down at the desk. "I want to say this right."

I try to summon some outrage at how he used my feelings of guilt, but that's not happening. If anything, I'm glad he found a way to get me back involved. He says he and Soul Identity need me, but I also need them. I want closure and a chance to regain some of my faith.

So I sit down next to him and reach out and hold onto his shoulder. "It's okay, Scott. I need this just as much as you. Thank you for getting me back involved."

He looks up at me, and a wide smile breaks over his face.

I gesture at the desks. "It's good to be here with you again." And slide my chair closer to him so our legs are touching each other.

We sit there smiling at each other for a few minutes. It's really hard to focus on work, but we have to. "If Alert's got eyes on you," I say, "Raff knows you're not really lying in a Massachusetts hospital."

He nods.

"And now you're back using your system to find both Xinya and the kid overseers, right?"

"I am assuming that we're hacked."

"So we have to move quickly," I say. "Before Raff can react."

"That's right," he says. "And we have to do two things at once: find and rescue the overseers he's holding, and get Xinya somewhere safe."

"Then how about this," I say. "Brandon and I will fly to China tomorrow night. We can bring back Xinya, and she may be able to help us."

"Perfect," he says. "Meanwhile, I'll keep looking for the kidnapped overseers."

I smile and say, "We have a plan."

He pulls me to my feet and wraps me in an embrace. "I have another plan," he whispers into my ear.

I run my hands down his sides and across his butt, which feels firmer than it was two years ago. "Show me. Now."

thirty-eight

YunTian Zuo buttoned up his coat and asked, "Are you ready to meet your brother?"

"I am," Xinya said.

The old man pulled on his cap. He took the scarf she held out for him. They walked outside of his apartment, he pulled the door shut.

"Will he be there, Mr. Zuo?"

"He will be waiting for you."

They walked for a mile in silence.

"Does he look like me?" Xinya asked as they turned onto the street where the restaurant stood.

He smiled at her. "I can tell you again. He is not as pretty as you, and he's already lost half of his hair. But you have the same intelligent eyes, and the same kind smile."

They reached the restaurant, and the waitress led them to the private room.

"I can't believe this moment has finally come," Xinya said. She looked at YunTian Zuo. "I wish I could freeze time right now."

"And never see your twin brother?"

She laughed. "No, of course I want to see him. But I never want to lose this final feeling of anticipation."

He laughed and said, "That sounds like something my dear wife would have said." He grabbed her hand. "I am happy for you, Xinya."

"Thank you, Mr. Zuo. Thank you for finding my brother."

He squeezed her hand. "I will leave you two alone. Have a wonderful reunion. And happy birthday to both of you."

She bowed, he bowed, and then YunTian Zuo left Xinya at the door.

But she didn't open it right away. She stood still, eyes closed, and thought about choosing paths.

For the first thirty-one years of her life, Xinya had walked the paths that others had chosen for her. She did well at school, moved to America, married Raff, and helped establish The Alert Foundation. She helped connect people to their previous lives.

None of those things required any conviction. She had no reason to be brave. No reason to choose a path of her own.

Eight years ago she felt the consequences of not being able to confront her husband. And she had vowed to learn how to stand up for what was right.

And she had done so: She left Raff, she saved Claudia from killing herself, she returned to communist China. And then she had helped Yun-Tian Zuo rescue many children and reunite them with their parents. She had begun to become convicted in her beliefs.

And now, finally, her brother waited for her on the other side of this door.

Was he as anxious as she? Had he also been searching for her? Did he also have a hole in his heart?

She opened the door confidently and let a broad smile stay on her face. "Feng GuoPing?"

A tall man sat at the table, facing the door. He stood up straight and nodded. "Xia Xinya?" he asked.

She nodded back. "Happy birthday, *Gege*," she said. "Today we start our fortieth year."

"I am the older twin?" he asked.

"Our father always said you were born first."

He smiled. "Then happy birthday to you, *Meimei*."

She laughed. "I like being somebody's little sister."

They sat down, and he said, "Until last week I didn't know I was a twin. I didn't know I was adopted. I thought I was an only child."

She looked at him closely. "I have known my whole life that you were out there, somewhere. I have felt you missing ever since I can remember."

He smiled. "When I was little, I used to pretend that I had an imaginary sister. It is nice to discover that you are real."

She frowned. "If I may ask, why did you wait a week before you met with me?"

He looked down at the table. "To be honest, I didn't believe Mr. Zuo when he told me about you, and about how I was adopted. I thought he was part of a scam to fool me."

"But here you are."

"Here I am." He glanced up at her. "Did you know that my adopted father passed away several years ago?"

"I am sorry to learn of your loss."

"Thank you. Fortunately, he did not suffer," he said. "Over this past weekend I flew to Xi'an and had a delicate conversation with my mother about where I came from, and why I look different from the rest of her and my father's brothers. When I told her that I had heard an adoption story from Mr. Zuo, she confirmed it."

"That was brave of your mother."

"She is a wonderful woman. You will have to meet her, *Meimei*."

"I am looking forward to it. And it would be my pleasure to introduce you to my—our—one remaining Auntie."

He smiled. "I can't wait."

The waitress came into the private room and took their lunch order. They discovered they shared a love for mushrooms and a hatred for squash. They saw they were both right-handed, and they had similar interests in mathematics and physics.

"But I don't work in the maths anymore," GuoPing said. "I had been a professor, but I was strongly recommended by my father's friends to change careers. Now I'm a lieutenant for the military police. My unit is responsible for communications when we are deployed."

"Communications between the different police units?"

"Between the police and the community. I am a liaison, making sure we don't have conflicts with the citizens, so no innocent people get hurt when we conduct our operations."

"Do you arrest bad people?"

"Our unit does."

She thought for a minute. "I wonder if you would be able to help me and Mr. Zuo with a problem we are having with a bad person."

"What kind of bad person?"

"A beggar king." She explained to him how she had been working with the old man for the past year, helping him rescue beggar kids and reunite them with their families. "You should see how happy the parents are when they get their children back."

"What would you like me to do?" he asked.

"We want him to stop kidnapping children," Xinya said. "But I will have to think about how you might help. In the meantime, let's get to know each other."

He smiled. "I want to learn about our family."

Xinya told him about growing up with no mother and a legless father. "Our relatives helped," she said. She told him about how her aunt and uncle had practically raised her.

"But it's not the same as having both a mother and father," GuoPing said. "I am sorry, *Meimei*. It seems I received the better childhood." He told her about being raised as the only son of a semi-important party official. "I heard stories growing up how the Cultural Revolution hurt many, but we were safe."

"I'm glad for you," Xinya said. Then she learned forward. "Do I have any nieces or nephews?"

At this, GuoPing hung his head. "No, *Meimei*. I am ashamed to admit that I have no children, and no wife, for you to meet."

"In this we are alike." She reached out her hand and grabbed his. "I am reunited with my brother. You are all the family I need."

thirty-nine

I'm sitting in a tiny conference room at the public library in downtown San Francisco; Brandon's ex-coworker from New York was only too happy to accommodate us. Those two went out to lunch to catch up on old times.

I've spent the past hour reading about Beijing. I looked for the park where Scott sees Xinya each morning, and I've grabbed two rooms at the closest English-speaking hotel. I stored its address, along with the photos of Xinya that Scott sent me, on my phone.

And now I have a chance to chat with Scott. I want to see him, so I plug in my earbuds and start a video call.

"Hey, gorgeous," he says, a smile lighting up his face.

I smile back. "Our visas are filed, and we'll have them in time for the flight to Beijing tonight."

"Great." He leans toward his phone, his smile getting even bigger. "Right after you guys headed to the airport, I got a hit against one of the overseers."

"You found them?"

"The cameras caught her for just a sec. Let me show you." He switches to the other camera on his phone and point it at the monitor on the wall. "This was filmed just a block away from The Alert Foundation," he says.

It's a video recording of the back door of a stone office building. Two yellow taxis pull up to a curb, and then a security guard steps outside the building, looks around, and motions behind him. Another two security guards come out, gripping the arms of three children wearing sunglasses. They are practically lifting them off their feet to keep them hustling toward the taxis.

And then the first guard trips on the sidewalk and drags the middle-sized child with him. The sunglasses fly off the girl's face, and for an instant she stares directly at the camera.

The video pauses there. Scott flips the camera back to himself, and he's smiling. "That little girl is one of the overseers," he says. "My tech is so awesome."

"Where are they now?" I ask.

"That's the bad news," he says. "The guards all had glasses, and the taxi windows were tinted, and I didn't get the license plates either, so I lost them. They're gone until somebody makes a mistake again."

"But now we're sure that Raff is holding them," I say. "I wonder if Xinya will have some ideas about where they'd be."

"After thirty-five years?"

"You never know." After another few minutes, when I disconnect and put away the earbuds, I think about how I wish Scott was coming to China with me.

A few minutes later Brandon returns from lunch. He's sporting two new food stains the size of half dollars down the front of his camouflage t-shirt. "We went to Chinatown and I brought you leftovers," he says, handing me a little box.

I open it up and find a half of an egg roll inside. "No thanks," I say, passing it back to him.

"I'm just kidding. You get your own dish." And he passes me a box of Szechuan eggplant and mushrooms on top of a bed of brown rice.

As I eat, I ask him about Xinya. "What are you going to say to her when you see her?"

"I've been thinking about that, and I want it to be meaningful," he says. "It's funny, but I've always imagined Xinya knows what's happening in my life."

"But she hasn't seen you since you were a teenager," I say.

"I know," he says. "It's just a feeling I have. Xinya knows what I'm do-ing. She encourages me, and at the same time, she keeps an eye on Raff."

I give him a funny look. "It's like she's your imaginary friend."

"I'm not crazy, really," he says.

We sit quietly for a moment. Then Brandon says, "I wonder if she ever found her brother."

"I guess we'll know soon enough." I point to his shirt. "Are you plan-ning on wearing this when you meet her?"

Brandon stares at me, his mouth in a big O. "God, I'm so stupid," he says. "I can't meet her when I'm looking like a slob. I need a new shirt, and I should get a haircut."

I check my watch. "You have time if you hurry."

Once Brandon leaves, my thoughts go back to Seattle. Mikk told me last night that he was going to rescue some of his clothes from the house. I decide to check in with him and see how it went with Rain.

The phone goes to voice mail, but I'm not deterred. This happens a lot with Mikk. On my fourth try, he picks up and says, "You found me."

"You finally answered," I reply. "How was your family visit?"

"I'm here at the house now," he says. "Rain appears to have moved. His suitcase is missing, and so is his toothbrush."

"Maybe Scott knows where he is." I launch Scott's app on my phone to see where Rain would have gone, and I see on the map that he's been in Bellevue, at one of the bimbos' houses, for the past few days. "That didn't take him long," I say.

"Where is he?" Mikk asks.

"Eastside. At some chick's house."

"Asshole," he says. "Hey Val, I found something. It's another letter from Claudia."

The night I left home I saw a letter from Claudia. "Is it called 'Just in case' or something like that?" I ask.

"That's the one."

"Is it long?"

"Just a few pages."

"Then do me a favor," I say. "Take a picture of each page and text them to me. I'll read them when I land in China."

forty

Xinya put water in the pot on the stove and stared at the calendar as she measured the tea.

It was six p.m. In just a few hours, she and YunTian Zuo would ask a beggar boy, Chun, to abandon his post and return to his family. Chun would be the twentieth child they had saved from the beggar king in the past two years. Twenty families reunited; twenty individual stories where joy had triumphed over anguish.

A knock on the door, and she opened it to let in YunTian Zuo. The old man accepted her offered cup of tea and sat at the tiny table with her.

"Chun's shift starts at nine this evening. Are you ready?" he asked.

"Almost," Xinya said. "I have not gotten Chun a new set of clothes, but we can stop at a shop along the way." She paused and looked at him. "Zuo YunTian, this time is riskier than usual. The city remains under martial law, and the student hunger strikers are still in Tiananmen Square. Are you sure it's wise to rescue him today?"

"The sooner we save him, the better," the old man said. "His family has been searching for over three years."

Xinya's brother came into the kitchen. He wore his police officer's uniform. Xinya got up to let him sit, then she brought him a cup of tea.

"Did I hear that you two have an adventure planned for this evening?" he asked.

Xinya looked at YunTian Zuo, who said, "Yes, GuoPing. We have a boy to rescue."

GuoPing frowned. "I received new orders this afternoon. I need to warn the workers to disperse before there is trouble. Tonight the army will advance into Beijing and restore order in the square. It is not a good day to be downtown, as the soldiers have been authorized to use whatever force is necessary to remove the students."

"This is the one day we know where Chun will be," YunTian Zuo said. "It's the best chance we will get."

"Then go early," GuoPing urged. "The army moves into the city at nine o'clock sharp."

Xinya and YunTian Zuo spent the rest of the evening preparing for Chun. They met again with his parents, then went shopping for a clean set of clothes for the boy. Finally, at eight-thirty in the evening, they arrived where Chun would be begging.

The street corner was at the east side of the Muxidi bridge that crossed the moat encircling Beijing's Inner City. The area was bustling with pedestrian and bicycle traffic. Fashionable apartments lined the street bordering the moat.

"There is plenty of money in this neighborhood," YunTian Zuo said. "Chun must be a productive beggar."

"Are you sure he'll be here tonight?" Xinya asked.

"I'm sure," YunTian Zuo said. "It is a rich area, and the protests bring extra business to the beggar king." He indicated with his chin down the long boulevard heading east from the bridge and into the city center. "Many people will come out here tonight, and many people make great begging."

"Why many people?" Xinya asked.

He pointed back at the bridge. "This is the logical way for the western army to reach the city. The bridge is a natural chokepoint. If the workers want to stop its advance, they'll do it here."

"Let's grab Chun quick, before the army gets here."

"Good idea."

They waited for Chun, but soon it was quarter until ten, and he still hadn't arrived.

A crowd had begun to form at the base of the bridge.

Xinya leaned toward her partner and said, "I don't like this. Let's get Chun tomorrow."

YunTian Zuo frowned. "It will be just as dangerous for Chun."

They heard what sounded like firecrackers popping on the other side of the river.

"That sounded like gunfire," Xinya said. "Can you see Chun?"

YunTian Zuo shifted his stance to get a better view. "Yes, he is setting up now."

"Then let's get him."

"We must wait for his watcher to leave."

She nodded. The crowd grew more restless. People pointed toward the bridge, and she turned around in time to see three young men come running across.

Two of the men had blood on their faces. The third's blue shirt was soaked on the right side with dripping blood.

"They're coming, and they're shooting at us," the third man cried. Then he collapsed on the road.

A roar went up, and Xinya grabbed YunTian's arm as at least a hundred people pushed two articulated trolley cars across the base of the bridge as a barricade.

"We must go," she yelled, trying to be heard over the noise. "I'll grab Chun."

"We both will get him," YunTian Zuo shouted. But they struggled against the press of the crowd, which surged toward the makeshift barrier.

Xinya held tight to the old man's arm as she dodged the onslaught of bodies. Several people ended up bouncing off, then sliding under, her grip.

At last they broke through into a relatively clear pocket, and she saw Chun at his position just a few yards ahead. Terror painted his face as he hugged the signpost.

Xinya dragged YunTian Zuo the final distance, and the two of them encircled Chun with their arms.

"Come with us, we can get you somewhere safe," Xinya yelled in the boy's ear.

"I must stay here," he wailed.

"You must come with us!"

But the boy wouldn't budge. And when Xinya pulled on his arms, he wrapped his legs around the signpost. A new mob of workers was almost on top of them, and she gave a mighty pull.

"I can assist!" It was GuoPing, her brother, in his military police uniform.

"*Gege*, help us!" she screamed.

GuoPing bent down and unwrapped the boy's legs from the post. Together the two of them carried Chun and dragged YunTian Zuo across the sidewalk and against the wall of the apartment building.

"Thank you," she said to her brother in an almost normal volume. "I am so glad you saw us."

GuoPing gritted his teeth. "You aren't safe here. The army is about to come across that bridge, and they'll use their tanks and armored carriers to bust through the trolley.

"Maybe not," YunTian Zuo said.

They looked where he was pointing. The protestors had set the trolley cars on fire. The flames illuminated the faces of the crowd gathered around.

"They will break through," GuoPing said. He pointed at the two tanks in front, followed by rows of soldiers carrying rifles tipped with bayonets. "I need to disperse this crowd before too many are killed."

Xinya heard cheering and looked up. Well-dressed men on the balconies above her appeared to be saluting the army. One of the men hurled an empty liquor bottle into the crowd. "Go home," he shouted at them. "Let the army do its duty!"

GuoPing stepped onto the sidewalk and pointed upward with his baton. "Restrain yourself, citizen," he shouted. "Do not incite violence."

The man laughed and threw another bottle at GuoPing, but it missed him and smashed harmlessly on the sidewalk.

GuoPing pointed at him, "I will return to arrest you!" He wheeled about and ran toward the burning trolley cars. Before he reached them, he faced Xinya and slightly bowed his head. When she nodded, he turned and ran into the crowd.

Xinya's arms still encircled Chun, who shivered and sobbed. "We must leave here," she told him.

"If I leave, I will die," he said.

"If you stay, you will die as well," YunTian Zuo said. "And so will we."

"Where will you take me?" Chun asked.

"Your parents have been searching for you for three years now. We will bring you home."

And even though this was the twentieth time, and even with the riot in full force all around them, Xinya's heart danced when the boy finally grasped that his parents wanted him to come home, no matter the damage caused to his body by the beggar king.

"We must get you somewhere safe," YunTian Zuo said. He moved from the wall and onto the sidewalk, then turned back toward Xinya and Chun. "We must all get somewhere safe."

Xinya grasped Chun's hand, but as she tugged him forward, the glass in the window behind his head shattered, and she wrapped him underneath her as she ducked to the ground.

Screams came from above. A man dropped from the balcony above her head and landed lifeless on the sidewalk next to YunTian Zuo. A gaping hole where his eye should have been showed her that he had been shot by the army.

"They're shooting, Zuo YunTian," she cried. "Lie down!" But as she reached out her arm toward him, he pitched forward and slammed into the ground.

A soldier towered above her. He planted his foot onto YunTian Zho's back and pulled on his rifle.

Xinya watched as if in slow motion as the bayonet slid out of the old man's back. She watched the drops of blood fall away from the steel. Her eyes locked on bayonet pointed at her. And when she realized the soldier was going to shoot, she shifted her body to protect Chun as best she could.

She looked directly into the soldier's eyes.

And just as he pulled the trigger, the soldier flew through the air and landed next to Xinya. The bullet aimed at her heart punctured the sleeve of her blouse and then the wall behind her. And her twin brother, her *Gege*, grabbed the soldier by the throat and yelled, "Run, *Meimei*!"

Xinya scooped up Chun in her arms and got him safely to her and her brother's apartment and waited all night, in the dark, mourning YunTian Zuo, and hoping and praying GuoPing was safe.

At seven in the morning, Xinya still sat hunched over the kitchen table, cupping a half-drunk cup of tea she had poured hours earlier. Chun still slept restlessly in her bed.

A knock on the door. She swallowed the lump in her throat. She got up, but paused and stood still for a moment with her eyes closed, bracing herself for the news. Then she walked quickly to the door and opened it.

Her brother stood there, a large gash across his forehead, and glorious in his torn uniform. "My keys are lost," he said.

"But you are found," she replied as she helped him stumble into their apartment.

forty-one

It's business class, courtesy of Soul Identity, for me and Brandon. My seat can lay flat into a skinny bed, and I plan to get plenty of rest on the fourteen-hour trip.

Brandon thinks differently. An hour into the flight, he gets testy with the flight attendants when the wi-fi stops. "This is unacceptable," he says. "The pilot should turn back and get a new airplane that works."

"Just get some sleep," I say.

"I have too much to do." He shuts the cover of his laptop. "I was half-way done with my online Mandarin proficiency test."

"You think Xinya has forgotten her English?"

"I just want to be prepared." He fiddles with his entertainment screen. "Maybe I can practice by watching Chinese movies."

"Sounds great," I say. I rummage through the toiletry bag they gave us, find the ear plugs and blindfold, and show them to him. "I plan on sleeping the rest of the trip. Tell them not to wake me up for the meals."

"And if there's an emergency?"

"Then wake me up," I say, which turns out to be a mistake, because three hours later, he's tapping my shoulder.

I lift up the blindfold, pull out the ear plugs, and press the buttons to turn my tiny bed back into a seat. "What's the emergency?" I ask him.

Brandon's hair is sticking up straight, and he's got a wild, over-caffeinated look in his eyes.

"You okay?" I ask.

He frowns. "I need some advice."

"Now?"

"You said I could wake you up in an emergency." And when I nod, he says, "I need to order new furniture for my apartment."

I stare at him, but he just looks back at me. So I ask, "What's the emergency?"

"If Xinya comes back with us, she's going to think I'm a slob. I could lose her."

I lean over and thumb the button to turn on his light. Then I look at him again. "Brandon, did you sleep at all?"

He shakes his head. "Too much to do."

"Not a wink?"

"Not yet. When I finish my work, I will have approximately twenty-three minutes left before we're scheduled to land. I should have time to take a quick nap then."

I stare at him for the next couple of minutes, and he's mumbling to himself as he's scribbling on a small pad of paper. Every few seconds he opens his mouth wide and wiggles his jaw back and forth, like he's trying to crack it.

"Brandon, are you taking any medications?" I ask.

"Yes I am," he says. "In fact, I just made a list of them." He flips back a few pages on his pad. "Right here."

I look at the scribbles on his pad. It's just a jumble of letters that don't quite align either horizontally or vertically. "Did you miss any doses with all your traveling and time zone changes?"

"I adjusted my dosage times when we landed in Seattle, and I'll do the same as we reach Beijing." Now he's leaning back in his seat, closing his eyes, and his words are slurring together.

"Did you drink any alcohol tonight?"

"The nice flight attendant brought me some port wine," he says.

"Is it okay to drink with your medicine?"

"Not really," he says. "My doctor says I can have one glass of wine on special occasions, as long as I sip it slowly throughout dinner."

So he's drunk, amplified by the altitude, and maybe even having an increased reaction from whatever medicine he's taking.

"Brandon, you have to drink even less when you're flying," I say. "And the alcohol is probably not mixing well with your medicine. You should sleep it off before we land."

He pops his eyes open and stares at me with the bug eyes. "But I need to prepare myself for meeting Xinya."

"What else can you possibly prepare?"

"I was going to review everything she ever told me about Raff. I don't want anything about me to remind her of that creep."

"Good idea," I say. "But you're nothing like Raff."

He turns to me. "You think I'm different?"

"Of course you are," I say. "You have compassion, where he just thinks about himself and his reputation."

"True." He's quiet for a moment. Then he says, "A few years ago Raff brought me and two other Alert employees to his lake house in upstate New York for the weekend. He and the receptionist were out paddling somewhere in the canoe, and me and another guy overstuffed the pizza oven with too much wood and had to call the fire department to get it under control. When Raff got back, I thought he was going to kill us both."

"For almost burning the place down?" I ask.

"No, for having the locals think that he couldn't control his own house. He said that he only gets one chance to establish the right reputation, and we blew it for him." Brandon is silent for a moment. "Raff never did invite me back after that. It's been, what, over twenty years now."

"See, you're nothing like that," I say, but he doesn't hear me, because he's fallen asleep.

I reach over to his armrest and press the flat-bed button. He's already snoring, and I rummage through his toiletry bag, snap his blindfold over his eyes, and pull his blanket up around his neck.

Now I'm wide awake. When the flight attendant come by and offers me my missed dinner, I skip right to dessert along with my own glass of port, but it appears I'm done sleeping.

My thoughts turn to Xinya. I think about how we have similar backgrounds: we both emigrated from our countries for opportunities in the States. We both got involved with Soul Identity soon after we arrived. And we both ended up marrying men who turned out to be bad guys.

In my case, I ended up with Rain because Xinya's husband abused her formulas and forced a fake match between us. Not her fault, but when she did find out that Raff was lying, she ran away and let him screw up my life.

The similarities don't stop there. Xinya and I both found enough courage to leave those husbands. And we each had another guy willing to do almost anything to get back into our lives.

The biggest difference between us is that Xinya doesn't know Brandon and I are on a collision course with her seemingly simple life in Beijing. I smile to myself and think about the irony. I'm about to up-end her routines, just like her formulas did to me over two years ago. Is this poetic justice?

Is it right to get her involved? I dwell on this question for an hour or so, and finally I decide that fair's fair; she can help get my life cleaned up.

Plus, Brandon seems to have left everything on hold for the past thirty-five years. The reunion, however it turns out, should help him unblock his life.

I shake Brandon awake an hour before we're supposed to land, as they've started serving us a light snack, and it would be good for him to eat. "You feeling better?" I ask.

"I am." He gives me a half-smile. "I got pretty loopy last night, didn't I?"

"You did," I say. "Are you ready to meet Xinya?"

"As ready as I'll ever be." He gives me a bashful look. "You're probably going to think I'm really weird."

"Is it weirder than having a string of girlfriends that each looked like Xinya?"

"It goes way beyond girlfriends," he says. "My hair stylist, my maid, my barista. I've surrounded myself with people who look and act like Xinya."

"You mean, who look and act like Xinya used to look and act," I say. "She must have changed in the past thirty-five years."

"I can't wait to find out," he says. "It's time to get my life moving forward again."

forty-two

Xinya woke up before the sun and lay in her cot, eyes wide open and heart pounding.

She had had a nightmare. Claudia Famosa had knocked on her Beijing apartment door, demanding that she re-run her formulas and kill her again, because the Estonian boy was not a good match for Val.

Xinya had been having one variation or another of this dream at least once a month ever since Claudia died and Xinya had returned to China. Although eight and a half years had passed, she still woke up in a cold sweat, scared that she couldn't help Claudia, and even more scared that she could.

The dream faded like it always did, and Xinya sat up, slid into her slippers, and padded to the kitchen.

The voice came from behind her as she prepared a special breakfast of tsa misua. "Longevity noodles are perfect for this momentous day."

Xinya turned and smiled at GuoPing. "Happy birthday, *Gege*."

He bowed and said, "Happy birthday, *Meimei*."

"It is our third birthday together," she said.

His brow furrowed, and he extended his thumb and forefinger. "I count only two."

She laughed and said, "Because nobody remembers their own birth. We were together for nine months in the womb, and for at least part of our first day."

He nodded. "Forty years ago. The day modern China was born."

Xinya poured hot water into the tea pot. "Will there be a National Day parade?"

"Yes, but it will be a subdued celebration," GuoPing said. "Our revered leaders are still recovering from what happened in June."

She closed her eyes and thought about YunTian Zuo and the hundreds of brave workers and students who died that day. "I am in your debt for saving my life," she said.

Now GuoPing smiled. "I am in your debt for reuniting us last year." But then his smile faltered. "*Meimei*, the purge continues, and I am afraid we will lose each other soon."

"I am ready to fight them, *Gege*." And it was true; Xinya had become a woman willing to stand up for what was right, no matter the risk.

"Yes, your bravery is impressive. But they are questioning my actions. Not yours."

As she poured the tea and the two of them sat at his tiny table, he explained that another police officer claimed he had witnessed GuoPing's assault on the soldier. "Last week he asked me for hush money."

"Did you give it to him?"

"Of course not. Paying him now will only lead to paying him again. This officer wants my job, and he will happily try to get rid of me. I believe the police will come to arrest me this morning."

Xinya reached out and grabbed GuoPing's hands. "Let us leave this country now, *Gege*. Before it is too late. Come with me to America."

He shook his head. "I will not run away from my homeland. If I must pay the price for saving your life, then I shall accept my fate."

The two sat silently for a few moments.

"The hole in my heart was finally repaired last year," she said.

"A flower blossomed and grew where once there was only desert." He let go of her hands and sipped his tea.

A staccato knock on the door, then it burst open with a loud bang. Two military police officers stood in the entrance, the younger one lowering his foot to the floor.

"Feng GuoPing, you are accused of breaking Article 102 of the Criminal Law," the older man on the right said as he pulled out a piece of paper and read aloud. "By impeding the righteous act of the martial law troops, and by inciting the overthrow of the political power of the dictatorship of the proletariat and the socialist system." He looked up and said, "Feng GuoPing, you are under arrest."

GuoPing looked at Xinya and gave a half smile. Then he turned back to the police officer. "I expect you to treat my guest with the utmost of respect."

"Of course," the officer said. He pointed at Xinya. "You must leave here immediately. This apartment is now property of the People's Republic."

Xinya stood up. "I must first say goodbye," she said.

"You will leave now, citizen."

She turned and faced the officer. "You will wait for me to say my farewell," she said evenly. "We are not animals, and you have no right to treat me like one."

"*Meimei*, just leave," GuoPing whispered. "Don't get in their way."

She grabbed his hands. "I will await your return."

He stared at her, a tear rolling down his cheeks. "Tell my mother goodbye," he said. "There will be no return for me, *Meimei*." He bowed his head.

"Is this true, officer?" she asked the older man.

He gave a brisk nod. "Nobody comes back from where he's going, citizen."

She turned back to her brother. "A momentous day," she said. "Happy birthday, dear *Gege*. You will forever be in my heart."

She turned and walked out the door and waited outside and caught one final glimpse of her brother as the police took him away from her forever.

forty-three

HELLO VALENTINA:

Here's that letter I mentioned on the phone. Sorry it took me a while to send it; I wanted to read it first. And then I had to figure out how to send all the photos of the pages in a single message.

As you'll soon see, it's a hell of a story. Claudia was quite the live wire. Too bad I never got the chance to meet her in person—she would have been lots of fun.

I also let Scott read it. He didn't seem surprised at all.

I hope my grandson isn't as dumb as I think he is. Be careful when you come back to Seattle.

Love you,
Mikk

forty-four

Dear Mr. Rain Ekko:

We are Madame Flora's granddaughters. You may have heard that she died a couple years ago in a terrible accident—so sad.

Anyway, we finally went through her papers, and we came across this sealed envelope addressed "To be opened only by the husband of Valentina Nikolskaya."

Val is our friend—how cool is that? As we were waiting for her to marry Scott Waverly so we could deliver it, next thing you know she breaks up with him and marries you instead—congratulations!

It took us too long to find your address, and as you can imagine we couldn't talk to Scott about this, but eventually we found you.

We hope to meet you soon, and we hope this letter from our Grandmother is good news. Let us know if you need anything from us!

Sincerely,
Rose and Marie Drabarni

forty-five

DEAR FUTURE HUSBAND OF VALENTINA NIKOLSKAYA:

Tomorrow evening is when I leave for India. I am prepared to face my own demise as I jumpstart your life.

If you're reading this letter, it means that The Alert Foundation has found you, and my and Fico's souls are reunited through your and Valentina's bodies, and somehow Madame Flora or her descendant got this letter into your hands.

The thought of us reading this letter in the future makes me so happy.

And while I'm sure you and Valentina are incredibly satisfied with each other, I thought it would be good to leave you another, very private, letter. One that will help you just in case things aren't as rosy as we both wish.

In my previous letters, which I deposited into our soul line account, I told you how Fico and I met, how we got married, and how he tragically died during our escape from Cuba. I painted the picture of a perfect three years of marriage that we had together. This is the public image that I want everybody to know. It will cement your reputation in the Soul Identity community as an honest and diligent man.

But now that you've married Val, it's time for you and me to be totally open and honest with ourselves. Because bad things can and will happen, dear me, and I want you to be well-prepared to handle them when they do.

In a way this letter serves as the confession I could never give to my priest. I hate burdening you with it, but I also know how strong-minded your soul is. Because you are me, and we are tough as nails.

But first, a warning: If you and Val are still in the innocent love phase, and you are still acting goo-goo with each other, put this letter down. Stop reading it, and wait until the darkness has found its way into your heart.

Are you still reading, future me? You're not just being curious and peeking to see if there is anything scandalous ahead? Don't say I didn't warn you.

You'll remember my letter where I told you how Fico and I lived in Havana, and Fico made the mistake of depositing the US lease check for

Guantanamo, and his even worse mistake of covering it up. This is what caused us to have to escape from Cuba with Camilo Cienfuegos.

I also told you how I was able to overcome Fico's infidelity by being a loving and kind and sexy wife for him.

Let me break the suspense and lay it all out there: Fico and I were not as happy together as I made us out to be. Because in reality he wasn't as wonderful as I made him out to be.

After I found the lipstick on his collar, I started to fantasize about finding my own opportunities to cheat on him. The grocery delivery boy, for example, had an incredible summer screwing me every which way possible. So did the postman. And the new priest. Once I started imagining being with other men, I couldn't, and wouldn't, bring my mind back under control.

I told myself that I had these imaginary affairs out of revenge, but in truth, dear me, each time I daydreamed about sleeping with another man, I felt liberated. They meant nothing to me except a way to have a whole lot of fun; I was committed to making our marriage work. When Fico came home each night, I was sweet, loving, and sexy to him. He never knew.

Or so I thought.

In October, when Cienfuegos offered me and Fico to accompany him on his escape, I spent some time thinking about the collection of imaginary lovers I was leaving behind. Each had been dear to me in their own way, and none had a clue of the ways I ravished them in my mind. Well, maybe the priest had noticed; I was going to confessional almost every day, and although I was careful not to name names, I did tell him that I dreamed of having sex all day long. At several of these sessions his voice was more strained and his breath heavier than usual, which only added to my fantasies of him bursting through the screen and pounding into me with his holy pole until I begged him to let me recover from the pleasure.

Does this sound terrible, future me? If you're anything at all like your soul line ancestor, I'm sure you understand. I'm guessing that you have your own imaginary couplings with Valentina's friends and the wives of your colleagues. Maybe you're surrounded by young and sexy girls who occupy your mind when you should be working.

But this isn't the big confession; it's just background. I want to tell you what happened during our escape from Cuba.

As I wrote before, Camilo Cienfuegos had planned to crash-land his airplane in the ocean and hop aboard his boat for the night-long trip to Florida. But it didn't go as smoothly as he had planned.

For starters, the landing in the ocean was rough. As we were about to enter the water, the plane's right wheel bumped on a floating log, and this caused the left wing to dip and plow through the next wave. The plane spun around and flipped over in the next few seconds. The three of us were tossed around the cabin, and I passed out. The next thing I knew, a dripping wet *Comandante* was shaking me awake.

"Didi!" he cried. "The plane is sinking, and we must get out now."

I looked, but couldn't find, Fico. "Where is my husband?"

"Already on the boat. His arm seems broken, so I brought him first." The *Comandante* pushed me toward the door. "You must swim down, under the wing, and then up to the surface," he said. "I'll be right behind you."

I took a big breath and pulled myself headfirst into the dark water. I kicked myself forward and soon enough headed to the surface, where the moonlit ocean was as calm as if we were in a quiet lagoon.

Cienfuegos surfaced just a few yards away from me. "Are you all right?" he asked. "Can you swim on your own?"

"I can. Where's your boat? Where's Fico?"

"Follow me," he said, and he swam past the sinking plane.

I kicked off my shoes and did my best to keep up. As we rounded the plane, I saw the powerboat only a hundred yards away. Within a few minutes the *Comandante* had pulled me up the ladder and onto the wooden deck.

"That was exciting," he said. "Sorry I have no towels."

"My husband?"

"In the bow."

I scampered to the front, and I was confronted by the sight of my unconscious husband lying face-down, his left arm reaching over his head but bent backward at an impossible angle at the elbow.

"Fico!" I cried.

He groaned and coughed up a few ounces of sea water.

I was about to kneel beside him, but the *Comandante* said, "Leave him for now. We must get this boat underway." So instead I pulled in the anchor, then coiled its rope, then held the light for Cienfuegos while he studied the map and aligned his compass.

Only after he started the engine and eased the throttle back did he let me see Fico again. He reached under his seat and pulled out a white box. "It's a medical kit," he said. "Fico needs a sling and some morphine."

I sorted through the kit and found the sling. We couldn't find the pain killers, but the *Comandante* pulled a half-empty bottle of rum out of a compartment under his seat. "This'll do the trick," he said.

I wanted to help, but he had me sit in the captain's chair and then he showed me how to steer the boat. "Call me if you see any lights," he said. "We can't be spotted."

And I sat there, future me, in the captain's chair, tears streaming down my cheeks while Fico screamed and cussed like he was dying. Cienfuegos came back after what felt like a year, and I rushed forward to my husband, who lay unconscious on his back, his arm in a sling.

Fico slept restlessly, and I forced as much rum as I could into him. I even took a few gulps myself. I stayed next to him, his head in my lap, until the dark sky on the right started to brighten into a dull orange, then the bright red of a glorious sunrise.

But then the next unplanned event: the engine went silent and we were left bobbing on the ocean.

I called to Cienfuegos, "Is everything okay?"

"My idiot pig of a master sergeant, who can't tell his ass from his elbow, didn't fill the tanks properly," he said. "Even the emergency tank is bone dry. We're fucked, Didi. Out of fuel in the middle of the god-damned ocean."

"How close are we to Florida?"

He came over and sat down next to Fico and me. "Just over thirty miles," he said. "But it might as well be a million."

I passed him the bottle of rum and he took a long gulp.

"Now what?" I asked.

He shrugged. "I've been through worse. Let's hope that we'll be fine."

But we weren't, future me. Just four days later, drifting aimlessly at sea, when we had no rum, only a tiny amount of dirty water we had collected from the single rain shower, and a single fish that we managed to catch, we were at our breaking point. Fico was feverish and slipping in and out of consciousness. The *Comandante* spent his days brooding and telling old war stories, and I lost myself to the same kinds of fantasies I had been having all summer. Only this time they involved Cienfuegos.

And this led us to the next unplanned event.

It all started in the evening. We were surprised by a drenching rain shower, and while Cienfuegos collected drinking water, I cleaned myself up as best I could. I went up to the bow, slipped out of my blouse and pants, laid them out flat, and gave my body a good rinsing.

The rain was hot and my daydreams even hotter. I stroked my breasts and wished it was somebody else's hands besides my own. The water trickled between my legs, and my fingers lingered as I rinsed and rubbed that area clean.

I was startled by a deep groan. I looked up, and there stood Camilo Cienfuegos, my *Comandante*, the object of my recent daydreams. He was halfway out of his shirt, his trousers unable to hide his huge erection.

"Didi…"

"*Comandante*…"

And then he stripped off his clothes, held me from behind, cupped my breasts, rubbed my body against his. He turned me around and slid down the wall and pulled me into his lap and thrust deep into me, and I couldn't breathe with the pleasure he brought.

Four days, future me. Four days of little food, almost no water, and an almost-dead, disabled husband. It was more than anybody could handle. I went for it, and it was the best sex of my life; more intense than any of my daydreams; better than it had ever been with Fico.

We sat on the deck, Cienfuegos still hard inside me, neither of us able to catch our breath, our arms tight around each other, the rain steaming off our hot skin.

And the next thing I heard was a sickening crack. The *Comandante's* arms went limp and I heard an ungodly scream come from behind me.

Somehow Fico's fever had finally broken at the most unfortunate of times. My husband had pulled himself up, lurched to the bow, grabbed the anchor I had left on the deck, and smashed it into Camillo Cienfuegos's head.

I scrambled out of Cienfuegos's lap, and his body slumped to the side, the anchor that slammed his skull hitting the deck with a thud. The Hero of Yaguajay was dead, future me, killed by my jealous husband.

Are you shocked by this story? By my behavior? I hope so, because I want you to learn the lesson that I'm about to share with you.

Fico lay collapsed on the deck, his energy gone after the exertion. I went to him, but he pushed me away, even after I put my clothes back on.

"All summer long," he whispered. "You have been fucking around all summer long. I know, Didi. You would talk and moan to your lovers as you slept."

"It's not true, Fico."

"It is."

"No, Fico." But how could I explain my daydreams to him? Especially after what he just witnessed.

"I hate you, Didi." His eyes flashed. "I hate you with every ounce of my body. I don't want to live with you. I don't want us to be in the States together. Or anywhere. I'd rather go to hell than spend my life with you."

"No, Fico!"

He pulled himself to his feet and shuffled over to Cienfuegos. He grabbed the anchor with his good arm. He lifted it up high and turned back to where I was sitting on the ground.

He was going to brain me with it, future me, just like he did to the *Comandante*.

I scrambled up and launched myself directly at him. My shoulder connected with his broken elbow, and he screamed. He took one, two, three steps to regain his balance, but he fell over the side of the boat and into the water with a splash.

My Fico, the love of my life, drowned. Not by saving me, but by almost killing me. When I was rescued three weeks later, it was the *Comandante's* rotting body, not Fico's, they found next to me.

Here's the lesson, future me, for you to engrave in your heart: if things go wrong, you can always rewrite the memories. Because this is precisely what I have done. Your beloved Val, my Fico, will never know how much they hated us. Their memories are limited to the ones we gave them in the letters I wrote.

Only the two of us know what truly happened. We hold the power to change history.

If you ever find yourself in the same situation, dear me, please remember that you always have a chance to restart. I did it, and you can too. If your relationship with Val falls apart and seems beyond repair, kill her if you must.

I truly hope you never have to read this letter, and that the work I did to reset our past helped shape our future into a happy one. But if I didn't succeed, I leave it in your hands to keep our legacy alive.

forty-six

After walking through several long and cavernous sections of the airport terminal, Brandon and I speed through the Chinese immigration and customs queues and find ourselves in the arrivals hall. I locate an ATM and withdraw two thousand yuan, and we follow the signs for the taxis.

After a half mile's walk, we get into a line that slowly snakes up to the green and white taxis. As we wait, my phone buzzes, and I read a text message from Scott.

"Found Xinya's address," it says. "Show this to your taxi driver." This is followed by a sequence of Chinese characters.

I tell Brandon and ask him, "It's only seven in the evening; do you want to go straight to Xinya's?"

He grins. "That would be perfect."

Our taxi driver speaks no English, but I hand him my phone. He reads the Chinese address and nods. He puts our luggage on top of the propane tank in his trunk, and we get into the back seats, which are covered in white sheets with handmade lace along their edges.

The doors close, and the TV monitors built into the seat backs come to life. They're showing images of dancing, food, and massages. Then there's an advertisement for what looks like breast augmentation.

"Can you understand what they're saying?" I ask Brandon.

"Mostly. It's just noise." He leans forward and speaks to the driver, who punches a button on the dashboard, and the monitors wink off.

The traffic is heavy, but the driver seems adept at working his way through it, and within an hour, he's pulling up to a squat concrete apartment building.

I pay the driver, collect my receipt, and he unloads our luggage. We bow to each other, and then he speeds off.

Brandon and I walk up to the front of the building and into its tiny foyer. A locked door with a metal grate blocks our access to the elevators. It has an intercom and a tiny screen.

"Can you read enough Chinese to find her?" I ask Brandon.

"Of course," he says. He taps the screen and tries to follow the prompts.

After ten minutes and a lot of cursing, I pull out my phone and load a translation app. I type in "Xinya Xia" and show him the resulting characters. "Is this the name you are looking for?"

He takes my phone, studies it, and then looks back at the screen. Two taps later, and he smiles. "I had to reverse the order, but it worked. It's dialing her number."

We hear three rings, and then a lady asks, "Wei?"

Brandon nudges me. "Answer her," he whispers.

"Is this Xinya Xia?" I ask. Hoping she still speaks English.

"Who is speaking, please?" the voice replies.

"Valentina Nikolskaya," I say.

Silence on the intercom for the next thirty seconds. Brandon and I look at each other. And just as I am about to say something, a bell chimes and the metal door swings open.

Brandon looks at me. "Do we know where to go?"

"Apartment 202."

We climb two flights of stairs and end up in a dark hallway. Apartment 202 is at the end on the right. There is another metal-grated door, but this one is unlocked, and we enter a narrow room that contains brooms, slippers, and coats. And the end of the hall is a brown wooden door, and I give it a solid knock.

The door opens immediately, and in front of me stands a tall and stately Chinese lady with bobbed gray hair. She's wearing a simple smock, and her face is lit up in a beautiful smile, dimples on each cheek.

She looks exactly like the lady in the images Scott showed to me.

"Valentina," she says. "I have been waiting so long for you to find me." She looks at Brandon, cocks her head to one side.

"Ms. Xia?" Brandon says. "It's me, Brandon Drumm."

Her hands fly to her mouth, then she rushes forward and grabs him by the shoulders. She peers into his eyes, smiles, and wraps him into a big hug. "Don't ever call me Ms. Xia again," she says. "I'm Xinya, okay?"

"Okay," he says. And when they let go of each other, the three of us enter her apartment.

Xinya leads Brandon and me to a couch, and excuses herself to get us some tea.

Brandon is all smiles. "She's so beautiful," he whispers.

I look around the room. "And she's single, too."

"How do you know?"

"Intuition," I say.

"I hope you're right."

Xinya comes back with a tray and three tiny teacups. She sits on the seat across from us, and we drink in silence, Brandon smiling goofily at her the whole time.

Where to start? "I read the letter you left me," I say.

Xinya raises her eyebrows. "I wrote no letter."

"It was inside your dissertation."

"Ah. That letter," she says. "You know that I have wronged you."

"I married the wrong person because of your formulas."

She frowns. "I assume the marriage did not work out for you."

I shake my head. "It's over."

"My formulas do not work," she says. "They never worked."

"Don't tell Raff that," Brandon says.

She looks at him. "How is my ex-husband?"

"Still trying to show the world how important he is," Brandon says. "He's turned you into the goddess of Alert. Your formulas are still in use. Your photographs are all over the place."

She shakes her head.

Brandon asks, "Have you found your brother?"

"I did," she says. "We had a wonderful year together before he was taken away from me."

"And now? Are you living alone?" Brandon asks. "I live by myself in New York City."

She smiles at him. "Me too, Brandon."

Brandon flashes me a grin.

Then Xinya leans forward and looks directly into my eyes. "Valentina, I offer you my utmost apologies for whatever pain I have caused you by not speaking up and not confronting Raff. I have spent my life learning to fight for what is right. I have tried to be braver and to make up for what I have done, but I suppose that doesn't lessen the bad feelings you have for me."

It hadn't lessened them at all, but here in Beijing, it does. I feel the residual anger in my body dissipate and flow out of me, replaced with a profound sense of relief and a feeling that everything will end up right in the world. I stand up and extend my hands to her. Xinya meets me, and we embrace for a long moment.

We pull apart, and Brandon and I both explain how Raff seems to have kidnapped the three child overseers, and how we need to get them before anything happens to Mr. Morgan.

"We think Raff is trying to hold Soul Identity hostage," I say. "We must rescue those kids."

"I have spent many years rescuing children," Xinya says. And she explains how she has been reuniting kidnapped boys with their parents. "But finally the one child policy has ended, and I believe my work is almost done."

"Perfect timing," Brandon says. "You can come with me. With us."

She studies him for a long minute. Then she says, "I have spent the last three decades knowing I had unfinished business in New York. Instead of facing Raff, I ran away. Now I am finally convicted enough, brave enough, and wise enough to fight back. I welcome the opportunity to help you stop him."

"We'd love to have your help," I say.

"Thank you," Xinya says. "But before I come, I do have a very important task that I must complete."

"What's that?" Brandon asks.

"I must confront the beggar king," she says. "He has done evil for almost thirty years, and it is time for him to stop."

Xinya explains to us how the beggar king has spent his career kidnapping young boys, maiming them, and converting them into beggars using terror and threats against their families. "I have rescued over four hundred of them," she says. "But he's still in business, and that must change."

"What else can you do?" Brandon asks.

"I am sure I can convince him to stop," she says. "But to do that, I must confront him directly."

"Is it safe?" I ask.

She turns to me. "Probably not. But I am convicted that this must stop. I have learned to be brave, Valentina, and not to find excuses when I know my cause is righteous. I only wish I had learned this earlier in life, so I could have stood up to my husband when I learned what he was planning with Claudia."

I like this Xinya. And apparently so does Brandon, who's only got eyes for her.

Xinya asks me, "When did Alert find Claudia's soul line descendant?"

"They didn't," I say. "Soul Identity found him. The collapse of the Soviet Union messed everything up. But three years ago, he injured his eyes, and when he got them checked, he got flagged. He was living in Seattle."

"And you're sure he's Claudia's descendant?"

I shrug. "His identity matches what's on record for her. But I've also seen some evidence that he had a year-older birth certificate. We believe that Raff set up a wrong account for Claudia, then paid his parents to make the descendant a year younger."

"That is exactly what he did," Xinya says. "When was the descendant born?"

"In October, either 1980 or 1981," I say.

She sits still for a minute. Then she says, "I may have something. What if you had proof that Claudia lived until November 1981?"

"You actually saved her from killing herself?" Brandon asks.

"I did," she says. "But by the time I found her, she had already sliced open her wrist. She got a bad infection from it, and she died not even a year later. She never left India."

"You had proof, but you never said anything?" I ask. Like, before I married Rain?

Xinya looks down at the floor. "Raff came to India and threatened me with my, my brother's, and Brandon's lives if I didn't disappear and keep my mouth shut. At that time, I was not able to face him."

"We're past that now," Brandon says to me.

"You're right, I'm sorry," I say. "It's hard for me when I hear of things that may have prevented me from wasting two years with Rain."

"Would it have stopped you?" Xinya asks. "Claudia once told me that the pull of destiny is almost impossible to ignore."

I think about it and decide that she has something there. "Good point," I say. "Though it still feels pretty crappy."

Brandon turns to me. "Proof of Claudia living past Rain's birth has the potential to destroy Raff's credibility."

"What kind of proof do you have?" I ask Xinya.

"I will show you," she says.

We follow her into a tiny kitchen. She opens the doors on a free-standing cabinet and points to the top shelf. "Brandon, can you reach up there? There's a tin box behind the paper plates."

He rummages for a minute, his arms over his head and deep inside the cabinet. Then he pulls out a metal box about a foot square. It's wrapped in engravings of elephants and mountains and Hindi script. "Is this it?" he asks.

"That's the one." She takes it, and we follow her back to the living room, where she places it on the table between her seat and the couch. "When I came here from India, all my possessions fit in this one box."

Xinya pries open the lid. She reaches in and pulls out a dark red booklet, a gold seal with five stars embossed on its cover. "My old Chinese passport," she says as she reaches back into the box.

Next she withdraws a small yellow pad of paper. "This is a letter from Claudia," she says. "She asked me to deliver this to her fake soul line descendant once Alert announced they had reunited him with you."

"Yet here it remains," I say.

Brandon turns me and says, "Val, you have to move past this."

"Sorry." I hold out my hand. "I can deliver it to Rain."

She gives it to me, and I tuck it into my laptop bag.

"Here it is," Xinya says. She has pulled out a sheet of paper covered in purple stamps. "This is Claudia's death certificate." She hands it to me.

I read a certification that Claudia Valdes y Famosa passed away from infection on the 8th of November, 1981 in Benares, India. It lists her Cuban passport number and her Indian tourist visa.

I pass it on to Brandon. "You think this is enough leverage to bargain with Raff?"

He laughs. "He will hand over the overseers when he sees this."

"You two don't deal with bad guys that much, do you?" Xinya asks. "I've seen what happens here with our beggar king. Raff would start killing the children. He'd never just hand them over to you."

She has a point. Maybe we are a bit too naïve to fight somebody like Raff. We would expect him to do something rational, but Xinya's right; he thinks differently, and there's children's lives at stake here.

I'm glad we came to Beijing. Xinya's got many years of experience fighting the same kinds of villains we needed to face. "How would you approach this, Xinya?" I ask.

"I would tell him what I wish he would change, but I'd settle for what matters most. For instance, I wouldn't worry about crushing his business; I'd focus on the children," she says. "I'd let him think he won on everything else, and if I'm lucky, he'd think that letting the children go was his idea."

"And this is what you're going to do with the beggar king?" I ask.

She nods. "What matters most for me is that he stops kidnapping and maiming children."

"So how about Brandon and I help you with the beggar king, and then you help us rescue the kids from Raff?"

She nods. Brandon nods. I nod. We have a deal.

forty-seven

Val–Beijing–Present Day

Xinya invites us to stay with her, so I cancel our hotel reservations. She prepares us a simple vegetarian dinner. When it's bedtime, I take the spare room that used to belong to her brother, and Brandon sleeps on the couch.

Jet lag sucks, and at 3 a.m. I am wide awake and staring at the ceiling. It's 9 p.m. in Seattle, so I call Scott.

"Did you find Xinya?" he asks.

"We're staying at her apartment."

"Cool. Do you trust her?"

"I do. She's a good person."

"Awesome." Then he says, "Hey, I want to talk about the letter from Claudia that Mikk emailed you."

"Where she basically told Rain to kill me if he's not happy?"

"That's the one. This is what I tried to warn you about in my first message. I'm pretty sure Rain was cooking up a plan to get rid of you," he says. "I want to confront him."

"You think that will help?" I ask.

"If he gets that he's not really Claudia's descendant, maybe he'll stop."

Somehow I doubt this. So I say, "How about I talk to him once I get back to Seattle?"

"Why wait?"

"Because I'll bring back more proof," I say. "Xinya has information about Claudia that will help us go after Raff, and may also convince Rain to lay off."

"That sounds almost magic. What's she got?"

"Proof about Rain not really being Claudia's descendant."

"I already can prove he was born a year earlier."

"You can raise suspicions about his birth certificate, not prove it like Xinya can."

"What does she have?"

"Claudia's death certificate a month after Rain's official birthday."

"That's definitely more convincing," he says. "Hey, that means Xinya was able to save Claudia after all."

"Sort of. She still died in India, just not on Raff's schedule."

"So we show the death certificate to Rain to get him to stop think-ing about killing you, and then we show it to Raff and threaten him with publicity if he doesn't give us the overseers." he says.

"That's what I thought," I say. "But Xinya says it won't work."

"Oh?"

"She says we're naïve, and don't know how to deal with evil people. Raff would probably start killing the kids," I say. "Scott, we can't afford to get this wrong."

He's silent for a minute. Then he asks, "What do you suggest?"

"Xinya has spent the past twenty-eight years finding and reuniting four hundred stolen children with their parents. She faces the Chinese equivalents of Raff and Rain every time she does this. And she wants to see Raff stopped. So I asked her to come with us to Seattle and help us work out a watertight plan."

"She's willing to return to the States?"

"She is, after we help her with her own problem." I explain to Scott what Xinya told us about the beggar king. "If nothing else, it should be good practice for us meeting with Raff."

"It sounds good," he says. "But be safe, okay? I just got you back, and I don't want to lose you again."

"Me either." And when I hang up, I try not to be upset at Xinya for the two years of time I lost with Scott. But I fail. This forgiveness busi-ness is hard work.

At six o'clock, Xinya knocks on my door and peeks her head inside. "We will leave in two hours," she says. "Would you like to practice some yoga with me first?"

"I'd love to," I say. Maybe it will bring me some peace.

In a few minutes I have donned my yoga top and shorts, and I come out to the living room. Xinya is sitting on the chair, wrapped in a towel, talking to Brandon. When she sees me, she stands up and says, "If we push the chair and table to the edges of the room, there's enough room for both of us."

"Great," I say. "But before we start, can you tell us what we're doing afterward?"

"We're paying a visit to the beggar king," she says. "I have asked him to meet us at Tiananmen Square, under the picture of Chairman Mao at the gatehouse."

"And what are you expecting of me and Brandon?"

"To bear witness to our agreement," she says. "I told them that I was bringing my associates from the States."

"So we just stand there?" Brandon asks.

She smiles. "You need to look tough. I told them that you were also providing me protection."

"Great," I say. "We're staying in public spaces, right?"

"That's right," she says. "Now let's practice our yoga." Xinya unwraps her towel, revealing a toned body in a tiny black sports bra and shorts.

"Wow," Brandon says. "You look incredible."

A tinge of red creeps into Xinya's cheeks, and she says, "For an old lady, you mean."

"I mean for anybody," he says. "I think I'll join you guys." He throws back his blanket. He's wearing a pair of camouflage boxer shorts. "I've never done yoga before; is it easy to follow along?"

"Come and try," I say.

We move the furniture back. Xinya hands us each a towel, and we lay them out on the floor.

"I alternate my days between yoga and tai chi," she says. "I learned this particular routine back in 1981, when I was in India with Claudia."

"This was in Benares?" I ask.

She nods. "Claudia was confined to the hospital. She had an old refrigerator that held her medications. I had to keep an eye out for other patients exchanging their prescriptions for Claudia's."

"Did she understand that Raff had tricked her?" Brandon asks.

Xinya nods. "I watched her go through many stages of grief. She first denied the truth and got angry that I destroyed her future. Then she was angry at Raff for tricking her. By the end, though, she was more philosophical about what happened." She kneels down, closes her eyes, and takes a deep breath. "She was able to make peace with herself."

I close my eyes and work on visualizing my finding that peace for my own life.

Xinya says, "I don't remember the names of the poses anymore. It takes about an hour to work through them. Just follow my lead."

And for the next hour we do our best to copy Xinya as she stretches and pulls and twists her body. The poses are similar, and they're held longer than what I practice in Seattle. It's a good workout.

During the poses, I try to imagine what it will be like confronting the beggar king of Beijing. I'm glad we're going to be in public areas, as it will be hard enough for Brandon and me to follow the nuances of the conversation.

By the end of the hour, Brandon has given up and collapsed on his towel, eyes only on Xinya as she goes through her poses. I'm sweating all over and trying to catch my breath.

Xinya, calm and composed with steady breathing, bows to us and says, "Namaste."

Brandon says, "Namaste. Let's go put your beggar king in his place."

forty-eight

Xinya sits up front with the driver, and Val and Brandon sit in the back of the taxi she hired to take the three of them to Tiananmen Square.

She turns around to check again on her passengers, and Brandon catches her eye. He smiles at her for what feels like the hundredth time that morning, and she smiles back.

Of course she smiles back. She's happy to see him after all these years. Though he doesn't seem to have progressed much in life since she left New York back in 1981. She wonders how much of this is because of his obsession with her, and if it can be fixed. But she'll have more time to think about Brandon once she settles things with the beggar king.

She had hoped to prepare for another year to negotiate with the beggar king, but when Val and Brandon showed up, she realized she was needed elsewhere. It was time to confront Raff.

The taxi takes them down the main street that borders the square. On the right-hand side, she sees the gatehouse. Right in the center hangs a large portrait of Chairman Mao. She points it out to Val and Brandon.

"What's the quote say?" Val asks.

"On the left it says that 'May the people's republic of the middle kingdom last ten thousand years.' It's a wish that China lasts forever."

"I studied this," Brandon says. "The phrase ten thousand years is special in Asian cultures. In China, it was only allowed to use in reference of the Emperor."

"You can see from the sign that we used it with Chairman Mao," Xinya says. "But nobody else since he died."

They get out of the taxi. Val pays the driver, and Xinya leads them through the metal detectors and into the Square.

Brandon points at the nearest lamppost, which has four video cameras hanging downward. "You think Scott can see us?" he asks.

"We may pop up on his screen if he's still tracking us," Val says. She smiles at the closest camera, opens her eyes wide, and waves. "Just in case he's paying attention."

As they approach the gatehouse, Xinya slows and grabs their arms. "Right ahead," she whispers. "Those three men. The beggar king is the one in the middle."

"He doesn't look like a beggar," Brandon says.

"No, he looks like a king," Xinya says.

The two men on the sides wear dark blue suits with white t-shirts, but the king wears a golden robe with large red cuffs at his wrists and neck. The robe is embroidered with images of dragons and warriors. His head is shaved bald, and he wears a fashionable pair of sunglasses.

"A somewhat modern king," Val says. "Is this how gangsters dress in China?"

"No," Xinya says. "They mostly try to look American. The beggar king is old school."

Xinya motions to Val and Brandon to walk on either side of her, and together they approach the trio.

As they draw closer, Xinya says, "In China, negotiations are polite and filled with compliments. Don't be fooled by this. The beggar king is not my friend."

"Got it," Val says.

The two groups get within five feet of each other. Xinya stares directly into the beggar king's eyes, then bows low. "Greetings, your excellency," she says in Chinese. "Thank you for making the time for this meeting."

The beggar king returns the bow. "At last we meet, Xia Xinya." He smiles. "We comrades have labored alongside each other for how long now?"

"Twenty-eight years." She smiles back. "We are a fixture in each other's businesses."

"I am honored that I could be of assistance to such a beautiful lady," he says. "How can I help you today?"

"I believe our relationship needs to enter a new phase," Xinya says. "But please permit me to spend a minute interpreting for my associates."

"Would you prefer to speak in their language?" he asks. He switches to English. "I was educated in Hong Kong church schools many years ago."

Xinya replies in English. "A less formal language would definitely help us get to the point faster."

"And we can follow along," Val adds.

Xinya steps back and holds out her arms. "Allow me to introduce my associates from America, Valentina Nikolskaya and Brandon Drumm."

After Val and Brandon shake hands with the beggar king, he says, "I hope it doesn't sound too rude, but let's get right to the point of our meeting." He points up at the lampposts and cameras. "I'm not comfortable being in public places for too long."

"Great," Xinya says. "But I need a minute. I had my speech worked out in Chinese."

"It will be more inspired when it comes directly from your heart," the beggar king replies.

She nods, closes her eyes for a minute, and thinks about her work of the past twenty-eight years. How she started helping YunTian Zuo, and how she continued his legacy after he was killed in 1989. She brings to mind the boys she has rescued and returned to their parents. And how frustrated she has become over the years at the seemingly never-ending supply of kidnapped and maimed children.

She opens her eyes. "The reason we are part of each other's business is that I have made it my mission in life to reunite lost children with their parents."

"That must be rewarding work," the beggar king says.

"It is," she says. "And over the years my business has gotten more efficient. After rescuing four hundred children, I have learned how to use technology to help. I am now able to find and reunite them with their parents within a month of them getting them on the streets."

"I have indeed noticed the dip in my profits from this branch of my business," he says.

"I am happy it has made an impact," she says. "But I remain concerned about two things: why these children are lost, and how their beautiful bodies are changed to become beggars."

He raises his eyebrows, but says nothing.

"Your excellency, the years take their toll on us. I have become an old lady, and I want to retire."

"I am sure my business will become much more profitable once you do so."

Xinya smiles. "You know, in other circumstances, I believe we could have been friends."

"It is possible."

She continues. "But I cannot retire until my mission is complete. I have heard that the children make up only a tiny fraction of all the enterprises you are involved in."

He smiles. "I have been fortunate in my ability to grow my father's once-small business."

"I need your help," she says.

He holds his arms wide. "Ask, and it's yours, Xinya Xia."

"I want to complete my life mission. Is it possible that we can make the children part of your business a part of history?"

The beggar king stares at her for a minute. He folds his arms and strokes his chin. "You are asking for a very big favor, Xinya Xia."

She nods. "I am."

"May I be unrefined and ask you your plans if I am unable to grant you this favor?"

She sighs. "This is an area that I would rather not dwell in, your excellency."

He stares at her.

"I have found a new court, your excellency, with a new judge. One that I believe is incorruptible."

"In over thirty years of business, Xinya Xia, I have never met an incorruptible judge."

"This judge, your excellency, is young and ambitious," she says. "Are you aware of my last rescue?"

"Two weeks ago?" he asks.

She nods. "That poor boy, whose left index finger is missing and whose right ear is torn off, is this judge's son."

"Ah." The beggar king sits stroking his chin. "I see where you are going with this."

She smiles. "At this point, the judge is very happy that his son has returned. But if I give him appropriate documentation, I believe he may have questions that will be uncomfortable for your business operations."

"I see." He remains quiet for another minute, and Xinya allows herself a small smile.

Then he says, "I must say that I'm disappointed. I expected more from you, Xinya Xia. Much more."

She frowns. "Excuse me?"

The beggar king chuckles. "At the very least you could have spent more time doing your homework. This judge, whom you believe is incorruptible, is in fact my nephew. The beggar boy, however, is not his child."

She sits still, blood pounding in her ears. "You set me up," she manages to say without her voice cracking.

He nods.

"Then it is good that I have another plan." But what, what, what could it be?

He stares at her.

After a minute of fast thinking, she says, "My associates here have provided me with their improved technology." She hopes Val and Brandon will back her up. "It is most impressive. By using it, I believe that I will be able to rescue the children the very first week they're on the streets. Maybe even the first day."

"That is interesting," the beggar king says. He looked at Brandon. "Can you tell me more about the technology?"

Brandon points to Val. "She's the expert, not me," he says.

The beggar king turns to Val.

Val briefly catches Xinya's eye, then clears her throat. "I am happy to tell you more," she says.

"Please," he says. A thin smile creeps over his lips. "This should be interesting."

"We combine our image and iris matching software with the public surveillance systems around the globe," she says. "China, in particular, is a good market for us, as the government has installed many cameras in public places."

"We do this?" Brandon asks.

"Of course we do," Val says.

Xinya whispers to Brandon, "You need to play along."

The beggar king folds his arms. "You are telling me that you can track people by their eyes, just using China's surveillance system?"

"I am."

"That seems impossible."

Val smiles. "It's amazing."

"Their technology will help me accomplish my life mission," Xinya says. "A game-changer for us, your excellency."

The beggar king strokes his chin again. Then he asks Val, "It sounds impressive, but can you demonstrate your technology for me?"

Xinya doesn't dare look at Val. Was the game up?

"I can," Val says. She pulls her phone out of her pocket. "I have an app installed that has been tracking me through Beijing."

"I have apps that track me, too" the beggar king says.

"But your apps don't really track you; they track your phone," Val says. "My app actually tracks me." She opens the app and shows it to the beggar king. "Check this out."

Xinya moves so she can also see the screen. On it is a photo of Val in the square, smiling at the camera in the lamppost. Val presses the map icon at the top, and the screen shows breadcrumbs from Xinya's apartment to Tiananmen Square.

"This shows where I've been today," Val says.

"Sorry, but it doesn't look special at all," the beggar king says. "Many apps do this."

"But watch this," Val says. She hands the phone to the beggar king. "Look, I have no other computing device on me." She turns and heads toward the closest lamppost. She walks past it, turns right, and goes to the next lamppost. Then she comes back to the group.

The screen has breadcrumbs showing Val's path, along with three photos of Val.

Val grins at Xinya, then says to the beggar king, "You see that two of the pictures are from the cameras, and I guess a tourist also snapped my picture and uploaded it on some social site."

The beggar king stares at the phone for a full minute, then he hands it back to Val. "Thank you," he says. "That is amazing." After another long pause, the beggar king turns to Xinya. "Please excuse me and my bodyguards for a moment."

Xinya bows, and the three men walk a hundred yards away. The beggar king takes out his phone and makes a call.

"My stomach is all in knots," Xinya says to Val.

"When he said that the judge was his nephew, I thought you were doomed," Val says.

"And then Xinya threw the problem at you, and you hit it out of the park," Brandon says. "Well played."

"Your technology is indeed marvelous," Xinya says.

"You inspired me, Xinya, with your conviction," Val says. "And I think Scott must be watching and helping us from back in Seattle, because there's no way his tech is really this good."

"However it works, I think the beggar king was impressed."

In five minutes the beggar king comes back and stands in front of Xinya. "You are a formidable opponent, Xinya Xia. I must confess that I have been considering how to gracefully exit this business. The judge was my last hope to find a way to best you."

Xina says, "It was a good idea, your excellency."

"But not good enough," he says. "Indeed the time has come to shut down this money-losing side of my business," he says. "I just called my lieutenants and gave them new orders. Starting immediately, nobody in my operations will ever kidnap or maim a child again. The children still with me are free to go."

At last!

Xinya bows her head and thinks of her journey over the past twenty-eight years. She thinks about the boys she could not save. She thinks about YunTian Zuo, who brought her in and gave his life to save the children. But most of all, she thinks about the boys who will never be separated from their parents. Never maimed, never threatened, never needing to be reunited.

She looks up at the beggar king, tears streaming down her cheeks. "What you have chosen to do is honorable," she says. "Thank you."

He smiles. "I wish you the very best retirement, Xinya Xia. You have earned it."

And with that he turns and walks away, his two guards hurrying to keep up with him.

forty-nine

Scott and Mikk join Xinya, Brandon, and me a little before noon on the day we land at SeaTac. We're up in his office using the center desks as an impromptu conference table.

"Just a quick summary so we're all on the same page," Scott says. "Archie's only got a few weeks before his tumor kills him, none of the overseers we've found are old enough to serve, and all of them are still missing."

"Your tech hasn't found any more overseers?" I ask.

He shakes his head. "I'm still looking, but it doesn't seem like there are any left." He turns to Xinya. "Your ex-husband Michael Rafferty kidnapped the ones we found."

"Are you sure about that?" she asks.

"Last week my tech spotted them in New York City, right outside of The Alert Foundation's offices," he says as he spins his laptop around and shows us the video of the girl's sunglasses coming off. "But not since then."

"You're blaming him because of this single video?" Xinya asks.

Scott shakes his head. "No, Xinya. I'm blaming him because he admitted it. This morning, Archie received a video message from Raff." His fingers glide over his screen, and we see an image of Michael Rafferty sitting at his desk.

Scott presses play, and Raff starts talking. "Hello Mr. Morgan," he says. "Last week my team discovered that your boy Scott Waverly is not in a coma after all."

"About time he figured it out," I say to Scott.

He nods and points at the screen.

Raff says, "Scott has probably told you all kinds of stories about me by now. But I want to tell my own version." He leans back in his chair. "I've been keeping all three overseers safe for you. I promise I will deliver them to you tomorrow morning, with absolutely no strings attached."

"That's got to be bullshit," Brandon says.

Then Raff leans into the camera and says, "The only thing you need to worry about is whether they'll be delivered alive or dead."

"Told you," Brandon says. "He's an asshole."

Raff sits back in his chair. "I have three reasonable requests for you to consider. If you agree to them, then the kids will arrive happy and healthy, and we can all be friends."

"What are they?" Mikk asks.

"It's a video," Scott says. "He'll tell you."

Raff raises his index finger. "First, Mr. Morgan, I hate competition. Soul Identity must immediately enter into an exclusive, perpetual contract with The Alert Foundation. This means you will sever all security and investigative ties with Scott Waverly, Valentina Nikolskaya, and their associates. You must ban them from any working relationships with Soul Identity and its affiliates."

"Now that's just mean," Mikk says.

Raff raises his middle finger, "Next, we need to keep the kids safe until they grow up. I want you to name me as your trustee, granting me your exclusive power of attorney, for exactly eleven years. This is when the youngest of the children overseers, who will be under my sole care, will reach the age of nineteen." He smiles. "I have prepared an agreement for you to sign, which I will attach to this message."

"Yikes," Brandon says.

Raff raises his ring finger. "Finally, you can't die on me. I have arranged a one-way trip for you to a cryogenic hibernation facility. They will freeze you, Mr. Morgan. Though you will be considered legally dead in the United States, Soul Identity will still consider you alive, and I will continue to be able to represent you and keep Soul Identity functional."

"How creepy," Mikk says.

"He stole that idea," Brandon says. "Every sci-fi movie freezes their astronauts."

Raff puts down his hand. "This is a good and reasonable deal, Mr. Morgan," he says. "One that prevents Soul Identity from being destroyed under your watch. One that keeps these innocent children alive." He pauses, licks his lips, and says, "I know you'll do the right thing. Please reply by midnight tonight if you agree to my requests. If I do not hear from you, I will assume you are not interested."

The video ends, and Scott turns his laptop back around.

"What was Mr. Morgan's reaction?" I ask him.

"Let's call him up," he says. "So you can hear for yourself." He taps on his laptop again, and when he makes the connection, he projects the video call to a monitor hanging from the wall.

Mr. Morgan is sitting at his desk in his office, a concerned expression on his face. "Hello, Scott," he says.

"Hey Archie," Scott replies. "You know most of my team, right?"

Mr. Morgan nods. "I presume the two new faces are Ms. Xia and Mr. Drumm?"

Xinya and Brandon nod their heads and smile.

"It is an honor to meet you both," the executive overseer of Soul Identity tells them.

Scott says, "Archie, my team wants to know what you're going to tell Michael Rafferty."

A pained expression crosses Mr. Morgan's face. "Before I answer, I want to say how difficult a decision this is. I have a sacred trust to secure the future of Soul Identity, and this weighs heavily on me."

"Sucks to be you," Mikk says. "But that's why you get the big bucks."

Mr. Morgan raises his eyebrows. "Mr. Ekko, how nice to see you again."

"You too, Archie," Mikk says. "Listen to me, you old coot. You can't say yes to that bastard!"

The overseer sighs. "My heart agrees and says I cannot. But my head wonders if we have any other choice to secure the future of Soul Identity. We have not found another overseer. My doctor says I cannot last six weeks, let alone six years."

"I'm sure we can come up with something better than what Raff is proposing," I say.

Scott says, "Let's play it out. Raff's proposal of becoming trustee while putting Archie on ice is interesting. What would happen if Archie named one of us as his trustee?"

"Xinya answered this already," I say. "Raff would start killing the children overseers."

"I will not bargain with their lives," Mr. Morgan says.

We all stop talking for a minute.

Then I say, "The only way we can succeed is if we rescue them."

"That's the problem," Scott says. "I haven't been able to find them."

"Even if we find where they are, would we have time?" I ask.

Scott say, "I've called George and Sue. They've assembled an extraction team and they're sitting in New York City, all ready to go. But we have nowhere to send them."

I turn to Xinya. "I know it's been thirty-five years, but do you have any idea where Raff could hide three children?"

She shakes her head.

"I know where Raff could hide them," Brandon says.

All eyes turn to Brandon.

"At his summer cabin," he says.

fifty

"Raff doesn't have a summer cabin," Scott says. "I've scoured the real estate records for both The Alert Foundation and Michael Rafferty. The only properties they own or lease is his apartment and the Alert offices."

"No, he has one," Brandon says. "I'm sure of it, because I've been there. It was twenty years ago."

Then I remember our flight to Beijing. "You mentioned this on the airplane," I say. "Upstate New York, right?"

Brandon nods. "It's not that far from Woodstock. My buddy and I were going to stop by and see the dairy farm where they had the festival." He laughed. "We didn't realize that Woodstock really took place in Bethel, sixty miles away."

"Did you get to the farm?" Mikk asks.

"Damn straight," Brandon says. He looks at me and says, "I know where the cabin is."

"You remember?" I ask.

He shakes his head. "But Raff gave me directions, and I'm a librarian. I'm sure I saved them."

"Are they in your apartment?" Scott asks. "I can send the extraction team over."

"They're online," Brandon says. "Everything sits in the cloud these days."

I slide him my laptop. "Pull them up, Brandon."

After a few minutes of typing, he smiles and says, "Found them. I told you guys he had a place."

I look at the screen, and there's a handwritten note with an address in Woodstock and driving directions from Manhattan. I pop it up onto another wall monitor.

"That looks like Raff's handwriting," Xinya says.

Scott walks over to the directions, snaps a picture of them, then dials his phone. "George," he says, "It's a long shot, but we have a lead on where the kids might be." He reads him the address, then messages the photo after he hangs up. "They'll check it out," he says. "We'll know in a few hours."

"What about your tech?" I ask him.

"Good question," he says. His fingers fly over the keyboard. A map appears on the monitor next to Mr. Morgan, and it begins to get filled in with imagery. I see a lake, along with several upscale waterfront houses.

"This is a live feed," he says. "I'll see if I can find any better security cameras in the area. Or maybe somebody's flying a drone that I can tap into."

"You can do that?" Brandon asks.

Scott smiles. "So many cameras in the world these days. But you still need to know where to look."

Mr. Morgan says, "Scott, I have a little less than nine hours before I will agree to Mr. Rafferty's demands. If you and your team can find any way at all to rescue those children, it would be most appreciated."

"We'll find them, Archie," Scott says.

"Nine hours," the executive overseer says. "Then I am out of options." He disconnects from the call.

Scott looks at Xinya. "If we do rescue the kids, Raff will still be a threat. We need to make sure he stops fighting us on this."

Xinya nods. "We need to make sure he stops all bad behavior."

Scott continues. "Val says you worked some serious magic when you convinced your beggar king to exit the business of kidnapping and maiming children."

She purses her lips. "If you rescue the children, Mr. Waverly, we will convince Raff to abandon his foolish quest of taking over Soul Identity," she says.

"Thank you," Scott says. He looks at me. "The jet is waiting for us at Boeing airfield. Let's get everybody on board."

"Where to?" I ask.

"New York City. If George and Sue find and rescue the kids, we'll have to immediately deal with Raff. And if they don't, we'll have to think of some other way to stop him."

"Is Raff even in New York?" I ask.

"Let's make sure," he says. He pulls out his phone, punches it, and says, "Michael Rafferty, please."

"You're calling him now?" I ask.

He nods, and says into the phone, "My name's Scott Waverly, ma'am. It's like life-and-death important. I'm sure Raff will take my call if you tell him who I am."

"You're crazy," I say.

He smiles, and then says, "Raff, how have you been?" A pause, then he says, "Yeah, the medical care was awesome. I feel as good as new. But we don't have time to chat, Raff. I'm calling about the message you sent Archie."

A full minute of Raff talking, with Scott listening politely. Then Scott says, "Whatever, Raff. We need to meet tonight. I think you'll want to hear what I have to say. Before you take any irreversible actions."

More talking, and Scott adds, "No, it has to be tonight." He looks at his watch and says, "How about at eleven o'clock tonight? Will that work for you?"

After another few minutes, he hangs up the phone. "He'll meet us at his Manhattan offices," he says. "In a bit less than eight hours. We'd better have some answers by then."

fifty-one

We land at LaGuardia at 9 p.m. and grab a limo to drive us downtown. Scott and I sit facing backward, and Mikk, Xinya, Brandon sit across from us. Bob the Dog is up front with the driver. Since we're early, we tell the driver to meander through midtown until the 11 o'clock meeting.

Scott's been conferencing with the extraction team since we left Seattle. It's a small team: George and Sue brought only Hans and Nigel, the contractors I met in Sterling. While we flew east, they used Scott's tech tied into their drones to scout the cabin. They've determined there are four security guards patrolling the property. They also know there are four people inside, of which three of them are small and may be children.

So now we're waiting in the back of the limo. We watch Scott's laptop screen as Hans creeps past the guards for a peek through the windows.

We see a living area with three children in the room. A teen-aged girl on a tablet, and a small boy and girl reading books on the couch.

"Can you catch their eyes?" Scott asks. "We need to verify these are the right kids."

"Just a sec," George says. We hear him say, "Hans, get them to look at you." The guy taps lightly on the window, and the older girl looks up from her tablet.

It's just a quick glance, but Scott captures the eyes and runs a check. Then he flashes me a big grin and hollers to George, "She's an overseer! Let's get 'em out of there."

"Roger that," Sue says over the radio. "Any operational parameters?"

"We need all three kids alive," Scott says. "And don't kill the guards, unless they shoot at you."

"Live guards have the risk of them calling for backup," she says.

"I know. But we don't know how much they know, and killing them brings more paperwork. Try your best."

"Give us sixty minutes to finalize an extraction plan," she says. "We'll be ready at 2245."

"Perfect. Talk to you soon," Scott says. He disconnects the call.

I've been thinking about how we'll negotiate with Raff. It's time to get some tips from Xinya. I turn to her and ask, "How did you know that the beggar king would agree to your demands?"

"Because I followed my formula," Xinya said. "It's how to get what you need from a very strong and very bad person."

"I love that it's a formula," Scott says.

"My whole life is made up of formulas," she says. "This one is simple. First, I showed him some respect. When you can't use force to get what you want from a bad person, you must acknowledge that what they do matters."

That made sense to me. The beggar king created an environment for people who couldn't make money in any usual way. Just affirming that she knew this helped Xinya bring him along.

"The next step was to tell him what I wanted, which was to retire," she says. "And then explain how my solution would hurt his business. That got him thinking on my behalf, looking for other ways I could accomplish my goal."

"It seems that bad guys have to be pretty smart for your formula to work on them," Scott says.

"You don't need formulas for dumb ones," Xinya says. "The beggar king was smart, and he indeed reached the right conclusion. He made the call to shut down his entire kidnapping and maiming operation."

I think about her formula. "You framed the problem so that you and he were on the same side of it," I say. "Then you both solved it together."

Xinya nods. "That's it."

Scott scratches his head for a minute. "It's like a Jedi mind trick," he declares. "It's brilliant."

"Thanks," Xinya says. "But even then, the beggar king had some surprises up his sleeve, and we had to adapt on the spot."

"Can we create a formula for Raff?" I ask.

"We can try," Scott says. "Let's see. First we're supposed to show him respect. Though he's a scumbag, so that's not going to be easy. He was planning to kill me, and he just told Archie to destroy our business."

"This is the guy who killed my son and saddled me with a lousy fake grandson," Mikk says. "This asshole doesn't deserve respect."

Xinya looks at me. "I know he's also wronged both of us, but if we don't show him that he's worthy of our respect, we won't get him to cooperate."

Xinya's asking me to ignore how Raff fucked up my life. But I did it with her, so why not him? "Okay, I'll find something nice to say," I say. "And I'll make it sincere." I turn to face Scott. "Anyway, I think that only Xinya and I should head up and meet Raff tonight. Remember how Feret almost killed us both in Venice. Let's not make it easy for Raff to eliminate us all."

Scott frowns. "You're sure you want just the two of you there?"

I nod. "He should know that he can't just take us out."

"That makes sense." He points at Xinya. "Back to the formula: what problem can we solve together with him?"

I have been toying with an idea since my flight back from Beijing, when I was thinking about how Xinya beat the beggar king. "What if Xinya's the problem," I say. "She wants to start reuniting people again, but for real this time. She's starting a new venture with me and Scott as her partners."

"Awesome," Scott says. "I love new ventures. But why will Raff view this as an existential threat?"

"We're going to expose him as a fraud," I say. "With irrefutable proof that he lied to Claudia, lied about Xinya, lied about Rain."

"I like that," Mikk says.

"It won't work," Xinya says. And when we all look at her, she says, "Remember that Raff has lots of experience in public relations. He can twist these stories to his advantage."

"Nobody's that good," Scott says. "You've seen the evidence we have."

I think about how Raff, once he got me hooked up with Rain, singlehandedly took his almost-dormant foundation and grew into a huge operation. Then I think about how confident he was when I visited his offices just a week before, even though Rain and I had just called it quits.

"Xinya's right," I say. "Raff's extremely confident. He can easily claim that it's us, and not himself, who can't be trusted: Xinya lied about the cancer, and I'm just upset that my marriage failed. No matter what evidence we show, he can lessen its damage."

And with that sobering thought, we all go silent and stare at the city streets outside our windows.

A few minutes later, Scott says, "There has to be something that Raff is threatened by."

"I know what threatens him," Brandon says. "It's the lack of rec-ognition. Raff needs to be important. Wherever he goes, he constantly reminds people how he helped them, and then he tries to be the most talked-about person in the room."

Xinya nods her head. "That sounds like the Raff I knew."

"Do we have something that threatens his importance?" Scott asks.

And then it hits me: "What if we made reuniting free?" I ask. "We charge nothing for finding connnections with your past. And since your tech is best, everyone will use us. Just like that, Alert loses all its influence."

"You'd make all my tech free?" Scott asks.

I don't answer right away. I think how Raff's malicious plans played out for me, and what I've been through the past two years. If we have ways to prevent this kind of turbulence, we must share them.

"It's our tech, partner," I say. "Nobody should have to deal with the shit we went through."

A moment of silence, and then Xinya says, "Letting everybody re-unite would be a dream come true. And it would stop Raff from ever faking another reunion."

Scott glances at Xinya, then back at me. "Okay," he says. "Just re-member that if Raff becomes Archie's trustee, none of this matters."

"You have to get those children overseers to safety before we meet Raff," I say.

Scott looks at his watch. "It's almost time," he says. "We can watch it happen." He flips the laptop around and dials into the conference line. "George, Sue? Are you guys ready?" he asks them.

"That's affirmative," Sue says.

"What's your plan?" I ask.

"My gadgets will lead the way," George says. "The drones are loaded with tranquilizer darts. We've already tagged the outside guards, and the drones will take them down first. Then we'll waltz in and get the kids."

"Let's do it," Scott says. "The drones have eyes?"

"They do," Sue says. "All units, prepare to launch drones in 5, 4, 3, 2, go go go!"

Scott's screen shows four night-vision video images of the ground re-ceding, fast flights to the guards' locations, then the ground coming close. All four screens show the back of each target guard, all four screens flash a three second countdown, and all four guards fall over.

"Nighty-night," George says. "That new tranquilizer worked even faster than I had hoped."

"Switching video," Sue says. "Let's get to the house." The four drone feeds switch to helmet-mounted cameras labeled George, Sue, Hans, and Nigel. We can see them each race to the house from different angles.

"They make it look easy," I say to Scott.

"These guys are awesome," he says. "Remember Dubnik?"

"George got shot by the Nazis in Dubnik," I say.

"I heard that," George says over the call. "I'm faster and smarter now. And don't forget: we won in Dubnik."

"Except for Madame Flora," Sue says. "But stop chit-chatting, George; we're about to go in."

In the next ten seconds we watch Hans and Nigel use their feet to kick down their doors, and George and Sue shatter their windows with their forearms. Hans disables the one guard by the front door, Nigel sweeps the downstairs for more guards, and George and Sue race to the living room.

In under a minute, the three children are gathered in the kitchen next to the unconscious guard. Scott quickly verifies their soul identities.

"They're definitely our overseers," he says. "Nice work, guys."

We high-five each other, and George and Sue lead the kids out to safety.

Scott looks at me and Xinya. "Kick Raff's ass," he says.

fifty-two

At precisely ten fifty-seven p.m., the limo pulls up in front of The Alert Foundation's midtown offices. I turn to Scott and say, "If I don't call you in ten minutes, come and get us. With the police."

He nods, gives me a quick kiss, and says, "Good luck."

Xinya and I climb out of the back and head into the building. I've got my laptop so we'll be able to conference with Scott.

In the elevator, I ask Xinya, "Are you ready to see your ex-husband?"

"I had hoped we would never meet again."

We reach Alert's floor and step into the hallway. The door to their lobby is unlocked, so we enter. The huge photo of Rain and me is still hanging there. Right next to it is the photograph of a much younger Xinya.

"I really don't like the décor," Xinya says.

I glance to the right. Raff's office door is open and the lights are on. I point it out to Xinya, and we walk toward it.

Raff is sitting at his desk, talking to somebody on his computer screen. He looks up and grins at me, but the smile falters when his gaze flips to Xinya.

"Hello, Raff," she says. "I'm back from the dead."

Raff sits still in his chair, his mouth wide open. But in two seconds he's smiling and getting to his feet. "Oh my God, it's a miracle!" he cries.

I remember that I'm supposed to be both complimentary and full of respect. "That's pretty funny," I say as I plaster on a smile.

"Please have a seat," he says, pointing to the couches.

The three of us sit down.

Raff asks, "Will Scott be joining us?"

"He'll be online," I say as I pull out my laptop and connect Scott. I set the laptop so the screen faces all three of us.

Raff puts his hands on his knees and says to the laptop, "Okay, Scott, you called this meeting. What can I do for you?" He looks at his watch. "As you may have heard, I have a busy night ahead of me. If we can wrap this up in a few minutes, it would be great."

Scott says, "I'll let the ladies take the lead for this conversation, Raff."
Raff turns to me.

His over-confident and slightly condescending expression turns my stomach. I turn to Xinya and say, "It must be weird to see The Alert Foundation after so many years away."

"It certainly has grown," she says.

"When I first came to the old offices two years ago, I think it was just Raff and a couple other employees." I turn to Raff, "All of this growth in the past few years. You must be very proud of what you've built."

He smiles. "I am, Valentina. It has been hard. I invested years to lay the groundwork for success, and now it's finally paying off."

"And the people you've helped," I say. "What an incredible feeling you must have, knowing how you've made it possible for them to enrich their lives."

Raff turns his head to one side and stares at me for a minute. "Yes," he eventually says. "It makes me feel great. Where are you going with this, Valentina?"

I smile. "You might have heard that Scott and I are back together as business partners."

"You hinted you were considering taking over his business the last time you dropped by," he says. "Back when Scott was in a coma."

"That's pretty observant of you," I say. "Even I wasn't sure at that point."

He smiles. "I've been doing this a long time; I pick up on things." Then he frowns and says, "I wish you had talked to me first, Valentina. You have picked the wrong team."

"It's possible," I say. "But this is why we're here. We have a problem that we think you can help us solve."

"That you're about to go out of business? Sorry, I can't help you with that."

I shake my head. "We've got a new partner, and we need some business advice."

Raff glances at Xinya. "Is that why you're here? You're their new partner?"

"I am." Xinya bows her head forward. "Before I never had the courage to stand up to you, Raff. Now I do."

He stares at her, then turns to me. "I have no idea what that means. But it's fine, because I don't really give a shit about your company."

"Thanks," I say. "That leads me to the problem we're facing," I say. "Which is?"

"We thought really hard about how we'd compete in this business climate." I stare at him. "We think the only answer is to make our tech freely available to whomever wants to reunite."

"Why would you do that?" he asks.

"Scale," Scott says through the laptop. "We want to reach the world, and the model that a tiny boutique agency like The Alert Foundation uses just won't cut it for us."

Raff looks at Scott, Xinya, and me in turn. "You guys are serious?" We all nod.

Then he laughs and slaps his knees. "You guys are hilarious. And if it wasn't for the fact that I'm going to be running Soul Identity real soon now, I might even be worried for The Alert Foundation's future."

I glance at Scott, who seems as puzzled as I am. I pull out my phone and send him a quick message: "Did we grab the wrong kids?"

"Hard to believe," he messages back. "We matched their identities."

"Maybe he grabbed them back. Can you check?"

He nods at me through the laptop, then the screen goes dark.

I tell Raff, "Scott will be back in a second." I hope my face doesn't betray my worry.

Raff smiles. "Is he about to mount a rescue?"

It seems he has taken them back. But I smile and say, "Have you read his books? He's done it before."

Raff laughs. "Please tell him that I welcome his attempt." He glances at his watch. "But he'd better hurry. After Archibald Morgan and I have our next chat, there will be no need for rescues."

My phone buzzes with a message from Scott. "Kids are on chopper to Sterling."

I type back, "Read their eyes again."

"No reader on the helicopter," he sends.

I look at Raff. "How do you know Scott isn't rescuing them right now?" I ask.

"Because my alarms would go off," he says. "And they have remained silent."

Xinya and I exchange glances. Could it be that Raff doesn't know we rescued three children from his cabin in Wookstock?

Raff stands up and says, "Wait a second." He puts his hands on his hips and stares first at me, then at Xinya. "You ladies disappoint me. You don't even know where the overseers are, do you?"

Now I'm really confused. But I bite my tongue and wait.

Raff sighs. "You never found my clues."

"You left clues?" I ask.

He laughs. "It seems I wasted my time. I sent the kids outside and had the girl lose her sunglasses. Maybe Scott's tech is not as good as I was led to believe."

"No, we saw that," I say. "It was a block from here."

"Great," he says. "And what about the tweet from the Chinese girl? Did you get that?"

I shake my head. "You let her tweet?"

He sighs. "It wasn't really her; I'm not that dumb. I used her account." He pulls out his phone and opens the app. "Here's the message."

I take his phone and read, "Help @soulidentity! Held in basement of Alert building."

"I didn't see it, but you sent it to the wrong handle," I say. I pull out my phone and type to Scott: "Raff says overseers are in the Alert basement. He tweeted a help message. You positive we grabbed the right kids?"

Scott writes back. "I saw no tweet. But now I'm getting worried."

Yikes. I look at Raff and shrug my shoulders. "Scott missed the tweet too."

"You're not even worthy opponents," he says. "I led you right to them, so I could show the world that you're nothing but thieves. Check this out." He gets up, walks to his desk, and swivels his monitor around so we can see three children sitting in what looks like large animal cages.

"You're holding them here, in this building?"

He smiles. "And you didn't even come and rescue them. No wonder I need to take over Soul Identity. Morgan hires losers. I'm going to call old Archibald now and get this over with. It's time for change."

Do we have the right kids or not? If we do, we save Soul Identity. But if we don't... Do I have enough faith in Scott's tech?

I do, and damn Raff for making me doubt myself. "Before you make that call," I say, "Answer me this. Where did you stash the real overseers?"

He swirls around to face me, a twitch in his right cheek. "Can't you see them?"

"They're not the real ones," I say. "They're decoys."

"I need no decoys with clowns like you."

I see his twitch is jumping faster now. "What if you stashed the real overseers somewhere else?"

"That's an interesting idea, Valentina," he says. "Crazy, but interesting."

"You'd never risk losing the real overseers."

He stares at me. "Are you so sure of yourself?"

"I am," and as he starts laughing, I go all in and add, "We've already been to Woodstock." And I hold my breath and hope I got it right.

"Shit!" Raff darts behind his desk and types at his keyboard. He brings up another screen, which shows video feeds of an empty house, front door wide open, side window broken, an unconscious guard in the kitchen, and an empty living room.

"We have them, Raff," I say. "You lost."

fifty-three

By the time Mr. Morgan sends his helicopter and we fly to Soul Identity headquarters in Sterling, it's six in the morning and we're all pretty exhausted.

Mr. Morgan himself is waiting to greet us next to the helipad. He's flanked by George and Sue. Nigel and Hans stand behind the trio with the three child overseers.

"Archie looks pretty happy," Scott says.

And he sure is: the executive overseer's got a big grin on his face, and when we get close, he pumps Scott's hand, then pulls me into a bear hug.

"Thank you, Ms. Nikolskaya," he says. "From the bottom of my heart."

"I think it's time you start calling me Val," I say.

He smiles. "Only if you promise to call me Archie."

"Deal."

Archie greets Mikk, Xinya, and Brandon, and he pets Bob the Dog. Then he wipes Bob's slobber onto a handkerchief. "I would like to introduce you to three very special people," he says.

The older girl steps forward. She's tall and slender, long black hair pulled back into a ponytail. She says something in Chinese. Xinya answers her, then tells us, "This is Ying, from Shanghai. She's says thank you, and she's happy to meet you."

The middle girl raises her hand. She's even shorter than Archie, but her brown curly hair adds six inches to her height. She's wearing white-rimmed glasses. "I'm Giselle," she says. "From Rio de Janeiro. Thank you for rescuing us."

"Don't forget me," the small boy with blond hair and blue eyes says. "I'm Simon, from Canterbury. That's in England."

I kneel down next to Simon and take his hand. "Somehow I don't think we could forget any of you," I say.

George says to us, "I understand you have been awake all night long. Come with me to the guest house to freshen up; we have room for everybody."

"Scott and Val, may I impose on you to spend a few minutes with me?" Archie asks.

George and Sue lead Xinya, Brandon, Mikk, and Bob the Dog down the path toward the guest house. Nigel and Hans take the children to a black limousine. Then Scott and I accompany Archie back to the headquarters building, through the reception, up the elevator, and into his office.

As we sit across from Archie on the couch, I notice how tired he looks. His left hand has a tremor, and the bags under his eyes are large enough to hang below his glasses.

"It is nice to see you two back together," he says. I give Scott's hand a squeeze and smile as he says, "I cannot thank you enough."

"You're welcome, Archie," Scott says. "And luckily, this time it has a happy ending."

"Indeed it does," Archie says. "Val, how long has it been since you worked in this building?"

I think about when I was running development for Soul Identity, tucked away in my little office in the dungeon. "Just about four years now," I say.

"That seems like forever ago," Scott says.

I couldn't agree more with him.

Archie says, "Tell me about your faith, Val."

I'm not sure where he's going, so I hedge a bit. "You mean in the whole Soul Identity idea?"

He smiles. "No, I mean your own personal journey. Take a few minutes to think about it."

I dwell on my personal journey for a while before answering. Archie and Scott are talking softly about business, so that gives me some time to get my thoughts in order.

"You know, Archie," I say when they wrap up. "When I came to work here, I thought Soul Identity helped me be a better person. The whole breathtaking idea of how my actions would affect my soul line descendants motivated me to do big things."

The overseer nods his head. "I remember those days."

"And then I met Scott," I say. "He looks at things differently than me. Just answering his questions made me stronger in what I believed. And all the adventures he somehow falls into taught me that what we do is much bigger than our own tiny soul lines. I gained a sense of purpose as I realized that we could help others in their own journey through life."

"I like that," Scott says. "The adventures part."

"Me too," I say. "But then Rain came along and introduced me to idea that I did have a past, and with it came obligations." I look at Scott and frown. "Your reactions horrified me, but I believed my past made me special, so it was easy for me to let you go."

Scott leans forward and opens his mouth, but I hold up my hand and say, "I know better now."

He sits back.

"I spent two years trying to make it work with Rain, because dammit, it was destined to work."

I pause for a moment and assemble my thoughts.

"When my marriage fell apart, I realized that trying to live by somebody else's grand plan of your future was at best random and at worst dangerous. I resented knowing that my connections came with obligations, and I wished I had never heard of Soul Identity."

I take Scott's hand again. "And then this guy came back and showed me that most of my supposed past was false: Claudia lied about her life with Fico, and Fico was not my soul line ancestor anyway."

"Maybe he's still alive," Scott says. "We should look someday."

"There's no need," I say. "I finally realized that what matters most is what you do and who you connect with in this life. Living only for the future is just as unhealthy as re-living the past."

The executive overseer asks, "And where does this leave you?"

I look at him and smile. "Every minute counts. We must make peace with and progress in our current lives. Soul Identity makes us confront our lives in the grand perspective of a past and future, and I love that. It brings me the strength to be happy with who I am today."

The three of us sit silently for a minute, which is helpful, because my heart is pounding.

"That was beautiful, Val," Archie says. "Thank you for sharing." After another minute he adds, "I find myself confronting my own life, or rather, the lack of life. I will not last the five years it will take for Ying to become the next overseer."

"I hate this," I say.

He gives me a sad smile. "I hate it as well. Especially since my heart, lungs, blood, and prostate all seem healthy. But the doctors have been pretty frank with me about my tumor, and I have come to accept my fate."

"What will happen to Soul Identity?" Scott asks.

"Good question," Archie says. "You know, as much as I despise Michael Rafferty, there is wisdom in the idea to put me on ice while a trustee runs the organization."

"That sounds nuts to me," I say. "You'd be killing yourself for an iffy, at best, solution. Who knows if the Match Committee would even agree that your frozen body is still considered alive?"

"As a matter of fact," he says, "I checked with the Match Committee. They believe that a frozen overseer is a dead overseer."

"There you have it," I say. "A dumb idea."

"But that provided the spark for a better idea," he says. "One that will pass muster with the Match Committee."

What was he up to? I glance at Scott, but his eyes remain focused on the overseer.

Archie says, "Last night I reacquainted myself with the story of Claudia Famosa y Valdes." He chuckles. "She was quite the woman. Her feistiness reminds me so much of Flora."

The two ladies definitely had many traits in common. But what was Archie getting at? "Because they both were willing to die for what they believed?" I ask.

"Yes, but this is also where they were the most different," Archie says. "Flora was willing to die for a principle: to right a wrong about the stolen gold. But Claudia, she was willing to die for her faith."

I think about Claudia's faith, built on a lie about her future carefully constructed by Raff. And on another lie about her past, carefully constructed by herself. "Her faith was misguided at best," I say.

"True," Archie says. "But misguided or not, faith is a very powerful aid to building courage, which right now is what I need the most."

"What do you need courage for?" Scott asks.

"For dying," the overseer says. "Not my body, as that will easily last five more years. But my mind, and I suppose my soul, will die when they invade my brain and excise the tumor. The doctors say my time is running out." He sighs. "I need the kind of courage that comes from faith like Claudia's."

"You're going to do the surgery?" I ask.

He nods. "The doctors have high confidence that I will survive, but the location of the tumor means my body will be an empty shell. It will be as if I have had a massive stroke."

"When will they operate?" Scott asks.

"As soon as possible," Archie says. "Before it spreads and we lose our glorious organization. The surgery is scheduled for this afternoon." He looks me in the eyes for a long minute, then in Scott's. "This, I am afraid, is our final goodbye."

"Hold on," I say. "How will this help save Soul Identity? Are you naming a trustee?"

"I am," he says. "Somebody I know can keep this organization going, and even grow it, until those children are ready to take over." He pauses. "Somebody whose faith I have come to respect. Somebody who would be superb as a trustee overseer."

I glance again at Scott. Was he ready? Could he handle running the organization? I ponder this, thinking about all that we have been through together, and how much he's grown since I met him, and all this thinking makes me miss what the overseer says next.

Then Archie's done talking and Scott's looking at me with a big grin on his face.

"Congratulations," I say to him. "You'll be the perfect trustee."

He gives me a weird look, then he turns to Archie. "She must have missed what you said," he says.

"It appears she did." The overseer grabs my hand. "Val, I want you to be my trustee. Will you spend the next five years in the service of Soul Identity?"

I glance at Scott, who's got tears beginning to overflow his eyes. "Tell him yes," he mock-whispers.

I face the executive overseer. "Of course, Mr. Morgan. I'd be honored."

fifty-four

Mikk and I take a drive in my new car to Anastasia's Capitol Hill apartment. After spending the past six weeks in Sterling, I'm finally closing the loop with Rain. Nastya has offered to let us meet on "neutral territory," as she put it.

"They actually let her highness drive?" Mikk asks.

"They really didn't want to," I say. "George and Sue say I need to take the limo, but I told them that it's just not me. I'm going to drive myself, ride my bike, and spend at least half my time here in Seattle."

"That seems wrong," he says. "I'd make Soul Identity pamper me like crazy. They can brush my teeth. Maybe even dress me in the morning. I'd even let them wipe my–"

"–I get the point," I say. "And at your age, you probably could use the help." I reach out and grab his hand. "I've missed you, Mikk."

"Me too, Valentina. I'm glad you're back. I've hated rattling around in that house by myself."

"Well, that's now over. Are you all set to move?" Mikk has decided to relocate himself into an assisted living facility downtown. It's loaded with former Soviet citizens, lots of vodka, and five shared dogs.

"I sold the furniture on Craigslist, and Rain's artwork on eBay. Now I've got a couple extra grand that he doesn't know about."

"He probably won't notice," I say.

"Are you really going to spend half your time in Seattle?" he asks.

"I am. Soul Identity bought the house next door to Scott, and we're going to use it as the home base for the children overseers. They're orphans, and I'm convinced that they need to grow up outside of Sterling."

"That's great," he says. "I heard from Brandon that he and Xinya are moving here too."

I smile. "Now that Xinya's our partner, she's intent on putting The Alert Foundation out of business. She's decided that she needs to be close to us. Brandon and she seem to have figured out something that works for them."

"Maybe they can buy my house," he says. "I still haven't listed it."

"Maybe," I say. "It would be nice to have them nearby. Brandon has offered to help us get the overseers settled and enrolled in school. He's going to curate an online reference library for them."

"He's certainly got the temperament for it," Mikk says. He's silent for a minute, and then he asks, "By the way, how's my friend Archibald doing?"

The executive overseer had the surgery to remove his brain tumor, and as his doctors had predicted, his body became an empty vessel. He seems to have no memory. Yesterday afternoon I stopped by the guest house, where George and Sue have converted the first floor into his special quarters. Archie sat in the same chair by the window, staring at the rolling fields. We didn't speak, but he never speaks any more.

I sigh. "He seems to be living in peace."

As I pull into Nastya's driveway, Mikk throws a quick glance my way. "I haven't seen the asshole since you left," he says.

"You mean, since we left," I say. "Remember that first night in the hotel in SoDo?"

He laughs. "The start of our adventures. I can't believe that was only two months ago."

I can't either. First the two weeks of flying all over the place as we stopped Raff and found the children overseers, then the craziness that has come with trying to wrap my arms around the global organization so I can be an effective trustee overseer.

I park the car and grab Mikk's arm as we walk to the front door. "Everything has changed since then, hasn't it?" I ask. "A new start for all of us."

"Yet everything remains the same," he says. "Let's not tell Rain that he's not really my grandson. I want him to feel guilty when he doesn't come to visit."

"That's not fair for him."

"Have it your way, your excellency." He looks me in the eyes. "I still consider you my granddaughter."

I kiss him on his wrinkled cheek. "I would be offended if you didn't."

I ring the doorbell, and Nastya immediately opens it. "He's not here yet," she says as she lets us in. "Come and have some tea."

As we sit down in her kitchen, she says, "So you won't leave Seattle after all."

I shake my head.

"I'm not giving your car back."

"Keep it," I say. "I bought myself a new one."

"Sweet. For that, I'll even serve you cake."

A minute later the doorbell rings, and Nastya lets Rain in. We move to the living room, and I sit next to Mikk on the couch while Rain and Nastya sit in the armchairs.

"This is cozy," Nastya says.

I look at my ex-husband and it's like looking at an old schoolmate: We've had some common experiences, but life has changed enough since then that we both know we'll never be more than Facebook friends.

But still. This is the guy who's had it in his head for a couple years now that Claudia had changed what happened between her and Fico.

"I want to get right to the point," I say.

"Good," he says. "The sooner I'm out of here, the better."

"You need to hear what I found out about Claudia and Fico."

Rain frowns. "Why do I want to know more about the bastards who fucked up my life?"

I smile. "You're going to love what I have to tell you." And for the next half hour, I explain how he wasn't Claudia's soul line descendant, and how Raff had pre-selected Rain and changed his birthdate, and how Claudia didn't even kill herself like she was supposed to.

Rain soaks it all in with a scowl on his face. "If you came to get the money back," he says, "It's gone. I've spent it all."

"That's all you can say?" Mikk asks. "After hearing how I'm not really your grandfather, and how you and Valentina were never destined to be together, your first words are about the money?"

Rain shrugs.

"It's okay, Mikk," I say, patting him on his knee. I turn back to Rain. "I read Claudia's confession to you about how Fico died, and her bright idea that you could always recycle my soul line."

Rain gives me a fierce stare, but when I don't flinch, he looks away.

"Would you really have me killed?"

He looks up at me. "Before we got divorced, I toyed with the idea. But in the end I decided it wasn't worth the effort."

"Wasn't worth it?"

"As I said, the money's all spent. Raff tried to squeeze me for a couple hundred grand to give me new dates and times for your soul line, but he wanted the cash up front, not when you came back." He made a fist. "And now I find out the prick was conning me. I'm going to kill him."

I think Raff would kick my ex-husband's ass. But I like the idea of the two thugs going after each other instead of me.

"I want to make a deal, Rain," I say. "It means no more fighting against me. No trying to have me killed." I look at him closely. "If you can do that, I have a parting gift for you from Claudia herself."

Another fierce stare, but I can see the fight has left his eyes. "Fine with me," he says.

And I'm relieved, even though I'm sure he's not being totally honest with me. I'll get George and Sue keep an eye on him. Maybe Scott too.

But in the meantime, I'll give him the benefit of the doubt. I open my purse and hand him Claudia's last letter, the one she gave to Xinya the day she died in the Indian hospital. Then Mikk and I say goodbye to him. I kiss Nastya on the cheek, and we're off for West Seattle, where I'll meet Scott after missing him like crazy for two long weeks.

As we drive over the West Seattle Bridge and into Alki, Mikk says, "I'm liking this new start already."

fifty-five

GREETINGS:

Eleven months ago, Xinya, my best friend in the world, was finally able to make me understand that I am not your soul line ancestor. You are not my descendant. In fact, I'm still alive, barely, and you're already a baby boy, living in Estonia. So there you have it.

And now, just like when I first wrote you, I don't know what to call you. Never-me? Future-me-no-longer?

Not that it matters, as I'll be dead soon. Xinya stopped me from killing myself, but I ended up with a nasty infection that these Indian doctors haven't been able to cure. I only get a few moments between my bouts of fever where I can think straight. I hope I can finish this letter to you.

I re-read the last few paragraphs, and I'm struck by the selfishness that still infects my soul. I shall call you Better-than-me. This is perfect, as it marries my own self-focus with the humility I now face as I realize that I not only made a mess of my own life, but most likely I have made a mess of yours.

Once upon a time I was a little girl, growing up with the pride and haughtiness of an owner's daughter, as well as the shame of having a dancing whore for a mother.

I married a bad boy, a revolutionary who didn't take his marriage, his job, or his life seriously enough. But then again, neither did I. We both were selfish; we both ran away when we faced trouble.

And then I fucked the wrong guy, and then I killed my husband. And then I did something truly evil: I tried to rewrite history by exploiting your, and baby Valentina's, lives. What kind of person could do this?

A desperate person, that's who. When Madame Flora first introduced me to Soul Identity, I saw a shortcut to redemption. With a few strokes of my pen, I could change my past and hope that my future self would atone for the sins I committed.

My faith was strong, Better-than-me. But soon enough, I realized that I needed more assurance than Soul Identity could offer. I needed to know that my plans would work.

And The Alert Foundation was perfect for me. They led me to Valentina, and holding that darling baby girl in my arms was the happiest day of my life. Never mind that Xinya has since told me that she's not really Fico's soul line descendant; at the time I believed, and it was amazing. It gave me the strength I needed to end my life.

I was willing to die, Better-than-me, so I could start over. And reading this again, it strikes me how my actions were not that different from an old Hindu woman I saw jumping on her husband's burning pyre last year.

When I have the courage to reflect on what I almost did, I realize that it wasn't my faith that was driving me to kill myself in Benares; it was desperation. I had no noble cause, just a desire to make my miserable life count for something, and a selfish motivation to find a shortcut way to get there.

Forgive me, as I have been slow to learn these lessons.

I will give this letter to Xinya. I believe that one day you'll receive it. I only hope it's in time for you to get your own life back on track. Hopefully you will meet Xinya, because she's an example of the kind of person I wish I could be. She's brave, she's full of purpose, and she finds fulfillment from helping others.

One last thing, Better-than-me. I was going to put every cent I owned into our soul line collection, but perhaps my faith in Soul Identity wasn't as strong as I claimed, because I withheld one of my dead husband's Swiss bank accounts from Raff's greedy hands.

The account details are with this letter. Since I don't know your name, I have instructed the bank to only release the funds to a person of Estonian descent, born on October 3, 1981.

Live your own life, Better-than-me, and not mine. Take no shortcuts as you do so. Make your life count. Make it wonderful.

Claudia Famosa y Valdes

Acknowledgements

Soul Integrity has stretched my writing skills as soundly and painfully as Bikram Yoga has stretched my ligaments. I wrote my characters into numerous dead-end plots, each one because I didn't understand them as well as I should have. Mario Goertzel, Hong Jia, Glaucia Young, and my daughters Alison and Holly helped me bring Raff, Xinya, and Claudia to life. I am so happy they daydreamed with me, read through the drafts, found inconsistencies, and kept me unblocked.

I asked a few trusted readers to read through and tear apart early drafts, including Neil Rubenking, Arlene Batchelder, Diya Sekhar, Hermineh Sanossian, Edyta Rozycki, Ben Hope, Bailey Ellis, Cherie Quek, Anna Gershnik, Christoper Messina, Marty Batchelder, Kristin Batchelder, Brady Anderson, Deepak Manohar, Bob Kennedy, Carolyn Liu, Brett Tanzer, Anthony Arrot, Kenneth Ray, Fanny Lalonde-Levesque, Jimmy Goldthwaite, and Matthew Cosensci. Their willingness encouraged me; those who also provided corrections and feedback helped make this book shine.

Jaime Dexter and Hal Berenson made generous bids at a charity auction, each winning the right to name a character. I hope Jaime's nephew, Brandon Drumm, enjoys his role. Hal's dog "Bob the Dog" was my first animal character, and he was a lot of fun.

Seven years is a long time to have this adventure rattling around inside my head. Thank you, Irina, my darling wife, for your encouragement, your continuous help, and for your tolerance when I spent all those hours brooding instead of listening. I love you.

About the Author

Dennis Batchelder lives with his family in West Seattle, Washington, and spends his off-hours writing the next Soul Identity novel.

Email: denbatch@gmail.com
Twitter: @denbatch
Facebook: www.facebook.com/denbatch
Web: www.dennisbatchelder.com